PRIMAL TRILOGY

RYAN KIRK

WATERSTONE
MEDIA

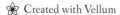 Created with Vellum

PART ONE
PRIMAL DAWN

For my daughter,
born during the writing of this book

ONE

TEV WOKE up before the sun rose, as was his custom. But today was different. Today he was driven by a greater purpose. His eyes opened, and without making a move or sound, he studied his surroundings. The other hunters of his clan slept nearby, but he paid them no mind. The sounds of their sleep came to his ears, the regular breathing and soft snores of the exhausted, and he knew he was the only one awake. Without even a whisper, he extricated himself from his sleeping pad, rolled it up tightly and tied it together with leather straps. He kept every sense alert to ensure his actions didn't disturb the sleep of those nearby. What he had to do, he had to do alone.

Tev knew his actions would have repercussions. Favored by the clan as he was, this decision might cost him a seat among the elders. There were reasons they always hunted together. The deep forests were dangerous, no matter how experienced one was. To wander alone in the woods was courting disaster. Some of their most respected hunters had tried what Tev was now doing, and they had never hunted again.

He looked over at the sleeping figure of Shet, the elder leading this hunt. He had more respect for the older man than he could say. Shet was a veteran of not just countless hunts, but years and trials. Despite his age, he still kept to the trail as though he were less than half as old, and his cunning made him a dangerous hunter. If there was anyone who could dissuade Tev, it would be Shet. But not today. It might cost him the respect of the elder, but if it saved the lives of the clan, Tev didn't see another way.

In his heart, Tev didn't think he was like the others. Where others had gone missing, he would succeed. He was a hunter, in the prime of his life, and the clan had never seen anyone with his skills. He trained harder than anyone else, and if he couldn't put those skills to the test for the good of the clan, what was the point?

Tev tested his gear to ensure it would remain silent as he moved. He didn't want to wake the other hunters, but more importantly, he didn't want to wake up anything else in the forest. They were not the top of the food chain here, and plenty of species nearby could stalk him by sound alone. Silence was safety.

Before he left, Tev looked to the sky, still dark before the dawn. She was still there, a good omen. He knelt to his knees and said a quick prayer to Lys, the goddess of the hunt. Skilled as he was, he would need her strength if he was going to succeed today. She had always looked out for him before. He took one last glance at her figure painted by the stars in the heavens, then stood up and left the peaceful confines of the camp without a second thought. Once the decision was made, there was only action.

Before he crested the ridge that would hide the camp from view, he glanced back at his fellow hunters. He hoped they would understand. Already the boar had taken two of them, and the clan was too small to sustain these losses. The arguments circled in his head one last time, but he was convinced this was the way. Far better to risk one hunter than several. The danger was greater to him, but if he could do anything to keep the clan safe, he wouldn't hesitate.

Beyond the boundaries of the camp, all his senses came alive. He had his spear and his blade, but his greatest weapon was his awareness. Sight, sound, smell and even taste would give him the information he needed to keep himself alive. A clear head and a calm mind. The mantra had been driven into him by the elders. Those skills were far more valuable to him than mere weapons.

He set out toward the rising sun. Memories threatened to disturb his focus. He was heading towards the area they had last seen the boar, the battleground where Tev had lost a friend. Tev hoped to pick up the trail from there. The boar was huge, one of the bigger ones he had ever seen. But far more intimidating than the beast's size was its intelligence. It had been hunted before and knew what traps Tev and his fellow hunters would try to lay. The boar never allowed itself to be surrounded, and it did not hide when it knew hunters were near. It bolted before it could be surrounded.

Peyt, Tev's fellow hunter and friend, had thought he was quicker and smarter, but the boar had proven him wrong faster than anyone could react. Peyt had tried to attack it from the side, an almost impossible spear throw from the distance attempted. To Peyt's credit, the spear had flown just centimeters above the boar's back, but Peyt had left himself undefended as the boar turned and charged. He had tried to defend himself with his knife, and the other hunters had converged to protect their brother, but everyone was too late. The boar got one tusk into Peyt's leg, and he wasn't much longer for the world. It was Tev who had led the ceremony of remembrance. He had said the final words and guided his friend's soul to Lys, who cared for all who died in the hunt.

Tev wasn't sure how he would outsmart the boar, but he knew he had to try. His clan needed food, and they couldn't risk anyone else. A part of him knew his attitude bordered on conceit, but he didn't view it that way. He had a certainty he could do this. He could kill the boar without putting his friends in danger. All he had to do was figure out how.

HE FOUND the place where they'd last seen the boar without difficulty. He knew the land well, but this place in particular was seared in his memory. A friend had fallen here. Marks were everywhere. The ground was trampled, and shallow pools of dried blood marked the place where Peyt had died. Tev's instinct was to glance away, but he took a long breath and focused. In the first light of the dawn, Tev knelt down and examined the scene with fresh eyes. His footprints and the prints of the other hunters were as clear as day to him. He could tell where each of his companions had been and how they had acted. The prints told a story, and he let his mind go blank and make the connections as he observed them.

Everywhere he looked he saw marks of the boar mixed in with the prints of his friends. Stepping with care, he circled the perimeter of the scene, looking for any sign as to where the boar had gone. He found one set of tracks, but they were leading to the battle, not away from it. Unperturbed, he continued his circuit, finally finding the tracks he was seeking.

While hunting boar was a challenge, tracking one,

especially one already wounded, was not. Once he located the tracks, they were easy to follow. The boar had left a trail of blood and disturbed plants so obvious a child could follow it. Tev wondered for a moment if the boar had died last night. There was more blood on the trail than he had expected. He was hopeful, but he proceeded as though the boar was still alive and well.

Despite the obviousness of the trail, Tev moved with caution. There was no telling where the boar had stopped and he didn't want to be taken by surprise. Once in a while he stopped and scanned the area around him, even though he knew he was on the right track. He sniffed the air and looked around for other signs he had missed. Information was safety. Awareness was his sharpest blade.

The sun was a quarter of the way above the horizon when Tev found his quarry. It wasn't sight that gave the boar away, but smell, an unmistakable scent Tev associated with shit. The odor was potent enough that the boar had to be within a dozen paces. Tev knelt down with perfect control, careful not to make a noise, and considered his options. He could attack the boar head-on, but it felt foolish. Tev was confident, but even he didn't want to risk his life in a one-on-one match with an intelligent beast. If it was injured, it was even more unpredictable.

In his silence, Tev could hear the labored breathing of his quarry. The boar was injured. It was time to end this hunt. Killing the boar would honor Peyt's memory. He just had to find the way.

Tev felt the wind change direction against his skin. It was a concerning development, but he didn't panic. Right now he was downwind of the boar, but if the wind shifted too far, the boar would pick up on Tev's scent. It would put Tev in much more danger. Tev kept his eyes moving, studying the environment, trying to gain an advantage on the boar.

His gaze paused on the branches above both him and the boar. An idea occurred to him. It wasn't traditional, or even the safest idea, but it might work. He ran the plan over and over in his mind, trying to get a better sense of the boar's location from its labored breathing.

Then it was time for action. Tev took two powerful and silent steps up to the tree, leaping off his left foot and planting his right foot high on the tree, above the level of his own waist. He pushed off his right foot and angled his momentum so he was flying straight up. He grabbed the lowest branch of the tree and hung there, studying the surrounding area. From this height, he could see the dark shape of the boar hidden in the undergrowth of the forest. Lys was with him. The boar was facing away from him and was about eight meters away.

Tev hung from the branch for a moment, watching the boar with a steady gaze to see if it had heard or noticed him. When he was confident he hadn't alarmed the creature, he pulled himself smoothly up onto the branch, causing only the slightest rustling of the leaves.

Perched on the branch, he paused one last time. He studied the branches between him and the boar, deciding how he would proceed. Once his mind was made up, there was no hesitation. He had to commit with all his heart.

Tev ran along the branch he was standing on, leaping to a new branch to get closer to the boar. The leaves rustled, but there was no helping it. He chose speed over stealth.

As he had expected, the boar's head immediately came up. It glanced from side to side, and Tev was counting on just a second or two of delay before the boar looked up. He was betting the boar had never been attacked from above, and his whole plan hung on just the slightest amount of confusion.

Tev leapt from the branch. He was still three meters away from the boar, but he knew he had the strength to make the jump, and if he waited any longer, he feared his element of surprise would disappear. He fell towards the boar, spear in hand.

His plan worked. Surprised and confused, the boar didn't break right away. Tev dropped towards it, leading the fall with his spear. His aim was true, stabbing the boar from above and piercing its vital organs. Tev didn't try to hold onto the spear. As soon as he thrust, he let go and focused on his own landing.

He hit the ground with his feet, bending at his knees to absorb as much impact as he could. He was moving too fast and too far forward, and he leapt into a roll over his shoulder, coming back to his feet with his long knife in hand.

It was good that he did. Boars were fierce fighters, warriors of the animal kingdom, and this one was no exception. The animal was dead, but it didn't know it yet.

The boar turned and charged. Armed with nothing but his knife, there was little Tev could do to stop it. With another spear he might have stood his ground, but he dove out of the way at the last possible moment, using the same roll over his shoulder. His body fell into relaxed readiness, prepared to move in any direction. At times like this, thought fell away, and Tev embraced his instincts.

Evading the boar was his best strategy. If he could gain even a few seconds, he could scamper up a tree and wait for the boar to die. Trying anything more would be pressing his luck.

The boar charged again, this time with less speed. Tev

assumed it was due to injury. He leapt out of the way again, but this time the boar's slower speed gave it time to adjust at the last moment, leaving a shallow gash along the outside edge of Tev's thigh.

The boar didn't give him a chance to think. It turned around and charged again. Tev reacted, his body and training taking over from his mind. His leg was weakened, and he didn't dare put too much pressure on it. As the boar got close, he threw his knife.

The knife wasn't balanced for throwing, and Tev counted himself lucky that it even caused a slight gash. But it did cause the boar to lower its head. Tev leapt, ignoring the pain that flared up in his injured leg. The boar tried to stab at him as he passed above it, but missed. Tev wrapped his hands around his spear, still jutting through the boar. He put all his weight against it, pulling the boar off its feet.

Both he and the boar landed hard on the ground, but the pain seemed to draw the last of the fight out of the boar. It struggled, just for a moment, before resting its head on the ground. Tev was ready for anything, but the light went out of the boar's eyes, and Tev was successful. He laid back and breathed a deep sigh of relief.

TWO

WHEN KINDRA WOKE UP, she was in a new star system. No matter how often it happened, there was still something about it that bordered on the magical. The scientist in her had a basic understanding of how space travel happened, but it was almost impossible to believe the light she had just left would take almost a hundred years to reach her now.

Perhaps the feeling was a side effect of the sedative. The first people to go through space jumps had succumbed to insanity, and to this day science couldn't explain why. Derreck, Kindra's captain, had done a jump awake once, and he refused to speak of it. Some of the less-controlled captains openly bragged about jumping without sedatives. But Kindra had jumped a lot, and she knew what she wanted. She strapped into her bunk and took her sedative. Once the computer was certain everyone was under, it initiated the jump.

The sedative was designed to last sixty minutes and disappear without a trace, leaving Kindra alert, but she didn't move. She had learned the hard way as a child during one of her first jumps. She might be awake, but she took a few minutes to catch up. Although she didn't consider herself spiritual, the only language she could use to describe the sensation was that of leaving a piece of her soul behind.

Kindra pressed her palms against her forehead and stretched out her eyes, forcing them to wakefulness. A soft groan escaped her lips as she undid the harness that kept her attached to the bunk during the jump. She had jumped well over a hundred times, but each one awakened her inner philosopher. Humanity had been debating whether they belonged in the stars ever since they had the ability to reach the moon. Ultimately, it didn't matter to her. She belonged here. It was why she took the risk of joining Fleet.

A few thoughts pulled up an old-fashioned analog clock in her vision, appearing to float about a meter in front of her face. It had been exactly one hour since the sedative flooded her system, a perfect jump once again. Even though only an hour had passed, she couldn't help but feel she was much older than she had been when she fell asleep. Just like every other time.

She was supposed to be reporting for duty, but years of experience had taught her it was much better to take the first few minutes after a jump to herself. She rolled her head from side to side, rejoicing as her neck popped and cracked. For the next few moments she did a basic warm-up. She stretched, rolled her limbs back and forth and did a few push-ups and squats, just enough to ensure everything was working the way it should.

When she finished, she spoiled herself with a quick shower. It would probably be the best she would have for a few weeks. The hot water warmed her body and erased the last bits of tension in her muscles. She stepped out, dried quickly, and threw on Fleet's latest attempt at a uniform.

Another focused thought brought a wave of information to her vision. The captain was already on the bridge and the rest of the crew were on their way. Even if she left now, she was certain to be the last to arrive. She didn't mind. It wasn't like the planet was going to disappear on them. She understood the importance of timetables, but some part of her, a childhood rebel that had never been tamed, enjoyed throwing off their schedules, even if it was just for a minute or two.

She overlaid a path to the dropship. This was the first time she'd been on this particular jumper, and it was clear the crew didn't like having guests very much. They were a long way from charted space, and the *Destiny* was one of Fleet's long-range jumpers. The crew were used to going months without regular human contact, and their social skills demonstrated that admirably. Kindra had barely left her room except for mess. One last glance ensured she hadn't forgotten anything. She had packed her gear on the dropship days ago and had already been through this procedure multiple times. Satisfied that everything was in its place, she thought off the lights and left the room.

AS KINDRA EXPECTED, she was the last to arrive. She paused after she passed the final bulkhead. Every time Kindra saw her, she took Kindra's breath away. It was Kindra's second home, the dropship *Vigilant*.

The ships that traveled between the stars were far too large to ever drop into atmosphere. Teams like Kindra's relied on dropships to ferry them between the jumpers and the planets they explored. Kindra had been crewed on the *Vigilant* for almost seven years now, but it still had the power to stop her in her tracks. Jumpers, because they never approached atmosphere, tended to look as though a child had glued them together. But the *Vigilant* was sleek, designed for atmospheric flight and exploration. In the cavernous hangers of the jumper it seemed small, but it would be her home again for the next few weeks.

Kindra could never place her finger on what it was about the dropship that stopped her. It was a sleek design, a tapered nose expanding to the body and smooth wings of the ship. One night, after a few too many drinks, she had tried to explain to a friend how she felt about the *Vigilant*. It was beautiful, yes, but there was a hint of menace to it as well, the ship as dark as night. It was well armed, but one would never guess just by looking at it. It was an implied danger, like a gorgeous man with just a hint of aggression in his bearing. Kindra had been embarrassed the next day, but it was still the best description she could muster.

Kindra shook her head. At the end of the day, it was just another dropship, no matter how she felt about it. It was the newest Fleet design, but it was still ten years old, and Fleet had at least four others she knew of.

The first person Kindra ran into was entirely unique within Fleet. Kenan was a monster of a man, at least fifteen centimeters taller than Kindra. Kindra had heard once that he had grown up in a low-gravity hab, but apart from his height you'd never guess it. Everything about Kenan screamed raw power. He joked that his muscles had muscles, and although Kindra's scientific sensibilities bristled at the inaccuracy, she had to give him credit. He was the strongest man she had ever met. As she approached, he easily slung a container over his shoulder that probably weighed twice as much as she did.

Unfortunately, his muscles weren't paired with an equal intelligence. He had once told Kindra he'd joined

Fleet so he could shoot at things all over the galaxy. Kindra had actually rolled her eyes, the first time she remembered doing so since she had been a girl. His greeting this morning wasn't any more enlightened. "Hey, babe! Glad to see you could join us on this one."

Kindra didn't give Kenan the pleasure of her response. He thrived on any attention, negative or otherwise. The two of them had never gotten along, and more than once Kindra had wondered what Derreck saw in him. She knew the two of them had a deep history, but neither of them talked about it very often. All she knew was that they had served together during the Rebellion conflicts. Although she didn't like Kenan, his respect for Derreck was obvious, and he would follow whatever order his captain gave.

Kindra walked past Kenan and almost ran into Eleta, who was hiding by the lift gate for the dropship. Her head was buried in some panel Kindra never knew existed. The two of them got along well, even though their minds worked in very different ways. Eleta was the engineer and mechanic on the ship, and was one of the most logical people Kindra had ever met. She was the type of person who believed everything had its place, and once it was there, you didn't dare mess with it. Despite their very different personalities, they enjoyed each other's company, and were united by a shared love of exploration.

Once on board the dropship, she passed Alston, their geologist. Kindra said hello, but there was no response from him. She suspected he had turned off all his inputs so he could focus on whatever task was at hand. Alston was, like Kenan, unique. He was driven by the pursuit of science, and couldn't care much about anything else. If they interacted more, she might not like him, but he was notoriously introverted. She figured the reason he was a geologist was because he understood rocks much better than he understood people.

Kindra dropped her small bundle of goods on her bunk and decided to say hi to Derreck. They'd be taking off soon, and although she was certain he knew she was aboard, she still wanted to check in.

She found him right where she expected him to be, sitting in the captain's chair on the small bridge. Derreck was the reason she stayed in Fleet, years after her initial tour of duty was over. When she had joined, she had been certain she'd only do a single tour; but serving under Derreck had been one of the best experiences of her life. She wasn't convinced she would become a lifer yet, but she was continually surprised to find that she was willing to consider it.

Derreck was one of the genuinely best men she had ever met. He was honest, hard-working, dedicated to his job, fun to be around, and attractive to boot. He was one of Fleet's stars, although there were some rumors he had intentionally passed up a handful of promotions to keep his current rank of captain. Kindra had never found the courage to ask him about it, but she could understand. Derreck was quiet about his past, but there was one thing that was obvious to anyone who met him. This was a man who loved space. He loved leading expeditions, and Kindra had never met anyone better at it. Sometimes, in her more cynical moments, she thought Derreck had the air of someone trying to escape something, but that was unfair to him. She didn't know what drove him, she just knew she would follow him anywhere in the galaxy.

Kindra walked in and overheard the last snippets of conversation. "Yes, captain. All our crew are on board," Derreck glanced at Kindra as he spoke, giving her a short wink. "We're just finishing getting our final supplies on board now. We should be off in about five minutes."

There was a burst of chatter on the other end of the line that Kindra didn't catch. Derreck shut down the channel. "They're disorganized even by Fleet standards."

Derreck turned around and looked at her. He didn't give her any snide remarks or demand to know where she'd been. Derreck knew each of his crew far better than they knew him, and there was no use hiding anything from him. It was another reason why Kindra admired his leadership. His look said it all, just as it always did. Derreck was generally a by-the-book sort of guy, and he didn't understand Kindra's little rebellions, but they had come to an unspoken agreement when he realized her small indiscretions were a reasonable price to pay for her expertise on missions. He may have disapproved, but he wouldn't take any action.

"Are you ready for this?"

Kindra nodded. Everyone knew there was something unusual about this mission, but only Kindra and Derreck had any real idea just how strange their mission would be. She knew he wasn't just asking a general question. He was wondering if they were up to the task before them. Kindra smiled. "We can do this."

Derreck returned the smile and leaned back in his captain's chair. "I certainly hope you're right."

THE BRIEFING WAS HELD in the galley of the *Vigilance*. Although the dropship was fairly large, most of its spaces were reserved for scientific inquiry, leaving little room for the crew's day-to-day activities. Like the galley, most spaces fulfilled more than one purpose.

Derreck entered last, no doubt having waited to make sure everyone was there before he started the meeting. He dimmed the lights and pulled up a hologram for all of them to study. The image wasn't perfect, and if Kindra squinted, she could still see the pixelation of the hologram. Apparently they still hadn't received the most recent survey data.

Kindra's mind wandered for a moment. Fleet had sent a survey probe far ahead of them, but the probe had never sent back any data. It was unusual, but Fleet wasn't working with the newest equipment, and malfunctions happened. They had sent a second probe once they'd jumped in-system, but from what Kindra could see, they hadn't gotten much information from that probe back yet. Even with all their technology, it took a long time to scan an entire planet.

"Listen up, everyone," said Derreck. "I know y'all have had quite a few questions about this mission, and the answers haven't been as forthcoming as you all would like. I can certainly understand if you're feeling a little bit left out of the loop, but this mission has a higher clearance level than our typical expeditions."

Alston looked over at Kenan. "Fleet has clearance levels now?"

Kenan shrugged, unconcerned.

Derreck looked over at Kindra. "Take it away."

Kindra did. "In front of you is our destination, a planet with a Fleet designation I won't even bother trying to remember. As y'all know, we're a long way from home. There have been expeditions that have gone farther, but not many. On one hand, our mission here is the same as it usually is. We drop down to explore the planet, take samples, and report everything to Fleet."

Kindra took a big breath before continuing. "However,

this planet is not typical. First, you need to know that a strong electromagnetic signal was observed coming from this planet about nine months ago. We detected it for about two months and then it disappeared. We weren't able to decipher anything useful about the signal, but it wasn't natural."

"In addition, preliminary scans of the planet made at range indicate this planet has an atmosphere and environment suitable for carbon-based life. I don't know a lot more than you do right now, but I'm hoping the situation will change as soon as I get the most recent information from the survey probe. What I can tell you is that from our initial scan, it appears the planet has a diverse range of flora."

Kindra let the information set in. Besides Kenan, everyone in the briefing was smart enough to put the pieces together. It was Alston who asked the question everyone was wondering.

"Are there any indications of intelligent life?"

Kindra shook her head. "That's what we're here to find out. This planet has as good a chance of harboring intelligent life as we've ever seen."

She paused and took a breath. "We're dropping into the heart of a mystery. Those signals would have originated almost a thousand years ago. Who knows what's happened since then? We haven't picked up anything, not even since we've been in-system. But we have to know."

Derreck took control of the briefing. "So, now you understand all the secrecy. Our mission is the same, but the stakes are higher than we've ever had. We're one of the best crews out here, which is why we drew this mission. We're burning hard for atmo and should make landfall in about twenty-eight hours. Use that time to prepare. I want everyone on top of their game."

Kenan spoke up. "So what happens if we make first contact?"

Derreck shrugged. "Fleet says discretion is in our hands. We don't have any idea what we might encounter, but Admiral Marshall told me he trusted our judgment. I'd prefer not to start an interstellar war, if we can avoid it." The smile on his face gave his joke away.

Eleta spoke up next. "Speaking of this mission, if what you're saying is true, why did the *Destiny* jump out? I was surprised to learn that. We're a long damn ways from charted space. If we're so far away and this planet is all that, why isn't the jumper staying in-system?"

Derreck appeared to debate with himself for a moment before he said, "This is supposed to be a secret, but you all deserve the truth. I can't give out many details, and frankly, I don't know all that much more than you. But there's another planet nearby which also indicated signs of life. It's about a forty light year jump, and Fleet decided to check them both out at the same time. Believe it or not, the other planet is even more likely to have intelligent life. I don't know what evidence Fleet is basing that decision on, but that's what I've been told. The *Destiny* will need to recharge before it can jump any further, so it will be at least three weeks before we can get any help from her. She is scheduled to rendezvous with us again in four weeks. But, we do have a jumping beacon if worse comes to worst. In that case, rescue will be a lot longer than four weeks; but it will come, and the *Vigilance* is stocked for a long mission."

Everyone looked around. A jumping beacon was a very expensive piece of equipment, and Fleet didn't have too many of them. Whatever happened to them, Fleet wanted to know about it.

Derreck looked around the room for any more questions, but there were none. Kindra was surprised. But then she realized, it wasn't that they didn't have questions, it was that all the answers they sought were down on the planet below them. A planet they would be on tomorrow.

THREE

ONCE TEV CAUGHT HIS BREATH, he said a short prayer of thanks to Lys for the boar, both for the fight it had given him and the food it would provide his clan. His ritual complete, he had one final problem to solve. In his eagerness to kill the boar, he hadn't considered how he would get it back to camp. The beast was much larger than he could carry, especially with the gash in his leg. With a sigh of resignation, he went to work building a makeshift litter out of downed branches and leather straps from his pack. He could get the boar back to camp, but the journey would be a difficult one.

The sun was well past its midpoint when Tev finally found his way back to the camp he had left early that morning. He collapsed to his knees in relief when the hunters watching the perimeter found him. His legs and arms ached from the sustained burden of the hike. His injured leg wanted nothing but rest. The hunters who found him picked up his burden, leaving Tev to walk into camp on his own.

He returned to mixed reactions. Some hunters looked

grateful for a day of rest. The injured hunters seemed especially grateful. Others gave him glares that would have broken bones if they could. Some were angry that he had put himself at risk. Others were angry he had stolen the honor of the kill. Tev met every look, accepting the unspoken opinion of each of his peers. Angry or delighted, there would be no lies, no pretense between them.

They decided to return home. With everyone taking turns carrying the boar and assisting the injured, they figured they could make it home before the sun set tomorrow. Tev didn't relish the idea of walking farther, but he accepted it as punishment for leaving his brothers and sisters behind. At least he didn't have to carry the boar on his own.

The party made it back just as the sun was setting the next day. Tev thought there was nothing more beautiful than the sight of cooking fires after a long journey. Their arrival had been expected, and the smell of cooking meat drove them all home as fast as their feet could carry them. The clan had been running low on food, but the boar would sustain them until the next hunting party returned.

Despite his kill, Tev was not given a place of honor at the feast. A part of him was angered by the slight, but it quickly diminished. He had fed the clan, and that was all that mattered; being popular was far less important to him. He took a place among the rest of the hunters, enjoying the meat and the company. Several of the injured hunters passed him skins of drink, and Tev drank freely.

The drums were brought out, and Tev, a little dizzy from drink, joined in. The beat started simply, and it was easy for him to keep pace. His musical skills lagged far behind his hunting skills, but he played enthusiastically.

When he couldn't keep the beat anymore, he passed

the drum on and began to dance. He wasn't skillful at making music, but he prided himself on his dancing. As the beats grew louder and more complex, the outside world slipped away. His whole existence became nothing but the rhythm, the pulsing heart of the world he lived in. The harder he danced, the more his thoughts disappeared, until he lost all sense of self and there was only the beat.

In time, the music faded, the beats becoming less complicated and more subdued. Tev came out of his trance, exhausted but elated. He left the ring and went to find something else to drink. When he did, he sat down on a log and watched as the younger boys continued to dance. Their energy seemed inexhaustible, even though he was only a few years older than them.

The shadows stirred, and Shet came and sat down next to Tev. "There are many stories about you on this hunt."

It was a statement, but also a question. Tev didn't want to have this conversation now.

"I did what I thought needed to be done."

"And why did you believe you needed to hunt that boar by yourself?"

Tev held his tongue. At the time, his intention had been clear, his path laid out before him so clearly there could be no question. But now, separated by time and distance, he wasn't so sure. "I didn't want anyone else to get hurt."

The older man nodded. "And did you not count yourself when you thought about this? Was your life meaningless to you?"

This time Tev didn't think. "It's better to risk one than many. I didn't want to say the words of remembrance over another friend. And besides, I was certain I could kill it."

Shet's eyes bored into Tev, and Tev couldn't help but

feel as though the elder saw into him, saw how he believed he was guided by Lys.

"Your intent was good, but your decision was foolish."

Tev's anger got the best of his control. "And what would you have done?"

"Trust. I would have trusted the rest of us. Trusted our traditions."

Tev wasn't sure what to say to that. His decision had seemed so right, and it still did. The boar was dead, and the clan was fed. Who was Shet to say he had been wrong? If not for his respect for the elder, he would have said as much.

"I didn't come here to criticize you. What is done is done. You are skilled, and one day, people will look to you for guidance. When that time comes, I want to make sure you are ready. Please, think about what I have said. If you hope to lead, you must think about us all, but you must trust us all as well."

Tev closed his fist and brought it to his chest to indicate his respect for the elder's words. Shet nodded, stood up, and walked off into the night. Tev looked up at the stars, wondering if he'd been right or wrong.

HE LOST all track of time as he watched the stars above. The sky spun lazily overhead. The Deer had already set, and Lys was not far behind. Those pinpricks of light gave him comfort. Every day the Hunter chased the Deer, and no matter what happened from day to day, Lys would continue to hunt. Just as Tev would keep chasing his prey.

Neera found him with his eyes half closed, enjoying the quiet serenity that came from being just far enough away from the celebration. He could hear the laughter and the joy, but he remained alone with his thoughts. She sat down next to him, and he allowed his gaze to wander over.

He thought Neera was the most beautiful woman he'd ever seen. She was as tall as him, and her thin coverings didn't hide her muscular legs and arms. Her hair was the color of night, and her eyes were dark, reminding him of fresh and fertile soil the night after a summer rain. She was a hunter, just like him, and although many of the men wouldn't admit it, she was one of their best. She and Tev had a friendly competition, many years old, to see who was better. Neither had definitively won yet.

She had twisted her ankle on a hunt a week ago and had stayed home to rest from the last expedition. Tev knew it pained her to miss a hunt.

Neera spoke. "There's quite a bit of an argument about you among the hunters. Some of them see you as a hero. Some see you as a fool."

He glanced over at her. "What do you think?"

She laughed. "Is there something that says you can be both?"

Tev laughed with her. Of all the hunters in the clan, Neera was the one he was closest to. They understood each other in a way that seemed almost like destiny to Tev. Neera always cheered him up, reminding him that life was only as serious as you made it. He loved her, but the sentiment was not returned.

"At the time, it made so much sense. I knew I could kill the boar on my own. I did it without risking anyone else's life. But now, I'm not so sure. It all turned out for the best, but I'm not sure it was the right decision."

Neera was silent for a moment before she replied. "Why worry about it? What's done is done, and you will continue to think about what is right. Next time, you will consider what you learned today and think more clearly."

Tev felt a weight lift off his shoulders. Neera was right.

"Anyway," she continued, "your problem is that you place others so far in front of yourself. I know that I, for one, would be greatly disappointed if you didn't return. And I'm not alone."

Tev took her words to heart. He wasn't sure what he should have done, but it was in the past.

"Thank you."

Neera nodded, and together they watched the stars for a while.

He stared at the night sky, his mind empty. But then he saw something he had never seen before. The stars all spun in one direction. It had always been so. But today there was a new one, brighter and larger than the rest, which traveled against the path of the stars. He pointed it out to Neera.

"Have you ever seen anything like that?"

Neera shook her head. Together they watched the rogue star as it spun against the rest of the night sky. A hint of fear tugged at Tev's heart. Whatever it was, Tev didn't think it was natural. It didn't fit in with the order of everything.

But he kept his thoughts to himself as they watched the star set against the wrong horizon.

FOUR

KINDRA COULDN'T HELP HERSELF. She saw the countdown timer running in the corner of her vision, and she knew that if she had any sense, she'd be joining Eleta in their bunks, which doubled as acceleration couches. Derreck wanted to give them as much time on the planet as possible, so they had burned hard after leaving the *Destiny*. They had slowed a bit to enter orbit, but after a few dozen quick orbits and their initial scans, it was time to slow to entry velocity.

Derreck's plan was unusual but efficient. On most missions they would spend more time in orbit gathering observations, but on this mission they had a survey probe in orbit doing much of the same work. Derreck judged it was more important for them to be on the surface for as long as possible. Working with Alston, they identified possible landing sites based on geologic stability. The info from the survey probe wasn't very refined, but it was enough to determine a safe landing site.

The burn to slow down for entry was often a rough one, but Derreck had warned them this particular burn would be even worse. They were still traveling through space far too fast to enter atmo. Not only that, but the *Vigilance* and all its crew would be fighting one-point-two G's of planetary gravity in addition to the G's from deceleration coming down. If she wasn't ensconced in her acceleration couch when the deceleration started, Kindra would be a mess on the floor for the others to clean up.

Despite this knowledge, she couldn't help herself. The information coming in from the survey probe was beyond fascinating. If she didn't know better, she would've assumed that she was looking at scans of Earth before the Collapse. There was a limit to how much information the survey probe could gather from its orbit in space, but everything she had studied so far indicated that this planet had the most diverse life humans had ever encountered since they left their home.

Scans revealed what appeared to be dozens of species of plants. There were grasslands, forests, mountains, and water. Kindra couldn't even begin to calculate the odds of finding what she was looking at. It seemed far too perfect to be real. In all of her experience, she had never encountered anything like this.

Life itself wasn't all that uncommon in the universe. Humans had visited dozens of planets that contained viral forms of life. The challenge, they had found, was finding life that had evolved past that. The conditions necessary to create viral life were easy to find, but to evolve into large multicellular organisms took an evolutionary leap that seemed nearly impossible.

As Kindra understood the problem, the challenge was evolution's balance sheet. Organisms needed to survive and reproduce, and the smaller you were, the easier it was to survive. Larger organisms needed to consume more energy to survive, reproduce and do everything needed to be alive. To grow in size, you needed to make the advantages worth the tremendous cost, and that was hard to find in the universe. Larger, multicellular life had only ever been found on two planets, and even then it qualified at best as fungi. What Kindra was seeing seemed impossible, and she couldn't tear her eyes away.

At one point she had been so much in doubt about her scans that she double-checked the records to ensure this wasn't a terraformed planet. Terraforming was a much more likely explanation, but there were no Fleet records of humans ever being in this part of space before. She was left with only one inescapable conclusion. They were about to explore a planet that had a high chance of supporting intelligent alien life.

Her mind wandered back to Derreck's comments at the briefing. If what he said was true, this planet wasn't even the best candidate for life. If that was the case, she couldn't even imagine what the other planet must be like. It would have to be another Earth. Despite her rationality, she couldn't shake the belief they were about to make discoveries that would change the course of human history.

Kindra was just about to go to her bunk when one final image caught her eye. She had asked the computer to flash images from the probe in front of her face with a two-second delay, and she saw a structure that seemed too circular to be natural. She recalled the image and studied it carefully. The odds of it being natural were astronomical. She tried calling up data from the three-dimensional scanner. Fortunately, an initial pass had been made of the area. She overlaid the images and gasped at the result.

In front of her, grainy and unrefined, was the unmistakable shape of a half-dome. She tried coming up with alternate explanations, but her mind would only see it as a habitation. She called to Derreck, busy piloting the dropship.

His voice came to her ear, "What is it? You need to be bunked by now."

Kindra shrugged off the comment. There were more important issues to discuss. "I think I found evidence of life."

There was silence on the other end of the line. Kindra could almost see Derreck debating options in his head.

"How sure are you?"

Kindra scanned the image again. It seemed unnatural, but there was no way of being certain. They didn't have the scan resolution yet for her to be sure, and there could be an alternate explanation, even if she couldn't come up with one now. Years of space exploration had taught her never to assume. "I'm not."

This time Derreck's voice came back much faster. "Okay, then we're dropping. We'll get the probe to scan more detailed images when we land and have communications back."

Kindra nodded. It was the smartest decision given what they knew.

Derreck's voice's shook her out of her reverie. "And Kindra?"

"Yes?"

"Get to your bunk. The retros are firing in about thirty seconds, and I think you'll want to be alive to see what's down there."

PERHAPS IT WAS JUST Kindra's imagination, but their entry into the atmosphere seemed endless. She had dropped onto over seventy different planets, but only this one had the chance of harboring intelligent life. The rational part of her mind understood she just wanted to get back to her data, but that didn't stop every second pressed into her bunk from feeling like purgatory.

Because Derreck had structured the mission around the chance that there might be intelligent life on the planet, Derreck and Alston had chosen a landing site on the night side of the planet. There was no hiding the flare of the dropship's engines, but Derreck's plan was to drop using as much glide as he could manage. The *Vigilance* flew well, but it was still large for flight. If all went according to plan, they would only fire the jets when they approached their landing zone. On the slight chance there was intelligent life down here, it increased their chances they wouldn't be spotted. But there were far too many unknowns to be certain.

From her perspective on the acceleration couch, Kindra felt Derreck follow his plan to perfection. She had made it to her bunk with only a few seconds to spare and had strapped herself in quickly. She finished just as they hit atmosphere, shaking the entire dropship as though it were a child's plaything. No matter how many times she endured entry, Kindra was always surprised that the *Vigilance* didn't tear apart from the forces.

As the dropship rattled around her, Kindra was pressed into her bunk by over four G's. The mattress, which Kindra set to very firm, molded itself to the pressures of entry, providing her body the support it needed to survive high gravities unharmed. Kindra had always wondered what sort of fluid dynamics were responsible for the qualities of her mattress, but ultimately, she didn't care enough to investigate. All she knew was that she could withstand much higher gravities in her bunk than outside of it.

The dropship came out of atmospheric entry without breaking apart, and Kindra could feel gravity loosening its crushing grip on her body as Derreck began their glide. She shuddered at the release, enjoying the sensation of freedom from forces that threatened to squash her like a bug. Kindra waited for the usual sound of the engines kicking in until she remembered that Derreck was planning on gliding to a low altitude before turning up the thrust.

For the first time since they hit atmosphere, Kindra willed her neurodisplay into being. She never left it open during reentry. The doctors said the nanos which helped form the network for the system reacted poorly to anything over two gravities, so she always turned it off for the few minutes of reentry. Her first act was to call up the dropship's flight system. She didn't have any control over the system, but she could see most of the same information streams Derreck did.

He was flying the *Vigilance* manually. She shook her head. In almost all circumstances, the dropship's AI was more than sufficient, but Derreck never seemed to trust it the way others did. At least, that was his claim. Kindra suspected it was only part of the truth. The greater part was that Derreck liked being in control of his dropship, and he loved to fly. This, the flying of a dropship manually in an unfamiliar atmosphere at one-point-two gravities, was what he lived for. Kindra worried sometimes, but her trust of Derreck overrode any fears she might have.

Kindra watched the numbers scroll down, their altitude dropping at an impressive rate. She frowned. She understood that in theory they were gliding, but she also knew they were in a dropship weighing more tons than she could easily count. Even with the wings generating lift, the dropship wouldn't float in the air. As she watched the numbers spin down, she realized the pressure on her body was lessening as well. In fact, she was getting to the point where the straps to her bunk were starting to hold her down. They were becoming weightless.

Derreck's voice came in through her ear. "Sorry, all, but this is going to be a bit rough. Prepare for G's again."

Kindra almost laughed. Derreck's words were an apology, but his voice was anything but. He was having the time of his life up there. She would bet anything he and Kenan were up on the bridge hooting and hollering like cowboys from American Western films. She turned her neurodisplay off again, grateful she at least didn't have to watch the numbers spinning downwards out of control anymore.

Derreck' voice in her ear was the only other warning she got. "Here it comes!" The excitement in his voice was that of a child unwrapping his first birthday gift.

The rockets kicked in, a familiar and comforting roar. Kindra wasn't sure she had ever felt them kick in with such strength before, but they'd never come in unpowered like this before either. She slammed back into her bunk, the mattress absorbing all the impact and rushing to support her body once again under powerful gravities. There wasn't any way of being sure, but she was pretty confident they were pushing more G's than they had on entry. Derreck might be having a little too much fun for her taste.

Despite the excitement of their descent, their landing was as smooth as anything Kindra had ever experienced. She could criticize Derreck for what he had put them through, but there was no doubting his skill as a pilot. She could just barely tell when their movement stopped. The engines were shut off, and the roar in her ears was replaced by silence, the sound that indicated they were ready to start a new mission. It took all her self-control not to slap away the restraining straps before Derreck gave the word.

"Everyone is free to move about. Status checks of your stations within five minutes."

He didn't have to tell Kindra twice. Every minute strapped to her gravity couch was a minute she wasn't staring at the information coming onto the screens. She pulled up the feed on her neurodisplay, but requested a more transparent version. The images were so interesting, she'd run into the walls of the dropship if she wasn't careful.

Kindra made it to her station and pulled up all the displays and information she could. She whistled to herself. There was no doubt they were someplace special. She'd been a lot of different places in her life, but this was something else. Derreck, Kenan, and Alston had selected a clearing in a forest. The amount of biodiversity within just a few steps of their dropship would be incredible. She took a brief minute just to immerse herself in the experience. She had been in forests before, but they had all been terraformed, and there was always something about them that just didn't seem quite right. It was almost impossible to put a finger on, but the feeling was consistent and well-documented. Humans could tell what was real and what was created.

Kindra shook her head and cleared her thoughts of romantic notions. They only had a few weeks here, and she was going to make the most of them. The scientist in her took over, and she began to run down her checklist. The first step was going to be to reserve time on the dropship's sensors. They had an amazing collection of tools and scanners onboard, but they'd all be fighting for time. She requested a few hours from the dropship's AI and quickly received notice she'd have access to sensors in six hours. It would seem like forever, but it would have to do. It would give her enough time to determine which tests she'd like to run.

The dropship's range was limited, but it would give her an in-depth analysis of the surrounding area. What they really needed was more information about the planet as a whole. She pulled up the scans from the survey probe and was frustrated by how much information was still lacking. Survey probes worked on the principle that time wasn't an issue. They collected information in bits and pieces, using multiple scans to increase the resolution of the survey. But it was slow, and Kindra wasn't feeling patient.

Suddenly, an idea occurred to her. Kindra pulled up the specs of the probe on the computer to check her hunch. She was right. She called Derreck.

Kindra waited while her display told her he was online with Alston. As soon as he finished, his voice came into her ear.

"What do you have for me?"

"Biology is green across the board. I haven't checked medical yet, but I'll let you know when I do."

Derreck hesitated for a moment, and Kindra saw the lecture forming, but he didn't even bother. He knew why she was distracted. "Just finish your checks as soon as you can."

He was about to sign off, but Kindra stopped him. "I'd like to reserve the S-band radar periodically on the survey probe."

Kindra could just about hear his frown. "To what end?"

"I can use it to pull up high resolution scans of some areas in question. I'd like to get a detailed image of some of the locations that indicate civilization. It will speed up the process substantially."

Derreck thought for a moment. Kindra knew what he was thinking. The S-band radar was almost never pointed down towards the planet. It was the radar used to detect any object that was small, typically between one and ten centimeters. Almost every jumper, dropship, and probe was equipped with one. In space, even small objects moving at high enough velocities could cause serious damage. The survey probe used it to detect any incoming debris or object and adjust its flight path to avoid it. If the radar turned its resolution down towards the planet, they would temporarily be blind to any dangers.

Kindra considered cajoling Derreck, but it would never work. He always made the best decision based on his own information.

"Fine. There shouldn't be any debris around the planet. Limit your scans to a few minutes each. We don't need that resolution planet-wide, but pick out the locations you think best and give the computer the orders. I'll ensure you have enough clearance."

Kindra contained her pleasure. "Thanks, Captain."

Derreck didn't respond, just signing off and going to the next person who was trying to get his attention.

Kindra smiled. She couldn't say why she felt this way, but she was certain they were going to discover something amazing down on this planet. She couldn't wait.

THEIR FIRST DAY on the planet passed too quickly for Kindra, or at least, the sunlight soon fled. The planet had a day/night cycle that lasted about twenty hours, and even in space Fleet observed a strict twenty-four-hour day. Humans may have left their home planet a long time ago, but traditions died hard. They had landed in the later part of the planet's evening, and dawn had soon been upon them. Derreck had confined them to the ship for the first day, and the only one who seemed disappointed was Kindra.

Kindra felt an attraction to this planet that defied rationality. It had started out as something subtle, an anxiousness she couldn't explain, but it was rapidly morphing into a physical desire. She wanted to be on the planet, wanted to run her hands through the soil and feel it slip through her hand. She wanted to feel the scratch of the bark of the trees against her skin. But instead she was trapped inside the dropship, its smooth and functional lines and surfaces everywhere she went. She considered asking others if they were feeling anything similar, but she was too embarrassed.

There were moments when she lost time. She would pull up all the external cameras on the dropship, and she would just sit in her chair and take in the view, limited as it was by the tall trees that surrounded them.

It was days like today that reminded her why she had become a biologist in the first place. Like most humans, she had grown up in a hab on a planet in the midst of terraforming. For as long as she could remember, she had been different. Growing up, none of her friends had ever questioned life in the hab. They accepted their day-to-day existence as the only one possible. But she never had.

Perhaps it was all the reading and viewing she had done as a child. She had always been curious, and her favorite study was that of the past. She had read all about Earth and what it had been like. There were entire libraries of film and text, and she had worked her way through as many of them as she could. The history courses on her tablet were all bland, just short descriptions of what life had been like. But with access to her parents' account, she discovered a trove of information.

What fascinated her more than anything else was the idea that humans had lived outdoors, with nothing between them and space but atmosphere. Some humans still did. There were planets that had been almost completely terraformed, planets where humans could go outside, but not too many, and they were prohibitively expensive to live on. Everyone wanted to get there, so it was difficult to do so. But on Earth, it had been normal to be outside. Kindra's imagination filled with thoughts of what it must have been like.

Her favorite childhood memories were her trips to the gardens. Her parents had always supported her curiosity and were always trying to find ways to give her new experiences she'd enjoy, and the gardens were always a sure bet. She was fascinated by plants, and if her parents could find a gardener willing to endure her questions, she'd pester them until she ran out of air. Her parents always joked that she was good for the plants because of the excess carbon dioxide she expelled.

As soon as she was able, Kindra had applied for a work permit in the gardens. Her dad, who had been high-ranking in the hab, had helped push her application through, and Kindra had spent every moment she could working there. It wasn't just that she'd enjoyed the place, she'd loved the work. She loved planting and the physical work it took to bring life from sterile ground. Through her work in the gardens she began to learn about the incredible amount of work it took to coax life to take root on a new planet.

The Rebellion conflicts changed everything. Kindra's hab had been spared, so she had been fortunate in that regard. But many of the positions off-world she'd dreamed of no longer existed. She wanted to study life in all its variety, and the only way to do that was to join Fleet. Her parents didn't want her joining. The organization was too new and unknown, but it was the only place that could give Kindra the opportunity to study life around the galaxy.

Kindra's reverie was interrupted by a beep from the computer. She came out of her trance and realized she had been staring at the outside screens for almost a half-hour. It was past mealtime with the crew, and the computer was still processing most of the data. She stood up and stretched, her joints creaking from long hours of disuse.

Night was falling, but Kindra wasn't tired yet, and her scheduled bunk time wasn't for a few hours. She decided she wanted to take a look at the stars, so she grabbed a meal pack and climbed the ladder to the upper level of the dropship. She figured she'd be able to use the viewing room.

Kindra was surprised when she found Derreck there. They sometimes called the room the observation deck, even if that wasn't accurate. There were no windows on the dropship. But each of the walls of the room, including the ceiling, was covered in viewscreens. They could be set to anything, and were sometimes used for more important work, but tradition demanded the viewscreens be set to the view of the outside world surrounding the dropship. It was where they all came to find some peace and to soak in the atmosphere of whatever new planet they were on.

Kindra didn't normally bother too much with the room. Most of the planets they landed on were barren, and unless there was something of interest happening outside, there was little reason to be there.

But as soon as she stepped onto the observation deck, she knew she would experience something new here today.

They were high in the trees, and from the vantage point of the cameras that fed into the viewscreens, the view seemed to go on forever. Evening was just setting, but the two moons of the planet reflected more than enough light for Kindra to see for kilometers. She had never seen a natural forest before, and Derreck was promptly forgotten as she watched the tops of the trees sway in the wind.

Derreck broke the silence, but when he did, he was quiet, as though he also felt the magic of the sight they were given. To speak too loudly would break the spell. "It's hard to believe, isn't it?"

Kindra nodded. Everything she could have said in response seemed inadequate. The feelings rushing through her were contradictory and powerful, and words failed her. She cycled through responses to Derreck' simple comment, finally settling on one. "Yes."

Their eyes met, and Derreck seemed to understand. Sometimes words just weren't sufficient. They were both explorers to the bone, and they understood at least a good part of what the other was feeling.

They stood in silence, taking in the view being provided to them of the outside. Kindra watched the trees and wondered if her ancestors had ever seen views like these, and if they had, how they had felt about them. Had they been awed every day, or had they taken it for granted?

Derreck's head moved, and Kindra knew he had gotten a notification on his neurodisplay. She felt a pang of sadness for him. The moment she had come up here she had turned hers off. She didn't want the view spoiled by anything humans had made. She wanted an uninterrupted experience. It wasn't hard for her to do, but Derreck wouldn't have the opportunity, no matter how much he might wish for it.

"The probe is going to be passing overhead in just a minute or two."

Kindra turned her eyes towards the sky. Despite an adult life lived in the void between the stars, she was still awed by the universe. Humans were just crawling their way across the Milky Way, and there was so much more to discover. Their ships, powerful as they were, could still only jump about a hundred light years with any reliability, and at that speed, the galaxy was still enormous.

Looking into space, whether she was landside or on a ship, always made her feel small and insignificant. Most people she knew were the same. For some, thoughts of the enormity of space made them uncomfortable, but most found space comforting. After all, in such a big place, any problems you worried about were essentially meaningless. It gave Kindra a proper perspective when she took things too seriously.

Derreck's voice broke her train of thought. He too, was staring at the stars, and Kindra imagined he was thinking the same as her. "Any constellations out there?"

Kindra smiled and shook her head. No matter how far they traveled, he would always be the same. There was something beautiful about Derreck. He was a veteran explorer and had been on more planets than most people even knew existed. He was a veteran of the Rebellion conflict too, and had the scars, both physical and emotional, to prove it. But despite a lifetime in space, he still maintained a sense of childhood wonder. Kindra wasn't sure she'd be able to do the same if she was as experienced as him.

Kindra's gaze took in the stars, looking for patterns. It was a practice as old as humanity, and a game Derreck always enjoyed playing. Everywhere they went, they saw mostly the same stars, but always in new arrangements. Derreck loved finding constellations and making up stories to go with them.

After a few seconds of searching, she thought she found one. She traced the image with her finger, trying to point out the right stars to Derreck. "It's an explorer. There are the legs, and there are the stars for the torso. You can see she's holding a telescope."

Derreck laughed softly. "So it is. Look, there's our probe."

Kindra didn't need to follow his finger. Their probe was crossing across the sky, a bright, quick-moving star from their vantage point. Kindra let her imagination run wild just for a moment and wondered what it would be like to live on this planet and see a star moving the wrong direction. They'd probably think it was a sign of some kind. They'd be disappointed to learn it was just a simple probe, also meaningless in the grand scheme of the universe.

Without warning, the space where the probe had been flared brightly. The viewscreens automatically adjusted the brightness after a second's delay, dimming the stars to nothingness. Kindra was shocked, but Derreck never lost his wits. He was already on his comm. "Kenan, what the hell just happened out there?"

The channel Derreck used was an open one to the entire crew, so Kindra could hear Kenan's response. "We lost the probe, sir."

Anger crept into Derreck' voice. "I can see that. I want to know why."

"Give me a few minutes, sir. Diagnostics were reading green across the board, so whatever happened wasn't internal."

Kindra was stunned. Losing one probe was could be

anything. Losing two probes was beyond the realm of coincidence.

Derreck shook his head and stormed out of the observation deck. Kindra looked back at the screens and saw the fading image of the nuclear explosion that had just happened, a perfect sphere of fire in the sky, and she wondered, just for a moment, if they were as safe on this planet as they thought they were.

FIVE

A FEW DAYS LATER, Tev was getting ready to join another hunt when Neera found him. There was a look of confusion on her face, but she spoke her mind before Tev could even ask.

"You're needed. There is someone from another clan here, and they come seeking aid."

Tev frowned. Visitors from other clans weren't all that unusual, even though they didn't come frequently. A clan asking for aid was something different though. Most clans Tev encountered would sooner die alone than ask for help from others.

Neera answered his unasked question. "He speaks about fire coming from the sky. They have already sent out a hunting party, but they seek aid from the surrounding clans."

Tev's mind flashed back to the star that had gone across the sky the wrong way. It seemed improbable that the incidents would be related, but he couldn't shake the idea that they were. He had never heard of fire from the sky. It seemed impossible, like a story told to children.

He grabbed his spear and followed Neera to where the clan was gathering. A small circle had formed around the foreign hunter, and Tev judged him immediately. He looked more like a messenger than a hunter, built more for running than fighting an animal.

The messenger was just beginning to tell his story.

". . . Two days ago we saw fire descend from the sky. I saw it with my own eyes, which is why I'm here today, so that you might believe me."

Tev interrupted the speaker. It was a rude action, but Tev didn't care. His story felt wrong.

"Tell us more about this fire from the sky. Are you sure you weren't taken with drink?"

The messenger glared at Tev but answered the question. "I was on watch that night and had nothing to drink. At first I thought it was a bright star, but it was going the wrong way, and as I watched, it got brighter and brighter. I was sure it was a star in the sky, but then it came lower and lower, and I saw it wasn't a star at all. It was some object descending on fire."

Tev didn't believe the messenger, but his interest was piqued. A star moving against the sky? Perhaps his own experience was connected.

The messenger continued. "What was most strange was that the column of fire slowed until it reached the ground. It landed softly, like a giant bird without wings. It landed about three days away from our home. We sent out a hunting party, led by the great Xan, the strongest of our hunters. Meanwhile, we have sought help from our neighbors. It was decreed by our elders."

Tev was uncomfortable. It sounded as though the messenger was honest, and Tev had heard of Xan. The man was something of a legend among hunters, and if he had been sent out, the clan the man came from was indeed serious about what they had seen. He would be foolish to ignore them.

But he was also foolish if he believed the story. Nothing descended on flames, and nothing slowed down as it fell. But precisely because these facts were so outlandish, Tev could almost believe the man. If it was a trap, wouldn't the man be able to make up a better story?

Tev turned to the elders, who were busy conversing in a group. Tev wondered which side of the argument they would take. The elders were a conservative bunch, so he didn't rank the messenger's odds too highly.

The elders turned around and faced the crowd. "We have decided to send some of our best hunters to help the clan."

Tev took half a step back. That wasn't what he had expected from the elders.

The camp moved into action. Once a decision was made, all that was left to do was to act. There was no debating the wisdom of the elders.

At least not publicly. Tev found Shet and took him aside. "Do you actually believe this man?"

Shet shrugged. "It is not about me believing him or not. It is more that we cannot afford not to believe him."

Tev frowned. "What do you mean?"

"There are stories about people from the sky. All of them urge caution."

Tev shook his head, unable to believe what he was hearing. "What do you mean, stories about people from the sky? I've never heard such stories. People don't come from the sky."

Shet shrugged again. "There are stories shared only among the elders. I do not understand them either, but we must be cautious. And so we will be. You will be among the hunters, of course."

Tev wanted to argue, but there was no point. Not with Shet. "What would you have of me?"

"Use your senses and your wisdom, Tev. I can feel the winds changing. Be ready for them."

SIX

ONE ASPECT of life in Fleet was that shit happened. Sometimes it was type of event rookies had nightmares about: hull collapses or radiation shielding failing. Ships were safe, but there were thousands of them in space at any time, and bad things happened. There had never been a system of transportation in human history that was perfectly safe, and the same was true of space travel.

Space could be dangerous for anyone, but it was more so for the explorers of Fleet. Other segments of Fleet stuck to well-traveled, well-populated sections of the galaxy. But explorers were beyond support, out on their own in the blackness. There were plenty of stories to go around about ships that had just disappeared. No one had the slightest clue what had happened to them. It was as if they and their crews had never existed.

When the probe exploded, the ship fell into chaos. Almost everyone had experiments running on the probe, and everyone had a responsibility to make sure they hadn't caused the malfunction. Without being asked, Kindra ran a full diagnostic on all her systems. She breathed a sigh of relief when she wasn't able to discover any problems.

Losing the probe was a blow to the team, and no one felt it more keenly than Kindra. Without the probe, they were essentially blind. The *Vigilance* had a full suite of sensors, but on land their distance was far too limited for Kindra's tastes. Without the survey probe they would have to settle for a detailed view of a smaller area instead of a more complete picture of the entire planet.

For Kindra, who had been excited to study and map out entire ecosystems, the loss of the probe was devastating. Without it, she was confined to a small area to study. She wouldn't be able to examine the connections between different systems on the planet with the detail she'd hoped for.

Although life on the ship returned to normal, the loss of the probe created a tension that hadn't been there before. Losing one probe could easily be explained away. Losing two probes around a planet without any meaningful orbital debris was another problem entirely. It could be that both probes had been unfortunate, but the odds of it were astronomical. It was much more likely something else was at play.

Even though everyone acknowledged that truth, there was no evidence either way. All the systems on the probe had checked out across the board. The probe had been communicating with the dropship constantly, and up to the last few milliseconds of its existence, it hadn't registered any problems. Most likely, the probe had impacted something. Due to the S-band radar being turned down towards the planet, there was no way of knowing for sure. Had it been hit by a piece of random debris, or had it been brought down intentionally? There weren't any answers.

With nothing else to go on, Derreck ordered the team back about their work. He told them he was rethinking on-world expeditions, but that was as far as his measures went.

It was the first time Kindra felt real fear while in Fleet. Their messages would only travel at light speed, which meant they were on their own. Kindra wondered if they had bitten off more than they could chew.

DESPITE THE LOSS of the probe, their team went about their work with practiced efficiency. They had explored dozens of new worlds, and despite the promise of this one, in every other way it was just another planet. Kenan would be the first one to place his foot on the world, as he always was. Kindra understood the protocol, but it didn't stop her from feeling a pang of jealousy every time she watched Kenan make first contact with a new world. She should have felt gratitude. Kenan went first because in many ways, Fleet considered him to be the most expendable. But just once, Kindra wanted to be first onto a new land.

The loss of the probe slowed them down. Derreck didn't want to let anybody out onto the surface until he was certain it was safe. They delayed a day, waiting for anything to happen, but nothing did. The forest was alive, but nothing came to bother them or the *Vigilance*. Every hour that passed was excruciating. Kindra wanted to send Kenan out to get samples, and she finally got Derreck to agree there didn't seem to be any danger.

Kindra helped Kenan into his exosuit, even though there wasn't much to do. Kenan could get into and out of his exosuit on his own, they were designed that way. But regs were regs, and Kindra had to check to ensure the suit was sealed properly. Even Kenan wasn't enough of an idiot to screw it up, though.

Their scans said the atmosphere was safe to breathe, but they wouldn't take any chances. All it would take was one curious microbe and they could all be in jeopardy.

Kenan gave Kindra one final, obnoxious smile, and put on the helmet to his exosuit. The visor dimmed as Kenan pulled up the displays feeding him whatever information he thought was important.

Kindra stepped away and Kenan powered up the rest of the suit, taking his first steps towards the airlock. As she watched him move, she couldn't help but be impressed. The exosuits were a new invention from Fleet headquarters. Humans had been armoring themselves for as long as historical records went back, but they had never created anything like this. The neural interface technology had only recently been developed.

The suits were heavy, ranging from fifty to well over a hundred kilos. Kenan's was on the heavy side, suitable for combat operations. But when you slipped into the suit, you didn't feel different at all. The key was a combination of two technologies. The first was the helmet. Sensors running from the base of the neck and all around the skull were able to read the electrical impulses in your mind. Once the suit was sufficiently calibrated, you could, at least in theory, do anything just by thinking about it. Everything from movement to environmental reports to combat was a simple thought away. In practice, the technology was still new, and many pilots struggled with neural control of the suits. But, it still helped the second technology.

Inside the suit was a system of responsive sensors. They amplified your natural motions by detecting them and feeding them to the suit. If you wanted to raise your arm, you simply began the motion. The suit would notice the change in body position and duplicate the motion. It was the primary driver for most pilots.

Kindra had logged over a hundred hours in the suits, and she was still amazed by their abilities. They amplified your strength and senses, and a skillful pilot could pick a flower or lift a girder with equal ease. Unlike Kenan, she didn't have her own dedicated suit. She and the other four shared the other suit, a basic multipurpose model, just over half the weight and size of Kenan's. It was still an impressive piece of technology, but it didn't match the capabilities of Kenan's suit.

Kenan stepped into the airlock and waited for the decontamination process to cycle. They were concerned not just about bringing microbes onto the ship, but also about delivering their microbes to the planet's surface. No system was perfect, but they did the best they could, and Kenan would be decontaminated both going and returning.

After she was certain Kenan was set and she had gone through the last parts of her checklist, Kindra returned to her station to get back to work. She had been upset to be pulled away from all the information coming across her screens. Even without the probe she was collecting a lifetime's worth of information.

Kindra pulled up three monitors when she got back to Biology. Two of them were dedicated to the information coming in from the ship's sensors, but the third was the feed from Kenan's suit. As much as she didn't care about Kenan, he was the first to step onto the planet, and he would collect a few samples for her. It was worth giving him at least a bit of attention.

Kindra went about her work, only half paying attention to Kenan's screen. The first part of the expedition was just getting Kenan away from the ship to prevent contamination of samples. When he started gathering her samples he would let her know. Until then she could focus on other data.

A flash in the monitor caught her eye. She looked up and saw a blip fading on Kenan's motion detector. Kindra shot to attention. She pulled up a wrap-around view so she could see even more than he could. She tapped into the audio between the dropship and Kenan. There was silence, so she clicked in. "Kenan, did you see the motion sensors?"

"Yeah, but it was a faint reading. Could have been anything."

Something twisted in Kindra's gut. After the probe, who knew what was out there? "Keep your eyes open. Everything coming across my screens indicates this planet is almost certain to support lifeforms we aren't familiar with. Who knows how they'll show up on motion sensors?"

She heard Kenan curse. "I suppose you're right. Oh well, at least it makes collecting samples more exciting."

Kindra kept her eyes glued to the screens, but nothing came up, and she wondered if she was worried about a danger that didn't exist. Despite the loss of the probe, they hadn't discovered any signs of intelligent life. They had to remain rational. She tuned in to Kenan's audio feed to hear what he was hearing. Mostly it was silence, the silence of a planet undeveloped by human hands. Kindra drank it in. Every once in a while, a breeze would come through and rustle the leaves of nearby trees. Kindra reveled in the sound, something she hadn't heard in months.

Another blip came across the sensors, and this time there was no doubt. Something else was out there with Kenan. Kindra was just about notify Derreck, but there was no need. His voice was already on the comms. "You've got company out there, Kenan. I'm aborting the mission. Come back in."

"Yes, sir."

The motion was behind Kenan, still faint. Kindra isolated the information from Kenan's suit and ran a basic analysis. The sensors were indicating a large object, so the faint readings meant it was moving slowly. It could only be intelligent life. A primal part of Kindra's mind went off, and she grew certain Kenan was being hunted. He was already on his way back in, and his exosuit was one of the most advanced around, so he shouldn't be in any danger, but she could still help him.

Kindra grabbed the video from Kenan's rear-mounted cameras. He couldn't use them while walking because of the disorientation, but she could. She started the computer on pattern recognition while she kept her eyes peeled on the screen. There didn't seem to be anything there. She blinked and switched the feed to infrared. There was a lot of heat, but in the distance, she could see something move, so carefully it didn't even trip Kenan's motion sensor. Kindra commandeered some of Kenan's sensors and focused on what was behind him.

She caught the movement again and pulled up the recordings. Her mind rebelled against what she was seeing. As a scientist, she was well aware of her own cognitive biases, but she couldn't help herself. Whatever was out there was bipedal. The odds of it were beyond astronomical.

"Derreck, check this out."

"That looks like a human."

Kindra sighed in relief. "I thought I might be going crazy for a moment."

There was a moment of silence as Derreck considered

the new information. Kindra had no answers for him. But he decided quickly.

"Kenan, you've got at least one bipedal creature thirty meters behind you. We'll watch your six for you, just get back to the ship, double-time."

Kenan didn't acknowledge, but his speed picked up. Worried, Kindra pulled up Kenan's vitals. His breath was steady, but his pulse was high, and his adrenaline was through the roof. It was far outside of non-combat parameters. She opened a private channel to Derreck.

"Derreck, his vitals are through the roof."

Derreck's answer was cryptic. "Memories. He'll be fine. We just need to get him back here."

Kindra watched the monitors, her worry mounting. She felt helpless, but she knew she was doing all she could.

Without warning, there was a large blip on the motion sensor. Kindra was still listening, and she didn't hear anything, but there were multiple creatures out there, and this one was less than ten meters behind Kenan. Time seemed to slow down and everything happened at once.

Kenan wasn't watching his six, but the motion was enough to draw all his attention. Like the well-trained combat veteran he was, he turned around and snapped his arm up and towards the target behind him.

Derreck saw it too and shouted through the comms. "Kenan, hold your fire!"

On the minimized monitor that showed Kenan's front view, Kindra saw the targeting reticule move away from the creature that had triggered the motion sensor. Kindra couldn't believe what she was looking at. It couldn't be, but she was looking at a human, clad in nothing but a loincloth and armed with a bow and arrow.

The creature, the human, drew his bow in one smooth

motion and launched an arrow straight at Derreck. Kindra flinched involuntarily, but the arrow bounced harmlessly off Kenan's armor. His exosuit could take most high-velocity projectiles without a problem. The arrow was less than a joke.

For a moment, it seemed like everything would still be fine. But then the woods around Kenan came alive. At least a half-dozen creatures emerged from behind trees, and Kindra lost her power of speech. How had they avoided detection? Two spears arced towards Kenan, and Kindra could see more were soon coming.

In theory, Kenan wasn't in any danger, but Derreck's voice over the channel was worried, more than Kindra thought he should be. "Shit. Kenan, retreat, now!"

But Derreck was still keyed into the private channel with Kindra, and it took him a few seconds to realize his mistake.

Kenan reacted. She heard the whine of the rifle attached to his arm, and the tree next to the first creature exploded. None of the other creatures even hesitated. Every one turned and sprinted away from Kenan. He aimed near one of them and pulled the trigger again, cutting down another two trees with a sustained burst.

Kindra couldn't believe what was happening in front of her eyes. How had this happened?

Derreck's voice penetrated through the fog of her mind. "Kenan! GODDAMNIT, CEASE FIRE!"

Kindra had never heard Derreck shout before, and it startled her back into action. It also caused Kenan to stop firing. She heard him mutter under his breath. "Only warning shots, sir."

He sounded like a child angry he had been scolded for doing something he had thought was okay.

Derreck's voice was lower, but his tone left no room for argument.

"Get back to the ship, immediately."

Kenan knew better than to say anything.

"Yes, sir."

Kindra released the breath she hadn't realized she'd been holding. Had they just opened fire on the first aliens humans had ever encountered?

SEVEN

THE NEXT DAY Tev and a group of his fellow hunters joined the messenger on the journey back to his home. Ever since Tev had heard the story, his mind had been racing with new thoughts. He thought about the odd star he had seen after the hunt. He tried to imagine what it would be like to see a ball of fire fly across the sky, and he wondered for the thousandth time if the two were somehow connected.

Tev shared his thoughts with Neera, but the best she could do was shrug. She did not dismiss his ideas, but there was also no evidence for them. Unlike him, Neera was comfortable with not knowing. She allowed herself to be uncertain until she learned the truth. It was a skill that Tev sometimes envied.

Fortunately, the journey itself distracted him. They were entering land he had never traveled before. Although he had roamed far and wide in his hunts, there were places the clan didn't go, and this far to the north had always been one of those places.

When he was younger, he had asked the elders why

travel to the north was forbidden, and they had given him a variety of answers. Some spoke about the inappropriateness of trespassing on the lands of another clan, others said it was a different type of land with dangers they didn't understand. Although the reasons differed, the rule always remained the same. There was a firm boundary to the north no one crossed. When they finally crossed the river that marked the northern boundary of his clan lands, Tev wondered what he would discover in this land, at once so new and so similar.

As they hiked, the land around them changed. The terrain they covered was still forested, but the trees thinned out as the land became steeper. Their progress slowed as they continued through unfamiliar territory.

As the two days passed, a friendly competition developed between the messenger and the hunters of Tev's clan. Tev prided himself on being the best hunter he knew, and it was soon obvious the messenger felt strongly about his own skills. The messenger shot a bow better than any Tev had ever seen, but Tev's familiarity with spear and blade couldn't be matched. Likewise, in the trees Tev had no equal. He could scamper from branch to branch and climb with the same ease as walking across flat ground. But as they left the dense forest and entered more mountainous terrain, the messenger was now the one at home, climbing from jagged stone to jagged stone as though he were walking up a set of steps.

As intense as the competition was, it remained friendly. Tev showed the messenger a stronger tree climbing technique, and in return Tev learned how to make more effective use of his legs while climbing rock walls. Together, their skills increased in tandem.

The final leg of the journey was a harrowing hike up the

sides of cliffs. The path was narrow, barely wide enough for one person to walk straight ahead, and at its narrowest, even that was untrue. At times Tev had to flatten himself against the rock wall and shuffle sideways until the path widened once again. There were times Tev doubted the messenger was actually leading them towards his home. Perhaps it was all an elaborate trap. There seemed to be no way a clan could make their home in such an inhospitable place.

But then they were there, among a series of caves that sheltered and protected the clan. A quick glance told Tev this was one of the safest locations a clan could make their home, and awe quickly replaced his doubt.

WHEN THEY ARRIVED, they found Xan and his hunting party recently returned. A small crowd had gathered around them, and Tev's group didn't receive much of a welcome. Tev and his fellow hunters joined the small crowd and listened as Xan spoke.

Tev's first impression of Xan filled him with respect. Xan was a tall man, lean and muscular. Scars were visible all across his body, and Tev noticed that a few of them were fresh. At the center of the circle, he stood up straight and spoke clearly, and Tev found it easy to listen to him.

The story he told was difficult to believe. Part of it was obvious. Xan spoke about how he and his fellow hunters had tracked the falling ball of fire. The beginning of the hunt was an important part of a hunt story, and Xan told it well, but Tev was far more interested in what happened after. His mind had been consumed by possibilities since he had left his home. He wanted answers.

As Xan continued, his story became more and more unusual. Xan spoke about hearing sounds he had never heard before, sounds he lacked the language to describe. He tried mimicking them, but to no avail. Then he told them all of a creature, a creature who seemed impossible.

"Like us, it seems to move on two legs. It has two arms and a place where the head is. But that is where it ends. It does not have skin like you or I have. It has skin made of some sort of rock, but rock made of bright colors. We struck it with arrows and with spears, but it did not bleed, and our weapons bounced off."

Tev kept his expression neutral, but he was having a hard time believing Xan's story. There were animals that had hides that were difficult to pierce, but everything living could be cut. Tev only knew Xan by reputation, and although he didn't seem like a hunter who would lie, he had to be mistaken.

"I do not know what power this creature has, but when it raised its arm, it made a shrill shriek, and a tree next to our hunter shattered as though it had been felled with one axe swing. We realized then that this was a hunt we were not prepared for. We returned to wait for our brothers and sisters, so we may once again pursue this most fearsome foe."

Tev ignored Xan's dramatics. While traditional, it was something Tev had little patience for. The legendary hunter's story had been full of exaggeration, but far too short on the details that Tev would have liked. But Xan was mobbed by the crowd, and Tev would have no chance of speaking to him for a while. He noticed, with a pang of jealousy, that Neera was among those who pressed to be closer to Xan.

What did strike Tev as interesting was the basic description Xan had given. He had said the creature looked much as they did, and Shet's words about people from the sky echoed in Tev's mind. Perhaps there was another connection here he didn't yet realize. He wandered the caves as his mind wandered over the possibilities.

AFTER XAN'S story was complete, the clan seemed to remember their manners. They had been obsessed with their greatest hunter's story, but they didn't forget their hospitality.

Tev and his fellow hunters were welcomed warmly by the clan. They received places to sleep and introduced themselves to hunters from other clans as well. Tev was surprised by how many clans had heeded the call. It was unlike so many to come to the aid of another.

That night there was a feast unlike any Tev had experienced before. Fish, caught from the streams below, made up the bulk of the meal. He had eaten fish before, but never of this size. The meat was tender and flavorful and entirely unlike anything he'd ever tasted. It was accompanied by a selection of fruits and plants, some of which were familiar and many that weren't. Tev tried everything, finding most of it to his liking.

After the feast was over, the crowd quieted down as a large bowl passed around the circle. Each person took a sip and Tev watched as their demeanor changed. Hunters who had been alert a moment before became glassy-eyed and lost in a world Tev could not see. Tev had heard of this practice before, but had never seen it in person.

He leaned over to the hunter next to him and asked what the liquid was. The hunter replied, "It is a holy gift, given to us by our ancestors. It is made with the crushed leaves of a plant that grows nearby, but a single sip will open your eyes to experiences you can't imagine. It is said that it will show you what you need to know."

Tev considered passing on the substance. He was a hunter tasked with pursuing a strange creature, and he needed his wits about him. But they were safe in the caves and he was a guest here. And he was curious, more than anything else. When the bowl came to him, he sipped without hesitation.

It took a moment for the liquid to kick in, but once it did, Tev's world shattered. Images and sensations burned across his mind faster than he could focus. He was no longer in the cave with other hunters, but was everywhere at once. He flew over mountains and trees and rivers and vast bodies of water. Everyone seemed small and their problems meaningless. And then everything went dark, a darkness unlike anything Tev had ever experienced, complete blackness.

A deep chill settled into his bones, a cold he thought he might die from. Then a single pinprick of light flashed across the sky. Small as it was, it was hot, setting his insides on fire. And then there was a rock, but it wasn't a rock. Tev didn't have the language to describe it, but he knew it had been made, like a boat sailing between the pinpricks of light. And somehow, it mattered, mattered more than anything Tev had ever done in his entire life.

Other images flashed through his mind, there and gone before he was even aware of their presence, but there was one image that stuck with him. A rock hurtling through the darkness, smooth and shiny. He opened his eyes, surprised to find he was no longer in the cave. He looked around and felt the wind whipping around him. Although it was dark, he knew he was in a very high place. Perhaps the highest place.

He spun around, suddenly certain he wasn't alone, and he wasn't. There was a woman there with him. At first he thought it was Neera, strong and confident. But as the figure became more solid, he realized it wasn't her. Deep in his gut, he knew he was standing with Lys, the goddess of the hunt.

She looked at him with sad eyes, eyes that had seen pain others had never experienced. She looked right at him, looked right through him, and spoke. He thought perhaps she was speaking to him, but he couldn't be sure. Her voice went through him as though he was just one of many people she spoke to.

"You have a very long way to go."

Tev looked around. He wasn't sure about anything, but he couldn't see anyone else and he felt compelled to respond. "I've already traveled a long way. Farther than I ever have before."

Lys shook her head. "You have barely even taken the first step," she said. "You cannot even conceive of how much farther you must go. You must chase your prey as far as your life can take you."

Then Tev was alone, standing on a high place in the dark. He shivered and opened his eyes and he was back in the cave, surrounded by the hunters he would travel with when the sun rose. He looked around and saw that the fire had gone out, untended by the glassy-eyed individuals scattered throughout the cave.

Moving silently, Tev built the fire back up to keep them warm through the long night. He laid back down, his dream running through his mind, the image of a rock in the blackness consuming his thoughts.

EIGHT

EVEN THOUGH KINDRA'S world was spiraling out of control, it had least had the decency to do it in slow motion. She was running towards the airlock where Kenan would re-enter, but she felt as though the air itself was dense, like she was running through a gaseous soup rather than the ultra-purified air of their dropship.

In the corner of her eye, Kenan's helmet cam allowed her to see what Kenan could see. From her observations, Kenan was the calmest of them all. Derreck was silent on the comms. He had given the order to return and there was little left for him to do but ponder his next decision. Kindra watched as Kenan's targeting reticule regularly scanned his path to make sure he was clear of threats.

She had never seen him in combat before. Besides Derreck, none of them had. But the bravado and machismo were gone. This was the real Kenan, focused and deadly. She pulled up his vitals. His hormones were all over the place. That was no surprise. Fleet had never seen any point in shutting down the hardwired fight-or-flight response. But his respiration was slow and steady.

Kindra reached the airlock minutes before Kenan did. Years of training took over, and her conscious mind slid away, replaced by the comforting checklists of routine. She could feel her own heart pounding in her chest, and she wasn't even in any danger.

Her checks were complete by the time Kenan returned. She could see him through the airlock window, assessing the surrounding territory one more time. But he hadn't been followed. He stepped backwards into the airlock, never turning his back to the wilderness beyond. He didn't lower his arm until the hatch was fully closed.

The airlock ran through the decontamination procedures. Kindra didn't see any reason they needed to rush, so she allowed the full cycle to run. She expected Kenan to complain, but he said nothing, waiting patiently for the cycle to complete. When it did, the airlock opened with a soft hiss and he stepped back into the dropship.

He didn't even give Kindra a chance to help him with his helmet. He pulled it off immediately, and Kindra was taken aback. Kenan was smiling. Not the half-smile he so often left plastered on his face, but a genuine smile. His eyes were bright, and he was grinning like he was a kid who had just gotten a gift he'd always wanted.

He didn't wait for Kindra. He stepped backwards into the exosuit storage container and waited as the container disassembled his suit around his body. The smile never left his face, and Kindra couldn't even begin to guess what was running through his mind.

She ran a quick diagnostic on his exosuit, but everything was in perfect condition. She wasn't surprised. The suit was designed to withstand impacts from advanced weaponry. There was almost no chance it would be harmed by mere arrows and spears.

Once the exosuit was off, she forced Kenan into a cursory examination, but she knew there was little point. There was no way he could have gotten even a scratch, and he hadn't. She took a quick blood sample to run some tests, but that was standard procedure after an exosuit mission on a new planet.

Derreck's voice spoke softly in her ear. "Kindra, I need to know what that was out there. It happened out of range of the ship sensors, so you'll have to rely on Kenan's exosuit data. Can you have a report for me in an hour?"

Kindra thought about what she had seen. "Can you give me two?"

Derreck didn't hesitate. "Sure. My quarters in two hours. There will be a team briefing in three."

"Yes, sir."

The line went dead, and Kindra walked quickly back to Biology, leaving Kenan to his post-mission checks. She needed to find out who they had just fired on.

AS DERRECK HAD PROMISED, three hours later the five of them were sitting down around the dinner table which doubled as their conference table. Kindra looked around the room to try to gauge the reactions of her fellow crew. Derreck's reaction she knew well enough. They had spent the last hour together going over Kindra's findings, as unbelievable as they were. He was angry at Kenan, but more disappointed by the way Kenan had handled himself. There was a backstory to Kenan's reaction, but she didn't know what it was and Derreck hadn't said anything.

Kenan was as cool as ever, and Kindra passed over him, trying to keep him as far out of her mind as possible. She was beyond furious at him. Pulling the trigger might have been the most disastrous event in all of human history. Humanity had been waiting hundreds of years to find another species, and the minute they did, they fired 137 high-velocity shells at them. Kenan didn't care. The smirk had returned to his face, and Kindra would have given a month's worth of hazard pay to kick it right off his face.

Eleta was the one who seemed most disturbed. Somewhere in her logical mind, the pieces weren't adding up, and she seemed deeply upset by what had just happened. Kindra had her work to distract her, but Eleta didn't. The ship and exosuit were in perfect working condition, so her life was largely routine at this point.

Alston was, well, Alston. He was as fascinated by the local geology as Kindra was by the life on the planet, and the fact that one of their crew had been fired upon didn't seem to register much in his mind. She suspected his biggest concern was what type of stone the arrowhead was made of.

Derreck called them to order and began the debriefing. He ran over the incident in moderate detail. Everyone chipped in their own piece, and Derreck detailed it all so they were on the same page. When he finished he glanced over at Kindra. "Kindra has some. . . interesting data on the incident. Kindra?"

Kindra nodded and pulled up some of the best holograms she'd been able to piece together. As a matter of course, Kenan's suit collected a wide array of data, and with a little manipulation, Kindra had produced a blurry image combining visual and infrared data streams.

There was a sharp intake of breath around the table. Only she and Derreck had seen this image before.

"As you can see, we've made first contact. As you can also see, even from a cursory glance, whatever we encountered looks awfully human."

She let everyone scan the image more closely before continuing, highlighting areas of the image as she spoke.

"Kenan's sensors are geared towards combat, and given the circumstances, we weren't able to get nearly as much information as I'd like, but from what I've been able to observe, the similarities between ourselves and this species go beyond remarkable. It's almost creepy, as unscientific as that term is. Kenan encountered a bipedal creature with a gait and stature similar to that of a human. I estimate this creature stands at about two meters tall and weighs approximately eighty kilos. Its temperature is almost thirty-seven degrees. It seems to have a human head as well: two eyes, nose, mouth, and ears, all on the head up here. It fired a bow and arrow much as a human would, if we were living thousands of years ago."

Kindra stopped and played the combined image as it shot the arrow at Kenan. She couldn't help but see the creature as human.

"I could bore you with speculation, but those are the facts."

Alston looked up from the hologram. "Forgive me for asking what seems an obvious question, but have you considered the possibility all this is meaningless? It seems to me we've just found some sort of crazy colony. Kindra, every stat you just mentioned falls squarely under the category of a healthy human. If it walks like a human, is the same size as a human, and shoots a bow and arrow like a human, why isn't it a human?"

Derreck interrupted Kindra before she could begin.

"The thought occurred to us, too. It's too much to be a coincidence, unless Kindra unearths some data that proves the theory wrong. I wondered if perhaps Fleet had some ulterior motive, and I went digging in the archives.

To make a long story short, there's no way they are human."

Alston shook his head. "Forgive me, Captain, but this history seems significant to me. I think I, for one, would like to hear the long story."

Derreck looked around and saw that Alston wasn't alone. "Very well. My first check was public archives. There was no surprise there, this planet has never been visited." Derreck paused. He looked around the room and spoke to the ship's AI. "*Vigilance*, pause recording. Captain's override."

Kindra's eyebrows went up at that. She glanced around and saw she wasn't the only one.

"What most people don't know is that there's another set of archives, not publicly available. The similarities Kindra picked up on were too much for me to dismiss, and even though I'm pretty high up in Fleet, they don't tell me everything. I don't want to say too much, because as you can probably guess, this is all highly classified. But Fleet does maintain a small subset of deep-expedition ships that can get involved in some highly unusual activities. I wondered if perhaps we had stumbled upon that. Perhaps one part of Fleet didn't know what another part was doing."

"But the search came up empty. Even according to the classified archives, this planet has never been visited before, and those archives go all the way back to the first colonies. Plus, all of us here know just how far from explored space we are. We're not as far as some of those deep expeditions, but we're well beyond the boundaries of current Fleet space. Why would anyone else be out here?"

Derreck shifted his voice back to the ship's AI. "*Vigilance*, resume recording."

"So, again, we come to the fact that as much as these

creatures may seem human, they aren't human. They can't be."

Alston wasn't so easily deterred. "What about concurrent evolution?"

This time it was Kindra who shook her head. "It's not impossible, of course. You can't prove something can't happen. But come on, Alston, you know as well as I do that the odds of something like that happening are beyond astronomical. There's no way that's the answer."

Alston shrugged but didn't say anything else.

Derreck gave everyone more time to ask questions, but everyone seemed preoccupied with their own thoughts.

"We now find ourselves in a difficult situation. We're all up to date with the information, so now the only question is what we do next. We weren't given very much guidance, but I think we're in over our heads. Our pick-up isn't for another twenty-two days, but our mission is officially over. I think we can all agree we have made first contact, and our only responsibility at this point is to communicate that fact to Fleet so they can decide on the next steps."

Kindra launched out of her seat. "Derreck, we can't just leave!"

He viewed her outburst calmly, as though he'd expected it. He probably had. "And why should we stay? There's no evidence to support this, but something is happening here. We've lost two probes and made contact with a species who considers us a danger."

"Derreck, everything you've said is exactly why we need to stay here!"

Kenan laughed out loud at that, silenced only by Derreck's vicious stare. It gave Kindra a chance to collect her thoughts.

"Derreck, we're already here, and there's still so much to

learn. None of you are biologists, but you've got to know just how unusual and special this planet is. Why not stay and gather more information? All of it will be useful for Fleet. We're explorers. This is exactly what we're supposed to be doing."

Derreck shook his head. "We can do research from orbit as well. That's not a compelling reason to stay here."

"Scans of the planet from orbit aren't nearly as useful as the research we can do down here. Besides, we all know the only thing Fleet is going to do is send another crew just like us here, if they can even pony up the resources for another mission. We are the only answer to finding out what's happening here."

Derreck nodded, acknowledging the truth of Kindra's point.

Eleta spoke up for the first time. "But we're in danger here. They shot at Kenan, and he shot at them. What if they come back with more weapons?"

Kenan rebutted that himself. "Eleta, we've got nothing to worry about. I could stand there and get shot at all day and it wouldn't bother me none. I may have overreacted a bit this last time, but I was taken by surprise. I could finish taking samples while they shot at me until their arms fell off."

Kindra saw Derreck's frown at Kenan's words. It was clear he didn't want any more contact with the creatures of the planet. She jumped in before Kenan could say any more. "There's no reason to think they'll return. Despite the inappropriateness of Kenan's reaction, you can be sure he terrified them all. They have no idea what our weaponry is like. And, if they do come back, we can just retreat and leave the planet. Simple as that."

Kindra looked around and saw everyone thinking about the choice. She couldn't believe they weren't as certain as she was. It had taken Fleet months to put together the resources for this trip. Despite their best intentions, it might be years before Fleet could afford to return, and Kindra couldn't live with that. There was too much work here to be done, too many questions to answer. And they were here, on a planet with intelligent life! How could anyone think about leaving?

"Come on. This is the biggest scientific discovery, perhaps of all time, and you want to leave? Think of everything we can learn. This is exactly why we signed on. We can't be deterred by the setbacks we've experienced. All of us are here because exploring the galaxy is in our blood. Let's make the discoveries that will change the course of human history."

She saw her words were having the desired effect. She knew her audience. Each of them had joined Fleet for different reasons, but there was a connecting thread that ran through all their lives. All of them considered themselves explorers. They loved to be on the edge of space, going places no one had gone before.

Kindra studied Derreck. Ultimately, he was the only one she needed to convince. He liked to pretend the ship was a democracy, and he considered everyone's opinions; but at the same time, he was the captain of the ship, responsible not just for their lives, but for all the decisions that were made. She had to imagine he would already be in the hottest of water for Kenan's firing on a new species. They'd catch the paused recording, too. Hell, there was every chance he would lose his position and get court-martialed as a result of all this.

But he was an explorer too, and just as curious as any of

them. He wasn't always a straight shooter, and Kindra was betting this was going to be one of those times.

Derreck called for a vote. He didn't say anything else. "Who wants to stay?"

One by one, the crew raised their hands. Kindra had been least sure about Eleta, but she raised her hand with the rest of them.

They all put their hands down and looked at Derreck expectantly. They all knew his was the only vote that mattered.

Kindra's bet paid off. "Fine, we'll stay. This will probably be the last tour for all of us, anyway. Might as well make the most of it."

Kindra let out a small whoop of joy before she was silenced by Derreck's glare.

"Here are the rules. First, every scientist is confined to the dropship. I'm not risking any of you on what could potentially be a hostile environment. Kindra, that means you, too. Second, any outside walks are going to be both of us, Kenan. I'll modify the second suit to be more combat worthy and take it out with you. We always go out together. Third, if there are any more encounters, we leave the planet immediately. I don't want us fucking this up more than we already have. Are we agreed?"

The tone of Derreck's voice made it clear they didn't have any choice but to agree. They all nodded, and the decision was made. The mission continued.

NINE

WHEN TEV WOKE UP, it was hard to decide what was real and what was imagined. Memories of his dream, if it could even be called that, floated on repeat through his mind. He felt the rocky ground beneath his fingers, and it seemed real, but what did he know for sure? Everything he remembered was as real to him as the soft snores he heard from the hunters still sleeping around the dying embers of the fire. He had felt the wind and heard the voice of Lys.

When he was a young boy, Tev had once gotten lost on a hunt. He had been too sure of his own abilities and had wandered too far. After four days the clan had given him up for dead.

But he hadn't died. Thirst wasn't a problem with all the streams that ran through the area, but hunger was a real issue. He hadn't been a very skilled hunter at that age, and he'd paid no attention to the women when they had tried to teach him about edible plants. He only remembered there were far more warnings than encouragements, and he was so afraid to eat anything dangerous that he had avoided eating any plants. Looking back, he understood his foolishness, but the decision had made sense to him at the time.

After four days Tev had forgotten what normal hunger felt like. The hunger he had experienced was all-consuming. It occupied every waking thought, and even in sleep he couldn't find relief. He had been certain he would die, and no trap he made seemed to work.

On the seventh day of his isolation he had come to the end of his will to survive. He found just enough food to keep him alive, but it wasn't enough. It was easier just to lie down and never move again, so that was what he did.

As he lied there, it was Lys who appeared to him. She beckoned to him, and in his delusion he crawled toward her. She was unspeakably beautiful, her radiance shining even in the darkness of the deep forest he had lost himself in. When he saw her, all he wanted was to be near her. He had never felt such a strong attraction to anyone. His desire overrode every instinct in his body, and he moved forward despite himself.

For every faltering step he took, she seemed to be one further away from him. He never actually saw her move, but he couldn't reach her. He became desperate, and he ran after her, completely unaware of his surroundings. He never saw the cliff, and even as an adult, he swore he took one step on air before losing the battle against the pull of their planet. Lys disappeared and Tev fell, plummeting almost ten meters down to the icy river below.

He was either guided by fate or incredibly lucky, as he landed in a deep pool carved out by countless years of falling water. He struggled to the surface, summoning a last bit of energy. When he broke the surface, a large branch was floating by. Without thought he grabbed on, and that was the last he remembered of his adventure.

When he woke up, he was surrounded by the concerned faces of the clan he had feared he would never see again. His birth-mother was closest, tears streaking her beautiful face. Tev didn't understand what had happened, and the story only came to him in bits and pieces as he recovered his strength. The clan had searched long and hard for him, but there came a point when they had given up hope. He was too young to survive on his own in the woods, and the hunters had found no trace of him. It was as though the forest had swallowed him whole.

The clan had packed up and moved, as was their way. Several days later they camped near a stream, and it was a little girl fetching water, Neera, who saw him drifting down the stream. Her shout had brought hunters immediately, and he had been rescued.

Tev didn't say much about what had happened to him. On one hand, he was embarrassed by his failure as a hunter. He was young and had thought himself capable of everything, but reality had made itself abundantly clear to him. On the other hand, there was an instinct that told him not to say too much about the vision he had. He couldn't explain it, but even at that young age, he had felt there was something sacred about what had happened to him. There was no way it could have been chance.

It was that incident that drove him to become the hunter he was today. It drove through his skull, more than any lecture from an elder could, how vital the skills of hunting and gathering were. Hunting wasn't just entertainment for the clan. It was survival. He threw himself into his studies with a vigor none of his peers could match, and soon he was the best hunter in the clan. Today he could survive out in the wild indefinitely.

He had thought long and hard about the vision he had seen that day. As a hunter, he focused every day on what could be observed. Smells, sights, sounds, feelings, and tastes were what allowed a person to survive. To trust in a greater power was foolish, a certain recipe for death.

But he also believed there was more to the world than what could be explained. He couldn't say why he felt so peaceful when he was alone in the woods, and if he could keep his mind quiet enough, there were times when he felt connected to all the life around him. He couldn't explain it, but he didn't feel the need to. It simply was, and that was enough for him. Perhaps it was a guiding principle, perhaps it was the gods of legends. Ultimately, it didn't matter much to him. He accepted there was more to the world than he understood.

So Tev didn't dismiss the experience he had gone through last night. It was the second time Lys had appeared to him, and the first time she had saved his life. If nothing else, he owed it to her to pay attention to what she had to say to him. But no matter how often he considered her words, they made no more sense to him.

Tev continued to turn the words over and over in his mind until the rest of the hunters came out of their stupor. As the camp prepared to leave on their hunt, Tev engraved the words on his heart and checked his own weapons, preparing to face a creature more dangerous than any he had hunted before.

TEV and the other hunters were each on a knee in a circle, accepting the blessings of the elders of the tribe. They were ready to go, and this was the last formality they needed to observe before beginning their journey.

Tev focused on the words of the blessing. There would be time later to think about the hunt, but his mind was swirling with memories of his dream. The elders were asking for Lys to give the hunters strength of leg and arm, and clarity of mind. The words were slightly different than those his own clan used, but the intent behind them was the same. Even a routine hunt could be dangerous for the hunter. Tev counted Lys as one of his greatest allies, and he had never been more certain she would guide him on the hunt. All his skills were for her service.

The hunters left the caves with little fanfare. Life was a daily battle, and although a tremendous burden had been laid on the hunters, there was work to be done while the sun was up. Tev, Neera, and the other hunters of his tribe fell into place near the middle of the column.

Tev's attention was half on the treacherous path leading away from the caves and half on the other hunters surrounding them. There was sometimes conflict between the clans, but it was rare. They didn't interact often, and were wary of one another, but there was little to drive them to combat. There was more than enough planet to go around.

Still, Shet had trained him to be aware of everything happening around him. Tev knew the difference between a successful hunter and a dead hunter was the hunter's mind and instincts. Prey was clever, and humans were not the apex predators in the ecosystem. But their minds set them apart. They could step into the thoughts of another creature, predict the creature's movements. Now Tev tried to step into the thoughts of the strangers around him.

Tev saw the party flush with excitement from the

celebration before. There were a handful of hunters who were quiet, composed, and alert, but they were in the minority. As Tev's eyes roamed over the group, his eyes met with a few others doing the same and a look of understanding passed between them. The hunters who were focused would be the ones to stay close to. They would do the best work of protecting each other.

While a few were wary, most were egotistical. Tev had no problem with the idea of pride. He was proud of his skills, but they were hard earned, and he knew his limits. There was a difference between pride and conceit, and too many of these hunters were the latter. True, they were a powerful hunting party, without doubt one of the strongest groups that had hunted together in the past several years, but their perceived strength could become a weakness. Tev developed a knot of worry in his gut.

He wanted to speak to Neera about his concerns, but she was too interested in Xan to pay much attention. Tev brushed aside his irritation. He was jealous, and angry that he was. He should be beyond such pettiness. Neera was a woman who was attracted to strength and skill, and even Tev couldn't fault Xan on either of those counts. The man was impressive.

So Tev bided his time, waiting to get a moment alone with Neera. But when the moment came, he hesitated. His concerns seemed so real, but when he tried to put them into words, they seemed silly. How was he supposed to tell her about the vision he had experienced?

Tev charged ahead, regardless of the consequences.

"Neera, I don't feel comfortable about this hunt."

She gave him an inquisitive look. "What do you mean?"

He gestured with his hand, indicating the entire party. "These hunters may all be very skilled, but they've never hunted together before. Instead of one strong group, we are several smaller groups. There is no order, and if the prey we face is as dangerous as Xan says, we're not going to have a chance."

Neera shook her head. "Maybe, but Xan himself is with us, and he seems confident. Maybe your fears are overblown."

Her respect for Xan was obvious, and it took Tev a supreme effort to push aside his jealousy. "There is something else, too, but I'm not sure how you are going to feel about it."

Her look made it clear she was running out of patience.

"Last night I was visited by Lys. It was as real as anything I'd ever experienced. I did not understand much of what she had to say, but I can't help feeling that this hunt is doomed."

Neera absorbed his thoughts in silence, and for a while they walked together without speaking. When she did speak, Tev had the feeling that every word she used was carefully considered, rehearsed.

"I don't know what was in the drink we had last night, but it was a powerful medicine. I'm not going to tell you that what you experienced wasn't real. I know you, and I know you wouldn't say anything unless you really believed it. But I don't think you should jump to conclusions. Maybe there's some truth in what you experienced, but maybe it was just a result of the drink we had. I had a strange experience, too, but I don't believe it was real."

Tev wanted to ask her what she had experienced, but she gave him a look that told him she knew what he wanted and he wasn't going to get it. Tev knew that look all too well.

Though he burned with curiosity, he contained himself. Neera nodded and moved up the line, back towards Xan.

Tev cursed silently. If there was anyone here who would take his words under consideration, it would be her. Her disbelief cut him deeper than he wanted to admit, but he had no choice but to keep moving forward towards their inevitable confrontation with the mysterious creature.

TEN

TIME WAS A FICKLE CONCEPT, Kindra decided. While science had made some incredible advances in understanding it from an objective standpoint, from a human perspective, it was anything but dependable.

They had been on the planet for twelve days, and at times Kindra couldn't convince herself they'd been here more than a day. Other times it felt as though she had done enough science to fill a lifetime. Even though they were limited without the probe, Kindra had enough data to study for several careers. Her lab was packed with samples, and if she chose, she could spend the rest of her years studying what she had already collected.

The planet was alive. It was a tremendous oversimplification, but Kindra was amazed by the constant interdependencies she was discovering. Everything from the dirt to the trees was connected, a web of relationships Kindra could spend the rest of her life untangling. Ecosystems weren't new to her, but almost every one she'd ever studied was artificially created and lacked the complexity of the systems she was uncovering.

There had been no further sightings of the creatures Kenan had attacked on his first excursion. At first, Derreck had kept the walks close to the dropship, but it appeared Kenan had predicted the creatures' behavior correctly. He had scared them away. Kindra couldn't decide how she felt about it. At times, she was glad they could continue their studies without complications. Derreck was on the fence about his decision, and she feared that if they made contact again, Derreck would pull them from the planet for good. But at the same time, the mystery surrounding the creatures was more than she could stand. Despite discovery after discovery, the one organism she wanted to study more than anything else wasn't coming back.

As the days had passed, Derreck had bent to the pressure from his crew to explore further and further from the dropship. They were on their own out here. Just as they always were.

Kindra focused her thoughts on the monitors in front of her. She had Derreck's view on one monitor and Kenan's on the other. They were over two kilometers away from the dropship, their furthest excursion yet. Despite the distance, no one was particularly worried. There had been no other contacts, and the planet didn't seem to have any other creatures capable of posing a threat to the exosuits.

Kindra was supposed to be supervising Derreck and Kenan, but their work was monotonous, and she kept sneaking a peek at the chemical analysis she was running on some soil samples. Derreck and Kenan were collecting rock samples for Alston, and Kindra couldn't think of anything more boring than drilling holes into the ground.

Both men were focused on the task at hand. As boring as Kindra found it, drilling with the laser they were using wasn't easy, and even a small mistake could be potentially dangerous. Kindra studied the carbon content of the soil for a moment before turning back to the monitors. Her eye was drawn to a faint signal on the motion detectors.

She didn't say anything immediately. Since Kenan's incident, Derreck had ordered the detectors boosted to full gain, and that led to false signals. Sometimes it seemed like even a leaf blowing in the wind could set them off.

Instead, Kindra pulled up more monitors, giving herself a wrap-around view from both of their suits. If something was out there, she should be able to spot it and warn them. She summoned a composite image, overlaying thermal imaging over the visual spectrum. Her eyes wandered over the monitors, looking for anything out of place.

She was just about to call it a false alarm when the motion detector faintly pinged again. With all the monitors pulled up, she quickly located the direction the signal was coming from. But as much as she studied the area, from both Derreck's and Kenan's rear cameras, she couldn't find anything. Two parts of her mind warred with each other, but there was no question it was much better to play it safe.

She keyed in the comms. "Hey, you guys, are you catching the blips on the motion detector?"

On the viewscreens, she saw the two of them stand up straight and stop drilling. Kenan turned around to face the woods they had their backs to. The movement threatened to make Kindra nauseous, so she averted her eyes.

Derreck's voice replied. "No. What are you seeing?"

"It's been faint, but I've gotten two hits from behind you. I've been studying the full spectrum images coming from your suits, but I can't make anything out. Just wanted to give you a heads-up, though."

"Appreciate it. Would you overlay the location on our

visors please? Kenan, check it out, but keep your weapons cold."

Kindra could imagine Kenan grumbling. Kenan always went about with his weapons hot and ready to fire, but ever since the incident, Derreck had been firm. He wasn't even allowed to boot up his weapons systems. If something happened, it would take Kenan at least ten seconds to bring his weapons online. Derreck figured it would give him enough time to think through what he was doing.

Still, Kenan went towards where Kindra had overlaid the detection. He scanned the area carefully, but there didn't seem to be anything there. "Nothing here, sir."

Derreck's voice was cautious. "False alarm?"

Kindra knew it was her call. She was the only one who had seen anything. "I think so. Sorry, sir."

"It's not a problem. Better safe than not."

Just as Derreck spoke, Kindra saw another motion hit on Kenan's monitors. It didn't appear on Derreck's. Kenan beat her to the punch.

"Solid motion, sir."

Kenan turned around, and Kindra's breath caught in her throat. In front of Kenan, about thirty meters away, was a man. There was no doubt of it in Kindra's mind. There was nothing else it could be. He was naked except for a loincloth. He was tall and muscular, and if Kindra's mind wasn't so consumed by everything else, she might have even found him handsome.

Kenan and the man looked at each other for what seemed like an eternity. Then the man raised his arms and yelled, a primal scream that chilled Kindra's heart even through the mic pickups. Kenan's calm voice came through next. "Sir, I'm looking right at someone, and they seem hostile. Permission to go weapons hot?"

Kindra couldn't believe what she was hearing. There was no way a man in a loincloth was dangerous to Kenan.

Derreck's voice, equally cool, answered. "Under no circumstances. Join up with me. We're collecting the sample and going back to the dropship."

Kenan acknowledged, but Kindra could hear the disappointment in his voice.

Then both Derreck and Kenan's motion detectors came alive with hits all around them. Kindra couldn't help but state the obvious.

"You two need to get out of there right now. You're surrounded."

ELEVEN

HUNTING WAS the pinnacle of experiences, in Tev's opinion. All his worries and fears fell away as the hunt progressed. There was no place here for preoccupation. Every sense and every muscle had to be primed and focused. Anything less brought danger to your doorstep.

It had been a difficult hike, taking most of the day to get to the site of the previous encounter. It was unlike any battleground Tev had ever seen before. He slipped into a soft, focused state, gathering all the information he could.

The first sight that drew Tev's attention was a felled tree. Tev had seen trees fall before, but trees only fell for one of two reasons: either their trunk snapped, or their roots pulled out of the ground. Neither was the case with this tree. The majority of the tree was almost a meter away from the rest of the trunk, but it looked as though the trunk had been blown out from the inside. Tev couldn't even imagine what kind of forces had to be in play for something like this to happen.

His gaze wandered, and he saw other trees that bore signs of damage. There were both deep and shallow gouges, and some small holes that went straight through the trees. Tev studied the damage with a mounting sense of unease. The damage was certainly the result of some sort of high-powered projectile, but he was certain there was no weapon he knew of that could create it. Whatever they were tracking was far more dangerous than they were.

Tev joined the rest of the group in examining the trampled ground where the creature had once stood. Its markings were heavy and distinct and unlike anything Tev had ever seen. The prints were shaped almost like a foot, but far too large. Something was wrong about them, and it took Tev a few seconds to identify the discrepancy. There weren't anything resembling toes. Every creature of size he knew had toes or claws to help stabilize themselves. How could the creature possibly manage to stand on two legs? It didn't make any sense.

He kept his concerns to himself. Most of the other hunters were only concerned with tracking the creature, a simple task considering the depth of its prints. The sun was beginning to set, but there wasn't any hesitation on the part of the group. They were confident the creature would be dead within the day, and the pursuit continued.

Tev followed the group, his eyes constantly scanning the ground for new signs. The creature, strong as it seemed to be, didn't have any woodcraft to speak of. Tev and his fellow hunters didn't even need to follow the tracks. The creature had left behind a disturbance even a child could follow with their eyes closed.

Tev considered the creature as they hiked. There were two possibilities in his mind. The first was that the creature was so strong it didn't need to worry about hiding its presence. The idea seemed a little strange to Tev, but he supposed it could be true. But every animal he knew of protected itself, no matter how strong it was.

The other idea, slowly growing in certainty in his mind, was that the creature wasn't from this area. It would explain the strangeness of the sign, and if there was any credence at all to the dream he'd had, perhaps that was what Lys had been hinting at.

The trail led upward until they broke through the tree line onto exposed rock. As easy as the trail had been to follow, it had still gone cold on them. Tev looked around. They were on top of a tall ridge, and it would take them some time to find the trail again. More importantly, the sun was going down. Begrudgingly, the others came to the same conclusion, and the advance halted for the day. They moved back into the edges of the woods for shelter and made camp for the night. When the sun rose again, they would track their quarry to the end.

TEV WAS up before the sun rose, as was his custom. He packed his gear onto his back and climbed back onto the ridge line. The rest of the camp wasn't up yet, and there was no chance Tev would try to hunt this prey alone, but he thought perhaps he could learn more about his prey without the distractions of others. Tev hiked to the highest place on the ridge line and settled in for a moment to take in the sights and sounds of the forest.

Tev listened to the sound of the breeze drifting through the pine trees and the birds making their morning calls. A peace fell over his heart, and he breathed in the cool morning air. There was no place he would rather be.

As his attention wandered, he gradually realized something wasn't as it should be. He had never been here before, but he had spent his entire life in the woods, and its ways had become his ways, and something was wrong. From a lifetime of experience, he didn't try to focus on any one sense. If he did, he knew he would lose the feeling. Instead, he allowed his attention to wander, almost as though he were in a daze. His mind, of its own accord, settled on the disturbance.

The sun was rising to the east, and in that direction, the birds were not singing. Along with the unusual silence, there was something else. At the limit of his hearing, there was a sound he struggled to recognize. It sounded almost like a high pitched whine, but faint. He shook his head and listened again, turning his head from side to side to focus on the direction of the sound.

There could be no mistaking it. Something unnatural was happening to the east. Tev stood up, only to find a few other hunters had also woken up early and were hiking to the top of the ridge. He waved them over, and in a few moments, all of them agreed the sound wasn't natural. The decision was made to wake the rest of the camp and follow Tev's discovery.

Curiosity overrode Tev's apprehensions, and he took the lead as the hunting party left their campsite. After hiking two kilometers, the sound became clear to everyone. It wasn't constant, but rose and fell at random intervals. Tev had never heard anything like it before.

A new sign drew his attention, something else out of place in the world he understood, shifting it ever so slightly again towards one that embraced mystery. He gestured to show the others what he saw. In the ground was a hole, perfectly round. Tev took his spear and put it down the hole. It ended near the bottom of his spear, almost two meters deep. Tev knelt and examined it. It hadn't been dug using any tool he could imagine. It was narrow, not much wider than his spear, but the edges were perfectly sharp.

Signs of the creature were everywhere, and as Tev took the time to stop and examine his surroundings, he realized there were more than one of them. There were two sets of prints, one on each side of the hole. The creatures must have worked together, Tev surmised. He studied the tracks. The shaping was almost identical, but one set of prints was a little larger than the other. Tev took note.

By the time he stood back up, many of the hunters had already moved on towards the sound of the noise. There was little doubt in anyone's mind that they were approaching the creature, and they were prepared. Bows had been strung and spears were in hand. They all crept forward, Xan in the lead, Tev far behind them all. Seeing the hole had raised his apprehensions once again.

From the moment he saw them, he was certain they were from a very long way away. There were two of them, just as he had guessed. His mind warred within him. At first glance, everything about them seemed so familiar; but at the same time, Tev had never seen anything like what he was looking at.

In so many ways they seemed just like him. They stood on two legs, using their hands as their primary way of interacting with the environment. But Xan's description of them had been accurate. They were made of rock, or at the very least, a hard surface. Together, the two of them were working with something else, pointing it at the ground. They must be making another hole.

The creatures weren't aware of the hunting party's presence, and for a few minutes, uncertainty reigned. Although Xan had acted as the unofficial leader, no one had actually designated him. The group, faced with their prey for the first time, hesitated, waiting for someone to take the first action.

Tev used the time to study the creatures more carefully. They moved in the same way he did, but their actions lacked the grace Tev associated with hunters. He watched as they stopped using the tool. One of the creatures knelt to the ground, an action Tev thought was clumsy. Another object was placed where the first tool had been, and Tev saw something coming out of it, going into the ground. The creature stood back up and pulled at the object, and Tev watched in amazement as it pulled out a perfectly round section of the ground. The section was placed in a tube and lined up with several other tubes. Tev nodded. He didn't understand what was happening, but he knew now where the holes came from.

The creatures grabbed the first machine and brought it back between them. Tev assumed they were going to make another hole. A hint of motion caught his eye, and he turned his head slowly. Xan was leading some of the hunters closer in.

Tev thought quickly, but he couldn't convince himself to move in closer. These creatures were entirely outside of his experience. There wasn't any hurry. The day was young and the creatures didn't seem to be going anyplace soon. Far better to be informed than dead, in Tev's own estimation. He stayed where he was, sheltered behind a large tree. He continued his study.

He examined the joints of the creatures. Many animals were vulnerable at the joints, and he wondered if that was true here. At first glance, it seemed like the creatures were entirely rock, but as Tev continued to watch, he saw hints that this wasn't true. Over the joints the rock seemed different, and as he watched the creatures move their heads, he could see the material move. So they weren't completely solid. Tev assumed if he was going to kill one of these creatures, it would have to be at one of these weak joints.

One of the creatures suddenly turned and looked into the woods, and Tev knew they had been spotted. He didn't know how these creatures sensed the world around them, but one of them, at least, was suspicious. The suspicious one stood and started walking towards the area where Xan had led a party of hunters forward. Tev watched with fascination, unable to will his feet to move quite yet.

Xan and the other hunters flattened themselves against trees. Tev evaluated their positions quickly and approved. They should be well hidden and were downwind of the creatures. There wasn't any more they could do.

The wind seemed to die down as the world held its breath. Tev watched as the creature stood at the edge of the clearing. Although he couldn't be sure why, Tev was convinced the creature was just about to turn around and head back to its partner.

But then Xan stepped out from behind the tree and let out his hunter's challenge. A part of Tev was impressed by the man's ferocity, but he couldn't help but think the other hunter had doomed them all.

TEV'S WORLD exploded into action. One hunter who had taken position behind Xan broke from cover and drew an arrow to his cheek in one smooth motion. The hunter released, and Tev was impressed by his aim and skill. The arrow flew true, striking the creature. Tev watched, fascinated, as the arrow bounced right off the creature's face. It confirmed his suspicions. If there was any weak point on these creatures, it was at their joints. The hunters' weapons weren't strong enough to do any other damage.

The other hunters didn't come to the same conclusion. All of them broke cover and charged at the creature that had wandered to the edge of the woods. Tev stayed behind his tree. Unless it was necessary, he wasn't planning on becoming prey for this creature.

The creature raised its arm and Tev flinched back. Xan's story had been true so far, and Tev remembered that the creature had a weapon in its arm. But nothing happened to the charging hunters, and Tev couldn't figure out why.

One hunter hurled a two-meter spear with all his might, and his aim was perfect. The spear hit the creature right in the chest, and Tev saw that it took a step back. Tev's head twitched as he processed the information. The spear had a fair amount of force, but not all that much. If that was enough to make the creature lose its balance, it wasn't as invulnerable as Tev had expected.

His heart stopped when he saw Neera in the pack of hunters charging the creature. He shouted for her to stop, but his voice was lost in the yells of dozens of hunters. Her passion overcame her reason, and he could see the bloodlust in her eyes. He almost left his tree, but couldn't bring himself to join the charge. It wasn't cowardice, he just didn't think they had a chance. Not like this.

The hunters reached the creature unharmed and swarmed him with their knives, their attacks completely ineffectual against the hard skin. At first, it didn't respond, as though it was unsure how to react. Tev had the fleeting impression it was like one of them trying to decide what to do about an annoying insect.

When it did react, the balance of the battle changed completely. With a few smooth motions it threw the hunters bodily away. They all rolled back to their feet, wary but unharmed.

Xan stepped in next, off to the side of the creature, where it shouldn't be able to see. He raised his arm up above his head in an attempt to bring his knife down on the creature's skull. But the creature turned before Xan could strike his blow. However it sensed the world around it, Tev saw it wasn't safe to assume it had any blind spots.

Xan was still fast enough to bring his blade down with tremendous force. The knife struck the rock skull of the creature and broke apart. Tev wasn't surprised, but all the same, he was disappointed. It had been an excellent strike.

Unfortunately, Xan paid the price for his attack. The creature lashed out with its arm, catching him full in the stomach. Xan doubled over as the impact of the punch knocked him backwards. He coughed up blood, and Tev wondered if his internal organs had been ruptured. He wasn't dead, but he might be soon.

Xan's sacrifice energized the rest of the hunters. Tev didn't blame them, even though his rational mind kept his body in check. He could feel the fire in his blood, the anger at seeing a fellow hunter injured. The hunters attacked with a fury, knives and arrows and spears striking all over. None of them had any effect, but the creature was disoriented. The creature tried to swipe at any hunter who got too close, but they had learned their lesson. They darted in and out, striking quickly and then retreating before they were hit.

One of the hunters, a young male Tev hadn't had the time to meet in person, snuck behind the creature and wrapped his body around one of the creature's legs. Muscles straining with effort, the hunter lifted the leg of the creature, shifting its balance. The other hunters seized the opportunity without hesitation. In less time than it took to take a deep breath, at least five other hunters had tackled the creature, bringing it to the ground.

As soon as it fell, even more hunters leapt on top of the creature, stabbing at it with anything sharp they had in their hands. Tev couldn't see if any of the strikes were doing any good. If there was a weakness to the creature, surely they would have found it by now.

Tev saw the second creature begin to come to the aid of the first one. From his vantage point Tev tried to yell out a warning, but none of the combatants could hear him over the sounds of their struggle. He debated for a moment and cursed. He didn't see that he had a choice. He couldn't let the others take on both creatures without him, no matter how unwise the decision seemed. Tev tracked the second creature's path and studied the terrain. The creature would pass near a rise in the ground about ten meters away from Tev's location. It would have to do.

Tev sprinted from cover. As soon as he did, the creature turned his way. There wasn't going to be any chance of sneaking up on it, but Tev didn't lose his resolve. He got up to full speed in just three steps and launched himself from the small rise. With a yell, he struck out with both feet, driving all his weight into the creature's head. The creature saw it coming and was already moving backwards, absorbing a small amount of the force before Tev could even strike. But despite the move, Tev still collided with the second creature with tremendous force, knocking it to the ground.

He landed on his side, taking a moment to catch his breath. He hadn't been sure that would work. Tev got to his feet faster than the creature. He thought he heard the creature grunt, and he had the sudden impression he wasn't seeing the creature as it actually was. What he had thought was skin was actually some sort of protective covering.

Tev didn't have time to follow the thought to its conclusion. He was knocked forward a step by a concussive wave. Behind him, the first creature had done something that had dazed every hunter on top of it. With a few powerful moves, the creature flung the limp bodies away from itself, struggling back to its feet. Tev could hear bones snapping as several of the unconscious hunters landed without muscular support.

Those who still could rushed the first creature, and Tev saw that Neera was among them. But his attention was distracted by the movement of the creature in front of him. It was back on its feet. Tev drew his long knife, which seemed to give the creature pause. He took the moment to study his opponent. Its skin, or armor, or whatever it was, was different than that of the first creature. There were bigger joints, and if Tev was going to defeat the opponent, it was in those spots he would have to strike.

The creature held up its hands, a gesture Tev recognized. It was the same gesture he would make to another hunter if he was surrendering or approaching in peace. It puzzled him, and Tev paused his attack. He couldn't keep up with everything happening around him.

He turned his head as he heard the battle behind him. Knives were clanging off the skin of the first creature, and Neera had planted herself front and center. The creature swung at her with surprising speed, but her reflexes were keen, and she dodged the attack. She struck back at the creature, but her knife was ineffective against it. The creature caught her with a short backhand, sending her skidding to the ground.

Rage swelled up in Tev. He didn't care what happened

to most of the hunters they were with, but Neera was another matter. He would give up his life for her without thought.

It was then the second creature in front of him moved. Tev didn't think, he just reacted. He leapt forward, catching the second creature by surprise. He lashed out with his knife and was delighted when the blade cut through the thick skin on the underside of the shoulder. The creature howled, a sound as human as anything Tev had ever heard. What was he fighting?

He didn't have time to answer the question. The howl of pain focused the attention of the first creature on the battle happening behind it. The creature grabbed one of the hunters in its left arm and picked him up, swinging him around and using him as a club against the others. With one swing the creature cleared the space around itself and released the hunter, sending him crashing into the trees.

The creature brought up its right arm, and Tev knew what was about to happen. He sprinted into the woods, terrified of the small black hole underneath the creature's arm. There was a whine, just as Xan had described it, and the woods in front of Tev exploded. Tev couldn't see what was causing it, but instinctively, he knew he didn't want to be between the creature's arm and the destroyed forest. He skidded to a stop and turned around, the destruction coming towards him as the creature adjusted his aim.

The second creature was down on its knees, suffering from whatever wound Tev had given it. Tev didn't stop to think. If there was one place that was safe, it was in the shadow of the second creature. There was no way the first creature would cause harm to the second.

Tev sprinted the other way, but the creature didn't stop its assault. Tev didn't know if it wasn't aware of what it was doing, or it didn't care. Either way, it continued to track Tev. The destruction licked at his feet, and desperate, he launched himself towards the second creature. As he did, he was punched in the gut with incredible force. Tev had never felt a power like this before. It was both sharp, as if he was being stabbed, and general, imparting a tremendous amount of energy into his body.

He lost all focus, crumpling in a heap behind the second creature. The first creature kept tracking, and the sound of screeching assaulted Tev's ears. The second creature fell backwards against Tev, crushing him underneath its weight. With a grunt, Tev managed to shift away from the creature, but when he looked down, he knew he didn't have long. There was a hole in his stomach, and blood and viscera were coming out. Tev was a pragmatist. He had seen the same injury dozens of times in animals and knew he was in for a slow death. Fortunately, he would pass out from blood loss soon enough. He just wanted to see if there was anything he could do for those who remained.

Tev managed to raise his head. The first creature was writhing around, and at first Tev thought perhaps one of the other hunters had landed a fatal blow. But as he watched, he noted there wasn't any sign of damage to the first creature. It seemed as strong and as healthy as ever. But it was still in pain. Some of the hunters, those not yet injured, crept closer to the creature. They had seen Tev damage the second one. They wouldn't give up until there wasn't any other choice left.

The hunters didn't have a chance. The creature, aware of their presence, raised both of its arms, and the whine started again. The hunters scattered like flies disturbed from their meal of a corpse. Tev caught a final glimpse of Neera. Their eyes locked, and Tev nodded at her. She understood what he was trying to say. She bowed slightly to him and summoned the hunters to her. Together they disappeared into the forest.

Tev watched Neera's back as she left. He had always loved her, but it was time for her to go on without him. This next journey wasn't one she should join him on. He understood what Lys had told him in his dream. She had been trying to warn him about his own end. Tev smiled. He looked forward to a never-ending hunt.

Tev didn't have any strength left. He laid his head down on the ground and closed his eyes, waiting for Lys one last time.

TWELVE

KINDRA STARED at all of her monitors, trying to understand what was happening. One moment the situation had been tense but peaceful, and suddenly all hell had broken loose. Kindra could see that Kenan was powering up his weapons systems despite Derreck ordering him not to. The people, whom Kindra couldn't think of in any way other than human, were swarming all over Kenan. But their attack was primitive, and if Kenan opened fire, it would be a massacre.

She was trying to track the action through both viewpoints, but wasn't able to. She had heard stories of commanders in fleet who could monitor multiple full-view displays at once, but she wasn't one of them. In desperation, she narrowed the two screens down to field of view for both Derreck and Kenan. That way, she was only looking forward. She felt like she could handle that much better.

Kenan's screen was still swarming with people, and when she looked over at Derreck's she could see he was running towards the action.

"Kenan, don't arm your weapons. I'm coming to help."

Kenan didn't respond. Kindra checked his vitals and saw that everything was spiked. She didn't think Kenan could hear Derreck even if he was screaming right in his ear. All Kenan was experiencing right now was a threat.

"Derreck, I don't think he can hear you."

Derreck's voice was desperate. "Kindra, you need to remote override his weapons systems. We can't let him fire on them."

"Yes, sir."

Kindra's fingers flew to the controls and she started entering the commands for a remote override. Her attention was distracted when Derreck's voice came into her ear again. "Oh, shit!"

Kindra looked at the readouts and saw Kenan's weapon system was active. She watched him throw off the last of the people on top of him. It was almost silly how much stronger Kenan's exosuit made him. Kindra couldn't tear her attention away.

She pulled her focus back to the boards. She had to finish sending the command before Kenan could do even more damage.

Derreck's grunt grabbed her again. She looked over at his screen and watched as his world twisted. Someone had hit him hard. She glanced down at his vitals, but everything seemed to be fine. She couldn't tear her eyes away from Derreck's screen. He was struggling back to his feet, but there was a person in front of him with a long and wicked-looking knife.

Her eyes darted back and forth between the screens. Too much was happening to keep track of. Kenan was throwing someone, and then Derreck's vital readings started going haywire. Derreck swore. On Kenan's screen, Kindra watched as Kenan tried to kill the person who had attacked

Derreck. The man moved with a strength and grace Kindra
had never seen before. He stopped right before he ran into
Kenan's crosshairs and sprinted back towards Derreck.

Kindra watched in horror as her brain tried to process
what was happening. The man dove, trying to use Derreck
as cover. Kenan's crosshairs floated over him and kept track,
and Kindra's time froze as Kenan shot Derreck right in the
chest. Derreck's vitals immediately disappeared, and Kenan
stopped firing.

There was a moment of silence. Kindra couldn't believe
what she had just seen, and Kenan seemed to be processing
what had happened. And then a scream came over the
channel, a primal yell. It was as though a man's soul was
being ripped from his body. Kindra slapped at controls,
trying to turn off the audio, but Kenan's scream echoed back
and forth in her mind, a perfect reverberating chamber.
After a few moments she wasn't sure if he was still yelling
or if she would just never get the sound out of her head.

Then Kenan lost it. He started firing at the trees.
Perhaps there were people out there, Kindra didn't know.
Her eyes were too blurry with tears. Derreck had been with
them just a few moments ago. Only a minute, maybe two,
had passed. How could this have happened? In the back of
her mind, she knew there were all sorts of procedures she
should be going through, but she couldn't process any of the
checks she was supposed to be doing.

Slowly, her mind reasserted itself. The first thing she
had to do was take care of Kenan. He needed to stop. His
exosuit had enough ammo to wage a small war, so there was
no chance of him being forced to quit there. She needed to
shut down his weapon systems. She punched the code into
the console and watched as his weapons powered down.

"Kenan, can you hear me?"

Kenan shook his head, and Kindra knew her voice was coming through, even if he didn't want to acknowledge it.

"Kenan, I need you to come back in."

His voice came through the channel, a voice she had never heard before. It was higher pitched, and the voice cracked. "They killed him."

Kindra's mind reeled. She had watched as Kenan shot Derreck, but she also knew the human mind reacted strangely under pressure. What had happened out there was in danger of cracking his sanity, if it hadn't already. As calmly as she could, she replied, "Kenan, I need you to come back in. Please."

There was no response, and Kindra saw on the screen that he was shaking his head again. Her mind raced, trying to think of ways to get him to come back. She had already decided that once he was back, she'd put him under sedation. He was too unstable right now to have running around the ship. He had already done more than enough damage.

Kindra saw him reach back towards his neck, and her heart raced. "Kenan, don't!"

If he heard her, he didn't care. With a quick yank, every screen she had on Kenan went dark. Kindra swore. He had pulled out every transponder he had on his suit. She didn't have any information on him. No visuals, no vitals, and most worrisome, no control over his suit anymore. Her first reaction was to try to scream at him, but she stopped herself. It wouldn't do any good. He had made his decision, and he couldn't hear her anymore.

Kindra rubbed her temples and took a deep breath. Her captain, her friend, was dead. Their soldier was off the grid, probably with a blood vengeance. It couldn't get much worse.

KINDRA WAS PACING THE ROOM, her eyes closed as she tried to think her way forward. The mission had gone so far south, she couldn't think of any way to recover. She had called a staff meeting that was supposed to start in an hour, but everyone shared her sense of shock and loss. They needed time apart to process this.

Her breathing was ragged and harsh, and it echoed softly in her ears. She frowned. That wasn't her breath. She opened her eyes, but she was alone in the room. Doubting her own sanity, she held her breath. Then there was a cough in her ears, and her eyes went wide. She looked at the screens. There was no way it should be true, but it had to be.

"Derreck?"

The only answer she got was a grunt, but it was more than enough for her. She let out a small squeal and a jump before getting ahold of herself once again. "Derreck, what's your status? Your vitals aren't coming through."

Derreck swore. "One minute."

The view on Derreck's screen, which had shown nothing but the sky of the planet, started to move, and Kindra's breath caught in her throat. She couldn't believe Derreck had lived through a direct hit on his suit. What had happened?

Derreck worked himself into a sitting position. There was another cough and a wet sound, and Kindra worried that although Derreck was alive, he wouldn't be for much longer. She watched as he flopped his left arm onto his leg and played with the command controls on the left wrist. Everything he did looked painful.

"Kenan hit one of the processors on the vitals system. I can't pull up any diagnostics for myself either."

Derreck pulled himself up a little straighter and swore. "Whatever happened, it can't be too good. I can't move my left arm at all except at the shoulder, and I feel like I've been kicked by a giant. I wish these scientific rigs were better armored."

On a hunch, Kindra pulled up the last known schematics of Kenan's exosuit. "He changed the round type. Kenan didn't have standard shells in there. He was firing full anti-personnel rounds."

Derreck swore again. "Well, that explains that."

Kindra didn't know what Derreck meant, but now wasn't the time for questions. She needed to get him back to the ship alive. "Let's not worry about that for now. Can you stand?"

In response, Derreck's camera swayed again, and Kindra could see he was about to make the effort. He paused for a moment and then stood, and Kindra's breath caught in her throat. He swayed from side to side, and the sound of his breath as he stood frightened her. It was ragged and wheezing, with an undertone of liquid that could only be blood. She figured he had to have a punctured lung. Without the first aid provided by the exosuit, he never would have lived.

Derreck might be on his feet, but he wasn't in good condition. Kindra wished she could get vitals on him, but she couldn't figure out how. The suit had a number of chemical delivery systems available, but without knowing exactly what he was going through, she hesitated to take any action. The wrong move could kill him.

"I can give you some painkillers if you want."

Derreck didn't answer for a moment, and Kindra feared

she had lost communication with him too. Then he shook his head. "I'm afraid that if the pain goes away, I won't have anything to hold on to."

Kindra grimaced, but there was nothing to say. Right now, Derreck was the only one who knew what he needed. All she could do was be around to offer whatever support she could.

One breath at a time, Derreck managed to stabilize himself. "It's official. My left arm is useless, and I might be too if I don't get back to the dropship now. Give me a sitrep."

Kindra shook her head. "That can wait, Derreck. We need you back now."

"Mission first." Derreck's tone allowed no room for argument. Kindra swore.

"Kenan is out of touch. I have no idea what's going on with him."

"Is he alive?"

"I assume so. His physical health seemed fine. He tore out communications from his suit, so we have no location and no way of getting in touch with him."

"I should be able to track him."

Kindra overrode Derreck. "No, Derreck. This isn't the time. Your life is in danger, and there's nothing Kenan is going to do in the next few hours that hasn't already been done. The damage exists. I'm more concerned about your life right now."

Derreck was silent for a moment. "I'm coming in."

Derreck scanned the ground one last time, and he came upon the native who had almost cut off his arm. Kindra gasped as Derreck kept his gaze on the creature. From everything Kindra could see, the creature was a young man, not much younger than Kindra herself.

"Do you want me to bring him in?"

Kindra shook her head. "There's no way we can do that!"

Derreck's voice gave away his exasperation. "Look, this whole mission has gone to hell. We're about as far from home as we can be, and in front of us we have what appears very much to be a human. We've fucked everything else up so far. Might as well try to get as much information as we can before we have to burn atmosphere."

Kindra couldn't deny her own curiosity. So many indications pointed towards human, but it was still impossible. It would be the discovery of a lifetime. There was no way she could refuse. "Can you handle it?"

"I think so, hold on."

Kindra watched as Derreck switched through his control schemes. The exosuits were controlled through a complex interchange of physical and mental inputs. Typically, most of the exosuit simply responded to the pressure the pilot exerted with his own body. If a person wanted to raise their arm, they simply started the motion. The suit sensed the motion beginning and mirrored it. But the helmets of the exosuit were also special. The helmet molded itself to the skull of the pilot, pressing sensors directly up against the pilot's head. They translated electrical impulses from the brain and moved the suit in accordance. The neural connections were primarily for balance and display functions on the helmet, but they could be used to move the suit. It just didn't happen often. Most people weren't very good at knowing how they were moving.

Derreck was switching the suit over to complete neural control. Kindra caught her breath. "Derreck, are you sure that's a good idea?"

He kept working as he responded. "I don't have a choice, Kindra. My body is giving out. This is the only way I have a chance."

"We can come get you."

"NO!"

Tears sprang from Kindra's eyes.

"There aren't any more exosuits, and we don't know this environment well enough to let you out without one. Even if we did, this area is crawling with people who want to kill us. You have to stay in the dropship."

"At least leave the creature behind!"

"Why? If it was me, physically doing it, sure, but it doesn't matter at all to the suit. Might as well."

Kindra couldn't find any fault with his logic, as much as she wished she could. Even though he was the one bleeding to death, he kept thinking clearly.

There was nothing to do but watch. Once transfer to neural control was complete, Derreck just stood there. Every move was agonizingly slow, and Kindra couldn't help but watch the mission clock. Depending on the rate of blood loss, Derreck might not have much time left.

"Derreck, do you want blood shut off to your left arm?"

Derreck only thought about it for a moment. "Do it."

Kindra sent the command to Derreck's suit and she heard him gasp from a new wave of pain. But he remained on his feet and stayed focused. She didn't know how he was managing it.

Derreck picked the young man up and threw him over his shoulder in what was known in Fleet as a safety carry. Kindra winced, expecting Derreck to grunt under a new wave of pain, but he didn't. It was the suit taking everything over now, guided by Derreck's mind. One step at a time, Derreck moved towards the dropship. Kindra pulled up

Derreck's positioning. He was less than a kilometer out, but at the speed he was moving, it would take him over twenty minutes to get back to the dropship.

Kindra's brain kicked into high gear. She could sit around and watch Derreck struggle, or she could make good use of her time. She was responsible for both biology and medical, and she would be responsible both for Derreck and for the creature he was bringing with him. Suddenly, twenty minutes didn't seem like enough time for everything that needed to be done.

She called Eleta as she walked swiftly to the medical bay. Eleta said she'd be willing to keep an eye on Derreck's progress. He didn't need any coaching from them, but Kindra needed to know if anything happened to him right away. She felt the burden of command on her shoulders.

Kindra was third in line for command of the ship, but it had never been anything but a joke for her. Below Derreck, they were all equals. But Fleet had suffered enough problems with ship command during the Rebellion, and now everyone was assigned a place for command. With Kenan out of touch and Derreck in danger, there was a very real chance she could find herself with her first command.

The thought had no place in her mind, and she pushed it away. Derreck was going to live. When she reached the medical bay, she summoned both of their medical pods to life. Her role as a doctor was limited, and that was good. She had more extensive training than the others, but she was still far from a full physician. Most everything could be done by the pods, but they still needed human supervision. She keyed in the emergency activation codes and they booted to life in under a minute.

The first pod she prepped for Derreck. She described his injuries as best she could. It would give the pod a focus for its scans and repair work. Typically, all the information could be communicated by the exosuit, but not with the biosensors offline. The second pod she prepared for the creature. She didn't know what to expect, but the creature had the approximate dimensions of a human being. She ensured perfect containment and restraint. The rest could come later,

Kindra finished less than fifteen minutes after leaving her desk in Biology. Just as she did, Eleta's voice spoke in her ear. "He's less than a hundred meters from the ramp."

Kindra didn't have time to wonder how Derreck had gotten back so quickly. Using neurocontrol, it should have taken longer than fifteen minutes to make it back. She rushed to the door, ready as she would ever be for Derreck's return.

When he first stepped into sight, Kindra couldn't help her gasp. She had only seen things from Derreck's perspective, and it didn't do his suffering justice. Blood leaked freely from his left armpit, and the trail he left was easy even for Kindra to follow. If those creatures were as dangerous as they seemed, they'd have no trouble tracking the ship now.

Even more disturbing was the crater on Derreck's chest. He had taken an anti-personnel round directly to the chest. The rounds were designed to expand on impact, being maximally lethal to non-armored personnel. Derreck was armored, but the armor on Derreck's exosuit was weak under the best of circumstances. It was a general purpose suit, not armored for combat like Kenan's. Kindra was certain they would find shrapnel in Derreck's chest. The fact that he was on his feet was remarkable. The fact that he had made it back to the ship was nothing less than a miracle.

Derreck collapsed on the deck of the airlock and Kindra

triggered the cycle. The airlock closed and began the decontamination process. It took a full minute and there was no way around it. Kindra opened a direct channel to Derreck. "Hold on, Derreck. I'm almost there."

Kindra summoned two small work drones, waiting impatiently for the cycle to finish.

When the decontamination was complete, Kindra slammed open the inner airlock. She ordered the work drones to pick Derreck up and drag him out of the airlock as gently as they could.

As soon as Derreck was out of the airlock, she closed it again. She expected the creature Derreck brought would remain unconscious for a while, but for now the chance of contamination was far too high. She summoned the drones to follow her.

Kindra got Derreck into the medical pod, which immediately began the process of repairing his body. It started out by scanning the area and deciding if it was safe to remove his exosuit or not. Kindra allowed the pod to proceed, channeling its feed into her own holographic viewscreens. The pod was far more capable than she was, and if a decision needed to be made, it would contact her.

While the pod went to work on Derreck, Kindra returned to the airlock. The creature was still unconscious, but Kindra flooded the airlock with a mild sedative just to be certain. Then she sent the drones in and placed a sample bag on the ground. They pushed the creature on top of the bag and sealed it around him. The membrane allowed gases through, so she wasn't worried about him being able to breathe. She keyed in a full decontamination process, then had the drones pick him up and bring him to medical.

A few minutes later, the creature was in the second pod, being restrained as the pod began running scans and tests.

Kindra slumped back against a wall of the medical unit and sighed as the pods went to work on the two men. Even though Derreck was her friend, and the other was an alien, she couldn't help but hope that both of them managed to live through their ordeal.

THIRTEEN

TEV CAME TO AWARENESS SLOWLY. His memories were the first to return, and they left a bitter taste in his mind. He remembered the actions of the hunters that had brought so many of them to the brink of destruction. But as devastated as he was, the anger couldn't take hold. It was as though he lacked the energy.

He remembered being pummeled by a power he couldn't understand. And then he thought he was dead. That would explain why he wasn't able to get angry. He had finally joined the great hunt with Lys. Tev opened his eyes, but he was greeted only by a perfect blackness, the like of which he had never experienced.

He tried to move, but found he couldn't. There was something holding him down, and as feeling returned to his body, he felt something soft and unnatural against his forehead, chest, wrists, hips, and ankles.

A moment of panic seized him, but he forced it down. The same exhaustion which prevented him from being angry also prevented him from being scared. Perhaps he was dead, but he didn't know. He had never heard of an afterlife where one was tied down.

Tev took a series of deep breaths, focusing on the rising and falling of his chest. He wiggled his toes, breathing a deep sigh of relief when he felt them move. He whispered, afraid of any more sound in this silent place. The words of his prayer caressed his ears, and he was grateful once again that his body seemed to work.

The world was still black, and it made no difference to Tev whether his eyes were open or closed. He closed his eyes and concentrated on the image of Lys, the one who had always been with him. Whatever happened, he knew she wouldn't abandon him. His breathing calmed and he could feel his heart slow down.

There was no way of tracking time, but Tev guessed that almost half a day passed before anything changed. Though his eyes were closed, he didn't allow himself to sleep. His body felt tired, but he was in a strange place, and he feared that if he slept again, he'd never wake up. He wasn't afraid of death, but if he could avoid it, he would.

When the lights came on, it was as though he had been slapped in the face. His entire world abruptly went white. He closed his eyes, and when he attempted to crack them open again, the light had dimmed.

Being able to see raised far more questions than he'd had before. The first thing he noticed was that he wasn't anywhere he had ever been before. The space was unlike anything he had seen, covered in textures he didn't understand. Images danced along some parts of the walls, and Tev had no idea what any of them meant.

His mind raced, but he could only come to one conclusion: he was in the lair of the creatures he had been hunting earlier. They were the only unknown Tev was aware of, and only they seemed capable of doing something like this. Tev's heart raced, but he focused on his breath and forced himself to study his surroundings.

The light continued to get brighter, and as it did, Tev noticed he wasn't alone in the room. There was another person, similar to but completely different from anyone Tev had ever seen. The man, for it looked like a man, was on a table much like the one Tev was lying on. The difference was the man's table wasn't covered. Tev was enclosed in some sort of clear tube. He could see through it, but the slight distortions made it clear that something was between him and the rest of the room.

Everything else was nonsense to him. The light was coming from the wall above him, but Tev didn't know how that was possible. Other lights flashed upon darker sections of the walls, but Tev wasn't sure how it was even possible for him to see what he was seeing.

Tev turned his attention to the only object in the room that made any sort of sense. He twisted his head around as far as he could to look at the other man. He was wearing clothing that covered much more of his body than Tev had ever worn. The man wasn't strapped to the table like Tev was, but he looked as though he was sleeping.

The man also had a complexion Tev hadn't ever seen before. His skin was pale, whiter than Tev had ever seen skin. It was almost as if the man had never been outside in the sun.

All of Tev's thoughts were washed away when one of the walls slid open and a woman came through. Tev's first instinct was to get away, but he recognized it was foolish before his body could start to respond. His body was still sluggish, and even if it hadn't been, he was still well secured to the table.

So he focused his attention on the woman. Like the man, she wore clothes from her neck all the way down to her feet. Her skin was closer in color to Tev's, but still different. She didn't move like anyone Tev had ever seen. Tev got a glance at her feet before they disappeared from view, and they were the only part of her that seemed misshapen to him. There was too much foot there, and she walked out of balance, shifting side to side with every step.

Tev couldn't focus on her feet for too long. She walked over to the table where he was and pressed her hand against the clear covering surrounding his tube. More lights lit up, and Tev wondered if the images had anything to do with him. The woman seemed to be staring at the lights intently. Finally, her gaze moved to Tev, and to him, it looked as though she was concerned.

She spoke to him, but Tev didn't understand. There was something familiar to her words, almost as if they sat on the edge of his understanding, begging him to pay closer attention, but no matter how hard he focused, he couldn't make out what she was saying.

He tried to respond, but the look of confusion on her face was enough to tell him she didn't understand what he was saying either.

After a few attempts, Tev stopped trying to speak to her. There was no use trying to communicate that way.

Tev tried another approach. He tried to move just one of his arms. He saw the woman track the motion with her eyes, and when she looked back at him, he tried to give her a quizzical look. She frowned and then nodded.

The woman turned away and Tev watched in fascination as a part of the wall slid out. She grabbed something and brought it back over to him. It was square and fit in her hand. She held it over him, and Tev saw his own reflection, as clear as day, for the first time. It wasn't that he didn't know what he looked like. He had seen his reflection in pools of water plenty of times. But this was a perfect reflection, not marred by ripples or dirt in the water.

Tev was fascinated by what he saw. These creatures, these people, seemed to have a technology far beyond that of his own people. He couldn't even guess how the object worked. The woman saw he understood, then angled the reflection downwards. When she reached his stomach, she stopped, and Tev saw what she was getting at. There was a fresh scar forming there, a large hole that was still open.

But although there was a hole in his skin, there was no blood. He struggled to understand. He was still alive, and the woman, at least from what Tev understood, seemed kind enough. She didn't seem like she was trying to hurt him in any way. Pieces started to fall together in his mind. Somehow, they were trying to help him.

Tev nodded, trying to show he understood. Then the woman pointed at the other man who was in the room with him. Tev nodded again. They were both being fixed. They probably still worried about him. He had tried to kill them, after all.

The two of them sat in silence for a few minutes, until finally the woman pointed at herself. "Kindra," she said.

Tev understood. He replied, "Tev."

The woman nodded, studying him for a few more moments. Then she stood up, saying something to him he didn't understand. But the tone of her voice was clear. At least for now, he wasn't in any danger. The wall slid shut behind her, and Tev's world plunged into darkness again.

TEV DRIFTED in and out of sleep, losing all track of time.

He could have been asleep for days or just minutes. With no light in the room, there was no way for him to judge the passage of time. Kindra came back to check on him every time he was awake. He tried to read the expression on her face. She seemed nice, but at the same time, there was a certain hardness to her. Tev didn't judge her for it.

He had plenty of time for thinking. Until just recently, he had been on a hunt to kill these creatures. The people in front of him had to be the same kind, and if that was true, it meant the ones he had fought were wearing some kind of armor, some kind of protection. He saw Kindra without armor, and if the other man was also being fixed, he had to be the one Tev had wounded.

He was still restrained, and with nothing to do but let his body heal, his mind often wandered. One subject he thought a lot about was what he was supposed to do next. He had been sent by his clan to hunt these creatures. Should he still? They seemed to be trying to help him, even after he had tried to kill them. Or was there more he didn't understand?

Tev wished he knew more. He wanted to know who these creatures were and why they were here. Did they mean to harm his people or not? Where did they come from? Tev had hiked hundreds of kilometers in his life, and had heard stories from much farther away. These creatures were outside of the experience of any story he had ever heard.

Complicating the decision, or perhaps simplifying it, was the fact that he was still restrained. Even if he wanted to do something, there was no way of doing so. He had tested his restraints, and no matter what he did, there was no give. So for now, he had to wait.

Tev also wondered how many of the creatures there

were. He only ever saw Kindra and the man called Derreck. Were they the only two here, or were there more of them? Tev didn't have the answers to the questions, and the lack of communication was starting to bother him.

One time the lights came on and Kindra came in. There was a look of hesitation on her face, but she seemed determined. Tev tensed up. He had never seen her like this before, and it indicated something important was about to happen.

Kindra paced the room a few times, for a reason Tev couldn't guess at. Finally, she stopped directly above him.

She held up her hands. In each one was a small item, almost like a small stone that was shaped strangely, another thing that would never occur in nature. As he watched, Kindra took one of the items and put it in her ear. She pulled her hair back and tilted her head so he could see it inside her ear. Then she gestured at him.

Tev nodded as best he could. He wasn't sure what was happening, but he knew that unless something changed, he would never make it out of this room. If escape was a possibility, he needed to figure out what these creatures were and how to kill them.

Kindra put on something over her hands, and with one final hesitation, opened the tube. Tev sniffed cautiously at the air. The smell was different than within the tube, but subtly. The air was different here, lacking the diversity of scents he was used to. Although he lacked the language to describe it, the best he could come up with was that the air here was empty.

Tev felt Kindra place the item gently in his ear. He wondered if he would feel pain, but none came. As soon as Kindra was satisfied with whatever she was doing, she stepped back and closed the tube again. Her hands ran over the now-familiar lights, and she seemed to be relieved by whatever she saw.

Kindra turned her attention back to Tev, and he could almost see her mind working. She pointed to herself and said her name. Then she pointed at Tev and named him, and at Derreck and named him. She went to one of the walls nearby, which opened to her touch. She pulled out Tev's sack, and as she pulled out his supplies one by one, Tev named them. He paid particular attention when she pulled out his weapons. He hadn't known they were so close. But it didn't matter. As long as he was restrained, there wasn't anything he could do about it. They might as well be over a mountain range for as useful as they were to him.

The process went on for some time, with Kindra making Tev attempt to name objects. Unfortunately, most of what was in the room he didn't have words for. Then she moved on to actions. She would act out doing something, and Tev would name what it was. If Kindra hadn't been so serious about it, so lost in what she was doing, Tev would have laughed. It was not what he had expected, not at all.

After this had gone on for a while, Kindra stopped acting. She seemed to stare off into nowhere, something Tev noticed she did quite often.

Then she spoke, and to Tev's amazement, he could understand what she was saying. Whatever was in his ear was making his language.

"Hello, Tev."

"Hello, Kindra," he replied.

Kindra hesitated, and Tev wondered what she would say next. He was amazed that he was able to understand her.

She found the question she was looking for. "Where do your people come from?"

Tev wondered what she was trying to get at. Was she asking for the location of his clan? There was no way he would tell her that. He answered with a question of his own. "Why are you here?"

Her eyes turned to him, trying to study him but failing to pierce him. "We're looking for life. Exploring."

Her answer made no sense to Tev. Life was everywhere. To look for it, all you had to do was open your eyes. Why would they need to explore for life?

He asked his next question before she could repeat hers. "Where do you come from?"

She pointed up. "The sky."

If Tev would have, he would have scrambled backwards away from her. Coming from the sky was impossible. It was the home of Lys and the other heroes. It was not for mortals to travel from. He was convinced that Kindra wasn't a god, but if that was true, why did she say she came from the sky?

Kindra seized on his confusion to ask him a question in return.

"Why were you out there?"

Tev looked her in the eyes, confusion replaced by anger. "To hunt you."

FOURTEEN

KINDRA FELT as though she was walking around in a constant state of shock, the entire planet trying to tilt and throw her off. It had only been three days since the incident, as they were now calling it, and everything kept shifting underneath her. First had been the challenge of healing Derreck. His wounds had nearly been fatal. The cut Tev had given him had severed an artery, and if not for the exosuit's medical systems, it would have been a fatal blow. But even that was no comparison to the shot Derreck had taken from Kenan. It had torn his suit up and left hundreds of pieces of shrapnel in his body. Kindra had no idea how Derreck had made it back alive.

Complications arose once the pod began treatment. The pod detected hemorrhaging in Derreck's brain. Between that and the repair work the nanos were conducting in his system, Kindra had no choice but to keep him in a coma while they did their work. Kindra would have done anything for his advice, but the pod estimated it would be several days before it would be safe to wake him. If they woke him now, Kindra worried his body wouldn't be able to take it. Unfortunately, they were on their own.

The tension between the crew members was palpable. They had faced difficult situations before, but they had never been split apart like this. In the past they had always been able to rely on each other to face challenges. But now, only three of the five of them were left. Kenan was rogue somewhere on the planet, and Derreck was in a forced coma in their medical wing. It made Kindra, third in command, their leader, and she felt lost like a child among the stars.

The three of them had argued every day. Everything was now in question. Should they stay or lift off? Should they search for Kenan or call him lost? But no question divided them more than what to do with the creature who called himself Tev. It had been an impulsive decision to make Derreck bring him to the ship in the first place, but now that he was here, they were all uncertain about how to proceed.

Kindra had saved his life. Tev's injuries, although not fatal by their standards, would have killed him. They had saved him, but to what end?

The three remaining crew members were sitting around the table, and it felt larger than it ever had before. Kindra rubbed the sleep from her eyes and started the meeting.

"Okay, I'll start. I've got a bombshell. Tev is human."

Stunned silence greeted her announcement. Eleta raised one eyebrow, the most intense question she could raise.

Kindra shrugged. "I don't know how. I don't have any answers. But he's made of DNA, just like we are, and his DNA matches ours. It looks like there may even be a shared ancestry, but I'll need to get to the main Fleet archives to find out."

"I've asked Tev about it, but his culture only has creation myths. There's nothing concrete I can draw on to explain my findings. But he is just as human as you or I."

Alston summed up his feelings succinctly. "That's a surprise."

Kindra nodded.

"But even if that's true, does it change our decisions?"

Kindra didn't know. It was the same argument they had been having for three days. None of them knew best how to proceed. They hadn't even decided what they wanted to do with Tev.

Unable to make a final decision, the dropship sat where it had landed. They all went about their daily routines, ensconced safely in the ship. Kindra checked on her patients a couple of times a day, each time trying to have more of a conversation with Tev. The more they spoke, the better the translators were able to translate. But as fascinating as Tev was, Kindra felt like she kept running up against a wall. All the evidence suggested a larger story, but if there was one, Tev didn't know it.

Eleta changed the subject. "There's something else you need to know. I've got news about Kenan."

Immediately, Kindra thought that perhaps Kenan had died. A part of her grieved. Although she didn't always like Kenan, he was a part of the crew, a part of their family. But more than that, she was relieved, and felt guilty for her relief.

Her thoughts were interrupted by Eleta. "Last night, he tried to make some more permanent modifications to his exosuit. In doing so, he accidentally turned on his communications array again. It was only on for about five minutes before he discovered it and disabled it again, but in that time, we got tracking data, visual logs, and suit data. It wasn't everything, but it was also too much."

"What do you mean?"

Eleta grimaced. "The first thing I did was look over his exosuit specs. I couldn't help it, but we've never put an exosuit through an experience like this before. Everything looked nominal at first, until I noticed this."

Eleta pulled up the stats from the exosuit, but Kindra didn't have any idea what she was looking at. Eleta seemed to think there was something important there, though. She kept looking at Kindra as though she should be amazed.

"I'm sorry, Eleta, but I don't know what I'm looking at."

Eleta shook her head, as though she was frustrated by a leader who didn't know what was happening.

"Look over here. This is his ammo readout." She pointed towards a section of the screen. "And here is his ammo readout from the last moment he was in contact with us." She pointed towards another section, and Kindra saw what Eleta was getting at. Kenan's ammo was lower than when he had left them. Significantly.

Kindra sat down. "You know what he's done?"

Eleta nodded. "I won't make you watch it, but he's been tracking the natives. He's found at least two encampments and has slaughtered them at each."

Kindra's world shifted, and she held onto the armrests of her seat as if she would fall out of the chair if she didn't. What had already happened had been horrible enough, but Kindra had started to wrap her mind around it. This was something else. This was inexcusable.

She sat there, completely lost, anger building inside her. They had done wrong. Before, the decision had been a straightforward one. Either stay or leave. But now their choice had even greater consequences. The only person on the ship who had any reasonable chance of helping them out was in a forced coma. To bring him back could kill him, but perhaps it was necessary.

Alston spoke. "I realize this may sound cold, but what does it matter? Fleet sent us out here to explore, and we have a little time left before the *Destiny* comes back to pick us up. There's nothing we can do about Kenan. None of us are trained in combat, and he's in an exosuit. I say, we keep going. We get all the information we can and leave when it's time. It's all we can do."

Kindra wanted to slap Alston. She understood where he was coming from, but he wasn't right. Kenan was out there murdering innocents. Something had to be done to stop him.

They argued, but they came to no decision, and Kindra didn't have any ideas she was comfortable ordering others to follow. They adjourned, no further decisions made. Kindra found herself walking towards medical, not even aware that was her destination until she was outside the door.

Perhaps she hoped Derreck would have some answers for her, that his very presence might help her.

Kindra stepped through the door, her presence turning up the lights, and she looked at the scene before her. Tev, as she expected, was awake and watching her carefully. Derreck was unconscious on the table next to him. She barely nodded to Tev, unable to face him after knowing what her people had done to his. She walked over to Derreck and held his hand in her own, wondering what he would do in this situation.

Of course, if it had been him, they never would have had this problem in the first place. Derreck demanded respect, and Kenan would do anything he said. But with

Derreck gone, the crew had collapsed like a house of cards in an earthquake. It was up to her now, and she wasn't ready.

Mostly, she wanted to leave. She wanted to be done with this planet. If they took off, it wasn't her problem anymore. They could rendezvous with the jumper and Fleet could take care of Kenan. She could find a nice small planet to go hide on.

But her conscience wouldn't let her. Like a petulant child, it kept screaming for her attention, reminding her it was her responsibility to make a decision. If she did nothing, the disaster would only get worse. Without any way of getting in touch of Kenan, she couldn't imagine him taking any other path than the one he was already walking.

But she also couldn't think of any way to stop him. They had one damaged general-purpose exosuit, and no one who was capable of doing anything with it. All of them were checked out on it, but none of them were great pilots. Kenan was, and if he was as unstable as he seemed, the exosuit wouldn't provide them more than a few seconds of protection.

Lost in her own thoughts, Kindra didn't say goodbye to Tev. She wandered out of medical, realizing she was far too tired to make any decision.

She called Eleta, letting her know that she needed to lie down for a while. Her mind was tired and running in circles. Eleta acknowledged, and Kindra told her she'd be awake in three hours. Kindra stumbled over to her bunk and lay down, her mind running through the same old problems. Sleep overcame her in a few moments, and for a while she was at peace.

When she sat bolt upright in her bunk, only two hours had passed. The idea was burned deep into her memory. As her heart calmed down, Kindra thought about what she was considering. It was the worst idea she had ever had, but it might also be her smartest. If it worked. She turned on her comms, hesitating before calling Eleta.

"Eleta? How soon can you have the exosuit repaired?"

FIFTEEN

TEV WASN'T sure what was happening, but he would have needed to be blind to miss that something was wrong. Kindra had been in and out of the medical bay constantly, and every time, her face was a mask of preoccupation. Their conversations, once important to her, were now over. She couldn't even meet his gaze. He would try to start a conversation, but she wouldn't respond, just doing whatever needed doing and then leaving again. When she came in with her eyes set on him, he knew a decision had been reached.

In her hands was a piece of what they called metal, shaped in a way Tev couldn't comprehend. But behind her came another person, the first time Tev had met anyone else from the crew. He had known Kindra wasn't alone, but she had never allowed anyone else into the bay with her. The woman looked similar to Kindra, and she held something black in her hand that she pointed at Tev.

Kindra introduced Eleta. "Tev, I have a problem, and maybe you can help me with it. But I need to try something first. I'm going to release some of your restraints, but I don't want you to do anything. Eleta has a weapon that will stop you if you do. Do you understand?"

Every muscle in Tev's body tensed up. If they removed some of his restraints, perhaps he'd have the chance to escape. But he watched as Eleta pointed the black thing in her hand at him, and he had an uncomfortable reminder of the battle where he'd been injured. These people possessed weapons he didn't understand. From the way she held herself, he didn't think Eleta was any more of a warrior than Kindra, but it probably wouldn't matter. Unless he was certain, he wouldn't make a move. He nodded, and Kindra stepped up and started removing his restraints. She took off everything above his waist, leaving the straps across his thighs and ankles. Even if he tried anything, he'd have to loosen those first, using valuable time he wouldn't have.

Kindra pointed to the metal thing she had brought into the room with her. "Tev, this is what we call a simulator. We put it over our heads." She took a moment to pause and demonstrate what she meant. Tev saw that the device covered her eyes and ears. She took it off.

"This lets us dream we are in different places. I want to put it on you, and I want to have you try some things. Then maybe you can help us. Is that okay with you?"

Tev didn't see how he had much choice, and besides, he was curious. He nodded.

Kindra approached and placed the simulator over his head. As he expected, his world went black and silent. Then he heard Kindra's voice. It wasn't coming from outside, as he had expected. Instead, it came from right next to his ear. It spooked him at first, but he wouldn't allow himself to show fear, not here.

"I'm going to put a picture in front of you." Tev could tell she was struggling to find language he could understand. It was a challenge that had raised its head repeatedly during their conversations. "You might think it is real, but it isn't. Just remember that."

It was all the warning Tev had before his world changed. Suddenly he was back in the woods of his planet, the land and terrain he knew so well. He turned his head from side to side, and as he did, his perspective changed. With his hands he could feel the table beneath him, but all around him he could see the forest. He could even hear the sounds of it in his ears. His mind realized it wasn't real, but he couldn't help but be impressed by how beautiful it was.

He spoke for the first time. "This is amazing, Kindra."

There was a hint of relief in her voice. "Good. Now, I'm going to change something. I am going to put armor on you, like the armor that Derreck wore. If you look down, you'll see it."

Tev did, and sure enough, he could see the armor covering his chest, arms, and legs.

"Okay, Tev, now it's time for the test. This might be hard, but I want you to dream you are moving. You can move however you want."

It seemed a strange command, but Tev decided to try it. He pictured himself walking forward, and after a few stumbles, it seemed as though he was moving forward. He could make a few steps, but then he'd think about how he was strapped to the table, and he'd fall over. After a few minutes of trying, Kindra recognized the problem.

"Tev, is it okay if I give you some medicine? It will numb your body, so you can focus on the test."

Tev, fascinated and curious, nodded. He didn't think through Kindra's words. But slowly the rest of his sensations faded away, and all that was left was the dream world. Once Tev couldn't feel his real limbs any more, imagining the movements became much easier. After about ten minutes of getting used to the world, he was running and jumping and climbing, just as he would if he was actually outside.

Kindra's voice interrupted Tev's play. There was something in her voice, but he couldn't quite place it. Maybe relief, maybe something else. "Tev, right now, I've been letting the dream act as though it was your real body. I'm going to change it now so your body moves like it would if it was wearing the armor. You're going to feel very different, but I want to see if you can move around in it."

Tev's curiosity was on fire. He wanted more. This experience was wholly unlike anything he had ever done before. He was eager for a new challenge. He stood still for a moment while Kindra changed his dream world. Then he tried moving again.

As Kindra had promised, the feeling was very different. Tev couldn't move as easily as he thought he should, and his balance seemed off, just a little. But he continued to focus, and soon walking felt just as natural as it ever had. Then it was time to press things harder. Tev started to jog, then to run. His stride, normally short and quick, was more powerful than ever, and once he mastered his balance, he sped through the forest faster than he could have imagined possible. He fell a few times, but there was no pain. He just stood himself up and kept moving.

Tev ran, the idea of movement freeing and liberating. He had always loved running through the woods, but this was something new, more powerful than before. A ravine opened up in front of him, and in a moment of recklessness he leapt across, imagining himself rolling as he cleared a space he never would have been able to leap on his own. He ran and ran, more free than he had ever been before.

Kindra's voice whispered into his ear and he slowed

down. "Tev, there's just one last test. Raise your right arm and imagine releasing the string on your bow."

Tev did as she asked, knowing already what was supposed to happen. The tree in front of him exploded, collapsing as its trunk was torn in half.

"I've added an animal to the dream. Can you hunt it?"

Tev's heart started to race, but after years of practice, he calmed his breath. Sure enough, there were tracks nearby, easy for him to follow. It was the first time he noticed a hint of artifice in the world he was in. No animal he knew would leave such an obvious trail. When he found the animal, it was a boar.

Tev smiled and watched as the boar made to run. He knew he could have raised his arm and shot it, but he wanted to test himself. He chased after it, his speed and endurance superior to the animal's. He ran it down, but unlike a real boar, this one never got tired. It kept running, and Tev kept up with it, finally leaping above it and using the weapon in his right arm to shoot it. He landed smoothly, a fierce fire and excitement burning through his body. This power, this experience, was something he never wanted to give up.

Kindra spoke. "Tev, I'm going to bring you back. You may not feel right for a few moments. Remember the rest of your body is numb."

Tev didn't want to leave, but before he could say no, his entire world went black. A few moments later the device came off his head. After the immersion in the dream world, the real world seemed to swim around his head. Kindra had been right. Not being able to feel his limbs was very disorienting, and he felt sick, his mind unable to keep up with the different sensations his body was going through. Kindra saw it and helped him lay down.

"I'm going to put you to sleep, Tev, so your body can reset. You'll wake up in about three hours."

She didn't wait for permission, and Tev was too disoriented to protest. She issued some commands to the table he was on and Tev's world faded to black.

SIXTEEN

THE LAST THREE members of the expedition sat around a table, the decision hanging between them, smothering conversation like a heavy blanket. It had been Kindra's idea, but she didn't feel comfortable making the choice alone. She wouldn't make it alone.

It was Alston who spoke up, logical and calm. "You're sure there's no other way?"

Kindra let out a sigh. It was the very question she'd been asking herself over and over. "No, I'm not. Perhaps there is another way. But if there is, I've got no idea what it is. I've been thinking and thinking, and as crazy as it seems, I still can't come up with anything better. I wish I could."

Eleta put aside Tev's brain scans, the images that had captured her attention for the past ten minutes. "Is it even our responsibility to make things right?"

"You know that I believe it is. What if Kenan continues to kill more people? Those are lives we might have had a chance to save."

Eleta glanced again at the brain scans. She had been right there, and even she still had trouble believing it.

"You're absolutely sure about the compatibility? If you aren't, the suit will likely kill him."

Kindra looked at the various scans and data the table was displaying before her. "I can't believe it either, but I am certain. Tev is perfectly human, just like we are. Not only that, his body and mind seem better wired for movement than ours. It gives him an advantage. There's no reason he can't pilot the suit."

Alston repeated the same question they'd already asked a dozen times. "How is that even possible? Derreck said he looked through the archives. There's never been an expedition out here. We're the first humans who have ever been here. Plus, they're primitives. They aren't even close to space travel."

Kindra shrugged. "I don't know. I have far more questions than answers. Where did the electromagnetic radiation we first detected even come from? We still haven't found any evidence there either. And yet the translator indicates that our languages have a root similarity. Tev uses the same units of time we do, even if they aren't measured as precisely."

Alston looked like his mind was ready to explode, and Kindra knew exactly how he felt. The data had been indicative at first, but as Kindra studied Tev more closely, she had no doubt about what she was saying. She didn't know how, but the facts were there. It didn't make any sense at all, but it was true.

Eleta still doubted. "Even if what you say is accurate, and I'm sure it is, piloting a suit seems insane."

That one Kindra had less worry about. "You watched the tests same as I did. After less than an hour in the simulation, he was running one of the suits as well as any of our top pilots, and he was using neural connections only.

Imagine what he would be capable of with physical feedback as well."

Eleta couldn't argue with that. She had been right there with Kindra, and both of them vividly remembered their own first simulation training. They had spent far more time on the ground staring into the dirt. What Tev had accomplished was beyond amazing. Kindra had theories about why it was true, but that wasn't up for debate right now. The fact was, she was convinced Tev could pilot one of their suits, and that was all that mattered.

Kindra glanced from Alston to Eleta, wondering if there were going to be any more questions. The jumper would be arriving in a few days, and she wanted everything put right by the time it arrived. "I don't want to do this without your support. Eleta, what do you think?"

Eleta leaned back in her seat and rubbed her eyes. "I don't like it at all, but every other option is even less palatable. I'll support you."

They both looked at Alston. Silence hung in the room as he considered his answer. When he spoke, he didn't justify himself. His reasons were his own, and Kindra knew he felt like they didn't need to be shared. "Yes."

The decision made, Kindra pushed them forward. "Okay. Eleta, I'll talk to Tev. Assuming he agrees, I'll want a test run within six hours. Make sure the kill switch is ready. Alston, I want you to double-check communications. I know it's not your field, but learn. After that, we're all taking a long break. If everything goes well, we'll send Tev out tomorrow at daybreak."

They both nodded and went about their tasks. They were going to send Tev to hunt one of their own.

KINDRA SAT next to Tev's bedside. He was restrained again, but not as tightly as before. She still didn't trust him completely, but their situation made them partners, whether they liked it or not. She hoped she could convince him of that as well.

"Tev, I'd like you to hunt one of my crew."

Tev's eyes lit up, a mixture of anticipation and wariness. She knew he would expect a trap. In his place, she would too.

Kindra decided how to break the news.

"When we came here, we didn't come to hurt you. We came to explore. We didn't even know you were here."

She let her words sink in before continuing.

"One of our crew, he isn't well. His mind is sick, and it broke when he fought against you. He wasn't supposed to attack you. But he's made it worse. He has hurt your people."

Tev tried to surge upright, fire and hate in his eyes. The restraints pulled tight on him. He looked like he wanted to shout, but he didn't allow himself to. Whatever his upbringing, Kindra thought, he was controlled.

"I know. I'm sorry. But I need to stop him. We're not here to hurt your people, but we can't stop him. We aren't warriors. Maybe you can."

Tev spoke, his voice a harsh growl. "I will."

Kindra pulled up a hologram of the general purpose exosuit. "You know that we have armor. We want to give you the suit to hunt Kenan. Kenan's suit is stronger and designed for fighting. Yours isn't. But it is the best we can do."

"Let me go. I will hunt Kenan for you."

"Tev, stop and breathe, just for a moment."

His nostrils flared, but her words must have sparked

something in him, because he did. After a few moments, she saw he was calmer, more rational than he had been earlier.

"There are some things I must know. First, do you trust me?"

Tev looked like he was about to tell her no, but stopped and fixed her with a stare. Kindra wanted to look away, but she forced herself to meet his eyes without flinching.

Finally, he spoke. "I want to, but I do not. Your people have hurt mine, and there is too much I don't know and don't understand."

Kindra recoiled. She had hoped he would trust her. If he didn't, she wasn't sure she could trust him. But she put herself in his place and tried to understand. They hadn't given him a lot of good reasons to trust them. She had healed him, but that paled in comparison to the numbers they had hurt.

"I understand. I want you to trust me too, so I will tell you the truth. First, we are going to let you try the actual suit, but it is only going to be a test. There won't be any weapons on it, and I can shut it down and trap you inside at any time."

She saw the anger in his eyes, but met it calmly.

"I want you to trust me, so I'm being honest. We shouldn't be letting you do this. We should just leave, but this is what is right. We need to test the suit first and make sure it is right for you. Today we test. Then you come back here and sleep. Tomorrow at first light we'll let you go hunting. That's the deal, and nothing will change that. Do you understand and agree?"

Tev was angry, but from where she sat, he didn't really have any other options, and he figured it out quickly enough. "Yes."

"Good. I'm going to let you go now."

Tev looked around the room. "No weapons?"

Kindra shook her head. "I trust you not to hurt me."

Tev seemed to take the statement seriously. "I will not hurt you, Kindra."

Kindra didn't know nearly enough about Tev's culture to understand him, but she got the sense that when he spoke, it was as good as a promise to him. Kindra released his restraints and allowed him to stand up. The bed stimulated his muscles, so there hadn't been any atrophy in the past few days. Even so, he stood and stretched out, and for the first time, Kindra got to watch him move as he normally would.

Tev was a lean man, not an ounce of fat on him. He wasn't large, but his muscles held a wiry strength, and Kindra knew if she had the time, she would find he was incredibly strong. But even watching him move was something else. He was grace personified in every movement.

In an act of trust, Kindra went over to the wall and opened up the bin that held all of Tev's possessions. She handed them all to him, including his weapons. His relief was palpable.

Their eyes met, and Kindra decided it was time to go past the point of no return. "Come on, Tev. Let's get you into your new suit."

SEVENTEEN

TEV WATCHED Kindra as she came over to put his helmet on. He watched the way her hands moved, learning the way to put it on correctly. Kindra's people called it an exosuit, but Tev just thought of it as armor, and it was the most powerful weapon he had ever possessed.

Kindra was fond of reminding him that this armor was not as strong as the one the other one had. Tev accepted her statement, even if it seemed hard to believe. He had felt the metal on his suit, and although there were still traces of the hole that had almost killed Derreck, Tev still had a hard time believing there was anything that could harm him. The suit made him so much stronger than any hunter who had ever come before.

Tev's thoughts wandered to the dream he had, back in the caves. More and more, he was convinced it had been less a dream and more a vision. These experiences with Kindra and her clan were so far out of the ordinary, it was a journey he never could have anticipated. He wondered where this path would end.

The tests yesterday had gone pretty well. Tev had

started out too eager, buoyed by the success he had felt in the dream world Kindra had put him in. But here in the real world, actions had consequences, as Tev discovered soon enough. Even in armor a fall could hurt, and he had fallen a lot. Kindra had asked him to come in a few times, but he had refused, driven to figure out how this armor worked. By the time night fell, Tev was running and leaping naturally through the woods. He still stumbled occasionally, but it was a small price to pay for the skill he gained.

More than once, Tev considered trying to run away with the armor, but it didn't make sense to do so. Kindra had told him they could shut it down at any time, and he didn't have any clue how to stop that from happening. And if Kindra was telling the truth about what her clan member was doing, it was Tev's responsibility to stay with them and stop him. Even if he didn't like it, his course was set for him.

He had fired the weapon for the first time yesterday. Kindra hadn't liked that, but Tev was coming to understand that though she was a leader, Kindra wasn't a hunter. She had an inner strength Tev respected, but out in the wild, she wouldn't live long. They had explained to him how the weapon worked. It was a weapon that threw small pieces of metal very fast. As usual, Kindra told Tev his armor wasn't as strong as Kenan's, but Tev barely heard, he was so fascinated by the new power he wielded.

They had him fire the weapon at a tree, and he watched in amazement as the tree exploded in front of him. His blood boiled, and he was excited about hunting once again.

Kindra finished attaching his helmet, and Tev watched as the pictures started appearing in front of him. They had told him what the pictures meant, but it was still new to him. Kindra's people didn't seem to trust their senses as much as Tev did his own. The suit told him what was around him, but Tev felt like despite it all, he was blind. He pushed the hesitation away as the suit started up.

Kindra gave him one last look. "Please, if you can, don't kill him. He has done horrible things, but he is also broken."

Tev looked at her. He did not want to lie to her. When he found Kenan, he was going to kill him. But he also needed Kindra to let him leave. "I will see what I can do."

He saw her expression clearly, and he knew she knew how he felt, but she wasn't going to call him out. She hated sending him out, but it was the only way to stop Kenan.

Without another word, Kindra stood away, and Tev walked towards the two doors that separated the ship he was in from the outside. He passed through the doors and was back out in his world, a free man once again. He took a deep breath, disappointed he couldn't smell the air yet.

Kindra's voice came in through his helmet, translated by the device in his ear. "I'm putting up a picture of where we knew Kenan was last. From there, you're going to need to find him."

Tev didn't bother replying. In front of him, an arrow appeared, pointing in the direction he was supposed to go. It was almost too easy.

Tev started running. Kindra protested, but Tev ignored her. He was so fast, and running used very little of his strength. It was a feeling he had a hard time describing. It was as though he had an unlimited supply of energy to draw on, a well that remained deep, no matter how much he drew from it. Tev never wanted to let the feeling go.

The ground flew under Tev's feet, and he found his mind reached a new soft focus. Every step was carefully placed. Although he felt light, he knew he was much heavier in the armor. As he had learned during the tests yesterday, a mistake could be painful, and more importantly, could damage the suit. But he was confident, and as he launched off of each foot, he was already planning his next step. Over and over, he fell into a trance that sped him across the land, his focus relaxed but complete.

And then it all stopped in a moment. Tev had a rough idea where he was, but he was in a clan's territory he hadn't been in since he was a child. He hadn't worried much about it, but his old life came rushing back to him when he came upon a camp in utter chaos. Homes were destroyed and bodies were everywhere. Tev had taken part in raids before, but he had never seen anything like this.

Tev didn't have to stop and examine what happened, but he did anyway. There were no arrows or spears, no sign any other clan had done this. This was Kenan's work. This is what Kindra wanted Tev to stop. Tev knelt to the ground, breathing deeply, trying to control his reaction. He heard Kindra breathing through the helmet, and knew she wanted to say something, but then there was only silence. There was nothing she could say to make this any better.

Tev was furious, his breath coming out in long, ragged bursts. There was a profound sense of wrongness here. Everything about Kindra and her people was wrong. Tev wanted to take the armor he was wearing and rip it off, to distance himself from anything that represented Kindra's clan. There was no way he would allow Kenan to live.

After a few minutes he got his breath under control. Once he did, it was only a few minutes before his rage cooled. He stood back up, a cold detachment settling over his mind. He examined the scene around him as though it were a hunting scene. These suits were easy to track, and all he had to do was figure out which way Kenan went.

He searched the ground, and after a few minutes found the track Kenan had left. As Tev expected, once found, it was easy to follow. Although the armor was very impressive, it didn't allow one the same freedom of movement, and even if it did, Tev was starting to understand his prey more clearly. His prey believed it was invincible. It didn't need to cover its tracks. That confidence would be part of what allowed Tev to kill it.

He was no longer running. Every step he took was deliberate and considered.

Kindra's voice was a whisper in his ear, and it sounded as though she had been crying. "I'm sorry, Tev."

He ignored her. She wasn't directly responsible, but her clan was, and he wasn't sure he could forgive them for what they had done. But none of that mattered now. All that mattered was revenge. He followed the tracks, his weapon ready for anything.

TEV CONTINUED HIS HUNT, unconcerned about the diminishing daylight. He figured he still had two hours of light left, easily. He kept following the trail, trusting his skill. Kenan could move, but he couldn't hide, and Tev would find him and kill him.

An hour later, Tev came upon a campground, the place where Kenan had rested. Tev halted his pursuit to scan the area more thoroughly. Tracks to and from the site led him to believe Kenan had spent more than one night here, and might have even left recently. He crouched down and examined the signs, wishing his helmet would stop flashing information across his vision.

The camp was crude and had several markings of someone who wasn't quite sure what they were doing. Nearby, a deer had been shot. Parts of it had been torn off and cooked. The more he tracked Kenan, the more he learned. The campsite reinforced what Kindra had told him. They didn't come from here. Everything about Kindra and her clan indicated they didn't know how to live in nature. They overcame nature.

Tev imagined what Kenan would be thinking, what weaknesses he would possess. Kindra told him Kenan was an excellent warrior, but he came from a people who believed they were the top of the food chain. Tev knew hunters who thought the same, and they were the ones who always met an untimely death. Even if humans were one of the most powerful creatures, the world was full of danger; and to lose focus was to welcome your end. It could be a poisonous insect you didn't pay enough attention to avoid, or a misplaced step that breaks a bone that then becomes infected.

Tev possessed the element of surprise. Kenan didn't know he was being hunted, so no matter how strong of a warrior he was, he was still prey. Tev would kill him.

Night was coming, and Tev had a choice to make. The signs were recent, and if Tev was forced to guess, he would guess Kenan had spent the last night here. The question was, would he again?

Tev's gut told him Kenan would return. Besides, there were several trails leading to and from the camp, and it would take Tev more time than he had left today to decide which track was the most recent and follow it. Better to wait here, at least for tonight, before deciding to track Kenan the next morning. He scanned the surrounding terrain. Kenan's camp was isolated, but there was a high point about a hundred meters towards the sunset.

He didn't hesitate. Moving quickly, Tev climbed the small ridge of rock. He laid down, resting his right arm in front of him, pointing his gun in the general direction of Kenan's camp.

The sun fell, and as it did, Tev's vision changed. Kindra told him about it as it happened, but he was still surprised to find that he could see, even though there wasn't any sun. Kindra called it night vision. Fortunately, Tev had become used to being amazed, and he took it in stride. The colors were off, but it wouldn't matter. All he needed to do was take one shot.

Tev's breath caught in his throat when he saw a light in his vision. He had learned about the motion tracker when Kindra had trained him. It was how Kenan and Derreck had known when people were behind them when the hunters had tried to kill them earlier. It was why Tev had decided to lay down and point his arm at the camp before Kenan came back. If he didn't move, Kenan wouldn't have a warning.

Tev forced his breath down, breathing in deeply and slowly. A few minutes later, Kenan came into view, wearing the terrible armor that had destroyed so many lives the last time Tev had seen it. Never again. Tev watched as Kenan sat down in his camp, his back to Tev.

Tev's hunting instincts kicked in. As much as he itched to pull the trigger, it was best to wait a few moments and make sure he had the best shot. Using his thoughts, as Kindra had taught him, he pulled up a small red circle that showed where his bullets would go. As he had worried, his aim was a little off. Moving slowly, Tev shifted his arm further to the left. He moved it a centimeter at a time, not sure what level of motion would cause Kenan's suit to alarm him. After a few minutes, Tev's weapon was in line with Kenan's head.

He almost pulled the trigger, but something held him

back. Something was bothering him, but it took him a few moments to realize what it was. He whispered to Kindra.

"Kindra, how accurate is this weapon?"

Her confusion was evident. "What do you mean?"

"I mean, will it hit what I'm pointing at from this distance?"

Kindra paused, and Tev imagined she was trying to figure out the answer to his question.

"At your distance, acceptable targeting is considered within half a meter."

Tev nodded to himself. Without a word, he slowly lowered his arm just a little further, watching the little red circle drift downwards over Kenan's back. He had a much better chance of hitting this target. He didn't wait, didn't hesitate at all. He pulled the trigger. His arm emitted the same whine he had once feared so much.

Tev saw something fly off of Kenan's back and saw him pitch forward. His heart leapt into his throat. He had killed the one who had brought so much pain to his people!

His elation was short lived. Kenan turned around and Tev felt a strong sense of déjà vu as Kenan brought his own weapon to bear. Tev moved, rolling to his right just as the dirt around him was torn up. He knew the armor might protect him, but there were no guarantees.

Tev dipped below the ridge line and got to his feet. He only thought for a moment, and his confidence was high. He took a running start and leapt off the ridge he'd been hiding on. The drop was a solid ten meters, but Tev landed and rolled out. He lost his balance just for a moment, but got the suit under control quickly.

Kenan was tracking him the entire time. Tev saw the arm come up again and darted to the left, against the direction of Kenan's movement. It wasn't much, but it was enough. Kenan's arm spit fire, but Tev was unhurt. Kenan shifted his aim and Tev leapt into the air, covering the last five meters between them in a moment.

But when he came down, Kenan wasn't there. He had side-stepped, and brought his weapon to point at Tev's back. Tev tried to turn but stumbled, his mind and body still unused to the suit. He slipped and fell as Kenan's bullets tore through the air above his head.

Tev caught his fall on his arms and churned his legs, driving himself right at Kenan. He came in underneath Kenan's arms, tackling him right across his midsection. But Kenan didn't fall. Instead, he backpedaled, somehow managing to keep his feet underneath him. At the same time, Tev felt a tremendous blow to his back, and he lost his balance once again. Kenan must have brought both elbows down on him.

Tev crashed to the ground. It took him a moment, but he raised himself up and saw Kenan's weapon pointing right at him. But nothing happened. Kenan seemed to glance at his arm, but Tev drove himself up to his feet, ready for more.

Kenan turned and ran. Tev wasn't sure what had happened, but he pursued. Kenan was fast, but Tev moved faster. The forest sped by them, the two suits of armor and the two pilots darting in between trees and over rocks. Tev would close the gap, only to trip and fall or run into a tree. If he had just been running, he could have done it, but to pursue was different, and Tev lacked the experience to keep his feet. Tev had never taken part in a hunt so fast-paced before and his entire body sang at the opportunity.

In front of him, Kenan leapt into the air, twisting his body behind him as he did. His arm came up and pointed at

Tev, and Tev sidestepped to the right. Above him, trees exploded as the bullets tore through wooden flesh.

Whatever had prevented Kenan from firing at him earlier wasn't a problem anymore. Tev watched, impressed despite himself, as Kenan's jump took him into a ravine. He landed moving backwards at high speed, absorbing the impact in his legs as though it were nothing. In that moment, Tev felt a hint of respect mixed in with all the rage towards Kenan. Whatever the man had done, Tev admired strength and skill, and those were qualities Kenan had plenty of.

Tev only paused for a moment before dropping into the ravine behind Kenan and continuing the chase. He tried taking a hasty shot, but it went wide. Kenan was running forward but shifting left or right frequently, making him a difficult target to hit. Still, the rocky walls of the ravine were closing in, and soon Kenan would have no place to run but forward. When he did, Tev would have him.

Tev was lining up another shot when Kenan took to the air again. He launched himself up towards one of the walls of the ravine. Kenan's foot pressed down into wall and he shot further up the ravine towards the opposite wall. Again, Kenan landed and leapt off of the opposite ravine wall, and Tev watched his enemy clear the entire ravine. Kenan took another shot from above that sent rock falling down all around Tev.

The hunter didn't even have time to think. His gut warned him that Kenan would only need a second or two to line up the final shot from above, and if he didn't move, he would be a sitting target down at the bottom of the ravine.

Tev jumped, trying to mirror the actions he had seen Kenan take. He leapt, placing one foot against one wall of the ravine, then pushed off and tried to plant his other foot against the opposite wall. Immediately, he could feel that he wasn't going to make it. His gut sank, but he pushed as hard as he could off his planted foot. He flew across the ravine, but instead of coming out on top, he smashed into the side of the wall. With a desperate grab, he reached up and one of his hands managed to find the edge of the ravine wall. He threw his second arm up, trying to find another handhold. The moment he felt like he had it, he pulled with all his might.

His own strength, amplified by the exosuit, threw him into the air. Tev, not expecting the strength of the suit, floundered in the air like a fish out of water before crashing to the ground, one of his arms sprawled over the ravine's edge.

The only thing Tev wanted to do was lay there and catch his breath, but fear coursed through his body. He knew Kenan had to be nearby, but in his confusion, Tev couldn't understand what he was seeing in front of his face. An alarm was softly wailing in his ear, and images were flashing quickly in front of him, the helmet distorting his view of the outside world. It was a private version of hell, knowing there was an enemy nearby and not being able to see him.

Tev rolled over onto his back. He struggled to sit up, but as he did, Kenan seemed to materialize out of nowhere. The warrior stood in front of Tev, seeming to debate what to do for a moment.

Tev wasn't going to give up. He tried to bring his right arm up while rolling to his left. If he could just get a shot off before Kenan, his sacrifice would be worth it. But Kenan wasn't planning on giving him the chance. Kenan stepped forward, grabbing Tev's right arm in his left hand. Tev tried to fight it, but Kenan and his suit were stronger than Tev's, and Tev was still too disoriented from his fall to do anything about it. He just sat there, frozen against his will, as Kenan raised his right arm and brought it to Tev's face.

Tev didn't even see what happened next. He didn't even have time to say a final prayer to Lys before his world went black.

EIGHTEEN

TEARS STREAMED down Kindra's face as she clenched her fist. She had never felt so helpless, so useless, in her entire life. If there had been another suit, Kindra would have climbed into it and chased Kenan down herself. Hell, she was considering just grabbing a pistol and walking out unprotected.

She didn't have any strong emotional attachment to Tev. But all the same, she was amazed by him. She searched her mind for the right words. She stumbled across *noble*, *primal*, and *decent*, but none of them fit her picture of him quite well enough. He was all of those qualities, but more. She couldn't place it, but watching Tev the past few days had changed her.

He reacted to captivity with an amazing calm, taking in all the information he could. When given the chance to simulate piloting a suit, he took to it with an ease she never would have believed possible. She tried to put herself in his position, but every time she did, she thought there was no way she would handle everything he had taken in stride.

Watching the hunt had been both terrifying and

exhilarating. She didn't fool herself. She knew that if she gave Tev the chance, he would kill Kenan, but after seeing firsthand what Kenan had done, Kindra wasn't sure she cared anymore. The scientific part of her brain detached, telling her it was interesting she was willing to kill a member of her own crew, but she didn't have the emotional space to be concerned.

Kindra had watched the entire chase, unable to tear her eyes away when Kenan raised his rifle and shot Tev in the face. She sobbed, anger and sorrow mixing together. No one had said anything, although she was certain the other two had been watching everything. They were out of options. It was time to prepare to launch.

After a few minutes, Kindra caught her breath and worked up the courage to look at the screens again. Her eye was immediately drawn to Tev's vitals, which were doing something they absolutely shouldn't be. They were still going, and going strong. She frowned and commanded Tev's suit to perform a self-diagnostic. A few seconds later the report flashed on the screen. There was a large amount of damage to the helmet, and plenty of minor damage to the rest of the suit, but there were no reported errors on the bioscanners. Tev was still alive.

Options raced through her mind. She keyed in the code to talk to him.

"Tev? Tev, are you there?"

She tried a couple of more times, but didn't get any answer. She gave up and studied her screens once again. Her thoughts were interrupted by Eleta's voice.

"Kindra, I just got a notice that our systems here are being accessed."

Kindra couldn't keep up. "What do you mean?"

There was a moment of silence, and Kindra could

imagine Eleta running commands through the system. "It's Kenan. He's accessing our survey data."

Fury built in Kindra. "Can you block his access?"

"No problem."

"Okay. Block it in about thirty seconds. I'm going to try to talk to him."

"Good luck."

Kindra keyed in for Kenan's suit. "Kenan? Kenan, I know you're there. Talk to me, you piece of shit."

Kenan's laughter was soft, and somehow far more terrifying than a laugh ever should be. "You know, Kindra, I don't think I've ever heard you swear before. I was starting to wonder if you even knew the words."

"Kenan, what the fuck are you doing? Come back in and stop this."

Kenan's voice was colder than Kindra had ever heard before. "I'm not going to stop until my enemy is gone."

"Kenan, Derreck is -"

"DON'T YOU EVER SAY HIS NAME TO ME," Kenan shouted, paralyzing Kindra with surprise. "He was the only good man I ever knew, and they killed him."

Kindra tried to interject, to let him know that Derreck was alive and on-board, but Kenan wasn't having any of it.

"No! Don't say another word, Kindra, or I swear I will come for you, too. All I want to know is who it was. Who did you send after me? I've seen the recorded pilot scores for each of you, and none of you can pilot a suit like that. That means one of you is Internal Security. Which one of you was the operative I killed?"

Kindra's head was spinning. She didn't know what Kenan was saying. There was no department of Internal Security. What was happening in his head? She could only stumble over half an answer.

"It wasn't one of us."

Kenan swore and cut the channel. Kindra screamed after him and tried to get him back on the line, but the comms had gone dead. Eleta, who had been listening to everything, spoke softly. "He cut everything again."

Kindra buried her head in her hands. "What did he get?"

"Not much. Just some information from a fly-by we did on our through atmo. But there is a problem."

Kindra didn't want to hear the problem. All she wanted was to put the dropship on autopilot and take it out into space and away from everything that had happened. Running from her problems had never sounded so appealing.

But duty, responsibility, and her inherent goodness prevented her from doing so. "What?"

"The maps he grabbed were annotated by you. You were pretty sure you had determined the location of several habitations."

Kindra's mind wandered. Studying the maps for signs of life seemed like it had happened lifetimes ago. Eleta was right. She had looked through the scans and identified places she felt were habitations. Since everything that had happened, she had barely thought about them. Knowing what they knew now, those locations were very likely habited. Kindra swore to herself. She had just led Kenan right to the site of his next massacre.

IT TOOK MORE time than Kindra wanted, but then again, everything took more time than she wanted. Every second seemed to rush by, one after the other, and each one felt like a life that Kindra was going to lose because of her inability to do anything. Time and time again she tried to reach Tev. His vitals remained unchanged, and finally, Kindra made a decision she wouldn't have otherwise. She injected adrenaline right into his system, waking him up.

She heard him gasp in shock as everything came back to him. Kindra had no visual, so all she could do was listen as he struggled to orient himself. There were grunts that sounded terrified. She checked the sensors, and he didn't seem to be in any danger. Kenan had left Tev alone, thinking he was dead.

"Tev? Tev, can you hear me?"

His breathing calmed. "Yes, Kindra, I can hear you."

"What's wrong?"

"There are too many pictures. It's very bright and I can't see anything."

Kindra struggled to imagine what Tev was saying, but then an idea came to her. While she was trying to wake Tev, Eleta had come down and worked through the footage of the fight, trying to determine everything that had happened. When the battle had started, Kenan had been using armor-piercing rounds. It was a logical choice against an exosuit, but because Kenan hadn't been planning on fighting against armored targets when he had originally left the dropship, he didn't have many armor-piercing rounds. He had run out just as he had Tev dead to rights.

He had switched to regular rounds, and that decision had saved Tev's life. They still had enough velocity to penetrate the helmet's armor, but Kenan's shot must have been just a few centimeters off-center, and the helmet had deflected the round upwards and out of the helmet, which was where some of the display controls were. If they were damaged, it might be flashing all sorts of information Tev couldn't understand.

Kindra switched off the area she suspected was the problem. Tev's breathing slowed even further, confirming her guess before he could even say anything.

Eleta's voice interrupted their conversation. "Kindra, if we shut down those displays, he won't be able to aim his weapon."

"But if we leave them on, he'll never move from where he is."

Eleta locked a stare on Kindra. Kindra knew exactly what was coming. "We need to think this through. Tev's already been beaten and almost lost his life. The armor he has is damaged, the display doesn't work, and he's still chasing someone with way more experience. It was a long shot to begin with. But now it's murder."

Kindra knew, but there wasn't any choice. Kenan was going to continue killing, and Tev was the only person who even had a chance.

Kindra spoke softly to Tev. She explained what had happened as simply as she could, and after a while, it seemed as though he understood. She tried to tell him how he wouldn't be able to aim his weapon any more.

"It's fine, Kindra. I think this is better."

She frowned. "What do you mean?"

"Your way, it isn't right. You don't trust yourselves."

Kindra tried to understand what Tev was saying, but couldn't make heads or tails of it.

"Can you make it so I can hear everything?"

Eleta answered. "Yes."

Tev seemed satisfied. "Now, I will hunt Kenan again. He is worthy prey."

"Tev, there's something else. Kenan, he is going to another place where your people live. He is going to kill them all."

"Do you know where?"

Kindra looked at the map and tried to describe the area as well as she could. Fortunately, Tev had an innate grasp of the surrounding land. Eventually, he had her stop. "I know where he is going."

There was a sound of distress in his voice, and Kindra wondered what the problem was. "What's wrong?"

"He's going to my home."

A part of Kindra wanted to call out to him, tell him to stop, but she couldn't. Tev was their only hope, as impossible as it was.

Kindra felt blind as she listened to Tev standing up. More than anything, she wished she could see what was happening, but there wasn't any way that could be. Sightless and distraught, Kindra listened as Tev began to hunt again.

NINETEEN

TEV WAS UP AND MOVING. Everything he had ever cared about was in danger. It was like he was living in a nightmare. No matter how fast he ran, it was as though he was trying to swim through the air. The ground passed underneath him so quickly he sometimes thought he was flying, but still he feared he wouldn't be fast enough.

As he ran, his mind found a relaxed focus once again. He would need to maintain it while fighting Kenan. He had lost to Kenan in their first fight. Even though he had possessed the element of surprise, Kenan had turned the tables on him.

Tev knew part of it was that Kenan was an excellent warrior with amazing command of his armor. There was no way Tev would beat him in a fair fight. But Tev was a hunter, and fair wasn't a concept that mattered to him.

He had two advantages, small as they were. The first was that he was faster than Kenan. In their chase, Tev had always gained on him, even though he had run into enough trees to build a village with. Kindra had told him Kenan's suit was supposed to be faster. So that was something. The other advantage he had was that he would have the element of surprise again. Kenan thought he was dead, and that he was one of Kindra's clan. Kenan wouldn't expect him again.

Tev wasn't sure how these advantages would come to his aid in another battle, but it was something to know he wasn't completely outmatched. He had hunted creatures that were faster and stronger than him before, and he had always come back home alive.

And now he was coming back home to a clan that was in danger. If Kenan got there before he did, Tev would never forgive himself. He pushed himself even harder, bounding the suit across the forest without hesitation.

WHEN TEV WAS within a kilometer of his village, he stopped to look and listen. There didn't seem to be any fire, and he didn't hear any sounds he would have associated with a massacre. His fear was that he had already come too late. Perhaps they were already all dead.

He walked now, years and years of training kicking in. No matter how dire the situation, it either hadn't happened yet or already had. Either way, rushing wouldn't solve anything. He needed to be aware.

Thankfully, there were no longer any pictures distracting him, images and words he didn't understand. His vision was clear, and he could hear better than he ever had before. Whatever Eleta had done, there were more sounds coming to his ears than he would have heard on his own. The woods were alive and speaking, and he listened to their words, deciphering the meaning given to those who paid attention.

As he crept towards the village, he let himself relax and become part of the forest. The exosuit made some noise, so he could never be completely silent. But he moved with all the grace he could manage, trying not to scare the wildlife nearby. With his mind focused, he scanned the sounds coming from the woods closer to the village. There was a place of near-silence, where the only calls he heard were those of animals crying about a predator. With sudden certainty, Tev knew that was where he would find Kenan.

Tev altered course, aiming for a place between Kenan and the village. With luck, he would intercept him before he could attack the village.

Step by step, Tev moved to head off Kenan. He moved slowly, afraid both of Kenan's motion sensors and of making any noise that would give him away. He didn't know how aware Kenan was of his surroundings, but after his first defeat, Tev would not give him any more chances. He wouldn't underestimate his opponent.

When Tev saw Kenan, it was all he could do not to charge him. His blood boiled with rage, and he wanted nothing more than to end this man's life. He raised his arm, realizing too late, even though he'd been told, that he had no circle to aim with. The motion must have set off Kenan's alarms, because he turned in surprise.

Tev fired the weapon, aiming his arm as well as he could. His first shots struck above Kenan, whining through the forest. Tev held his fire and moved his arm down, tracing his fire onto Kenan. He was rewarded by several impacts.

Tev couldn't tell how much damage he had done, but Kenan's armor must have been much thicker than his own, because Kenan kept his feet and his head. He saw the now-familiar view of Kenan's right arm coming up to finish the job he had started. Tev bolted to the side, surprised when

Kenan didn't fire at him. He wasn't sure if something was wrong or if Kenan had something else in mind.

Tev tried to angle towards Kenan as Kenan turned and started sprinting towards the village. Tev swore to himself. He had hoped that by stopping Kenan before he got to the village it would remain safe, but Kenan was trying to bring the battle in that direction. It was almost as though he sensed Tev's intentions and sought to frustrate them.

Again Tev found himself chasing after his opponent. They were only a hundred meters from the village, and every meter seemed far too small for Tev, each step covering far too much space. With a sinking feeling, he realized there was no way he would stop Kenan before he reached the village. He considered firing at him, but held back. He couldn't aim, and if he missed, the village was right beyond. It was a foolish risk.

Kenan didn't have any of the same compunctions. As soon as he could, he started firing haphazardly into the village. The village had already been awakened by the strange noises coming from the woods, but they weren't prepared for what was coming their way. Kenan missed a step, and Tev caught up with him, tackling him from behind.

The two of them went crashing to the ground, the unfamiliar sound of metal on metal tearing through Tev's enhanced ears. Tev rolled to his feet and watched as Kenan struggled to his. A thought raced through Tev's mind, but he didn't have time to process it. He charged Kenan as he got to his feet, knocking him down to the ground once again. Tev pointed his arm towards Kenan's chest and fired, sending more bullets into the already damaged armor. At least one of them must have gotten through, as Tev saw blood squirt from the armor.

Kenan knocked Tev's arm away with his foot, and Tev stopped firing just in time to avoid hitting two of the younger girls of the village, frozen in their attempt to leave their homes.

Tev listened as Kenan's own bullets whizzed past his head. He grabbed Kenan's wrist, preventing him from moving his aim any closer. Kenan responded by curling his armored knees as close to his chest as he could and lashing out with both feet. The kick caught Tev in the chest, throwing him several meters backwards. He felt the armor collapse and crunch around his chest.

Tev laid on the ground for a few moments, dazed from the blow. But then the sound of Kenan firing his weapon came to his ears, and Tev felt a sinking feeling in his gut. Every second he wasted was a second his people died.

Tev struggled to his feet. Kenan was working his way further into the village. Tev limped after Kenan, worried that the exosuit didn't seem to be responding to his commands as smoothly as it had before. He needed to finish this, and finish it soon.

As soon as he poked his head around the corner of a hut, Kenan snapped his arm towards him and fired. Tev spun out of the way, but Kenan kept firing, tearing up the hut Tev had meant to use for cover. Tev ducked low to the ground. He hoped that Kenan would assume he would keep moving in the same direction. He tried to focus on the sound of the bullets as they passed overhead.

Although it was nothing but a guess, when Tev thought the bullets were past him, he spun back out, coming around the hut from the same direction he had at first. Kenan was still firing a steady stream of bullets, but his aim was several meters off. He calmly started to bring his arm back to Tev as Tev charged forward.

Tev sensed Kenan bracing for the impact. The foreign warrior brought his right foot back and settled his weight lower. He was going to meet Tev strength for strength, and Tev knew that in that battle, Kenan's suit would beat his own.

Tev didn't think, but a lifetime of fighting through crisis had taught him skills he would never consciously understand. He came in low and underneath Kenan's right arm, clutching it in both of his hands. As he came up outside of Kenan's arm, he held on tightly with muscles enhanced by an armor he still didn't fully comprehend. Tev's rising caused Kenan's arm to twist. The warrior tried to twist with it, but could only go so far. Tev couldn't hear the arm break, but from the unnatural angle he forced it into, it had to have.

Tev kept twisting, trying to break the weapon on Kenan's arm. He didn't know how these weapons worked, but if they were anything like a bow, they didn't react well to pressures put on them at unnatural angles. He was so focused on trying to break the weapon he didn't see Kenan's knee spinning around to catch him in the stomach.

The armor crumpled around him again, and Tev felt a moment of gratitude that Kenan's strike hadn't landed any higher. If it had, it would have collapsed the armor around his chest completely, and Tev was certain he would have been killed.

A calm focus descended on Tev. He could feel his death lurking nearby, and something in his body responded to the threat he felt. Suddenly, the world around him seemed to move in slow motion, and he saw with a clarity he had never possessed before. He saw Kenan's left arm coming back to strike him in the chest, and he saw how the warrior was putting everything into it.

Tev shifted his weight, just slightly, and watched as Kenan's left sailed harmlessly past his body. He grabbed the arm and shifted the weight of his hips, trying to break Kenan's other arm. Kenan, wise to what was happening, allowed Tev his motion, allowing the suit to roll forward into the dirt. Tev leapt into the air, driving his feet down onto Kenan as he tried to get back up. His feet crushed into Kenan's chest, collapsing the armor already weakened by Tev's bullets.

For a moment, everything was a tangle of arms and legs and armor, but Tev got to his feet first, screamed, and brought his foot down on Kenan's chest with all his armor-enhanced strength, right where he had fired his bullets earlier, right where he had just landed. Kenan's body, armor and all, curled around Tev's foot. Tev tried to remove his foot, but Kenan wrapped his left arm tightly around it, trying to bring him down. Tev was balanced well, however, and nothing Kenan could do would shift him.

Tev raised his right arm slightly, pointing it at Kenan's head. Kenan stopped struggling, knowing there was no way he could stop what was going to happen. Tev imagined the weapon firing, and he didn't stop until Kenan's helmet was gone.

TWENTY

IT TOOK Tev a few minutes to realize it was all over. After everything that had happened, it was finished. Kenan was the man who had tried to kill his clan, and now he was dead. If Kindra was as good as her word, the danger to his people had passed.

But at the same time, everything had changed. The village he had grown up in, the place he called home, was gone. He stood there, stupefied, as he looked at the hut where he had had his first kiss. It hadn't been with Neera, but another village girl to try to make Neera jealous. Shet's house was torn to bits, and all around him were bodies. Not as many as there could have been, but more than he could take. It was worse because he knew who each one was.

Without warning, he felt something ricochet off his head. He frowned, then realized what had happened. His people were shooting at him. He was surrounded, and at an unspoken signal, arrows flew towards him.

Even damaged, his armor had no problem deflecting the arrows and stones thrown his way. He realized just how much stronger Kindra's people were than his own. In that moment, in that suit, he felt more out of place than he ever had in his life. He loved the suit. Loved how much strength it gave him and how much power he was capable of. He hated himself for how much he loved it.

Tev debated, but only for a moment. Kindra wanted the suit back. She had made that clear when he left. Tev didn't know what would happen to him when he returned it, but he had to keep his word. All he knew was that he had things to say before he left. There were things he had to make right. He hoped Kindra would allow him to return to his people, but he couldn't be sure. After everything, he wasn't sure he could bring himself to trust her.

As the arrows bounced harmlessly off of him, he raised his arms, and after a few seconds, they stopped shooting at him, confused. Still moving slowly, so as not to alarm anyone, Tev hit the latch that disengaged his helmet. There was a hiss of air as the suit depressurized, and Tev pulled the helmet off.

He could almost hear the sudden intake of breath as everyone saw who was underneath the helmet. Tev looked around and met every face. He didn't know what to say, and he wasn't alone in that sentiment.

It was Shet who stepped forward first. Tev was glad to see he had made it through the battle alive.

"Tev, is that you?"

He nodded, and the words started to rush out. He told them everything. How he had been captured and how he had discovered the creatures were people just like them, with weapons Tev couldn't understand. He explained how they had come from the sky, and how he had been given the suit to kill the one who killed his people.

When he was done, all he saw were blank looks on the faces of those around him. The only one who seemed thoughtful was Shet, but then again, he always seemed that way.

Tev turned around slowly, wondering what would happen next. Half his clan looked upon him in awe, and half looked at him as though they were ready to fire an arrow at his unprotected head. But everyone's expressions changed when Neera stepped forward.

Tev hadn't seen her earlier. If he had, he never would have been able to fight well. His heart raced, and he searched her face for clues as to how she was feeling. But her face was a mask of stone, the only clue to her emotions the tears streaming down her face. She didn't say a word. She just wound up and slapped him, harder than he'd ever been slapped before. The suit kept him locked in place, only his face snapping around from the impact. He felt his cheek instantly become warm.

Without another word she turned around. Tev stopped her. "Neera!"

She paused and looked at him over her shoulder. Tev knew he wouldn't have another chance.

"I've always loved you, Neera. I just wanted you to know."

There was an almost imperceptible flicker across her face, but she kept walking, leaving the circle that surrounded him. Tev's heart broke, but he hadn't expected anything else. He turned back to Shet.

"I need to return to the people who gave me this armor. They require it."

The elder nodded. "Will you return?"

"If I can." Tev looked around the circle. Neera's actions had changed many of the expressions on their faces. Now most of them were more angry than awe-inspired. He looked the elder in the eye. He didn't want to ask, but he had to. "Should I?"

The elder looked at Tev. He studied the faces around him. The silence rang in Tev's ears. When Shet spoke, it was loudly enough for all to hear. "You will always be a part of this clan, Tev."

Tev understood. He stood up straighter and addressed the crowd. "I know how you feel. But I will do everything I can to protect the clan. Even if it means my life. Remember me well."

The hunters, perhaps as a sign of respect, perhaps out of habit, replied. "Remember him well."

With that, Tev tried to look one last time for Neera, but she was nowhere to be seen. He put on his helmet and spoke softly. "Kindra, are you there?"

"Yes. Even though I can't see, I heard everything that happened. How are you?"

Tev didn't know how to respond. He was angry at everything that had happened. Excited and afraid of an unknown future. But most of all, his heart broke at Neera's treatment of him. He didn't know how to respond. "The hunt always goes on."

Either Kindra understood, or she was so confused she didn't know how to answer him. As Tev was about to leave, Kindra asked him for one last favor. "Please bring Kenan's body. We need the suit and his remains."

Tev considered arguing, but there was no point. Kindra seemed to be as much his clan now as his own people were. He picked up Kenan's body and slung him haphazardly over his shoulder, and with one last look at his home, left.

THE NEXT DAY, Tev sat with Kindra in their dropship, as

they called it. He had brought back Kenan's body, and although Kindra's crew was horrified, they didn't say anything to Tev. What had happened had happened, and there was no going back.

Somewhat to Tev's surprise, Kindra didn't kill him. After he was out of the suit, she gave him food he didn't recognize and told him he needed to stay with them for at least another day. Kindra's clan still had decisions to make, and she couldn't let him go until they decided. Tev had resigned himself to death, so he didn't mind. Another day was another day. He spent the evening praying to Lys and sleeping deeply.

The next morning Kindra and Tev broke their fast together, and Kindra told him what she had discovered. She talked about the fact that they were the same. Tev didn't find it as surprising as Kindra seemed to. They looked the same and acted the same, and he didn't understand why it was such a big deal that they were the same. In his mind, he couldn't imagine them being different.

Tev met the rest of Kindra's clan. Alston was silent, and Eleta he had already briefly met. He was surprised there weren't more people, and although he could tell Eleta kept a weapon on him while he was nearby, they talked for most of the day.

When they were done, Kindra made Tev an offer he hadn't expected.

"Tev, we are leaving here tomorrow. When we do, I was wondering if you would like to come with us."

"To the sky?"

Kindra nodded. "To the sky."

Tev asked for time to think about it, and asked if it was okay if he camped outside that evening. To his surprise, again, Kindra agreed. "You can leave if you want. This isn't a trap, and we won't search for you. But, given everything that has happened, it makes sense to bring you with us. There are going to be a lot of people who don't believe us."

"What would it be like?"

Kindra shook her head. "I don't know. Many people will want to do tests on you, tests like we did here. I will try to keep you safe, and Fleet is made up of good people. But the universe is in chaos, and I'm not sure what will happen. You will see more than you can ever imagine."

Tev took her up on her offer to camp outside. He was given all his gear, and that evening, for the first time in what seemed like forever, he sat out under the stars next to a fire. It felt right and natural, unlike many of his experiences over the past few days.

Kindra surprised him one last time by coming out, unprotected, to be with him. She mentioned something about running some tests on Kenan to prove it was safe, but apparently she wasn't worried anymore. They talked late into the evening, and Tev pointed out Lys in the stars. Kindra laughed and told Tev she had seen the same constellation and called it an explorer.

Kindra told him about growing up and wanting to study life, and Tev talked about learning how to hunt. As the fire burned down, Kindra stood up and gave Tev's shoulder a squeeze. "We'll leave tomorrow when the sun is high. Please let me know what you decide."

Tev nodded. He knew he wouldn't be sleeping at all this night. And that was fine. He sat in the darkness and listened to the world around him. It was his world, and there was a part of him that couldn't imagine leaving it. There was so much beauty, and the past few days had made him realize how much of his own world he still hadn't explored. Then he thought of Neera slapping him, and he thought that no matter how beautiful his world was, there was no place for him here anymore. He had gone on a hunt the others wouldn't understand and couldn't accept.

Kindra's words tumbled through his mind. According to her, there were other worlds out there, worlds both like this one and worlds that were very different, but through all of them, there were more people. Despite himself, Tev was starting to trust Kindra. But would all the other people be as trustworthy? What if others came and tried to kill his people like Kenan had? Tev knew, better than any other of his clan, just how useless their weapons were against the weapons of Kindra's clan. If he was going to protect his clan, didn't it mean leaving and fighting for them in other places?

Tev's mind ran back and forth. To find solace, he started whittling an image of Lys. It was an old practice for him, an active meditation that allowed him to focus.

As the sun rose, Tev still didn't have answers. All he knew was that this next day would change his life, and possibly the lives of everyone who lived on his world, the lives of all the people he cared about.

THERE WAS a rustle in the woods behind Tev, and despite a night without sleep, he was on his feet with his long knife in his hand in an instant. His first instinct was to worry that the clans had arranged another expedition to kill Kindra's clan.

The truth was even more surprising. Only one person stepped out of the woods, and it was Neera.

Tev stood there, his mouth open. Neera laughed at him.

"So, even though so much has happened to us, you still can't get your words straight when you're around me?"

Tev laughed, a sudden courage overcoming his natural

hesitance. "I think talking to you is the most terrifying thing I do."

Neera laughed, and a tension Tev didn't even know he was carrying faded away.

She came and stood next to him, and together they admired the ship only a few dozen meters away. "That's the ship they came in?"

Tev nodded. "They offered to take me up into the sky with them. They are leaving today."

A comfortable silence descended over the two of them, and there was a part of Tev that wanted Neera to make the decision for him. If she decided she wanted to be with him, there was no way he would leave. But if not, maybe there really wasn't anything for him here.

Neera turned her head from the ship and looked at Tev. "Those things you said yesterday, are they true?"

Tev didn't hesitate. "Yes, but I think you've known that for a while now."

She smiled, and Tev's heart was as light as it ever had been. "Yes, I have."

"And you?"

She sighed. "For so long, I'm not sure I've known that answer. Most things in life are clear to me, but when it comes to my own emotions, I don't know. There are other strong hunters out there who would provide well and give me strong children. But yesterday, when I saw you in that armor, my heart broke in a way I didn't think was possible. You and I have known each other since we were children, and yes, Tev, I love you. It just took losing you for me to recognize it."

Tev's heart both sank and rejoiced at the same time. "You haven't lost me. The decision is mine to make. I'll tell them I will stay here."

Neera shook her head sadly. "No. You need to go with them. I don't know what is going on, but if there is anyone who can protect our people and figure it out, it's you. When I saw you yesterday, I was angrier than I'd ever been, but then I realized that if it had been anyone else, our clan would probably be dead. You're curious, Tev. You're always focused on learning more. It makes you a strong hunter, and it makes you the only person I know who can make this journey. It's a hunt far longer than anyone else has ever taken."

Echoes of Lys' words spoke to him, and a chill went down his spine.

Neera smiled at him, and he could see she was about to cry again. "And even if you can't admit it to yourself, you want to go, don't you?"

Tev nodded. He did. He wanted Neera and he wanted to leave. Two desires that would never mix. He cursed himself.

Neera leaned in close to him, and their lips met, lingering, unlocking a passion both of them knew would only be satisfied once.

Their love was quick and furious, and when they finished, Tev kept his arms wrapped around Neera, unwilling to let her go.

Neera squirmed in his arms, turning around so she could face him. She pushed herself gently away and allowed Tev to drink in the sight of her in the morning light. He was certain that no matter how far he traveled, he would never see anything more beautiful.

"Tev, I want you to leave with no regrets. I will always keep you in my heart, and I will remember you, every day. And if you come back, I would love to see you again."

Tev's own tears started to trickle down his cheeks. A

part of him wanted to ask her to wait for him, but he knew it was foolish. She wouldn't, and she wouldn't expect him to. She had given all she could.

Tev gave her the last image of Lys he had carved. Something he hoped she would remember him by.

"I don't know what will happen, but I will do everything I can to come back."

She nodded, and with one last kiss, they separated.

Tev spoke again. "I will remember you, every day."

She laughed and gestured at herself. "You think you'll be able to forget this?"

Tev knew he wouldn't, and he was crying as he turned around, walking to the ship, which opened up for him. He stepped inside, and as the doors closed, he kept his eyes on Neera, watching as he left his world for good.

TEV DIDN'T BOTHER GOING to the screens to see what Neera did after he left. She would go back to the clan and continue on her journey, just as he would continue on his. Kindra, sensing his turmoil, didn't come to get him until they were about to take off.

"Tev, did you want to come see this?"

Mostly, Tev wanted to hide, but his curiosity overrode his reluctance. He stood up and followed Kindra to the observation viewscreens. They took off, and for the first time in his life, Tev was flying. He had a moment of panic, but he was expecting it and quickly found his mental balance once again. He watched with fascination as he saw the world he had grown up in fall below him. Kindra angled the screens down so Tev could watch as they flew.

Tev worried what would happen if they fell, but he trusted Kindra and allowed his fascination free rein. He could see landmarks he had grown up with, but soon even they became so small he could barely see them as they climbed higher and higher. From there, his attention turned to the sky as it turned slowly from blue to black.

Tev didn't understand what was happening. He thought the sky would be blue forever, but Kindra told him the sky wasn't blue everywhere. She told him that on different worlds it had different colors, but in between the worlds, in the space they were now, the sky was black, cold and empty.

Tev tried to understand, but he wasn't sure he could. He accepted. If he was going to live like this, there was going to be so much for him to learn. He would have time.

Kindra eventually had to leave him. They were meeting up with a ship even bigger than this one, and she had work she had to do before they met. Tev didn't have any guess what was next for him, but as he watched the stars off in the distance, all he knew was that he was ready to follow the hunt for as long as he could, chasing new prey until the day he died.

PART TWO

PRIMAL DARKNESS

For Bryce

PROLOGUE

TEV LOOKED out from the observation deck of the jumper *Destiny*, his breath taken away by the unimaginable vista. Stars, each one a tiny explosion of light, shone constantly at him. The change in appearance was such a small difference, but one that fascinated him every time he stopped to stare.

Back home, Tev had always liked to look up at the stars. He had memorized dozens of constellations. The sky was full of stories, myths, and legends. He had watched Lys chase the deer around the sky more times than he could count, and her never-ending chase had always comforted him. He could navigate by the stars, their lights and shapes as familiar to him as the weight of his knife.

But they had always twinkled back home. They had been alive, full of energy and vitality. Out here, in space, they were cold and unblinking, their light hitting his eyes as straight as an arrow.

Out here, he was lost. The constellations that had once provided him such familiar comfort were gone. His hunt had taken him so far even the sky had changed.

Every day Tev studied everything he could get his hands on. Part of him was driven by a desire to learn. He burned to know more about space and space travel. But there was more to his research than just curiosity. He was in a new environment, and if he was going to survive, to become the best hunter out here in space, he needed to master his new surroundings. Right now, Tev was prey. But it wouldn't always be that way. He had learned how to hunt once, and he could learn again.

But learning how to hunt wasn't enough. His studies kept him busy, but not fulfilled. His days were full, but his heart was empty. He missed his home, but more than anything, he missed his clan. He hadn't been ejected from his clan, not quite, but he hadn't been welcomed back either. The *Destiny* was where he lived, but the jumpship didn't feel like home.

Tev compared his experience to the concept of being in orbit. He had learned that orbit was nothing more than a constant process of falling, like tripping and never hitting the ground. That was how he felt most days. He was falling and falling but never found the solid bottom.

Tev prayed, but for the first time in his life his prayers felt inadequate. He had prayed to Lys every day since he was a child, and he had been convinced that Lys always looked after him. But out here, his belief seemed so small. Could Lys watch over all the planets that existed? It was one task to watch over the hunters of a few clans, but to watch over all this space? Tev continued to pray every day, but where the tradition had once provided him comfort, now all it gave him was a few moments of silence to himself.

Even though he was with Kindra and the crew of the *Vigilance*, the dropship that had landed on his planet, Tev felt more alone than ever. He had always had his clan. Even if he wasn't partnered, there were always people around who he trusted and confided in.

The crew he met on *Destiny* were kind enough. Everyone was interested in him, and the questions he received were driven by genuine curiosity. But he didn't have the years of companionship, the experiences of shared danger, with anyone here. He was closer to Kindra than anyone, but there was a distance between them that Tev wasn't sure could be bridged.

She might not have been able to watch, but she had heard the battle Tev held with her clan member. Although she knew Tev had done the right thing in killing Kenan, and had even helped him do it, she wasn't a hunter. Tev could see the change in her, see how she doubted herself. He wanted to help, but she wouldn't let him get close enough to speak about the events.

Derreck became the center of Tev's new world. The captain of the *Vigilance* was healing, thanks to the greater skills and resources of the jumper. It would be some time before he was at full strength, but Tev took every opportunity to visit with the captain. Like him, the man was a hunter, but he was also an explorer and warrior. The language barrier was a challenge, even with the translators, but there was a shared understanding between them. Tev had killed Derreck's clan member; but Derreck, unlike Kindra, had found peace with the events that had happened on Tev's home planet.

Then there were the mysteries, the questions that had no answers, the questions he had never been forced to think about before. The day-to-day concerns he had once obsessed endlessly over seemed so small and insignificant now it was laughable. To think, his biggest worry had been if he could mate with Neera. Out here, in the vastness, what did that even matter?

Kindra said that he and her clan were related, but how could that be if they came from different planets? Tev couldn't even begin to wrap his mind around the problem. There was no way they could be related, but they were.

Tev stared into the unblinking void of space, adrift between worlds.

ONE

TEV DIDN'T like the medicines that put him to sleep for the jumps between the stars. Kindra had explained why they were needed, but he still didn't like that he was giving away control of his body, even if only for an hour. He had argued, but when he saw the fear in her eyes, he relented. She had explained the concept of jumping, the process by which jumpships leapt amazing distances across the stars, but she hadn't been able to explain why humans needed to be asleep. All she could say was that jumping caused people to lose their minds.

At home, when Tev slept, he could wake instantly, a skill honed over years and years of training. As a hunter, it was essential to wake up and be aware in the same moment. With the drugs that was next to impossible. It took Tev a few minutes, at least, to bring his awareness back to full focus.

Those first minutes after he came out of jump sleep were miserable. After every jump he rolled out of his bunk as soon as possible, challenging his system to catch up. But he always had a hard time getting his feet under him, and his body always seemed to be a second behind the commands he gave it. He was used to his body's instant response, and the inability of his limbs to keep up with his thoughts was beyond disconcerting. It was terrifying.

They had been jumping for months now. Despite the power of the jumpships, all humanity could do was crawl across the stars. Each jump could cover about a hundred light-years, but *Destiny* could only jump twice before she needed to stop to charge her capacitors. Combined with the fact that most jumpship captains liked to keep a jump in reserve in case of emergency, their progress had been slow.

Despite Tev's inability to get used to jumping, and his general sense of being adrift, the past months had contained bright spots. He was learning more every day. On top of that, on the jumpship, he was well-known. At first, many of the crew had stared at him, but over time he had gotten to know more of them. The language was sometimes a barrier, but the translator Kindra had given him back on his home planet had worked wonders in that regard, and Tev was learning their language quickly. Among those he was comfortable with he sometimes tried to speak their tongue without the aid of the translator.

What was more challenging were the concepts that governed Kindra's people. There was so much he didn't know, so much that Kindra's people took for granted. Often Tev would have to stop someone and ask what they meant, and would have to keep asking until they could reduce it to the simplest terms. Even then, sometimes the concepts were impossible for him to understand.

One concept Tev found bizarre was the idea of money. In his clan all was shared. If one suffered from lack of food or water, it was only because the entire clan suffered from the same. Items were often traded back and forth, but Tev didn't understand currency. He knew crew on the ship took the idea very seriously, but there was nothing physical that traded hands. No matter how many times the concept was explained to him, he still felt lost and confused.

It was endlessly frustrating. In the forests he called his home, he understood deep in his body what was happening. He could hear the call of the birds and know a predator was nearby. He could look at the tracks in the dirt and know, without a moment's hesitation, what had occurred there.

But out here he was learning just how little he knew, and at times, his ignorance angered him. Too many people spoke to him like he was a child, and he recognized that by their standards he only possessed the understanding of a child. But they were foolish, too. Tev judged the crew of the *Destiny* by the way they walked, by the flabbiness of their skin. He may be a stranger in their home, but if their roles were reversed, the people here would need his protection.

At times the challenge made Tev want to give up. Those were the days when he wanted to go home and retreat into a comfortable existence. Unfortunately, that wasn't an option. Tev's only direction was forward, towards Kindra's home planet. The moment of doubt would pass, and he would push even harder than before. He had always wanted to be the best hunter, and that meant perseverance. So although it was frustrating, he didn't allow himself the luxury of sulking. Time and time again, he forced his mind open to understand new concepts.

There were other bright spots in his life too, and the brightest of those was that they continued to let him pilot the suit. He knew it had been a matter of fierce debate among Kindra's people, but Kindra had fought for the privilege for him. The suit had been repaired, and all the weapons had been removed, but they allowed him to pilot it around the jumpship, and even a handful of times outside the ship.

Wearing the suit was the closest Tev came to pure bliss. His first experiences with it had been difficult, but as he had grown used to the power and feedback, the suit had become like a second skin to him, a skin that gave him power and ability beyond his wildest dreams. He had quickly adapted to the suit on the ship, but taking it out into space had been something else entirely.

They had matched him with another pilot, a hunter from another dropship like Kindra's. The pilot was an older man, a man Tev had immediately liked. Kindra had tried to explain gravity to Tev, but he hadn't truly understood until he went out the airlock, tethered to the older man.

Flying in space had taken more than a little practice, but Tev was learning quickly. At first, the emptiness of space had messed with his intuition, but he quickly learned the value of small changes in speed, and he had become intimately familiar with the laws of motion.

Like all of life, there were ups and downs, but Tev was finding a tenuous balance, a balance that was about to be upset again. They were approaching the frontier of Kindra's people.

THE JUMP HAD ENDED MUCH LIKE any other, but that changed quickly. Tev was, as usual, trying to get his body to respond to his commands when the lights in his bunk room flashed orange.

Tev noted the lights but kept practicing his movements. Kindra had drilled into him the importance of the lights, but her people were too cautious. He knew he was supposed to get into his bunk, but he didn't want to interrupt his physical challenge. He didn't want to waste a single jump of practice, and besides, all the warning lights he had seen so far had proven to be false alarms. There was no reason to think this would be any different.

Suddenly, Tev felt his feet come unglued from the floor, and he immediately regretted his decision. Deep in the ship, he could hear the hum he had learned to associate with the artificial gravity increase, and gravity returned to normal. Tev only fell a few centimeters, but his body was unbalanced, and he couldn't command his legs to get under his center of gravity quickly enough. He fell roughly to the floor, grunting in annoyance.

A few seconds later, Kindra's voice came though his earpiece, as Tev suspected it would. "Tev, are you okay?"

Tev fought the impulse to groan against the pain of his recent fall. He grimaced and spoke as normally as he could, glad she couldn't see his face. "Yes. What's wrong?"

"I don't know, yet. But I got an order. They want you in your suit, now."

Tev's mind raced as he tried to put the pieces together. From the gravity changes, it was clear the old jumper had been forced to make a quick maneuver; but if there was any trouble, he didn't understand why they would ask him into his suit. He knew, even if they never said as much, that the only real reason he was allowed to pilot was because they were testing him. He had never imagined he would be used in an actual situation.

Regardless, Tev would never say no to any opportunity to pilot the suit. "I'm on my way."

Kindra took a few seconds to respond, and Tev imagined she was doing multiple tasks at once. It was behavior he had observed in her and her clan many times, and it still frustrated him. He couldn't understand why they allowed the machines into their bodies. At best they served as nothing more than a distraction, but at worst, they were a desecration. When Kindra responded, her voice sounded as though she was somewhere far away, focused on something else. "Great. I'll meet you there and help you suit up."

Getting his feet underneath him, Tev stood and exited his bunk room. His mind was still a second ahead of his body, but he knew another minute or two would cure that. He could walk relatively quickly, and so long as there weren't any more sudden gravity shifts, he would be fine.

The hallways of the *Destiny* were a nightmare. He had grown up in a world full of textures and sights, but here in the jumpship, everything was a flat gray color. Kindra told him that most people used the technology they had embedded to paint pictures over the hallways, making them appear to be all sorts of different passages. But Tev, unaugmented, saw only meter after meter of flat, gray hallway.

There weren't even any directions in the ship. The crew relied on their implants to overlay their directions for them. Tev found the entire situation ridiculous. Kindra's people relied on their technology far too much. If something ever happened to their electronics, they would be helpless.

It had taken Tev a long time to figure out how to find different places in the ship, and at times he still got lost, but he had no problem finding the room where his suit was stored. That was a route firmly stored in his memory.

He got there before Kindra, but didn't waste any time. He had put the suit on dozens of times now and knew the order of operations. While she was still on her way, he began donning the suit.

Kindra arrived a few moments after he did. Without a word, she saw where he was in the process and jumped in to help. Together, they had him inside the suit in under a minute. The last piece was the helmet which settled over his head with a soft click and a hiss as the suit pressurized itself. The display came up in front of him, a minimalist display programmed for him by Eleta, the *Vigilance*'s technology wizard. It allowed him to focus on his own senses instead of the blast of visual information the pilots of Kindra's clan preferred.

With the suit on, Tev waited for his orders. Kindra was doing the same. He could see her eyes flashing left and right, and he knew she was reading something coming across her vision. Mentally, he shook his head. There was a better way to live, but that idea was something they would never see eye-to-eye on.

Kindra finished reading and focused on him. "There is a ton of debris in the system we jumped into. The scraps weren't large enough to trigger our warning systems prior to the jump, but they were large enough that the captain had to pull emergency evasive maneuvers in-system. It looks like a large ship was destroyed here recently, and there is a dropship broadcasting a distress beacon."

Tev didn't understand everything, but he understood enough. There was another ship in trouble.

"What do they want me to do?"

Kindra shook her head. "For now, nothing. A while ago they assigned you to the powered suit reserves for certain mission parameters, so the computer sent me an automated order for you. Other suits are on the rescue mission, but they are asking you to stand by."

Tev nodded. Now that he was in the suit, he wanted nothing more than to move around, but he forced his body to be still. He imagined that he was out on the hunt, and that his success required patience and calm. He focused on taking deep breaths, holding them for a second, and then releasing them. When the moment came, he would be ready.

After a few minutes of his deep breathing, Tev entered a trance-like state. He was aware of everything but his own body, and his muscles relaxed. He lost track of time as he waited.

Kindra's voice snapped him back to the present. "Are you sure, sir?"

There was a moment's pause, and then she replied. "Yes, sir. Understood, sir."

She looked up at Tev. "They need you. The rescue suits are working as fast as they can, but the rescue is going to be a close call. They've located survivors, but oxygen is running low in the space they are trapped in."

As Kindra spoke, a floating droid came into the room with several cylinders Tev recognized as containers that stored air. He understood what he needed to do as Kindra was speaking. He turned around so the droid could attach the tanks to his exosuit.

Tev caught Kindra's final words. "Deliver the oxygen, but be careful. The captain said the environment outside is dangerous."

Tev nodded and Kindra left the room. He turned and stepped towards the airlock, trying his best to contain his excitement.

AS SOON AS the airlock opened, Tev was thrust into a world unlike any he had grown up in, different even than the limited training experiences he'd been in.

He had trained in space several times now, but every time space had been empty, devoid of anything but the jumpship he now called home. In front of him, space was anything but empty. On his display, pieces of junk were highlighted with a dim green outline. For once, Tev was grateful for the extra information. In the darkness of space, many of the pieces would have been almost invisible to the naked eye.

Unfortunately, the area in front of him was packed full of the green outlines. At times, Tev could see safe paths through the debris, but as he watched, they would close again.

Immediately, Tev realized the danger. He knew that his suit needed to stay in one piece if he was to remain protected against the extreme environment of space. It was armored, so it could probably take several hits from the fragments, but every hit was a risk he didn't want to take. All it would take was one unlucky strike and he would be on his last hunt.

Tev took a deep breath, befriending the fear he felt. Kindra spoke in his ear. "The ship you need to get to is here."

A brighter, yellow outline came up on his display and then faded again. Tev squinted, but in the cloud of debris, he had a hard time making out the ship without the outline.

"Leave the outline up, please."

A second later, the brighter yellow outline returned, and Tev saw where he had to go. "Is there anything else I need to know?"

"No. Time is important, but you've got a window. It's more important that you get there safely. Several lives depend on it."

Tev nodded and pushed himself with his legs out of the airlock, being careful not to jump with all his strength. If there was one lesson he had learned in his space training, it was that small changes made a huge difference. If he started even approaching the edge of control, there was no way he would make it to the ship in one piece.

Tev took a moment to get readjusted to the realities of space. There was no up or down anymore, no direction for his body to get used to. He kept his head pointed towards the disabled dropship and gave himself a small thrust to increase his velocity. Small omnidirectional thrusters had been added across his suit, with the largest being on his back and chest. They were controlled through mental manipulation, with the suit interpreting his commands and directing thrust as necessary. It wasn't a perfect system, but it allowed for a fair degree of mobility in space.

Tev worked hard not to focus on any one object. Everything around him was moving, and he had to be constantly aware. His display warned him when objects were heading his direction, and he would respond with gentle thrusts to move himself out of the way. So long as he knew of the debris well before it came near him, just the slightest firing of a thruster was all he needed to change his trajectory away from that of the debris.

Throughout his flight, Tev only had one close call, when a vector adjustment brought him into line with another, closer piece of debris. He cursed himself and adjusted with a stronger thrust. He barely passed by the larger piece of debris, but more challenging, it took him several small adjustments to get his course back on track. Once he did, he breathed a deep sigh of relief. He wasn't sure what kind of support he would have out here if he lost control. The debris might kill him before anyone else could get to him.

Tev slowed his velocity as he approached the other dropship, and for the first time, he allowed his mind to wander and wonder what had happened here. The dropship was full of holes, and Tev could see that many were caused by explosions outside the ship. He also wasn't sure where all the debris had come from. There seemed to be far too much to have come from a single dropship.

Tev's questions disappeared as he used gentle thrusts to turn his feet towards the damaged dropship. In his mind, the dropship changed from being up to being down. With a few more gentle thoughts, he landed, the electromagnetic soles of his suit engaging against the hull, keeping him locked down.

Kindra answered his question before he could even ask it, highlighting the location on the dropship where he needed to go. Tev moved with more ease, more familiar with the mechanics of moving on the hull of a ship from his practice.

Tev found the hole Kindra had highlighted without a problem, dropping down after taking a brief look at his landing position. The ship's artificial gravity was out, but through a combination of gentle thrusts and the pull of magnets on his feet, Tev was able to move almost normally through the ship. Kindra overlaid the route on his display. All he had to do was follow the arrows.

Kindra's voice was soft, as though she was afraid to disturb him. "You're making good time. So long as you get there within the next five minutes, there shouldn't be any problem with the air supplies."

Tev grunted his acknowledgment. The interior of the ship was a maze, and he needed to focus on his surroundings.

He turned a corner and took a deep breath as he came face to face with the body of a crew member of the ship. It was a woman who had managed to attach a harness to an anchor point. When her section of the ship had been breached, she hadn't been sucked out into space, but space had come for her, nonetheless. Tev, out of habit, said a short prayer to Lys before stopping himself. The woman hadn't been a hunter, and even if Lys could hear his prayer, Tev didn't think she would grant it. He kept moving towards the rest of the rescue mission.

The first sign he got that something was wrong was Kindra's voice shouting at him. All he heard was his name, but it was too late. About a dozen meters in front of him, an explosion blew the floor plating into the ceiling. The explosion only lasted for a fraction of a second, but Tev felt the entire ship twist and buckle underneath him.

Tev had never felt anything like it in his life. In his limited experience, a ship was always solid. It was like the ground, something firm and steady you could trust to be underneath you. Suddenly, that was no longer true.

The entire corridor twisted, with the wall becoming the new floor, and the opposite wall becoming the ceiling. Tev's boots kept him anchored, but still he twisted. The experience was incredibly disorienting. Tev could feel the composite materials groaning underneath his feet.

Tev's instincts kicked in. He was in a dangerous place and needed to escape. In front of him, a gash opened in the hull, and Tev could see more and more stars out in the void of space as the hallway separated. Fortunately, all the air was already gone from the section of the ship Tev was in, so he didn't have to worry about decompression. He looked at his display and saw Kindra's navigational arrow, still pointing towards the same hallway he had been traveling down.

Tev realized it was only the part of the ship he was in that was breaking apart. His destination was still intact. He moved, his suit reacting to his mental commands. He ran forward, using a strong boost of thrust to get his body moving in the right direction. As the hallway continued to twist around him, Tev made a step and ran along the wall, and then the ceiling as the twisting continued. He made it to the gash that was ever-widening and leapt, trying to focus on his thrusters.

His aim had been true, and he was crossing the void of space towards the same hallway he had originally been walking in, but he was moving too fast. His actions had been too powerful. Acting on instinct, he used his thrusters to spin his body around so he was heading feet first towards the hallway.

Tev landed and absorbed the impact with his legs. The magnets clicked back on, and he was locked in place. For the moment, he was safe. He took a deep breath and looked around. With the angle he had come in at, his boots had locked him against the ceiling of the hallway, so it was a little disorienting to look forward. But when he looked behind him, he saw the entire back section of the ship tear apart, the section of the hallway he had been in a tangled mess.

"Are you okay?" Kindra asked.

Tev grunted. It had been close. Very close. Gingerly, he rotated around so he was facing the hallway right side up. He didn't need to, but it helped his perspective. He started moving forward quickly. The crew only had a few minutes left for him to get them the oxygen.

TWO

A MAN SHOULD NEVER BE able to stand without a head, but that was the image that kept haunting Kindra. She knew she was dreaming, but rationality didn't stand a chance against the flood of emotions battering her from all directions.

Kenan stood in front of her, or at least, his blood-covered suit did. Tev had lost visual before his final battle with Kenan, and at first, Kindra had been grateful. She hadn't needed to watch the end. Now, she wasn't so sure. Her imagination and guilt seemed more than happy to fill in the blanks in her knowledge, and Kenan's death was always a wretched affair in her nightmares.

Kindra was trying to explain herself to Kenan, for what felt like the thousandth time. But even without a face his judgment was clear. She had murdered him. The fact was simple. She didn't pull the trigger, but she armed the weapon and pointed it in the right direction. She was every bit the murderer that Tev was.

Her alarm pulled her out of the nightmare, but scraps of the dream followed her into wakefulness, imprinting on her memories. She pressed her palms to her eyes, as though the pressure would somehow erase the images.

After a few minutes the images faded. They weren't gone though. They never left. It had been weeks, months since the events on Tev's planet, and Kindra was beginning to wonder if the guilt would ever fade.

She rolled haphazardly out of her bunk, disgruntled that her shift was beginning again.

KINDRA HAD NEVER HAD any desire to be a captain, and almost every day she developed a greater appreciation for everything Derreck had done on a day-to-day basis. She had thought her own report needs were overwhelming, but she had never seen a captain's paperwork.

Derreck was recovering in sick bay, but it would still be a matter of weeks before he was at full strength and cleared for duty. She knew the forced bedrest was eating him alive, but on the bright side, at least he had volunteered to help with some of the paperwork. He had to be bored if he was stooping so low.

Even so, the number of reports she had to file was getting ridiculous. Fleet was becoming more and more organized, and the closer they got to central space, the more report requests were filtered through local commands. Every report she filed in *Destiny*'s servers spawned two more. Kindra rubbed her eyes and stood up.

A message popped up in the corner of her vision, reminding her that she had a commander's meeting in a few minutes. The reminder elicited a full-blown groan. She was well aware of the meeting and had hoped the reporting would take her mind off of it. She had begged Derreck to go, but he had smiled and reminded her he wasn't currently the commanding officer on their little dropship. Even if he tried, the security on the jumper wouldn't let him anywhere near the meeting room.

This was the last major meeting before their last series of jumps towards Haven. Captain Absalon, the captain of the jumpship *Destiny*, would soon be inundated with the work necessary to jump within the central systems. The commanders needed to meet to decide their actions. They also needed to share the results of the experiments they had been performing while in transit.

With a sigh, Kindra walked towards the meeting space. A part of her wanted to meet with Tev beforehand, considering a fair amount of the meeting would focus on him. But she couldn't bring herself to do it. Tev was more delighted than he had been since he had left his home planet. His rescue a few weeks ago had made him something of a hero among the crew of the *Destiny*, and he was eating up all the attention. She didn't want to bring him down by discussing what the future might hold.

Even though she had a hard time acknowledging the truth, she still struggled to speak with him. Once they met up with *Destiny* after leaving Tev's planet, everything felt as though it had changed. Kindra's nightmares began, and although she was still Tev's primary connection to her world, there was a distance she didn't know how to bridge. She didn't know how to relate to him in the space between worlds.

When she entered the meeting room, Kindra was reminded of just how spartan a space Captain Absalon preferred. The meeting room was the most secure on the ship, located near the heart of the jumper and virtually immune to any surveillance. The walls of the room were the same flat gray as the rest of the jumper, but nano usage wasn't allowed in the room, so Kindra couldn't even hang a painting in her neurodisplay without setting off at least four alarms.

Captain Absalon opened the meeting with the usual formalities. He spoke about the rescue and what the results had been. Thanks to Tev's actions, and those of the pilots who had initially gone over, they had rescued close to twenty people. Those who had survived had little information to report, but it was obvious they had been attacked. By who was a matter of fierce speculation around the jumper. From what Kindra had overheard, about half the ship blamed pirates, the other half claimed the rebellion was beginning again. Absalon let the commanders know that their investigation so far hadn't turned up any concrete leads.

Absalon turned the meeting over to his second-in-command, Freya. Freya brought up a display that Kindra recognized as the video feed from Tev's suit, with a side display that mapped Tev's neural connections with the suit. Kindra's stomach twisted as she wondered what was coming next.

Kindra respected Freya. She had been a combat pilot before going into command, and she had a no-nonsense way of going about her business. But beyond that, she was still friendly. Most commanders she had met were stuffy and full of themselves. Captain Absalon was a great example. But Freya was personable and sometimes pushed the boundaries of acceptable behavior for an Executive Officer. Kindra appreciated that.

Freya began, her voice loud in the small space of the conference room. "One of our main concerns this meeting, as we all know, is the alien being known as Tev. Based on Kindra's recommendation, he has had relatively free rein on the ship, and has been training as a pilot of our exosuits.

"A few weeks ago that decision paid off. Thanks to Tev's efforts, in tandem with our own pilots, we were able to rescue nineteen Fleet personnel. Personnel that would be dead if Tev hadn't gotten them the oxygen they needed to survive.

"None of this is news. It's all anybody has been talking about. What I want to bring to the group is this footage and data from a portion of the rescue."

Kindra had watched the footage time and time again, but her stomach still twisted in knots as she watched the hallway Tev had been in shift and crumple around him. The entire clip lasted less than a minute, but it was all Kindra could do to sit through the entire video again. Tev had come close to meeting his end on that rescue.

Freya continued, "For those of you at this table who are pilots, the footage speaks for itself. For those who aren't, let me be clear. There are only a handful of pilots in the entire galaxy capable of what Tev managed to do on his fourteenth time in space. Although the data is technical, if you look at the graph on the right, you can see that Tev's neural connection with the suit is off the charts, and he isn't even enhanced with nanos."

Commander Mala, the commander of the other dropship housed in the *Destiny*, spoke up. "So why does any of this matter? He's a great pilot, so what?"

"When we get to central space, and home, one of the greatest questions we will face is what we do with Tev. I want to make it clear, as a pilot, that Tev may have a value even beyond being the first alien we've ever encountered. There will be those in Fleet that will view him only as a specimen, and I want to make it abundantly clear that he is far more than that. I would have him on my wing any time."

Absalon wanted to keep the meeting moving, which Kindra appreciated. The only thing worse than a meeting was a long meeting. "You've made your point. Let's move on to see all the data we've collected."

Absalon motioned to Mala to start with her findings. Kindra leaned forward. This was the part of the meeting she was most interested in. What Mala and her dropship had found still amazed her.

Mala spoke. "As everyone knows, we were assigned to study a planet which looked exceptionally promising for signs of life. Not only did an early analysis indicate an atmosphere and an environment conducive to life, but we detected electromagnetic signals emanating from the planet itself. My team went in certain we would make first contact.

"However, our discoveries were bizarre. What we found was a planet where a civilization had once existed. We found buildings, vehicles, and plenty of bodies. What we didn't find is anyone alive. Some of their technology was still up and running, which was the source of the electromagnetic readings. Although we weren't able to do a full scan of the planet in the time we had, we weren't able to find a sign of life."

Absalon waved away the introduction. "None of this is new. Please focus on what your team has discovered while we've been in transit back."

Mala nodded. "Since we left, we've been analyzing all the data we gathered, and what we're finding defies any explanation I can come up with. The technology is not similar to anything I've ever encountered before, but at the same time, is definitely human. We ran a search through *Destiny*'s mainframe, and there wasn't a single match. My technician has looked inside at some of the code, and it's the same thing. It doesn't match any code in our databases, but the similarities are too striking to be ignored.

"DNA testing of the bodies indicates the same. Like Tev, the DNA is human, but doesn't match up with anything in our database.

"The only final note is that we weren't able to uncover any records that would lead us to understand exactly what happened to the civilization there. From some of our core samples we've detected large amounts of radiation, indicative perhaps of a dirty bomb or nuclear fallout, but we don't have enough evidence to make a definite conclusion."

Absalon turned to Kindra. "And what else have you discovered?"

Kindra shook her head. "Nothing that sheds any light on the mystery. Our initial findings still hold true. Tev is human, but no amount of questioning or exploration of his people's legends provide the slightest clue how that can be."

Absalon nodded, the disappointment evident on his face. "So we've made first contact with an alien species that turns out to be human, and we discover a long-dead civilization that is also human, but humans have never been in this part of space before?"

Kindra and Mala nodded in unison, and Absalon rubbed his forehead in frustration. "Great."

"So, the question is, what do we do when we get back?"

Kindra spoke up before anyone else could. She had been thinking over this problem for a while. "I recommend that we give Tev the status of a foreign ambassador."

Absalon looked up, a frown on his face. "That designation hasn't been used since before the Rebellion Conflict, back when there were separate governments."

Kindra knew she had to make her argument carefully.

"That's true, but the regulations are still on the books, and the designation can be assigned by a jumpship captain. Doing so would mean that Tev will have some degree of protection when we land on Haven."

Absalon nodded. Like many of the crew, he had grown to view Tev as more crew than alien. "It's not much, but I suppose it's better than nothing. I'll make the notations in the system before we get any further towards the central stars."

KINDRA LEFT THE MEETING EXHAUSTED. Even with Absalon pushing them to make decisions as quickly as possible, it had still taken hours. There was too much to go over.

They had talked a little about Kindra's actions on Tev's home planet. When they returned to Haven, she would receive an administrative review. There were a wide range of possibilities open. Most people seemed to agree that she would be held innocent for her actions, but there was a slight chance that she would be found guilty of ordering the killing of Fleet personnel. Depending on how the panel viewed her actions, the result of that could be anything from expulsion from Fleet to execution.

Kindra didn't care. How Fleet felt about her actions didn't matter to her. She just wanted her life to return to normal, wanted the dreams to stop. Ever since that day, she had been carrying a weight, and Fleet's judgment wouldn't affect that one way or the other.

At times she worried about her career, but it never stuck. Both Derreck and Absalon had written her letters of support, and she had been left in command of *Vigilance*. In all likelihood, it would only be a review, but it made her nervous all the same.

She needed someone to talk to, and out here, there was only one person she felt she could trust. She followed the arrows in her vision to sick bay.

Derreck was looking much better than he had even a few days ago. The *Destiny* had far better medical facilities than their dropship, and they had brought Derreck out of his induced coma not long after their reunion. It had been touch and go for a while, but he had come out of the coma with his attitude as positive as ever.

His smile was so wide when he saw her that Kindra couldn't help but grin in return. "The brave warrior returns from the scene of battle. How did it go?"

Kindra filled Derreck in as best she could. He focused on her as she spoke, and she could almost imagine him taking mental notes.

When she finished, he leaned back in his bed, a look of deep thought on his face. Kindra tolerated his silence for a few minutes, but it seemed he was thinking about something else, and Kindra was too curious not to ask.

"What's on your mind?"

Derreck glanced at her, a look of concern on his face. With a gesture, he pulled up a file he had been looking at. It was the same file Freya had pulled up in their meeting, the video feed from Tev's suit in addition to the neural connection data. The only difference was that this one was annotated.

"Freya filed a report with Absalon yesterday, and I've been reading and re-reading it."

Kindra nodded. "I've seen that, although without the annotations. Freya showed it in the meeting. She said kind things about Tev."

Derreck laughed. "I bet she would." He pointed at the annotations. "Do you understand these?"

Kindra took a look and shook her head. To her, they all looked like gibberish.

"These are annotations we use when we are breaking apart combat scenarios. It's a system we're taught in officer school. The language allows us to analyze and break down an event and help people improve their piloting."

Kindra nodded. "What's the problem?"

Derreck paused, as though he was choosing his words. "I don't have any direct proof of my suspicions, but when I look at these annotations, I get the strong sense that Freya is looking at Tev as a combatant. You're absolutely correct when you say that Freya has been complimentary. Even in these annotations, she gives Tev some high praise. But she gives Tev praise as one combat pilot to another."

Kindra shook her head. She wasn't sure what Derreck was getting at, and he noticed her confusion.

"Okay, let me break it down into two parts for you. The first part we've already talked about. Freya sees Tev as an incredible combat pilot. Agreed?"

Kindra nodded. She trusted Derreck with her life, and if he was seeing something in the annotations, she believed him. Freya had been very complimentary during the meeting.

"The second part of my concern is one of the reports you submitted, a report which has been read over a dozen times by just the command structure of this jumper."

That fact really confused Kindra. She was fairly certain that no one ever read a single word she wrote.

Derreck noticed her hesitation and clarified. "It was the report about why you believe Tev made such a good pilot with such little training."

Kindra knew the report Derreck was talking about. One of many questions she had been trying to answer while in transit was why Tev could pilot the exosuits as well as he could, especially without any enhancements. Her theory wasn't bulletproof, but she was almost certain she was right.

Kindra believed that Tev's skill in the suit had everything to do with his upbringing. Research had long ago proven that there was a connection between movement proficiency and neural development. It was why most people went through rigorous gymnastics training in their youth.

Tev was different though. Not only did he grow up in an environment that was far more diverse than Kindra's, he had moved and hunted in that environment every day since he was born. He had years and years of movement experience, climbing trees and rocks, swimming in streams, and stalking prey over all sorts of terrain. Tev moved like that all day, every day. In contrast, even the most intense gymnastic training classes lasted at most an hour or two a day. Because of his environment, Tev's brain had developed an impressive ability to control movement, which was picked up and then amplified by the exosuit system.

Kindra had written her theory into the report, including the relevant links to research she thought might help make the connection. She never dreamed her theory would be read, and certainly not often.

"What does my report have to do with anything?"

"Think about it. You've stated many times that although Tev is considered an excellent hunter by his own people, he is far from alone. You've said there are many hunters in their culture who are just as good or better than he is. If your theory about environmental factors being the deciding reason why Tev is such a good pilot is correct, can you make the connection?"

Kindra's mind raced. "Are you saying Fleet might want to recruit even more of Tev's people to strengthen the ranks of our combat pilots?"

Derreck nodded. "Exactly."

Kindra shook her head. "I have a hard time believing Fleet would be so interested in the military applications of first contact. The Rebellion Conflict is over. Everything Fleet does is about looking forward now."

"I wish I was as optimistic as you. You joined the service near the end of the rebellion, right?"

Kindra nodded.

"You know I served through all of it. Fleet won that war, but not because we always fought with more honor than the other side. We did horrible things as well, and I don't think that part of us just leaves after the war is over."

"That's a pretty pessimistic view of life."

"Then let's put a better spin on it. Let's say Fleet is completely benevolent from top to bottom. Even if that's true, we live in a dangerous galaxy. We still don't know what or who blew up those dropships we had to rescue, and strains of the rebellion still thrive throughout peripheral space, no matter how much Fleet would like us to believe otherwise. Even if Fleet was benevolent, wouldn't it make sense they would want to strengthen themselves in case more conflict developed?"

Kindra hated to agree, but she saw what Derreck was getting at. A flood of anger surged through her, anger at herself for not seeing the truth sooner.

Derreck must have seen the frustration in her eyes. "Don't blame yourself. You've done your duties well. I just think this is something we will need to be careful of when we get to Haven and meet with the Senate."

"What should we do?"

Derreck gave a small shrug, one of the largest gestures he could perform without pain. "I'm not entirely sure. Tev is closer to you than anyone else. If Fleet treats him like an ambassador instead of a test subject, I would encourage you to use your influence with him in whatever way you see best. It's not that I don't trust Fleet. On the whole, they do a good job, but humans are always looking for new weapons, and I don't want to think that we've found one for them."

Kindra nodded. "I'll keep an eye out for it. Thanks for letting me know."

After making sure that Derreck had everything he needed, Kindra left the sick bay, more filled with worries than she had been before she had come in.

THREE

TEV HAD ALREADY SEEN MORE wonders than any of his ancestors, and yet every day continued to amaze him. In his youth, he had thought the lands of his clan were endless. As an adult, he had wondered if it would ever be possible to explore the entire world he lived on. Now, to think the world he had known was only a small part of the entire galaxy, and that the galaxy was only one part of the entire universe.

Tev had always known about the stars, known that they were other suns that were a long way away. It was what the legends of his clan had taught him. But it was one thing to hear something, and another to experience the truth firsthand. He was a man who had grown up using only his two feet to get around. To imagine the distances he now traveled was beyond his comprehension.

He found that oftentimes, it was easiest not to think of things in terms of scale. If he did, what was right in front of him often became overwhelming. Instead, he focused only on his surroundings without placing them in context. In a hallway of the jumper, he focused only on the fact that he was in a hallway, not that he was in a hallway in a machine larger than the land his clan used to set up camp. Or that the same machine could jump unbelievable distances in the blink of an eye.

Kindra had invited him to the deck where he could look out into space. They were only a few hours away from their destination, and Kindra wanted to show him where they were going. Together, they gazed at the planet below.

"Welcome to Haven, Tev."

The planet was huge, and although he didn't trust his memories, Haven looked as though it was larger than the planet he had grown up on. He asked Kindra, and she told him he was right. Haven was almost twice as big as his planet.

"This is the center of humanity. Or at least, we used to think so. I'm not sure what to think since you came around. But after Earth collapsed, this was the planet that became the hub of everything. It's near the center of explored space, for what that's worth, but more important is the industry that started here."

Kindra had to explain the concept of industry, but in Haven's case, it was simple. She pointed off in the distance, into the blackness of space. "Out there, there are a bunch of tiny planets that look a lot like the moon you are used to. They are made of the same rocks we use to build our spaceships. Here, at Haven, we use those rocks to build our ships."

Kindra pointed to a giant machine off in the distance, and Tev saw what looked like a spaceship, but wasn't quite. It was more like he was looking at a ship with the skin taken off, and he could see inside, see into the bones of the machine.

Tev wanted to ask more questions, but Kindra was

already pointing down towards the planet. Sometimes she, and all the crew, had a tendency to take their world for granted. Tev was flooded with questions, but he held onto them for now.

"Below us is the city we are going to."

Tev looked down and saw that Kindra was pointing to lights on the planet's surface. They were on the dark side of the planet, so all Tev could see was an enormous cluster of lights surrounded by near perfect darkness.

Tev's sense of scale was far from refined, but from what he knew, it seemed like the lights covered an amazing amount of distance. "How big is the city?"

"Billions of people live there."

Tev shook his head. He couldn't even understand how billions of people lived in the same place. But that wasn't the question he had asked. "No, how big is it?" Tev held his arms out wide, and Kindra laughed.

"Sorry, generally when we ask that question we mean population. I'm not sure." Her eyes flashed around, and Tev knew she was looking up the information. "It's over five hundred kilometers across at its narrowest points."

If Tev hadn't become so used to being amazed in the past weeks, he would have sat down. It would take days and days to walk across the city.

"How can that be?"

Kindra shrugged. "In space, it's much easier to build cities. All the services are concentrated, and it's easy to make things bigger. How you lived on your planet? No one lives like that in my clan."

Tev felt a sense of vertigo, a sensation he was becoming more and more familiar with. "How can you live like this?"

Kindra smiled and shrugged. "It's all we've ever known."

Again, Tev was overwhelmed. Despite his best efforts, the feeling still occurred more often than he cared to admit. "I don't think I'm the best person to be here. Shet, or another elder from another clan, they should be here. This is too big."

Kindra put her hand on Tev's shoulder. He tensed for a moment, his body reacting to what it perceived as a threat. Then his conscious mind took over and he relaxed.

"Do you think one of your elders would have been able to take in everything that you've seen?"

Tev knew what she meant. Neera, the woman he loved back on his home planet, had said something similar before he left. He wasn't the right choice because of his hunting skill, no matter how much pride he took in his abilities. He was right because of his curiosity and his open mind. It would be tough for an elder to be here.

"You're right. Shet would have died in amazement by now."

Kindra laughed, and together they stared off into space in silence.

TEV WALKED alongside Derreck as the captain used his wheelchair to get around. He continued to get better every day, but it would still be a week or two before the doctors allowed him to walk longer distances. His handicap still irritated Derreck to no end, but he tried to keep a smile on his face.

Tev respected Derreck for that, among many other things. Tev had always been a bad patient growing up. Every time he was injured or sick, he was up and running around long before he should have. Derreck didn't even have the choice. He was monitored constantly by his doctors. If he tried to do too much, he received immediate warnings.

Mostly, their journey was made in silence. They had been on Haven for a few days now, and Tev was still getting used to the city. On their first journey he had closed his eyes and focused on his breath, trying to shut out all the external noises and sights. Everything was so loud and bright. He didn't understand how people could even think in such a space.

There had been some debate about where Tev should stay, but in the end it had been decided that Tev would stay with Derreck. Derreck offered Tev a bed, but Tev found the floor to be more similar to what he was used to. Inside Derreck's apartment, they kept the lights dim and the rooms quiet.

The past few days had been all about exploration. Tev had taken his time, only exploring a bit at once. His first journey had only been about a hundred paces out Derreck's front door, but that had been more than enough for him. He returned to Derreck's place and tried again later that day.

Today was their first real journey of any distance outside of Derreck's apartment. Tev claimed he was ready, but even so, travel was difficult for him. His senses, used to the sights and sounds of the forest, were overwhelmed by everything happening around him. Derreck kept moving forward, and when Tev asked questions, he answered, but otherwise, he gave Tev the time he needed to adjust. Tev still had a hard time believing Derreck could move so easily from one world to the next.

"Do you like living here?"

Derreck chuckled. "Not really. That's why I'm out in space most of the time."

Eventually they came to a building. Tev recognized the

image that Fleet put on their ships and suits, but other than that, Tev saw nothing different about it. The structure was tall and large, but so was every building nearby.

Tev didn't want to say as much, but he was excited for the day's activities. He would test himself against the warriors of Derreck's clan. He was excited to see how he compared, but the feeling didn't seem to be shared by Derreck. Tev noticed that Derreck's tone changed whenever he talked about the tests. For some reason, Derreck didn't like the idea, but Tev thought it was fantastic. This was an opportunity for him to compete against some of the best people in the galaxy. He hoped that he could learn from them.

They entered the building and Derreck introduced Tev to several people. Tev didn't pay any attention to their names, but he paid attention to their stance and bearing. He was amazed by just how poorly most people in the city walked. He had noticed the problem in space too, but it seemed to be everywhere in Kindra's society.

These men and women were different. Their bodies were always in balance, and Tev could tell several of them were ready to strike at any moment. He approved. These were people he had something in common with.

After introductions, Tev and the others were brought to a room that overlooked several other rooms. Tev was impressed. The rooms were all very different and didn't even seem like rooms to him. They were large and had entirely separate environments in each one. One room was bare: four walls, a floor and ceiling, and nothing else. The second looked like it was a city street, but one that had been attacked. Walls were crumbling and debris littered the ground. The third room was a forest, and Tev felt immediately at home. He hadn't seen any green spaces since landing, and the sight of grass and trees soothed his spirit.

Derreck gave Tev instructions. Tev would take part in three separate fights, so long as he was willing. In each room, he would face a different opponent, a fighter who was considered great in that environment. Derreck explained that they wouldn't be wearing any armor or protection, and instead everyone was relying on an honor system not to hurt each other. He showed Tev how to indicate surrender in the event he was losing. Tev understood. It was the same way he fought with clan members at home.

Without further ado, Tev and his fellow warriors went down to the first room. One warrior stepped forward, a young woman with a fierce countenance. Tev glanced her over. She was one of the strongest women he had ever seen, far stronger than Neera was. He probably outweighed her by at least five kilos, but she wouldn't be an opponent to take lightly.

The first room was the bare room where the environment wouldn't have any effect.

Derreck nodded, and the fight commenced. Tev was tempted to rush in, but something about his opponent made him wary. To an untrained eye, it might look as though she was open to attack, but Tev decided it was a feint. She wanted to lure him in closer. He tried striking at her instead.

Tev lashed out with his fists but hit nothing but air. She moved around his attacks with ease, not even flinching. Tev tried a combination of punches and kicks, and the woman stepped back, allowing the strikes to pass harmlessly in front of her.

Tev was in a dilemma. Striking wasn't working. He would have to be more aggressive if he wanted to hit her, but he worried that if he was, he would be falling into the trap she was setting for him. He came in for another series of punches.

This time, she didn't dodge, but stepped inside his attack and delivered a fierce punch to his stomach. He could tell she had pulled her punch at the last moment, but the blow still knocked him backwards. She didn't give him a chance to recover, leaping at him and pulling him to the ground.

Tev had always thought he was a good wrestler, but within moments she had him pinned with her arm across his throat. He slapped the ground twice, and she let go and let him stand up.

Tev wasn't angry. Whoever this woman was, she was a far better warrior than he was. He wasn't even sure what had happened once they were on the ground. She had moved with such surety he never had a chance. He thanked her for the match and asked if sometime she might show him some of her techniques. The woman looked at Derreck for approval and then nodded. Tev was grateful. He could tell he would have much to learn, especially when it came to combat.

As a group, they moved towards the second room, the city that had been destroyed. Tev explored the room for a few minutes, getting a feel for where everything was. His opponent, a slim man, did the same.

Derreck came forward and explained that for this fight, they would use weapons. Tev hesitated for a moment, but as Derreck continued, his hesitation disappeared. Derreck gave Tev a handgun, a small silver weapon that fit nicely in his hand. He explained that all Tev had to do was point it at his opponent and pull the trigger before his opponent could do the same to him.

Derreck explained that the guns didn't fire anything. They simply determined whether the opponent had been hit fatally.

Tev nodded his understanding, and the two warriors separated to opposite edges of the room. Tev was smiling the entire way. This was learning he never could have received at home. His senses felt alive, a rare occurrence in the artificial worlds of Kindra and her people. This was fun.

The lights dimmed, and Tev knew the contest had begun. He didn't rush. The time had come to hunt his prey. He scanned his surroundings, deciding on his best course of action. He thought about taking to the rooftops. Most people didn't look up or down, so it would give him an advantage.

Tev found a place where he could climb a wall, flattening himself against the rooftop. Slowly, he peeked his head over the roof and looked around. He didn't see any sign of his opponent. He worked his way to the center of the roof and came up to a crouch. If his opponent was on the ground, he should be safe from view.

He didn't want to make the same mistake he was hoping his opponent would make. He took a moment to look across the other rooftops, but in the dim light he couldn't make out any other shapes moving. The path looked clear.

Tev mapped out his next steps, running and leaping across a narrow gap to a nearby rooftop. Once there, he stopped and repeated the procedure, peeking out onto the streets and checking the other rooftops. Then he listened.

The temptation when hunting was always to rush. Sometimes it was necessary to use haste, but those times were rare. Much more often it paid to remain still, to move slowly. Patience wasn't a practice Tev enjoyed, but he could be as still as a stone for as long as it took. He could feel the familiar tension in his body, and he had to fight the urge to move, to do anything.

He continued to listen, but he couldn't hear anything. After a few minutes passed, Tev moved to the next rooftop. They were in a big room, and it might take them some time to find each other. He didn't mind. If he could find his opponent first, he would easily win the match.

Tev leapt to the next rooftop, his landing silent. Again, he repeated the procedure of checking the streets and rooftops. Once he was certain he couldn't see anything, he remained still and listened. The urge to move was stronger than ever. A part of Tev's mind kept reminding him that he wasn't just the hunter. He was also the hunted. Tev kept his focus and stillness. He wouldn't succumb to foolish decisions.

He heard a sound not far from the building he was on. It was soft, as though someone had accidentally kicked a pebble. His instinct was to run towards the noise, but he resisted. Making sounds appear in other places was an old trick, and he wouldn't fall for it if it was one. Instead, he moved carefully, gun in front of him, towards the edge of the roof, his eyes scanning left and right over and over as he approached.

He approached the edge but saw nothing, which most likely meant the sound had been made as a distraction. Suddenly, he heard a sound directly beneath him. His eyes tracked down and saw movement. Tev only had time to react. He stepped backwards, and he heard the click of a trigger below. Tev panicked, but the lights didn't come back up, so he must not have been hit.

Tev debated and discarded options. His advantage had been neutralized, and most of his actions would expose him to the warrior below. His best idea was to get down to ground level. He figured at most, his opponent could cover two of four sides. Tev just had to decide on a side and let himself down.

He listened, hoping he could catch some sound from below, but this environment wasn't very conducive to it. In the woods, there were leaves and branches which cracked and gave away a person's position, but here there was only the same hard rock found everywhere else. Unless someone's footfalls were heavy, there was no way of making out where they were.

Tev chose the side of the building opposite of where the shots had come from. It was a guess only, but he figured that at least for a minute his opponent would stay in place. He peeked over the edge before dropping down. Out of the corner of his eye, he caught motion once again, and he shoved himself back on top of the roof as he heard several clicks.

The lights didn't turn on, but Tev wasn't surprised. It hadn't been much of a chance. If his opponent had been a little more patient, he might have been able to shoot Tev as he was descending, but he had reacted too hastily.

Tev was getting frustrated. Ultimately, this was only a game, and he was losing. It was time to play around and see what happened. He stood up and sprinted back the way he had come.

Tev's actions forced his opponent to make a decision. If the warrior wanted to keep track of Tev, he would need to give chase. Otherwise they would go back to playing a big game of hide and seek. Tev assumed the warrior would chase him.

He was right. The warrior stood up from behind the rubble he was using as cover and chased after Tev. Tev pointed his gun and pulled the trigger a few times, but he was running and aiming to the side. He missed all his shots, but as he leapt across the rooftops, the warrior didn't hit him either.

Tev kept running, heading for the first roof he had climbed onto. He could hear the warrior down in the street below. He couldn't see his opponent, but he decided they were running just about parallel. When he leaped between the rooftops, he saw his opponent clearly for a fraction of a second. He pulled the trigger repeatedly, and below him he saw his opponent doing the same.

Tev was so distracted he forgot about his landing, and he lost his balance as soon as his feet touched the other rooftop. He rolled to his feet, but as he did, the lights came up. Someone had been hit.

He wasn't sure if he had won or not, but that had been some of the most fun he had had in a while.

Tev walked to the edge of the roof and allowed himself to drop from it. He landed and rolled smoothly to his feet. His opponent was grinning ear to ear, and he stepped forward, his hand extended. Tev had already learned about the handshake, and he took the other man's hand and shook it firmly.

His opponent spoke. "I don't know who won, but that was one of the best duels I've ever been in. Thank you."

"Thank you. You were brilliant."

Derreck rolled up to them. "Well, I have bad news. Both of you died. Tev, technically you got off your shot last, but it was close. For all intents and purposes, you tied, although if you want to get picky, he won," Derreck finished by pointing his thumb at the warrior.

Tev nodded. A part of him chided himself for letting himself go at the end, but it had all been fun.

Derreck looked over at Tev. "Ready for a third match, or do you want to take a break?"

There was nothing Tev wanted more. "Let's go."

The third room was the closest Tev had felt to home in a very long time. A part of him recognized the fact he had only been gone for months, but still, Tev's journey seemed like it had been much longer. His life had changed an enormous amount in a very short time.

The room could almost pass as the forest Tev grew up in. He dug his toes into the dirt floor and exhaled a deep sigh he didn't realize he had been holding on to. His body missed the diversity of angles and feelings of the forest. Everything in this world was smooth and hard and shiny. He didn't like it.

For the last time, Derreck gave instructions. Each warrior was given what appeared to Tev to be a stick, about half a meter long. Derreck pointed to the end and told Tev that if he could touch the point to the other person, he would win.

Tev watched as the other warrior spun his stick in fancy patterns. Clearly, the man had received a lot of training in the weapon. Tev didn't care. He was at home here in the forest. There wasn't any way he'd lose.

Derreck gave Tev the opportunity to wander into the forest first. He said he'd send the other man in after him in a while. Tev resisted the urge to skip into the forest. The only things missing were the sounds and traces of wildlife, but Tev wasn't going to be picky. It was a blessing to be here. Tev felt almost as though Lys was looking over him once again.

Within a few minutes, he found the place where he wanted to stage the battle. It was surrounded by trees and bushes and gave Tev ample opportunity to hide and move around. The other soldier wouldn't have a chance against him.

Tev found a place that gave him good cover, and he crouched down into it. Here in the woods, he was certain to detect the other man. The ground was covered in sticks and leaves, and Tev was certain the man wouldn't have any ability to move quietly in such an environment.

He was right. It was several minutes later when he heard the soft crunch of a footstep on the leaves. The man had come from a different direction than Tev had suspected, but that wasn't surprising. The man would want the element of surprise, so he wouldn't chase Tev directly, not in a room that was still pretty small, all things considered.

Tev tracked the sound with interest, not feeling any need to break from cover. The woods were his home, and he wouldn't be drawn out. He heard a noise in a different place, and he took a few moments to place it. The man had thrown a stick in a different direction, trying to throw off Tev's idea of where he was. It wasn't working. The man didn't have any idea how to move in the woods, and it was proving impossible for him to move silently.

Eventually the man came into the clearing near Tev's hiding place. Tev didn't wait. As soon as he had a clear opportunity, he took it, leaping forward and trying to hit the man.

Tev didn't count on the man's incredible reflexes. Tev didn't have any doubt he had surprised the man, but his opponent moved with speed, blocking Tev's strike before it landed.

If it came down to a battle with the sticks, Tev knew he would lose. This man was trained in exactly this style, and Tev wasn't. But Tev was home. He darted off to the side, narrowly dodging the man's return attack. The man chased him towards a set of two trees, set about a meter and a half apart from one another.

Tev leapt at one tree just as the man swung at him, the stick passing just centimeters behind Tev's back. Tev's right foot struck the tree, and he planted it there, holding for just a fraction of a second as the man approached.

His opponent must have thought Tev would try climbing the tree. He had watched Tev scale the building in the previous room and must have expected him to go high. But Tev had other plans. He shoved off his right foot towards the second tree to his left. The soldier's overhand swing passed harmlessly to Tev's right.

Tev bounced off the other tree with his left foot, ending up behind the man who was desperately trying to turn to keep up with Tev. As he passed, Tev slapped him gently with his stick. He landed off balance, but allowed his body to collapse and roll back to its feet.

When he stood back up, the other man had a look of disbelief on his face. "I'd heard that you could move really well, and I saw hints of that in the other room, but I've never seen anything like that before. Impressive."

Tev smiled. "Thank you. Your reaction was also very fast. I thought for sure I'd defeat you on my first strike."

The man accepted the compliment as the others approached. Derreck was grinning from ear to ear, and Tev saw all the other men were making a swiping gesture towards him, a gesture Tev had learned signified the exchange of money from one person to another. Tev still didn't understand why these people worried so much about their money.

Derreck spoke, his enthusiasm contagious. "I told you he was good."

The last soldier Tev had fought grumbled in return, making the same swiping motion. "I guess so, sir."

Derreck laughed and addressed the group. "That's enough fun for one day. Y'all care to join us for some food? It's on me."

A chorus of grumbles answered him, but they all left together, discussing their most recent battle.

FOUR

KINDRA WASN'T sure what she was experiencing. She knew what she was supposed to feel: Fear, trepidation, nervousness. But she couldn't bring herself to feel any of those things. When it came to the administrative review, the only emotion she could come up with was boredom.

She knew she wasn't looking forward to it. She imagined that they would review evidence of her actions on Tev's planet, and she'd rather not look through that again. Her actions haunted her memories every day. She didn't need to see them played out in front of her.

Try as she might, she couldn't bring herself to care about the review. She was responsible for killing a person. Worse, the person had been a member of her own crew. She had never liked him much, but that didn't matter. This wasn't a review to find the truth. She already knew the truth. Everyone already knew the truth. This was to decide on her career, and that seemed much less important to her than her own sanity.

At times, she considered just giving up and resigning.

This was a battle for her to fight alone. No one else had anything to do with it. Her decision would end her career in Fleet, but she wasn't sure that was such a bad idea anymore.

She didn't know what kept her going, but her mind wandered as she went through the preparation for the administrative review. She took a nice, long shower, finding comfort in the steam that curled around her. Afterwards she put on her dress uniform, a piece of clothing she hadn't worn a single day since she graduated from the academy. She added a handful of decorations she'd been awarded for her service, decorations she'd thrown in a drawer in her apartment and never bothered to put on until today.

Fleet had sent a car for her, a gesture she didn't know how to interpret and didn't care enough to figure out. She climbed in the back and was promptly lost in thought as the car sped away. The only thought she remembered having was that Tev would have found this ride fascinating. She smiled at the thought, but it was short-lived.

Kindra followed the directions to her review, surprised the meeting was as high up Fleet Headquarters as it was.

When she got to the room she was instructed to wait outside, which she did without complaint. Even the waiting rooms this high up in Headquarters were ornate. She thought that even the walls of the waiting area were lined with real wood. An extravagant expense if it was true.

Kindra wasn't sure how best to spend her time, so she sat there, her mind as vacant as ever. She realized her name had been called twice before she responded. She shook her head to clear the cobwebs and stood up, straightening her dress uniform.

Inside the meeting room sat more brass than Kindra had ever seen in her life. Under any other circumstance, she would have found them intimidating. Instead, all she could think was that this was the most expensive set of actions she had ever taken. Millions of credits of time must be being spent in this room every hour, all to judge her decisions. The whole process seemed foolish. Wasteful. Almost funny.

Kindra fought her urge to smile and stood ramrod straight, waiting to be addressed.

"Commander, at ease, please."

Kindra relaxed her stance. She figured she was supposed to know who the people in front of her were, but she didn't. She'd never had to pay too much attention to the chain of command above her. The woman who had spoken could have been her grandma, though. She had gray hair and a smile on her face, with just a hint of steel in her eyes. Kindra automatically liked her.

The same woman seemed to be in charge, whatever that meant here. "Commander, we've reviewed logs from the alien's suit, the *Vigilance*, and Lieutenant Kenan's suit. We've read your reports, and we've talked for hours among ourselves. To say that you found yourself in a difficult situation is an understatement, and there's no need to go over what happened here. Your reports were straightforward and in line with everything documented about the event. We believe you have been honest about the events."

The woman's voice was plain and soft-spoken, devoid of judgment. Kindra found it soothing.

"We only have one question for you, and it's a vague one, intentionally. We know the facts of what happened, but what we want to know is, how do you feel about the actions you took on your last mission?"

Kindra frowned. She hadn't been sure what she was

expecting, but that question wasn't it. She didn't answer right away, thinking about her answer.

Eventually the silence became uncomfortable, and she spoke just to fill the space. "To be honest, ma'am, I really don't know. I hate what happened. I'm sure that our actions saved many lives of the aliens and potentially salvaged a chance for future relations with them. But did I make the best decisions? Was there a better way? I keep thinking there had to be, but I can't think of what it was."

Kindra felt like she was rambling, and that the less she said, the better off she was, so she stopped. The various admirals looked around at each other, and Kindra caught one of the men give a slight nod to the gray-haired woman.

The woman turned to Kindra.

"Commander, it is the judgment of this review board that you acted in the best interests of Fleet. You are hereby declared innocent of all charges and will keep your rank and pay. Is there anything you would like to add, or do you have any questions?"

Kindra thought she would have felt something, but she felt exactly the same as she had when she walked in the room. She shook her head. "No, ma'am. Thank you, ma'am."

The woman nodded. "Very well, commander, you are dismissed."

THAT NIGHT, Kindra didn't know what to do. There was only one person she could think of to talk to, and she worried that she was getting desperate. She thought about calling almost a dozen times before she finally did it.

Derreck answered right away, and as soon as he heard her voice, he told her where to meet him.

An hour later the two of them met at a small bar Kindra had never heard of. She hadn't grown up on Haven like Derreck, and his knowledge of small and unique places always surprised her. The place didn't even show up on her net results. She wasn't even sure how that was possible.

The bar was cozy and intimate, with only a few booths and several stools around the bar. Derreck was already there when she arrived, sitting in a booth. Kindra frowned. She didn't see his wheelchair anywhere. She asked him about it as soon as she sat down.

"I hate that thing. The docs say I'll be fully cleared next week, but I know I can move short distances."

Kindra shook her head. Derreck must be driving the doctors mad.

"What's wrong?"

"I'm thinking about leaving Fleet."

A range of reactions passed over Derreck's face, but he was a good poker player, and he settled into a concerned frown after just a moment. "I received the notice that you'd been cleared." He paused, studying her carefully. "But you don't feel that way, do you?"

Kindra had an urge to just let everything out, to ramble on, but the scientist that lived inside her wouldn't let her. She needed to be focused and precise.

"Derreck, I signed up so I could explore the galaxy. I want to study life and how it evolves across the planets. Fighting was never a part of what I wanted to do."

Derreck nodded, taking in her words. Kindra wasn't sure how he would respond. She trusted him though. He wouldn't ask her to stay if he didn't think it was in her best interest.

"Do you think that everything happening around Tev is important?"

Kindra knew where Derreck was trying to go. "Absolutely! His discovery is probably the most important event in humanity's history. But I'm not sure this journey is worth the cost to me. There are other biologists out there who could handle this situation better."

Derreck's response was immediate. "No, there aren't."

Kindra wanted to interrupt him, but he held up his hand.

"Look in my eyes."

Kindra, surprised by the command in his voice, obeyed.

"I know you feel guilty over Kenan's death. I know that and I'm glad of it. If you didn't feel guilt you wouldn't be the person that I believe you are. But I've seen combat, and I know, without a doubt, no one could have done better than you did in that situation. Not any commander I've ever met, and certainly not a scientist. Do you believe me?"

Emotions warred within Kindra. She knew he believed he was telling the truth, and she wanted desperately to believe him, but she couldn't do it.

The silence stretched between them. Finally, Derreck spoke, "I don't know what else to tell you. I know the guilt you're feeling. In a perfect world, I'd be able to tell you that nothing like that will ever happen again, but you know I can't. The truth is, our duty can be horrible, but this is what we signed up for. You need to decide if the impact you'll have is worth the risk."

Kindra nodded. "What do you think I should do?"

Derreck shrugged. "If I were you, I'd stay in Fleet. We need people like you, people who care and will always try to make the right decisions. Losing you would be a tragedy."

Derreck ordered another round of drinks for them, and Kindra could feel the alcohol dulling the edge of the pain she was feeling. After getting halfway through her second drink, Kindra worked up the courage to ask the other question that had plagued her. "How is he doing?"

Her captain didn't need to ask who she was talking about. "Okay. He hides his discomfort well, but he's having a hard time adjusting to our way of life. Everything is foreign to him. I realize this sounds manipulative after your confession, but he needs you. You're the anchor between the two worlds for him."

Kindra nodded, the words struggling to find purchase in her distracted mind. "I heard that Fleet ran some combat tests on him."

"Yeah. The results were interesting. He's good, but he's outclassed by Fleet's best. As a fighter, I'd say he's only average, maybe a little above. It's his movement that's fascinating, though. Give him an environment to work in, and the way he moves through it instantly elevates his abilities. That ability to move is what makes him so dangerous in a suit. As I've been watching him, I'm more and more convinced your theory is right. I'm also convinced that with training, he could be one of the best suit pilots we've ever seen."

"You sound like you want that to happen."

Derreck's grin vanished. "Look, I'm concerned by the possibilities, but I have to admit, it's really fun to watch him learn the suits better."

Kindra shook her head. The phrase *boys will be boys* ran through her head, but it wasn't one she applied to Derreck often.

They finished their drinks, and Derreck left her with one last thought. "I don't think it's my position to tell you what to do with your life. For what it's worth, I want you to remain in Fleet. But, I think that at the very least, you should talk to Tev. He needs you, and I think, perhaps, you need him. Hell, take him out on a date. Relax and enjoy each other's company. It would do both of you some good."

"I'll think about it."

Derreck nodded as he hailed a car, leaving Kindra alone once again, deciding what to do.

FIVE

A FEW DAYS later there was a knock at Tev's door, or more accurately, Derreck's door. Tev wondered who it could be. Most of his days were spent exploring, a little on his own, but mostly with Derreck. The knowledge pained him a little, but even after a few weeks the planet of Haven was still too strange to him. He didn't feel safe when he was alone. With Derreck along to guide him, he felt much better and could focus on learning, rather than on his own safety. It was evening, and Derreck was out, and he wasn't the type of person to get visitors.

Tev was supposed to be able to check who was at the door, but he had forgotten what Derreck had shown him. Instead, he grabbed his knife and opened the door.

Kindra was there, an uncertain smile on her face. A smile that disappeared the moment she saw Tev's knife.

"Is everything okay?"

Tev spun the knife and hid it behind his back, fooling no one. "I'm fine. Sorry. I just get a little nervous sometimes."

Kindra nodded, the smile slowly returning to her face.

She still looked uncertain, as if she thought she should smile, but couldn't quite convince herself.

"Are you going to invite me in?"

Tev, feeling foolish, did. Together they walked to Derreck's living room. On the way Tev sheathed his knife and put it down on a counter.

The two of them sat on separate couches, looking across the room at each other. Tev wasn't sure what he should do. He wanted to talk to Kindra, but everything he thought of fled his mind before he could form the words. He cursed silently to himself. His interactions with her had been difficult, and he didn't want them to be. He was just about to force out an awkward question to start a conversation when he noticed Kindra wringing her hands.

"What's wrong?"

"Tev, I wanted to ask you about Kenan."

Tev's stomach tightened. That was the last thing he wanted to talk about with Kindra.

"What about?"

"How ... how do you feel about what we did?"

Tev wasn't quite sure what Kindra wanted him to say, but he was an honest man, and it was easiest to follow his first instinct. "I'm sorry that I had to kill one of your clan, but we did a good thing. He would have killed many more of my people."

"I know that, but, how do you live with it?"

Suddenly, Tev understood. He knew why Kindra was here, what she was really asking about.

"It's because you don't have to kill to survive."

Kindra looked confused, so Tev explained.

"At home, we have to kill other animals to survive. Not just for food, but sometimes because other animals are dangerous to us. You don't have that. No other animal can hurt you here. Where I grew up, we learned that we must kill or be killed."

Kindra shook her head. "Murder isn't that simple."

Tev stood up, surprised by how frustrated he was. "Yes, sometimes it is. He would have killed many. We saved many. That is all there is."

Kindra was taken aback by the violence in Tev's answer. His tone penetrated the guilt she was feeling. Tev could see that easily.

Gradually, Kindra's entire demeanor changed. Her shoulders slumped and straightened again. Tev studied her. She hadn't found her answer, not yet. But she was one step closer.

"Do you want to come out to eat with me?"

Tev debated. He had already been out today with Derreck, and leaving the apartment twice in one day seemed like a lot. But Kindra was in front of him and talking to him, and he wanted to keep her that way. Tev nodded, and Kindra stood up and led the way.

Throughout the journey, Kindra seemed content. It was different for her after being so distant the past few months. Tev enjoyed the change in her. They soon reached the restaurant Kindra had chosen and were seated immediately.

As often happened, their conversation turned to the different aspects of Kindra's culture. Tev always kept a mental list of the new things he had seen, and whenever he got a chance, he asked people about them. He most often asked Derreck, but tried to split his questions between all the people he interacted with. He worried that if he ever asked one person too many questions, they would get frustrated.

Their food came out, and it was yet another type of food Tev had never seen before. This was some sort of long, stringy food, with meat and sauce covering it. Tev was still mastering the use of the fork, and this food didn't seem to want to work with the skills he had. Kindra laughed at his challenge and showed him how to twirl his fork to keep the strings attached. Tev didn't understand. Eating with hands was much easier, but every time he did so here, he received stares from others.

The meal was delicious, and eventually the conversation became focused on Tev.

"What do you think of our planet so far?"

Tev was at a loss for words. Everything about Kindra's planet was amazing, but no matter how awe-inspiring it was, Tev felt that there was something missing here. He tried to explain his feeling to Kindra, but found that he couldn't. The truth was, he wasn't sure what was missing. All he knew was that he didn't feel complete here, the way he did on his home planet.

Kindra listened to him struggle to find the words but eventually interjected. "Do you want to go back?"

It was the very question Tev had been struggling with.

"I do. Everything I know is there. All of this, this is too much for me. I'm a hunter, but out here, my food is brought to me. What am I, then?"

Kindra looked like she was about to reply, but Tev interrupted her.

"You know what really scares me? What if I go back, and I don't fit in there anymore, either? What if I don't fit in any world?"

Kindra didn't respond, but Tev could see his words had struck her, somehow. She was thinking deeply about something. Finally, she reached across the table and took his hand in hers.

"Tev, I don't have the answers for you. But I will always be there if you need me. I want you to know that."

Tev took heart. It was surprising how much he trusted Kindra. He felt her hand on his, softer than any skin he had ever known. Even Neera had never had such soft skin. For the first time, he thought about Kindra in a new light.

Kindra removed her hand and leaned back. "That got far too serious too fast. This was supposed to be a celebration."

Tev's mind raced, faced with ideas and thoughts he hadn't encountered before. For months he had been obsessing about losing Neera, but the entire time, Kindra had been right in front of him. At first, she had been alien to him, but as time had gone on, that feeling had gone away. Now she was just Kindra, a friend.

Tev pushed his mind into the present and smiled. Kindra returned the smile. "Tev, have you ever had wine?"

Tev shook his head. He didn't know what wine was. Kindra laughed and ordered some from the man who brought them food.

He had been expecting food, so he was surprised when the man brought out liquid in a bottle. He poured a little into one of Kindra's glasses and she smelled it and took a sip. She nodded at the man, and he poured more into her glass, and then some into Tev's.

Tev cautiously sniffed at the drink, frowning at what he smelled. It was both sweet and not. He took sip, amazed by the different flavors assaulting his tongue. He wasn't sure if he liked it or not, but he took a few more sips, trying to understand everything he was tasting. Kindra watched the entire process with a grin on her face.

Almost immediately, Tev felt the effects of the drink. He looked at Kindra. "Is this alcohol?"

She laughed, confirmation enough for Tev.

The evening continued as Tev asked more and more questions. Kindra kept refilling both their glasses, and at one time they both found themselves helpless with laughter. Some of the other restaurant patrons shot angry glares their way.

When the bottle was gone, Tev had almost worked up the courage to ask Kindra to come back with him to the apartment.

A moment of happy silence descended on the two of them, and Tev was just about to ask when Kindra's eyes glanced up and to the right, her tell that she had just received a message. Tev was upset. Kindra and her people were never present.

"I thought you'd turned it off?"

Kindra frowned. "I did."

In a moment, Kindra's entire demeanor changed. "It's Derreck. He pushed through my barriers. Whatever it is, it's got to be something serious."

SIX

KINDRA'S MIND was a disorganized mess. There were too many thoughts and not nearly enough space or time to deal with them all. The fact she had let herself get thoroughly drunk with Tev wasn't helping either. She had ordered her nanos to help clean out her bloodstream, but she had let herself go much further than she probably should have, and it would take them at least an hour to get her sober.

Some small part of her conscience was screaming at her about poor decisions, but the rest of her just didn't care all that much. It was the first time she had relaxed in months, and even if the evening had ended early, it had been fantastic. If she was given the chance to go back in time, she was certain she would do the same again.

Tev was fantastic company. Being in Fleet generally meant you didn't have too many friends. You moved around a lot and were gone for long periods of time. Usually, Kindra didn't mind, but when it came time to take a deep breath and think about life, there weren't always a lot of options. Asking Tev to join her had been a whim, but it had been the best call.

To Tev, everything was new. He had never had pasta, had never had wine. Everything was fresh to him, and his curiosity simply wouldn't be sated. It made Kindra think about how she was living her own life. In a way, she wished she could be more like him, amazed and questioning the parts of life that she took for granted. Tev would make a wonderful scientist.

But no matter how she tried, Fleet inserted itself into her world. Derreck met them on their way to the senate buildings. No doubt he had tracked her and Tev to meet them en route. His eyes took in Kindra and her dress, but he didn't say anything. Kindra allowed herself a sad smile. Tev wouldn't notice the dress because to him, all the clothing he saw was bizarre. She hadn't dressed up for him, but she was sure Derreck would take it that way.

Kindra closed off that part of her mind. It had been a fun evening while it lasted, but now there was business to take care of. "What's going on?"

Derreck shook his head. "I'm not sure, but whatever it is, the senate is worked up about it. There's been a tremendous increase in encrypted traffic heading to and from Haven in the past few days. There's something happening, something big, but I don't know what it is."

"Do you think it has to do with Tev?"

Her captain shrugged. "I really don't know. I worry that it does, though. My summons specifically requested that he join us, and that doesn't bode well."

Tev had overheard the entire discussion, but when Kindra looked at him, he turned away. She would have given any amount of money to know what he was thinking, but she had seen him like this before. Every once in a while, the enormity of what he was going through would hit him, and when it did, he needed a few minutes alone to think.

Kindra had to give Tev credit. He had experienced more than he could have imagined, and the world he grew up in was entirely different from the one he currently lived in. If not for his open and curious mind, he would have gone mad, or at least been frozen in fear.

They got to the senate chambers in little time. From the outside, the building was nondescript, built during a time of colonization where little thought was given to form. The building was one large rectangular block, rising three stories in the air. It was an artifact of an age before the planet had been terraformed. It still had an airlock. Various petitions had been submitted over the years to have the building torn down and replaced with a newer, more modern version, but there was a sense of history, a connection to old Earth, and even though the building was an eyesore, no one could bring themselves to tear it down.

Kindra, Tev, and Derreck entered the building together, completely unsure of what type of disaster they were walking into.

ONCE INSIDE THE BUILDING, the three of them were treated like celebrities. Kindra had only been in the senate building a handful of times before, but her memories were of security checkpoints and guards. Today they were escorted through corridors without a single security checkpoint to stand in their way. Under other circumstances, Kindra might have been honored by the treatment. Today, it made her stomach sink.

The three of them were escorted to a small room. The moment they entered, Kindra was surprised to see the other faces present. The first and most important was President Jackson herself. She had a recognizable face, with a strong jaw and sharp eyes. Kindra had never been a supporter of Jackson's policies, but she had a difficult job and kept the planets together. Arrayed to either side of Jackson were a handful of very important people. Kindra recognized Fleet Admiral Tooney and a group of top scientists.

Her first instinct was to run out of the room. Whatever was happening here, right now, wasn't something she wanted to be a part of. She wanted to go back to the restaurant, order dessert, drink another bottle of wine while talking with Tev and then go home and sleep for a day.

President Jackson made a motion for them to sit down, and Kindra and the others obeyed. Just like she was in public, she was in private. She got right to business, her voice cold and commanding.

"Thank you all for coming on such short notice. Ambassador Tev, it's a pleasure to meet you in person, although I wish the circumstances were better."

Kindra kept a blank face, but her mind was racing. It was clear Fleet didn't know what to do with Tev. This was his first official meeting in any capacity. Jackson was being polite to Tev, giving him an honorific that was a matter of no small debate. If her understanding of Jackson's character was at all accurate, it meant there was something happening and Jackson wanted Tev on her side. Kindra's heart sank even further.

President Jackson continued. "I'll get right to the point. Recently, there has been an increase in rebellion activity across the periphery worlds. Unfortunately, some of the fighting has even worked its way into central space."

Jackson continued. "The reason I've called you in is that a rebellion agent recently accessed files pertaining to your last mission. Our counterintelligence tells us that they are planning to launch a mission to Tev's home world, and the other world explored by the *Destiny*, as soon as they are able."

Kindra couldn't keep up. When she thought of the remainder of the rebellion, she thought of small groups of farmers on far periphery worlds. She didn't imagine an organized movement that had the resources to send a jumpship to Tev's home planet. It was too much to take in. She couldn't understand how everything was connected. "Why?"

It was Derreck who answered. He seemed to have already put everything together. "Weapons."

Jackson nodded, but the answer did nothing to aid Kindra's understanding. Derreck saw her look and answered before she could ask another question.

"Two things. We are certain that civilization was wiped out on the second planet due to some type of weaponry. The report talked about an advanced civilization destroyed. It would be reasonable to assume, reading that report, that there might be weaponry on the planet to be exploited. But it's your report, Kindra, they are most interested in."

Suddenly, the connections fused in Kindra's mind. If her theory about Tev's abilities was correct, it meant that there would literally be hundreds and perhaps thousands of top-rated pilots on a planet, pilots who could be easily coerced because of their lack of technology. It would be an easy matter to hold a village hostage. Hell, one armed dropship in orbit could control the entire planet. Kindra saw how her report could be interpreted.

Kindra looked to Jackson. "What are we going to do?"

Jackson pursed her lips, as though the answer was distasteful to her. "Unfortunately, there's not much we can do. Not as much as I'd like, anyhow. Fleet is already spread thin. Our resources are all committed right now. The only thing I can do is send *Destiny*."

Derreck raised his eyebrows at that. "*Destiny* isn't outfitted for that kind of duty. She's a long-range exploration vessel. Her armament is defensive at best. What kind of resources are we up against?"

It was Fleet Admiral Tooney who responded. "Fortunately, not too much. The hold-outs that haven't signed the treaty have been embargoed, so they aren't doing well. We're slowly choking them into submission. At best we're looking at a heavy jumper with two dropships, and that's if they commit everything we think they have left."

Derreck leaned back, and Kindra wished she could read his mind.

"That's still more than the *Destiny*."

"Yes, but it's not insurmountable. Frankly, this can't come down to combat. Even if we win, it's going to put a tremendous drain on Fleet resources. This is a race, pure and simple. The good news is, we should have an advantage. The distance from here to Tev's planet is shorter than what we believe they'll have to travel. We calculate that we have at least two weeks to prepare, and even so, it gives us a few weeks on-planet before they arrive."

Derreck didn't look like the answer satisfied him in the least. "And what are we supposed to do when we get there? They'll still have the ability to overpower us."

President Jackson looked directly at Tev. "That's where we need the help of our ambassador."

Kindra watched everyone at the room. Derreck made a connection that Kindra didn't. "You're planning on loading up *Destiny* with a bunch of suits, aren't you?"

Kindra almost collapsed in her chair. Fleet wanted the pilots just as much as the rebellion did. She closed her eyes tightly, trying to shut out the world. When she joined Fleet, it was because they were transitioning from combat to exploration. She had never wanted to fight. She had never wanted any of this. A few hours ago, she had decided to stand by Tev, but the urge to quit, to put it all behind her, was stronger than ever.

"Ambassador Tev, I don't know how much you've followed, but I'll try to keep this simple. Your planet is in danger. There is another group of people who are interested in coming to your planet and harming your people. Our goal is to stop them. Will you help us?"

Tev looked from Kindra to President Jackson and back, not sure what was best to say. Kindra wanted to open her mouth, to tell him to dismiss Jackson, but she couldn't do it.

Tev responded as best as he knew how. "I will do everything I can to protect my people."

President Jackson nodded, a look of relief on her face. "That is good, Tev. Thank you. Would you step outside for a moment? I need to discuss something with these two."

Tev nodded and stepped outside. As soon as the door sealed, Jackson fixed both of them with a stare. "I know you two may not like what's happening here, but there's far more at stake than just the lives on Tev's planet. We cannot allow the Rebellion Conflict to restart. If it does, I fear the civilization we have built is going to collapse. You get to that planet first, and you make sure his people join Fleet. Is that clear?"

Kindra's tongue loosened, and she was about to unleash a tirade against Jackson, but Derreck's voice was clear and loud. "Yes, ma'am. We'll be happy to make sure it happens."

With that he stood up, his hand virtually dragging Kindra up and out of her chair. He didn't even give Kindra time to tell the president to go to hell.

IT SEEMED like an unusual place to hold a meeting, but these were unusual times. The bar was dark and quiet, the sort of place Kindra associated with suspense holos. She and the rest of the crew of the *Vigilance* sat around a small table, drinks in their hands, courtesy of Derreck. They were in a corner booth, surrounded by high seat backs that absorbed the already quiet sounds of the bar.

Derreck nodded at Eleta, their systems engineer and Kindra's closest friend aboard the ship—although that wasn't saying too much in the world outside of Fleet. She put a small device on the table and thumbed it on. After a check of her personal display, she returned Derreck's nod. Kindra frowned. They were going to some extent to make this meeting private.

Alston, their geologist, was the most uninterested of the crew, but that was to be expected. He didn't seem to care about people in general, their problems at most a distraction to him. He spoke first, annoyance in his voice. "Okay, Derreck, you got us all into your favorite bar. Why all the secrecy?"

Kindra resisted the urge to slap him. As annoying as he was, Alston was an excellent geologist, and fit in well with the crew, mostly by hiding in corners and keeping busy with his own work. He wouldn't care much about Tev or the danger they had put his planet in.

Derreck chose his words with care. They were walking a fine line, and Kindra knew Derreck faced a decision that didn't have a winning scenario for him. Either he could coerce Tev's people into becoming warriors for Fleet, or he could act treasonously and have his rank and command stripped from him. She knew he didn't want either of those events to come to pass.

"We've just received new orders from Fleet. We're shipping out in a few weeks at the most."

There was a chorus of groans, but all of them were half-hearted. All the crew felt most at home when they were out in space. It was frustrating to have their leave cut so short, but all of them would rather be flying. Kindra couldn't decide if that was true for her though, not anymore.

Derreck outlined the meeting with the senate and what their orders were. He spoke bluntly. He and Kindra had left Tev in Derreck's apartment for this meeting. Despite everything that had happened, Tev was still something of an outsider among the crew, and his presence would only complicate the meeting. Derreck needed everyone to speak freely, which meant no Tev.

When he finished, there was a moment of silence around the table. Alston broke it. "Okay, so why all the secrecy?"

"I have a real problem with the way Fleet is going about this. They've all but said that we should take Tev's planet by force if we can't persuade them to join us. I'm certain Captain Absalon will have orders that say exactly that, unfortunately."

Alston's eyes drilled into Derreck the same way they peered at his precious rocks. "What are you asking, Derreck? Get to the point."

"Fine. I don't know what to do, but I'm considering disobeying orders down the road. For now, I think we need to go along with it. If we don't, we'll be scrubbed from the mission, and perhaps from duty, so they can give *Vigilance* to another crew. But depending on how everything turns out, I want to know if you'll back me up if I go against the orders of Fleet."

Everyone took a few moments to sip at their drinks. Eleta answered first. "I don't much care either way. I'll go along with whatever happens. My tour is almost up anyway, and I wasn't sure if I was going to re-up. If I get kicked out of Fleet, maybe I can finally find a nice guy and settle down." She gave a wink to Kindra, who smiled her gratitude.

Everyone's eyes turned to Alston. He didn't flinch. He didn't care about anyone else's opinion. "If I say no?"

Derreck shrugged. "I'm not doing this unless everyone is behind me. Whatever happens, I'm not going to have my crew at odds with one another. I'd probably ask for all of us to be scrubbed from the mission and see what happens."

Alston turned his glass in his hands, seeming to consider the bubbles as they floated to the top. "What if the senate is right? It may sound horrible to coerce an entire people into our service, but what if by doing so, we can save the lives of many more people?"

Kindra couldn't let that question slide. "That's a dangerous question. Once we start thinking that way, we allow ourselves to do all sorts of horrible actions for the greater good."

"But isn't that exactly the point? Maybe we need to consider the greater good instead. I'm not arguing that turning Tev's people into our soldiers is the right idea, but maybe it's the best."

Kindra was about to argue, but it was Derreck who spoke, his soft voice carrying an air of command Kindra had never heard from him outside a mission before. "I can appreciate the logic, Alston, and maybe, maybe there's something to it. But you didn't serve during the rebellion.

Both sides did horrible things, to each other and to their own people, because they believed it served the greater good. Who knows how history will judge? That's not up to me to decide. But I know this: I don't want to live in a society that willingly tramples on those who can't fight to make life better for the majority. I've seen firsthand what that looks like, and that's not where I want to live."

Alston fixed his eyes on Derreck once again, considering his words and bearing. Kindra wished she understood her shipmate better. He was relentlessly logical and seemed to be uncaring, but that assumption had been proven wrong several times before. She was certain he was a complex man, but he never let anything show.

When Alston spoke, his answer was simple. "I'm in."

Derreck nodded. "Thank you."

Eleta asked, "So, what do you want us to do?"

"For now, I want us to prepare. Eleta, I want you to do a full upgrade of your systems, both offensive and defensive. I don't even care where you find them. Find the best tools to do anything that may be necessary."

Kindra watched as Eleta's eyes lit up. Derreck had made a dream of hers come true. Kindra knew her friend had a taste for hacking systems that was sometimes hard to satisfy.

"Alston, I want you on requisitions. I would like it if we are set for any materials that may be useful, and I want the *Vigilance* to have everything she needs for exosuit repair as well."

"Kindra, your job is to upgrade the sick bay as well as you can. Our facilities are good, but I want us to be able to go further in case it's necessary. Get your hands on whatever you can. Does anyone have any questions?"

It was quiet around the table as everyone considered what they would need to do.

"Good. I do have one last item, and I don't know how you all will feel about it. I want to make Tev part of our crew."

Eleta looked up. "What do you mean?"

"We need someone to replace Kenan. I recognize how bizarre it might be to have him replaced by the man who killed him, but I think it's the right thing to do. It's time Tev becomes part of our crew. Maybe it's just symbolic, but I think it's important."

Kindra didn't respond right away. She knew she was okay with Tev being part of the crew, but this felt like a decision that needed to rest on Alston and Eleta's shoulders. The two of them glanced at each other, and some sort of unspoken agreement passed between them. They turned to Derreck and nodded.

"Good. Let's get moving. The faster we can be ready, the better off we will be."

Eleta and Alston stood up, but Derreck grabbed Kindra's arm, keeping her seated. She nodded at the others to go on without her, and she looked into Derreck's eyes.

"Yes?"

"Given our conversation earlier, I need to know what you're thinking. If you're still thinking about leaving Fleet, I won't have you on this mission."

Kindra shook her head. "I can't leave. Not now. I will see this through. After, though, who knows?"

Derreck held her eyes with his own, trying to find something there. Whatever he was looking for, he must have been satisfied. "Good. It would have been a shame to leave without you."

SEVEN

AS THEIR TRANSPORT lifted off from Haven, Tev took the time to look down on the world he was leaving. It was the second world he had ever been on, and it couldn't have been more different from the first. Tev was torn about his departure.

On one hand, he was glad. Haven was far too crowded, full of right angles and people who weren't aware, who weren't even capable of good movement. It was so far from what he was used to, and although he had spent months on the surface, he had never truly gotten used to it. More than once he had decided he wasn't made for space exploration. The universe was too strange.

On his home planet, Tev had known who he was. He was a hunter in a clan, one of the best, in his own opinion. He had been respected, at least before Kindra and her clan arrived. But out here, in the vastness of space and on another planet, he didn't know who he was. He had heard the term *alien* plenty of times, but that didn't seem like him. Kindra said he was human, just like they were.

Tev longed for his home. He wanted to be back in a

place he understood. In his previous life, before Kindra had landed, he had always wanted more, always wanted to explore a little farther. But now, he was thinking he had explored far enough.

Still, there was a small, insistent part of him that wouldn't let him settle for the easy answer. He didn't know how many times he had remembered the dream he once had, but in it Lys had told him that he needed to hunt farther than anyone had before. His rational mind told him he had already fulfilled the requirements of the vision, but the same insistent voice in his mind reminded him that judgment wasn't for him to decide.

Exploring hadn't always been fun, but he had to admit he had opened himself up to far more experiences and sensations than he had ever believed possible. There were benefits to everything he was doing. Perhaps he just needed to keep a more positive mindset.

Tev's thoughts were interrupted by Kindra's entrance onto the observation deck. They stood side by side for a while without saying anything, but it was Kindra who broke first, as it always was.

"So, now that you've been on our home world, what do you think?"

"Many things. This world is so different from my own. I can't believe that two places can be so unalike. The people are very different, too. I know you say we are all human, but even if we share the same bodies, our souls seem hardly recognizable to each other."

Kindra considered Tev's words. "I don't know if I agree. I think that really, all of us are far more alike than we care to admit. Almost all of us want the same things, it just takes a lot of work to get others to be sympathetic."

Tev dismissed the subject. He had never been one to

take such debates too seriously. There were more pressing concerns on his mind. "Kindra, what can we do to protect my people?"

Kindra's mood changed in an instant. Tev could easily see how distraught the most recent turn of events had been for her. But Tev wouldn't let her escape the question. He had come into space hoping that somehow his presence would help him protect his people back on his home planet. Now that belief was being called into question. He wanted to do something, but he didn't understand everything that was happening. If there was one person who would not lie to him, it would be Kindra.

"I'm not sure what we can do. I want your people to be safe as well, but I worry that there are very powerful people who want to use your people to serve them."

Tev contained his anger. Rage did no one any good. His intentions were already set. He would do anything, include sacrificing his own life, if it meant that he could protect his people.

TEV AWOKE from the jump meds, and his body struggled to keep up, as it always did. The first two months of travel had been dull and routine, and Tev had a hard time containing his energy. He wanted to do something, to take some action that would protect his people, but there was nothing to do. For the moment, he was nothing more than a glorified passenger.

This jump was different. As Tev was finally finding his balance on his feet again, the lights in his room dimmed and turned orange. He sank lower in case the gravity on the jumper fluctuated again. He still refused to return to his bunk.

There were no shifts in gravity, and soon the orange flashing lights turned off. Tev debated his course of action, but decided to continue normally until someone gave him further instructions. It only took a few minutes for Derreck's voice to come through the translator Tev wore. "Tev, could you come up to the bridge, please?"

Derreck's voice was calm, but that didn't mean anything. Tev knew Derreck well enough to know that he wouldn't betray any of his emotions in a stressful situation. The more chaos a man like Derreck found himself in, the calmer he would get. It was one of his most powerful traits.

Tev followed his memory, only taking two wrong turns on the path to the bridge. It was a windowless room in the center of the jumper. Captain Absalon was there, as was Derreck.

Derreck looked up from a display he was staring at when Tev entered the bridge. "Tev. Thanks for coming. There's something I wanted to show you." He handed Tev a computer pad, and Tev looked at the image on it. He saw another ship, but it looked about as different from the *Destiny* as one could. The *Destiny* looked like it had been built by a group of children, a blocky structure with attachments and additions growing out of it from all directions.

The ship Derreck had him looking at was something different. It had smooth, sleek lines, and although Tev could see that it had plenty evidence of damage, it was a design that radiated a sense of danger.

"Is this why the lights turned orange?"

Derreck nodded. "Yes. The ship is currently on the other side of the sun. It's about fifteen light-minutes away."

Tev shook his head. He didn't understand. He knew there was a difference between a light-minute and a minute, but his mind wasn't able to process just how different they were. Fifteen minutes away didn't seem like very far, especially considering how fast ships moved out here.

"Are we in danger?"

Derreck looked over at Captain Absalon, who shook his head. "Apparently the other ship isn't too worried about us. They haven't done anything to attack us yet, and we are a long way away from each other. We should be safe for now."

"Why did you call me up here?"

Derreck grinned at Tev's direct line of questioning. "I wanted to show you the ship. I've fought against her before, actually. She's named *Hellbringer*, and she's one of the most advanced jumpers in the galaxy, although that's not saying as much these days. I heard rumors she had been destroyed, but apparently the rumors of her death have been greatly exaggerated. But, there is a problem that I wanted to make you aware of."

Tev followed Derreck as he walked to another screen in the bridge. Derreck entered some commands using his neural interface, and the screen in front of them changed to a handful of points scattered across the entire screen.

"Here's the problem. We thought we would have a head start on the other ship, but if it's here, either it started far closer than we expected, or that ship can somehow jump more than twice without recharging. If that's the case, we're screwed one way or the other. We'll never be able to keep up.

"But that seems unlikely. We don't have knowledge of any technology that would allow for that to happen, so we need to assume the ship started from a different place than we were expecting."

Derreck pointed to a place on the board. One of the

points lit up. "This is where we are." Another point lit up. "And this is where your home planet is. Now, do me a favor and draw the fastest way to get from one place to another."

Tev studied the points. From their location, there was only one route that made sense. There were plenty of paths they could choose, but if they wanted to go as fast as possible, there was really only one way. Tev traced it with his finger, and Derreck nodded. "You already get it. Unless they are willing to jump into the void of space, which I don't believe they are, they will be following the same path we are. It will be a race to your planet, unless we can figure out a way to slow them down."

TEV SLIPPED into the suit like it had become his second skin, which it felt like, in a way. He remembered his first experiences, stumbling around as though he had had far too much to drink. Now he could move with a grace his old opponent Kenan would have been jealous of.

Derreck noticed it, too, as Tev took a few steps. "Damn, Tev. You've gotten really good. I've been watching most of your training feeds from a first-person perspective, but when I look at what you're able to do now, in person, well, damn."

Tev smiled at the compliment. Derreck was no slouch with the exosuits either, so the comment meant a lot to him. Derreck wasn't the type of person who gave a compliment unless he meant it.

As soon as they were ready, Derreck led them out the airlock into space. Tev, as he almost always did, took a moment to look out at the stars in all their vastness. He looked for the other ship, but couldn't see any sign of it.

"Where's the *Hellbringer*?"

Derreck laughed, and an arrow showed up on Tev's display. He followed it, but couldn't see that it was pointing to anything.

"You can't see it. We're too far away for us to see it with our eyes. I don't even think the magnification on our suits would do the trick."

Derreck detached from the hull of the *Destiny*, instructing Tev to do the same. With some very gentle thrusts, they pulled away from the jumper until they could see all of it at once. Derreck started his lecture.

"The most important thing I can teach you is this: when it comes to space combat, we don't destroy jumpers."

Tev frowned. That didn't make any sense to him. If you destroyed the jumper, then it would solve all of their problems. Why would you not? He didn't hesitate to ask.

Derreck, to his credit, didn't laugh at Tev's question. "It's because jumpers are too valuable. They take forever to build and to test, and the expense is incredible. Fleet has only built one in the past ten years. They're just too expensive and too important to destroy. You need to remember, if the jumpers get destroyed, we have no other way of connecting to each other across the galaxy."

"But why does that matter? You still have an entire planet."

"True, but remember that the vast majority of planets aren't like yours. Even Haven doesn't have the resources necessary to support all the people who live there. If the jumpers disappeared, so would much of humanity. It's too much of a risk, and so, for now, we never attack jumpers."

Tev still wasn't convinced. If the jumper was the problem, destroying it still seemed the most straightforward solution. If he could destroy the *Hellbringer*, he wouldn't hesitate.

Derreck interjected. "I know what you're thinking, and I understand how you might feel, and how, from your perspective, it might even make sense. Let me put it another way. I would happily sacrifice myself, the *Vigilance*, and all her crew if it would save your people from harm."

Tev heard the truth in Derreck's voice. The warrior was an ally, and a strong one.

Derreck continued, "But, if you did anything to destroy that jumper, I would kill you myself."

The statement rocked Tev to his core. Over the past couple of months, he had come to trust Derreck deeply, and there was no doubting that Derreck believed in what he was saying. Tev didn't understand why, but he understood he couldn't lose the captain's support.

"I don't understand, but if that is how you feel, I won't destroy the jumper."

"Good. Now, instead of being so serious, let's have some fun. Just because we can't destroy the jumper doesn't mean we can't attack it."

For the next hour, Derreck gave Tev more information than he could take in. The reason exosuits were so popular was because they made for great weapons in all the different situations warriors found themselves in. They were most often used in ground combat, but with the unspoken rule that no jumper be destroyed, they made for great ship-to-ship combat tools as well.

Derreck talked about attacking the access points of a ship to gain entry. He highlighted the parts of the jumper that warriors could strike, like the places that provided air for the ship, or the bridge. Everything that was important was usually located near the center of the ship, so most battles became about trying to reach the center of the jumper.

Once they were done out in space and on the hull, Derreck took Tev inside the ship and demonstrated some of the basics of combat in corridors, how to use the different weaponry of the exosuits to their greatest advantage.

When he was finished lecturing, Derreck smiled and looked at Tev. "Now, are you ready to practice?"

Tev was, more than anything. Listening to Derreck was fascinating, and Derreck interrupted himself frequently to demonstrate techniques first-hand. He then had Tev practice them until he got them down. But it still wasn't the same as going through the entire process.

"Here's the situation. You need to get to this room," Derreck said, as a room highlighted itself on Tev's display, "all in one piece. I've requested that this area be clear for the next hour or so, so it will just be the two of us. Your suit is set to training mode, as is mine, so you'll be able to shoot at me and our suits will simulate hits. Good luck!"

For the next hour, Tev "killed" Derreck far less often than Derreck killed him, but he learned fast, and he won the last three run-throughs. When he finally got out of the exosuit, he was exhausted, but he also knew he was ready to take on the opposing jumper. They just needed to give him the chance.

EIGHT

EVERYTHING about this mission felt off to Kindra, as though she couldn't quite awaken from her jump meds. She had joined Fleet after the end of the Rebellion Conflict, and she wasn't prepared for what life was like when combat became part of the equation. Memories of her actions on Tev's planet were never far away.

Their lives had become a strange mixture of tension and boredom, a mix that ate away at a person's rationality. Kindra remembered reading a history book when she was young, a book about seafaring navies back on Earth. She had been fascinated, because much of Fleet was based on the same principles. Now, the sea was space.

Kindra had gone far beyond the scope of her required reading, learning about ships and submarines. She had always been interested in the submarines, using the abyss of the deep ocean as their cover. She had been on edge of her seat as she read about the earliest submarines, sitting quietly in the water, hoping the more powerful ships above would lose them.

In her mind, what she was going through was almost

identical to the challenges of those first submariners. They knew the enemy was out there. Sometimes the other jumper was close enough that if you pulled up the viewscreen on its maximum magnification, you could even see it. Other times it was on the other side of a star, or far enough away that no amount of onboard magnification would allow you to see it.

Kindra also knew that like the submarines of old, facing surface ships, the other jumper was much stronger than the *Destiny*. She wasn't an expert in interstellar combat, but the one time she had asked Derreck why they didn't just attack, he scoffed as though she was suggesting that they try to build a jumpship using only a hammer and two nails.

Kindra watched the way that Derreck trained with Tev. There was a newfound intensity to the training, an urgency that had never been there before. Derreck was trying to teach Tev everything he knew about space combat, and Tev was a sponge, soaking up everything Derreck offered. In the years they had been flying together, Kindra had never seen Derreck like this. He had always been cool and collected, never perturbed by any situation, no matter how out of hand it seemed to get. But the presence of the rebellion ship was rattling him on a deeper level.

Not for the first time, Kindra wished she understood her captain better. Derreck was the reason she had remained with Fleet after her first tour, and to see him distractible and worried was difficult for her to swallow. She knew he had been a hero in the Rebellion Conflict, but there weren't any records of his deeds. All she knew was that Fleet had given him pretty much every medal they had. He never spoke of his actions, and nothing he did had ever made it to the public record. All she could do was guess.

Even though they didn't attack *Hellbringer*, they weren't being attacked by the other ship. The reasons why were an endless source of speculation among the crew. In theory, the *Hellbringer* could attack and disable the *Destiny* whenever it pleased. But they were left alone.

When Kindra had asked Derreck, he developed a far-off look before he came back to himself.

"I think there are two things happening. First, at the heart of it all, this is a race, and there's a chance they might figure out a way to win the race before we even arrive. If that's the case, they can achieve their objectives without risking any of their resources. Second, it comes down to the materials they carry on board. We don't know how much they have on that ship. It's capable of holding far more dropships and weaponry than we can, but that doesn't mean it's full. The rebellion has been largely defeated, so it could be an empty jumper. The only problem is, we won't know unless we attack. Even if the ship is largely empty, what's inside is still a huge proportion of everything the rebellion has left. Every suit and dropship they lose is a much bigger loss to them than it is to us. They'll be searching for a way to attack us with minimal risk."

What developed was an interstellar chess match, a standoff that wasn't a draw, but that didn't have a clear winner. Most of space travel and combat came down to a matter of energy. The amount of energy necessary to fold space and complete the jump was enormous, powered by the ship's capacitors. Most jumpers, including the *Destiny*, had only enough energy to make two jumps. After that, they had to recharge.

The problem was, the same energy needed to jump was used to defend the ship. *Destiny* used a full complement of missiles and point defense lasers for self-defense, but her main weapon, a single large laser, was powered by the same capacitors as the jump drive. It left Captain Absalon with a choice. He could take one free shot with the laser, but after that, if he took any more, it cost the *Destiny* a jump. Likewise, if they jumped twice in a row without recharging, they would only have one shot with the laser.

They weren't alone in their problem, though. The *Hellbringer* had the same capacitors as the *Destiny*, so she was always forced to make the same choice.

What developed from these facts was a slow and ponderous chase, an interstellar game of chicken to see who would break first. Right now, both captains were playing a conservative game. They would jump once and recharge at the next system, always leaving the maximum amount of power in their capacitors.

There were risky ways to win, but so far, neither captain seemed willing to take the chance. If they wanted to, the ships could jump into empty space, not towards an inhabited system. The option was more and more likely as they left central space and reached the frontier, but it was a chance no one wanted to take. If something went wrong, there wasn't an easy way of getting rescued. The *Destiny* carried one jump-capable emergency beacon, but even so, it would be weeks, at the very least, before they were rescued. No one wanted their jumper to break in the middle of empty space, so both captains would try to keep their ships near stars.

Regardless, the pressure of the interstellar chase was wearing on the crew of the *Destiny*. Kindra could see it on the faces of everyone she saw, and she knew that before long, something would have to happen. Humans simply couldn't keep themselves under this type of tension for long before they broke.

It was only a matter of time.

KINDRA AWOKE from her jump meds to complete chaos. The klaxons were sounding and everything in her room was flashing red. It wasn't easy to come to awareness after any jump, but to awake to such a cacophony was debilitating. Kindra fought the urge to throw up as she stumbled out of bed.

Just as she had her feet underneath her, the entire ship rocked, and the artificial gravity gave out for a moment, sending her on an arcing trajectory her mind couldn't work fast enough to process.

The commands came through her neurodisplay. Battle stations, all pilots to their exosuits. Kindra opened the channel to Tev, the vomit still rising in her throat.

"Tev, are you awake? Are you okay?"

"Yes." His voice was as calm as ever. She wasn't sure how he managed such composure under these types of situations.

"You have been ordered to get into your suit as fast as you can."

"Derreck already told me. I am on my way now."

Kindra tried to get her legs under her, but her foot gave out as soon as it touched the floor. Something was wrong with her ankle. There wasn't any way she would be able to help Tev.

"Tev, I'm hurt. It's not serious, but I won't be able to assist. You must get into your suit on your own."

"I will. Be safe."

Kindra could tell from the tone of his voice that he didn't want to be talking with her. Right now he would be focused on what he needed to do. That was okay. He had gotten into his suit on his own dozens of times. He didn't need her help, even though she liked to think he did. Her orders were clear. She needed to report to the bridge.

Derreck, now healed, was being used as an exosuit pilot, which put Kindra in temporary command of the *Vigilance*. Kindra called for a hover sled to come take her to the bridge.

While she waited, she felt herself pressed into the floor once again. Kindra wanted to call up the information on what was happening outside, but in a moment of panic, decided that she would rather not know, at least not right now. If they were making such sudden moves, it could only mean they were in combat.

When the hover sled arrived, Kindra strapped herself onto it and left for the bridge. It would take her a few minutes to get there, and she finally faced her fears and looked at what was happening outside the ship. If she came onto the bridge without knowing what was happening, her career would definitely be over.

The information she pulled up didn't reassure her. The *Hellbringer* was only a couple thousand kilometers away from them, practically spitting distance in interstellar terms. She had launched a series of missiles at the *Destiny*, and at least a few of them had gotten through the point defense lasers.

Kindra was confused. She thought that no one ever fired directly on jumpers. They were the only devices capable of connecting humanity throughout the stars. Had the rebellion fallen so far that they would stoop to such depths just to achieve their objective? Another glance at the monitor showed her that she had been incorrect. The *Hellbringer* had launched missiles at *Destiny*, but they had all been non-nuclear, and they had all been aimed at the dropship ports. *Hellbringer* wasn't trying to kill *Destiny*, she was just trying to tear out her claws. If *Destiny* couldn't launch any dropships, its capability to defend itself and attack the *Hellbringer* would be severely limited. *Hellbringer* would be more or less invincible.

Kindra had just reached that conclusion when the hover sled entered the bridge. Captain Absalon looked at her with a cool, appraising eye. "Are you fit for duty?"

"I am, sir."

"Good."

The captain turned back to his screens, and Kindra was impressed by the lack of noise and activity in the bridge. She had thought that during combat people would be yelling out orders to each other, but she realized just how foolish that was. The mechanics of space combat were incredibly intricate, and *Destiny*'s AI was far more adept at combat than any human on the bridge. There were decisions to be made, but they were few and far between. Most space combat was triggered by humans and then waged by their AIs. There was little for the captain to do but watch and issue commands as necessary.

Kindra wasn't sure what was expected of her, so she found a corner where she could be out of the way and observe the proceedings. While she did, she pulled up more information on the attack. In the last star system the *Hellbringer* had jumped out first. As had become the tradition, *Destiny* had followed as soon as their capacitors were fully charged.

When they reached the current star system, they had jumped dangerously close to *Hellbringer*. There wasn't any way of knowing exactly where the other ship had jumped to, so the AI, when making its calculations, had simply chosen one of the known jump points in the star system. Apparently this particular system had two points within close proximity to one another, and the ships had chosen them. While the humans on *Destiny* had been in their drug-induced sleep, the other ship had launched a missile attack, seeing an opportunity to gain the upper hand.

Destiny, not needing to sleep like the humans onboard, had fought against the attack as well as it was able. For the most part, it had been successful, but one missile had gotten through and struck the port where the *Vigilance* was housed. There was damage there, but nothing that couldn't be repaired in time. That must have been the explosion that happened right after Kindra had come to.

She watched as her display showed the dance of missiles happening in the space between the two jumpers. The *Hellbringer* had more missile tubes, but *Destiny*'s defense systems were managing to keep pace with the difference.

Finally, the words she had been waiting for echoed in the bridge.

"*Destiny* reports that all attacks have ceased. She wants to know if she should switch to offensive capabilities."

Captain Absalon seemed to consider his options. Kindra watched him as he glanced into the corner of his vision, checking for some information only he could see. "Does it look like they are planning on launching any dropships from any of their ports?"

"No, sir. *Hellbringer* is quiet."

There was a silence on the bridge as Absalon debated what he wanted to do. "No, don't launch an attack. Keep the ship running on code orange. We don't have the missiles necessary to get past that ship's defenses."

Kindra looked around the bridge. Was that all there was to the battle? It seemed anticlimactic. Perhaps it was just because she had watched too many holos, but in her mind, a space battle should have been far more dramatic.

Kindra's thoughts were broken by the communications officer. "Sir, we're being hailed by the *Hellbringer*."

"Put it up."

An image floated onto the viewscreen, visible to the entire bridge crew.

"Hello, Captain Absalon. My name is Captain Nicks of the *Hellbringer*. We are in the middle of periphery space, and we both know from here on out it only becomes more desolate. I'd like the chance to meet with an officer from your ship to discuss the cessation of hostilities."

Absalon didn't reply, and Kindra figured he was trying to work out Nicks' play. *Hellbringer* outclassed *Destiny*, but even though it had every opportunity to take *Destiny* for her own, she held back. There was something going on that Kindra didn't understand, and she suspected that Absalon didn't either. They weren't in a position to negotiate. *Vigilance* was trapped in her berth, and if *Hellbringer* was serious about taking the *Destiny*, there was little they'd be able to stop it. The fight would become an exosuit battle within the corridors, and there was no telling who would win that.

Absalon's voice interrupted her concentration. "You'll guarantee safe passage?"

Nicks nodded.

"Verbal, please."

"Yes, your officer will have safe passage."

Absalon nodded. Ultimately, Kindra decided, he didn't have a lot of options. He had to take what was presented to him, or he might lose his ship completely.

The viewscreen cut out, and Absalon looked around the bridge crew. "I need strategies for defeating that ship in combat. Take everything we've learned from the latest exchange. I want *Destiny* working on why *Hellbringer* hasn't tried to board us yet, and I want your most creative suggestions for taking that bastard down."

Absalon's eyes focused on Kindra. "It looks like you will be making up our diplomatic mission today."

Kindra froze, and Absalon grabbed her arm, almost pulling her out of the hover sled. Together they left the bridge and headed towards the shuttle bay.

Kindra's mind was flooded with questions, but the only one she could get out was the obvious one. "Why me?"

"Frankly, because right now you're the highest-ranking officer we have who's expendable."

Understanding stabbed into Kindra like a knife. Everyone above her on the ship was ranked as an exosuit pilot. Only she wasn't qualified for combat. They had plenty of suits. Their mission parameters had seen to that. What they needed was pilots, and she wasn't one. Absalon's logic made sense, but she didn't like it.

"What am I supposed to do?"

"Not much. Go over there and see what they want to talk about. Whatever their offer, simply say you aren't in a position to make concessions and that you must return to the *Destiny* for a final decision. If they are as good as their word, they'll let you come back."

"And if they aren't?"

Absalon paused and looked at her. "Let me be clear. I don't want to lose you, but if I have to choose between this ship and your life, my decision is easy. I've got confirmation that they guaranteed safe passage, so if they refuse it, their ship and everybody onboard becomes war criminals. Perhaps that's a risk they're willing to take, but I doubt it."

Kindra was hardly reassured by the captain's explanation. "Is there anything else?"

"Yes. Gather as much information as you can. Store the

memories in your nanos from your approach to the moment you leave the ship. Anything you see or hear might be important to us, so bring back as much information as you can."

Kindra nodded, trying to look far more confident than she felt.

THERE WAS little fanfare as they got to the shuttle bay. Kindra's hover sled brought her as close to the pilot's seat as it could, and she was able to hobble the rest of the way. Absalon had given her a small shuttle that looked like it might fall apart if she made too much noise, further increasing her discomfort with this new plan. It was clear that although Absalon didn't wish her harm, he was risking as little as possible.

Just before he closed the hatch behind him, Kindra remembered something and turned around. "I'm not a pilot. Aren't you sending someone with me?"

"Normally, yes, but I don't want to risk any pilots. It's a standard operation, and I'll have *Destiny* guide you in."

With that, Absalon shut the hatch and Kindra could feel the pressure on her ears changing. Moments later, the shuttle powered up and began a launch sequence with absolutely no input from Kindra.

The sequence didn't make Kindra feel any better. She didn't mind AIs. Modern life would be impossible without them, but all the same, she wished she had a little more control over what was happening.

The shuttle launched, and moments later, Kindra was flying between the two jumpers. She tried hard not to think about the fact she was crossing the space that less than half an hour ago had been lit up with spherical explosions and destruction. The space between two jumpers that had been in combat just a while ago was not a relaxing place to be.

But there was nothing for it, and as her shuttle approached *Hellbringer*, Kindra used the nanos embedded in her mind to start recording her memories. It wasn't something she did often, as the results were often somewhat unpredictable, but she had a good two hours' worth of recording capabilities in her head if she needed them.

As she approached the *Hellbringer*, she couldn't help but feel that the ship hadn't been named well. From the glances Kindra had seen in their viewscreens, the ship appeared to have beautiful lines, and now that she was so much closer, she saw them for herself. Many jumpers, like *Destiny*, cared little for aesthetics. They never entered atmosphere, and they were rarely called upon to execute dynamic in-system thrusts, so they were often built in whatever way was cheapest. Because of this, they weren't too pleasing to look at.

Hellbringer was different. Kindra didn't know why the ship was designed how it was, but it was a sleek ship, with graceful lines that reminded Kindra a little bit of *Vigilance*. It made her respect the ship more than she expected to. It was hard to be mad at the rebellion when they flew ships like this.

"Kindra, we're handing you over to the *Hellbringer* right now. Good luck."

Kindra didn't bother responding. The handover between the two AIs was seamless, and she didn't even notice when one computer took over from the other. Her tiny shuttle docked on the *Hellbringer* without a problem.

Once aboard, the shuttle doors opened, and Kindra was greeted by three people whom she assumed were officers. All of them wore sidearms, but none of them appeared hostile. Kindra realized she hadn't even thought about bringing a weapon with her. Another reason Absalon had chosen her: She was about as nonthreatening as a human could be.

"Ma'am, if you'd please come with us, Captain Nicks is expecting you in his office."

Kindra nodded, and they led her through the ship. Remembering her mission, Kindra did her best to look around at everything she could, trying to take in as much information as possible. She didn't have a military upbringing, so to her, everything appeared much the same as it would on any other jumper. If she hadn't actually known better, she'd say there wasn't much difference between the two ships.

She chastised herself. Again she had been led astray by holos that portrayed the rebellion in different ways. Of course the ships would run largely the same. The differences between the leftover rebellion and Fleet were political, but ultimately, there were only a few ways to run ships in space.

Kindra didn't notice anything of importance, and before she knew it, she was at the captain's office. The door opened and one officer gestured for her to step in. Mindlessly, she obeyed.

Her first glance at the room stopped her in her tracks. Captain Nicks' quarters were a joy to behold. There were relics from the past, beautiful paintings, and even a wonderful sculpture within. It was one of the most impressive collections Kindra had ever seen, and seeing it in a rebellion captain's office was disconcerting. She couldn't help but stare.

Captain Nicks himself stood to greet her. He was a man of middle age, about fifteen years older than Kindra, if she had to guess. He approached her with several smooth steps and extended his hand in a warm welcome. Kindra took it, not sure what protocol in these types of situations was.

"Welcome, commander."

Kindra frowned. Apparently the captain already knew her rank, which meant he knew who she was. He was more prepared for this meeting than she was, although that didn't take all that much.

Nick saw the look of confusion on her face. "Don't think too much of it. Fleet personnel records are public, and with just a little work, it's easy to know who everyone is on one ship. Once control of your shuttle was handed over to our AI, your personnel folder popped up, and I was able to browse it. I was interested to see who they would send over."

Kindra was at a loss. She didn't know what she was supposed to do here. "It's a pleasure to meet you, sir."

Nicks smiled, and Kindra realized just how ridiculous she must sound. Were people supposed to be polite to their enemies? All she knew was that she didn't want to say something that would result in violence.

"You can relax, commander. I've looked over your record, and it allows me to come to certain conclusions. You're a scientist, and the only reason you're second-in-command on *Vigilance* is because the previous executive officer was killed on the very planet we are now racing towards. That's a story I'd love to hear someday, but for now, let's get to the point. You were sent here by Captain Absalon because you're the highest ranking officer on his jumper that isn't exosuit-certified. He gave you instructions to be nothing more than a glorified messenger, and ultimately, he considers you to be expendable. Am I close?"

Kindra didn't know what to do. Her first impulse was to

lie, but she was a poor liar, and she couldn't come up with anything that would convince Nicks, anyway. Whatever his allegiance, he seemed a competent commander.

Nicks didn't seem to be bothered by her silence. "I'll assume I'm close. Don't worry. I would have rather had Captain Absalon come over himself so we could talk about what's really happening here, but I'll let him fear for his own safety. You can deliver a message to him."

"What do you want?"

"We know Fleet is searching for a weapon capable of destroying all opposition. I've seen our intelligence reports, and although we aren't as capable as we once were, the evidence is clear. I know you believe you've discovered a weapon that will change the balance of power in the galaxy."

Nicks' eyes bored into her, and suddenly his expression changed. "You don't know, do you?"

Kindra had started the conversation confused. It was only getting worse.

"You think this is only about protecting the alien planet, don't you?"

Nicks stood and paced, as though he had learned something that changed everything. Finally, he stopped and stared at Kindra.

"I won't go into politics with you because that's pointless. You believe in Fleet, and there's nothing I can say in the next few minutes that will change that. But, Fleet isn't as benevolent as you might think it is. They won't succeed in their real mission. You can pass that along.

"As such, my only demand is this: leave off this foolish pursuit. My ship far overpowers yours, both in terms of jumpers and in terms of the military onboard. As much as I detest Fleet, I don't want to kill people like you, Kindra, who only believe you are doing your jobs and exploring the galaxy."

Nicks paused, as though he was waiting for a response. Kindra searched for the appropriate one, but had trouble finding it. "That's it? You wanted me to come all the way over here, just so you could ask us to give up?"

Nicks nodded. "Yes. I didn't realize how little Fleet was passing on to its crew. I'm sure you're recording this, so I'll say this once. We know you have the weapon, and we know you are heading back to the planet. But, even with your weapon, we are certain we can beat you. I'd like to avoid loss of life if I can."

Everything was upside-down in Kindra's mind. Nicks kept referring to a weapon, but was he talking about Tev? Tev was interesting, but Nicks kept referring to a weapon, not a person. Regardless, Kindra decided this was an occasion where discretion was in her best interests, so she didn't say or ask anything.

"Is there anything else you'd like to mention?"

Nicks shook his head and then seemed to reconsider. "Only one other thing. The rebellion will never die, and we will never let Fleet crush us under their heel."

"I'll let Captain Absalon know."

Nicks stood again. "I'm sorry that we had to meet under such circumstances, but despite that, it was a pleasure meeting you, commander. Perhaps one day we can meet again when we can be on the same side of the table."

Kindra nodded, and before she knew what had happened, she was back on her shuttle, safely on the way to *Destiny*.

AS SOON AS SHE LANDED, she was taken to meet

with Captain Absalon in his office. Mala, Absalon, and Derreck were all there, and Kindra couldn't help but feel as though she was in front of a firing squad, one that shot stares instead of bullets. She also couldn't help but compare the difference between the two offices she'd been in. Nicks', decorated with beautiful art, and Absalon's, as bare as an office could be.

As her hover sled brought her to the command office, they downloaded all of her memories, and Kindra was glad to have them out of her head. She didn't have any desire to be human memory storage.

Destiny's AI was running an analysis of her memories, but the results would still take a few minutes. Until then, they asked her questions, more questions than she thought were reasonable. They didn't care about what actually happened. For that, they could get a much more objective view from the memories embedded in her nanos. What they wanted were impressions.

"He seemed sincere. I'll admit that I'm not the best lie detector, but there was a passion to what he was saying. At the very least, he believes he will do whatever he can to prevent us from reaching Tev's planet again."

Her answer seemed not to sit well with the rest of the leadership.

Derreck was the one who voiced their concern. "But if he wants us out of the picture so badly, why wouldn't he take his opportunities? He just had his best shot and didn't finish it."

Kindra countered. "What if he was being honest? What if he doesn't want to kill us?"

Absalon scoffed. "Sometime you should read the file on Captain Nicks. If there is one thing that is true about him, it's that he is a believer in the cause of the rebellion. He has shown on several occasions that he will do anything necessary to further that cause. On that count, he was lying to you."

More than anything, Kindra wanted to ask about Nicks belief in a weapon. Where had that idea come from? She thought that he believed in what he was saying, but to the best of her knowledge, there was no weapon on the ship that should have the rebel captain worked up. However, she decided now was not the time to ask. It was the type of question that she wanted to ask Derreck alone, because he would give her the straightest answer.

Mala floated an idea across the table. "Do you think he wants us to get farther out into frontier space? If so, any attack he makes will be far more detrimental to us. It will take us longer to get word back to command, giving him more time to do whatever he plans on doing."

Absalon nodded. "It's the only thing I can think of that makes any sense. On the other hand, he'd only be buying himself a few extra weeks, which doesn't seem like that big of a deal when we look at the grand scheme of what they are trying to accomplish. Every jump he lets us take is a jump that we get closer to our goal, and it increases his risk. It still seems like it would make far more sense for him to attack now when he's got an opportunity he can't beat."

Ever since Kindra's return, *Destiny* had been moving away from *Hellbringer*. No matter what happened, they wanted to have more space between the two ships. *Hellbringer* hadn't responded at all, allowing the distance to increase without concern.

There was a beep, and everyone at the meeting received a notification that the AI had finished analyzing Kindra's memories. Absalon flipped through several highlighted sections before stopping at one in particular. It was an image, clearly enlarged and enhanced from Kindra's original memory. She didn't remember seeing it at all, but something had happened in the corner of her vision.

The image was of a hanger bay, and inside was something Kindra wouldn't have believed possible. There were exosuits. More exosuits than Kindra had ever seen in one place before. She queried the AI, which counted 93 suits, but suspected based on the estimated dimensions of the hanger that there were at least 144 present. Kindra sat back in her hover sled, astounded by the number.

How had the rebellion managed to get their hands on that number of suits? Kindra didn't know how many Fleet had, but 144 would be a substantial percentage. Another query to the AI let her know that at present, *Destiny* had 36 suits onboard, but only 24 pilots. If it came to combat, the *Hellbringer* would overwhelm them with almost no difficulty at all.

Derreck whistled to himself. "Damn."

Absalon sat back in his own chair, clearly concerned. "If they have that type of force, we don't stand any chance against an assault. They could take us out whenever they pleased. Nicks wasn't lying about that, apparently."

Derreck responded. "They may have that many suits, but what if they don't have the pilots? What if they are in a situation much like ours?"

Absalon looked up. "Is that a risk you are willing to take? Even if they only have pilots for half those suits, they would still destroy us. We know that *Hellbringer* is the last rebellion combat jumper. It would make sense if they placed all their eggs in one basket and focused their efforts."

There was silence around the table as they pondered what it was they were supposed to do, so far from any support.

NINE

TEV HAD RESPONDED to Derreck's summons, and now he found himself back on the *Vigilance* after a long hiatus. On the *Destiny*, there wasn't much reason to visit the docked dropship, but Derreck had found one.

The rest of the crew were present as well. Eleta and Alston were there, and Kindra and Derreck came aboard only a few minutes after Tev. He wondered what Derreck was up to. He knew they were being chased by another ship, knew that they were looking at possibly having to fight, but none of that would explain why they were meeting here, of all places.

Derreck looked at Eleta, who nodded to him. The captain wanted to make sure no one was listening. What was he up to?

Derreck answered the question himself by getting right to the point. "Everyone, I'm worried about what is going on aboard this ship."

No one responded, waiting for him to continue. Tev instinctively looked at Alston, whose face was impassive.

"It's hard for this not to sound paranoid, and maybe it is,

but all of you have heard about the intelligence Kindra received when she went aboard the *Hellbringer*. They have the strength necessary to wipe us all out, and yet they don't do it. I've talked to Absalon about it several times, but I haven't been satisfied with his answers. Captain Nick referred to a special weapon when Kindra visited his ship. Everyone seems to think he was talking about Tev, but I'm just not convinced. I think there's more going on here than we are being told."

Alston spoke up, an action that didn't surprise Tev. He knew the man studied rocks, and the way his mind worked was remarkable. He wasn't burdened by concerns for ethics like so many people were. Results were all that mattered to him.

"Derreck, please be specific. What do you want?"

Derreck looked around. "The reason I asked you here is because I want to learn more. Captain Absalon will not tell us anything we don't already know. Perhaps I'm overreacting, but my duty is to Fleet and the safety of the planets that it protects. I'm not losing sight of that."

"So what do you want us to do?" It was Eleta, leaning forward to hear what would happen next.

"First, I want to reaffirm that we're all in this together. We're far, far away from anyone that can help us, and I need to know that everyone here has each other's backs. If not, we might as well not even try. What I'm proposing is a method for us to learn what's going on. Once we know more, than we decide, as a group, what actions we want to take. That's the deal. But whatever we decide, we all abide by."

Everyone looked around the table at each other, their gazes eventually falling on Alston.

He swept his hand at them, as though trying to clear

them all away. "Fine. I don't know if I agree, but I'll back you all up. You all can trust me."

Tev couldn't help but smile to himself. Alston was a pain, but he was as much a part of the crew as anyone else. They wouldn't act without him, and he wouldn't allow himself to be left behind. It was an interesting dynamic that Tev enjoyed observing.

"So, what's the plan?" asked Kindra.

Derreck smiled. "Well, I was thinking we could send in a spy." He glanced over at Tev, who couldn't figure out at what was in store for him.

TEV WASN'T certain if Derreck was just very good at guessing the moves of his opponents, or if he had some way of being able to tell the future. Either way, everything he had predicted came to pass.

About a week after the meeting on the Vigilance the call came through his earpiece. Captain Absalon asked for Tev to come visit in his office. Tev had never been there before, but he called Kindra and she was able to guide him there. He rehearsed the checklist of everything he needed to do, making sure he was prepared for whatever happened. It really wasn't all that complicated, but he was nervous all the same.

Tev entered Absalon's office shortly after he was asked to appear. Absalon turned around from the viewscreen, which displayed a large map. Tev had been studying the same map over and over, because it showed just how close they were getting to his home planet. He was looking forward to the smell of boar roasting over a fire, the juices slowly cooking as the meat was spun, the fat crackling in the fire. Kindra and her kind may be far more advanced than his own, but it didn't mean they had everything figured out.

Absalon's office was one of the most barren rooms Tev had been in since leaving Haven. Most people filled their offices and spaces with pictures, holos, and trinkets. Tev had noticed that even though most people could project images using the machines in their bodies, most preferred physical items in their own spaces. He understood. The virtual items they had were useful, but they didn't carry the same emotional impact as something physical, something you could touch.

Tev stepped up to the map, and as he did, the viewscreen changed to an image Tev had never seen before. It looked like a map, but of what, Tev wasn't certain.

Absalon stepped next to him. "It's beautiful, isn't it?"

Tev nodded. "What is it?"

"It's a map of old Earth. This is where all of humanity came from. It's where you came from too, if your genetics are any indication."

They took a moment, and Absalon showed him the map in more detail. He pointed out the different lands and said a bit about them all. There had been great civilizations, and he said the map they were looking at was a map of the entire planet. Some of the nations had covered more land than Tev could imagine ever walking. And the water. There was more water than he had imagined possible, but water you couldn't drink.

Tev marveled at everything he was learning. It was a constant temptation to think of everything as a legend, to think of everything in the same way he thought of Lys and her endless hunt. No one knew for sure if Lys was real. Tev had always believed in her, but wasn't sure if she had been an actual person. But everything Absalon was telling him was something true, something his people had concrete proof of.

Eventually, Tev had to stop thinking about it. If he thought too much about all the new information, it became overwhelming. He needed to change the subject and think about something else.

"What can I do for you, Captain Absalon?"

Absalon motioned to his desk and indicated the two of them should sit down. It was another custom Tev still hadn't gotten used to. On his planet, if something important needed to be discussed, it was discussed around a fire, standing up, or while walking from place to place. Never sitting down. Sitting was a posture of ease, not suitable for important words.

As they sat, Tev looked around the office. In one of his pockets there was a small disk he needed to leave on Absalon's desk. It was a simple task, complicated only by the fact that Absalon couldn't see Tev placing it, and if their plan was going to work, couldn't notice it any time soon. Tev was dismayed to see that Absalon's desk was spotless and clean, with no good place to hide the disk. Eleta had made one side adhesive, but Tev still needed to physically plant it some place Absalon wouldn't see.

Absalon began by thanking Tev for everything he had done, but changed his tone quickly when he realized Tev wasn't paying much attention.

"Tev, there are going to be serious things happening at your planet soon, and I want to make sure you are ready for them."

Tev focused his attention on Absalon, which was all that the captain seemed to want. He explained what Tev already knew through Kindra, that the other people wanted to come to his planet and make the hunters fight for them.

Eventually, Absalon got to the point.

"Tev, I want you to fight with us. I know that *Vigilance* has adopted you as crew, but I'd also like to post you with *Destiny*. We will have a battle on our hands soon, and with you fighting with us, we will have a much better chance. You'll be able to pilot an exosuit in battle and help protect your people in the process."

Tev didn't understand all the politics involved. He had always assumed that if it came to a battle, he would be used. A clan didn't only send out one hunter when threatened by a whole pack of large cats. They sent out all the hunters. He assumed Kindra and her people would do the same.

Regardless, there was no question in his mind what he would choose. "Of course."

Absalon's reaction wasn't exactly what Tev expected. There was relief there, but there was something else, something Tev couldn't identify.

"Thank you, Tev. I'm going to put you in a squad with Major Aki, who will command your group. I promise that with your help, Fleet will protect your people for all time. You're doing something great."

That was starting to lay it on a bit thick. Tev wasn't sure what was happening, but he could tell when someone wasn't being completely honest, and Absalon wasn't.

Absalon stood up and turned back to the viewscreen behind his desk. Tev seized the opportunity, slipping the disk underneath Absalon's desk and holding it there to make sure it stuck. It did, and Tev masked the movement by standing up, mirroring Absalon's action. Absalon turned around, but he didn't turn around fast enough to notice anything untoward. Tev was in the clear.

Absalon motioned Tev to come around the desk and join him at the viewscreen, which Tev did. The captain switched the image back to the original map showing the route to Tev's planet. Absalon pointed out Tev's homeworld and smiled. "Don't worry, you're almost home."

Tev nodded, a fake smile on his own face. He knew they were almost home, and was excited for that possibility. But he worried about what would happen when they got there. He wasn't sure if his arrival would herald a new age for his people, or if it would bring about their doom.

TEN

KINDRA FELT as though she was a dry twig, ready to snap at any moment. It was a bizarre feeling, because from most anyone's perspective, the mission so far had gone as well as could be expected. Granted, they were being trailed by the *Hellbringer*, but so far there hadn't been any casualties.

But the tension was seeping into her soul. She had joined Fleet for a simple purpose: she wanted to explore the galaxy. She wanted to find places where life could thrive. It had never occurred to her how dangerous it might be if all her dreams came true.

Exploring Tev's planet, at least at first, had been the pinnacle of her career, of her life. To find a planet that supported diverse ecosystems had been a dream come true, a dream that she had never even been able to give her whole heart to because of just how unlikely it was. It had turned into a nightmare as first contact threatened to become a war, but on the whole, she still felt a sense of accomplishment for their discovery. She had thought the worst was over.

It seemed, though, that the worst was yet to come. In her mind, what Fleet needed to do was straightforward.

They needed to protect Tev's planet the way they protected natural spaces for a while back on old Earth. Ideally, they would minimize contact and build up a relationship slowly, ensuring that Tev's people had a chance to thrive and grow with only as much interference as they chose.

The universe seemed to conspire against that idea, though. Kindra was concerned about the current actions of Fleet, but she had believed in Fleet for most of her life, and it was hard to shake the belief that they had everyone's best interests in mind. She had served for several years, and the people she had grown to know and love were good people, capable of making good decisions. Derreck was the epitome of that belief. She knew he had a past he didn't want to talk about, but she also believed that same past was what gave him the wisdom to make good decisions today.

When the remnants of the rebellion came into play, though, everything was thrown into confusion. Fleet's actions became more debatable, and she was questioning everything she believed in. Was she on the right side of history? Were they the good or the bad? The fact that she couldn't answer the question easily tormented her daily.

The problem was compounded by the knowledge that everything was on a timer. They were only a handful of jumps away from Tev's planet, and there was less and less time to decide. The end game was approaching, and Kindra wasn't sure which side of the table she was playing on. She wasn't even sure what pieces were on the board, or how she could win.

Derreck's most recent message to her wasn't easing her mind, either. He had called her to his quarters, an urgency in his voice. There was only one reason she could think of. Their bug in Captain Absalon's office must have finally picked up on something they could use, or at least, something they needed to do. Kindra checked her display and saw that no one else was heading towards Derreck's quarters, so whatever he was debating was between just the two of them.

The door opened to her, but when it closed again, she heard the lock cycle behind her. Derreck held up his hand for a moment, switching on a device Kindra recognized as something Eleta had scrapped together. It would jam any potential listening sensors. Only once it was on did Derreck turn to her.

"Thanks for coming."

"What's wrong, Derreck? You've got me worried. Did you find something about the weapon that Nick was talking about?"

Derreck nodded. "I think so. Eleta's hacking has unlocked a series of files I have never encountered before. We're not all the way through the encryption on them yet, but they are reports from Mala's mission. They found something on that other planet that they aren't talking about. I hope to figure out what that is soon enough, but my gut tells me it's the weapon Nick was referring to.

"That's not why I called you here. I found something else, something bigger, and I need to talk about it with someone."

Kindra frowned. "That's not terrifying," she said, the sarcasm dripping from her voice. It wasn't like her, but Derreck was always their rock. Her rock. If there was something happening he wasn't sure about, something he needed to discuss, she wasn't sure she wanted to be part of it. Perhaps she'd made the wrong decision in coming on this mission. Maybe she should have remained on Haven.

But her path had brought her here, and she was a firm believer in the idea that even if you couldn't change your circumstances, you were always in control of your actions. She wouldn't run away. She couldn't. So, she sat down, leaning forward, ready to listen.

Derreck took a deep breath and spoke slowly. "I found plans for the colonization of Tev's planet in Captain Absalon's secure files."

For a moment, Kindra didn't feel anything. The enormity of what Derreck was saying seemed to knock the emotion right out of her. It was a temporary shock though, and anger found its way back to her heart quickly enough. She resisted the urge to scream, her voice coming out in a forced whisper instead.

"Are you serious?"

Derreck nodded.

"What do you know?"

"The plans haven't been developed too far, yet, but the outline is there for a plan of colonization. They've used all of our survey data and mapped out cities and farms. It would be the first major self-sufficient colony ever."

"And Tev's people?"

"That the big question mark on their plan. I've seen everything from discussions of possible treaties for land to extermination."

Kindra couldn't sit down any longer. She stood up, her legs covering the short spaces between walls in just a stride or two before turning around. It must have looked ridiculous, but she didn't care. She needed to move or she wouldn't be able to think.

"What can Fleet be thinking?"

Derreck spoke softly, not because he thought he was hiding from surveillance devices, but because he wanted Kindra to calm down. "I know how they think, Kindra, and I can see them doing something like this."

She stared lasers at him. "Explain it to me, then."

"You'd know it too, if you thought about it, even a little."

Kindra did think about it, but she still couldn't figure out what Derreck was talking about. She shook her head.

Derreck took another deep breath and exhaled. "You need to step back and look at the big picture. Right now, so many people seem to think that everything is going well, but very few people seem to understand how tenuous it all is. From one perspective, there have never been more humans than there are today. We live on hundreds of planets scattered across lightyears. You'd think we are more resilient than we've ever been. But that's not true. Name one planet that is entirely self-sufficient with a large human population."

It dawned on Kindra. Of all the planets that came to mind, there were maybe only one or two that were self-sufficient, and they were very small. Everyone required trade.

"That's why Fleet thinks how it does. Since the war, almost every jumper we have left is being used to maintain the trade that keeps the planets alive. Haven would be gone inside of a month if it couldn't trade. Other planets are even worse off. Terraforming will someday change that, but that day is still hundreds of years away. Until then, humanity is hanging by a thread out here in the stars. Tev's planet is valuable. More valuable than anything we can imagine. It's a planet that doesn't require any terraforming. We can move there next week and start building. It could be self-sufficient from the beginning, become the new cradle of humanity.

"Trust me, if Fleet could spare more jumpers, I can guarantee they'd all be heading this way with colonists. Hell, Fleet may already be working on plans like that. If not for the fact that information travels slowly through space,

I'm sure they'd have already recalled all the jumpers like *Destiny* that are out exploring the stars."

Kindra sat back down, making sure her jaw was closed. Derreck was right. She had never considered just how tenuous an existence humanity was hanging on to. Humans were everywhere, but if the network of jumpers failed, many planets would simply cease to exist. Even in the best case, their populations would be wiped out and they would have to slowly rebuild. They'd be isolated, possibly forever. The idea was terrifying to her.

"But, Derreck, we can't just destroy a people!"

"Kindra, I know what you're saying, and trust me, there's a part of me that agrees. I want to live in a galaxy where all life is honored and protected, but I also understand the utilitarian argument. You've estimated the population of Tev's planet to be a few thousand at most, right? Maybe that's worth the cost of humanity's future."

Kindra almost slapped Derreck, but held off. "You can't really believe that, can you? Lives are so much more than numbers, and our future is more than a balance sheet."

Derreck held up his hands. "I know you hate the idea, and I do too, but I'm trying to be rational, trying to decide what the best thing to do is, here."

Kindra huffed and fought the urge to drive her fist against the wall. It would feel good, emotionally, but it would only hurt her hand. Derreck didn't say anything else, at least not for a few moments. When he did speak up, his voice was changed, filled with an uncertainty Kindra had never heard in all the years of serving under him.

"Kindra, I'm not sure what to do. The records are just plans and ideas. I can't find any evidence anything has actually begun, but I feel a responsibility, a need to do right by Tev and his people, but also by Fleet. I don't know where to stand, here."

Her captain's words seemed to shift Kindra's view, just slightly, and she saw everything from a different angle. Derreck wasn't trying to rationalize Fleet's ideas to justify them, he was torn himself and trying to decide what to do. He was trying to make the best, most rational choice. His head hung limp off his shoulders, and Kindra knelt in front of him to meet his eyes. In a rare moment, a second of courage, she gently grabbed his chin and lifted it so that their eyes met. She stared into his eyes and saw the confusion and the doubt.

Her voice was soft, but as firm as steel. She wasn't sure where the words came from, but she spoke them with a conviction that surprised even her. "I don't know what the right answer is, Derreck. But I do know this: our futures are shaped by the choices we make, the decisions about how we want to live. If we want a galaxy where all human life is honored and protected, that means we need to make the choices that bring that future about."

Her words seemed to have the desired effect. Derreck's shoulders and back straightened. He looked forward instead of down, his eyes focusing off into the distance.

"You're right, of course. Thank you."

Kindra stood back up, feeling suddenly awkward for kneeling in front of Derreck that way. They had always respected each other, but they had never been close, not like that.

She could see the change in him. His mind was racing, and she waited for him to tell her what conclusions he had come to.

Derreck stood up. "I'm still not sure exactly what to do,

but we can handle one problem at a time. First, we can't tell Tev any of this."

Kindra was just about to object when Derreck interrupted her. "It's not about keeping secrets from him. It's about keeping him safe. Right now, he's valuable to Fleet, because he can shift the will of his people once we get to his planet. But if he gets any wind of Fleet's ideas, he becomes a liability to them. We will be in a combat situation in a few jumps, and if Absalon wanted to get rid of him, it would be far too easy to do. For now, he needs to stay in the dark, for his own safety."

Kindra didn't like it, but she saw the wisdom in Derreck's suggestion. "Very well. For now, we can keep it from him, but if it becomes an emergency, we need to let him know."

Derreck nodded his agreement.

"Is there anything else we can do?"

Derreck shrugged. "Maybe. I'm going to keep digging through the data files I can get my hands on, and I'll try to do some more suit training with Tev, even though he's to the point where he should be teaching me. I want you to try to think outside of the box. You're the one who brought the crew back after Kenan defected. I'm a military man, and I think like one. I'm sure you'll come up with something I never would have considered."

Kindra smiled, a grim smile forced by circumstances. There was nothing else to say, so she took her leave, her mind racing with ways to try to save Tev and his people.

ELEVEN

TEV WOKE up from the jump as disoriented as always. Despite the frequent practice, coming out of the sleep was still disconcerting. He had asked Kindra how the drugs worked, and while she had explained them, the concepts were too far beyond his understanding. All he knew was that he went to sleep, and when he woke up, it took far too long to feel normal again.

This jump was normal, at first, but soon fell into chaos. Orange lights flashed in his room, and Tev knew that the event they had all feared was coming to pass. They were still several jumps away from his planet, his home, but with each jump the expectation of attack had grown. They were far from central space now, and even the periphery was a distant memory. They were a place where no help could come.

There was a lot beyond Tev's control. He didn't understand jumpship combat, and he certainly didn't understand how the ship worked. There nothing he could do now about any of those facts. But he could pilot a suit. That was something he could do better than almost anyone, and he felt a mix of excitement and fear as he walked towards the hangar where it was stored.

Derreck's voice spoke into his ear. "Not so fast, Tev. Things will happen slowly for a while here. Come to the briefing room, first."

He gave Tev directions, and Tev turned around, finding himself in the briefing room a few minutes later. Other pilots were gathering there, and when everyone arrived there were 24 of them, including Tev. It seemed like such a small number. Tev had been part of much larger hunting parties. This one seemed puny in comparison.

Captain Absalon stepped into the room with Derreck right behind. Derreck grabbed a seat next to Tev while Absalon went to the front of the room and pulled up a display.

"Okay, ladies and gentlemen, the moment we've all been waiting for is finally here. *Hellbringer* was here before us, and she's burning towards us at a decent speed. Although it's too early to tell for sure, it looks like we're going to be dealing with a classic boarding scenario." Absalon looked over at Tev. "Tev, that means the other ship is going to get very close, close enough that we can't use our shipboard defensive weapons. Then they'll send over their suits and try to take over our ship.

"I want to take the party to them, first. The intelligence we've collected indicates they've got quite a few advantages on us, but there is one element we still have, and that's surprise. They are taking the offensive, and will expect us to take defensive positions inside our ship. Instead, we're going to attack them first. Hopefully we can catch them while a bunch of their suits are still in hangars and launch tubes. If so, maybe we can take them with their pants down."

Tev listened intensely. He didn't understand the

strategies of space combat, but he understood striking first. He nodded in appreciation. Absalon was a bold commander, and Tev respected that.

"We're going to separate the two commands. As much as I'd love to keep everyone together on the attack, I don't feel confident sending everybody over there. Instead, all three lances in Aki's command will attack the *Hellbringer*, with support with one final lance from Commander Jen's command. The other two lances will hang out back here, covering the different entry points. I won't lie to you. We'll be spread thin, but it's the best balance we can come up with. Your commanders have specific orders for you."

Tev looked over at Derreck, who was upset. As the meeting disbanded, Tev saw that Derreck was looking at something using his display that Tev couldn't see.

Finally, Derreck looked over at Tev. "Come with me."

Tev followed, wondering what made Derreck so frustrated. Together, they approached Captain Absalon. Derreck didn't hesitate. "Sir, I think it's a mistake to send Tev in."

Absalon looked back at Derreck, and a look seemed to pass between them that Tev didn't understand. Something was happening under the surface, something that wouldn't be spoken by either of the men, but something far more important than Tev's assignment.

"Commander, Tev has been training with Aki's lance for months now. That lance is part of the attack on the *Hellbringer*. Tell me how that's a mistake."

"Sir, he's not just a pilot. He's also our only ambassador to an entire planet. If something happens to him, it will cause even bigger problems down the road. Let us switch spots. He can be in a defensive position here, and I'll join his squad on the attack on the *Hellbringer*."

"Denied, commander. I hear you, but let me remind you that Tev is potentially our best pilot. If we don't stop *Hellbringer*, it's not going to matter whether he's the only ambassador to the planet. We'll never make it. We need to keep our priorities in line. Do you understand?"

Tev looked at Derreck. It seemed obvious that Derreck was a very long way away from understanding, but he bit his lip and nodded.

Absalon turned his back to them. "Good. You're dismissed."

As the two men walked towards their exosuits, Derreck seemed lost in thought. Tev needed to know what he was heading into, though. "What was that all about?"

Derreck glanced at Tev and then looked straight forward again. "I am not convinced Fleet has your best interests at heart, Tev. I don't really want to say anything else, but stay alert out there. Stay safe, stay with your team, and no matter what happens, don't try to be a hero. You need to stay alive, more than anything else."

Tev nodded. He wasn't afraid of death, not really, but it wasn't something he was going to go searching for. When they got to their exosuits, Tev saw that Kindra was at his, waiting for him.

As he began suiting up, he saw that Kindra was nervous as well. It was clear there was something happening he wasn't being told about. He met Kindra's gaze and held it, repeating the same question he had asked Derreck.

Kindra shook her head. "It's a lot to say, Tev, and I'd tell you, but they want you on station in less than three minutes. Derreck and I are worried that Fleet might be almost as bad as the rebellion ship. We're not quite sure what to do, but there is one thing we know. We need you with us, so even though you are going out to fight, we need you to stay alive."

Tev laughed softly to himself. "That's poor advice for a man going into combat."

Kindra's smile at Tev's joke became a frown. Before she put on his helmet she leaned forward and gave him a quick peck on his cheek. She looked embarrassed by it, and Tev was completely surprised, so there was an awkward silence between the two of them as she put on his helmet. When his suit checks were complete, she gave him one last glance. "Be safe, Tev."

"I will. Do everything you can here. I trust you to watch my back."

Kindra nodded, and Tev walked towards the launch bays, taking a deep breath before his first fight in space.

TEV WAS on the launch pad with the rest of his squad, but for now, there was very little happening. They had needed to hurry so they would be ready when the moment came, but the moment seemed a long way off in Tev's mind. If not for his years of waiting for prey, he thought he would have gone mad with anticipation.

Kindra's breathing was a steady reassurance in Tev's helmet. She had boarded the *Vigilance* and was in the command chair, promoted yet again so that Derreck could be used as an exosuit pilot. She would be with him the entire time.

In the corner of his viewscreen, a display started counting down from two minutes. They were getting ready to launch. Tev smiled, and all four members of his squad grabbed hold of the small rocket they were clustered around. Tev had never used one before, but he was excited for the opportunity.

As the time marched down to zero, Tev followed the

lead of his squad by crouching down while holding on to the small rocket. When the timer hit zero, the launch bay door opened with one lightning-quick motion. Tev and his team were sucked out into the vacuum of space, the initial shock dampened by the suit itself. If it had just been Tev holding on to the rocket, he wondered if his arm would have gotten torn off.

He understood the basics of what was supposed to happen next. The space in between the two jumpers, although only a few kilometers wide, was some of the most dangerous space around. Tev and his squad needed to get to the *Hellbringer* as quickly as possible, hence the violent ejection and the rocket.

Captain Absalon was trying to give his squads the best chance possible. Moments before Tev and the others launched, he had ejected tons of debris, reflective material, and decoys into the space between the ships. At the same time, *Destiny*'s AI launched an all-out assault on *Hellbringer*'s AI, trying to scramble, jam, and cause as much trouble as possible.

All of this was designed for one purpose. With the help of the rocket, Tev and the other exosuits would have less than a minute between the ships. But while the jumpers would never destroy each other, they would be happy to destroy any suits in space. As Tev watched, a missile struck out from *Hellbringer*, exploding debris off to their right.

At this point, all Tev could do was hold on for the ride. The rocket they held on to was nothing more than fuel, nozzles, countermeasures, and a simple targeting computer. It bobbed and weaved through space in near-random patterns, trying to balance safety and speed in their boarding.

With nothing to do, Tev just watched. He saw debris

being vaporized and fired upon, and at one point he was certain he saw another suit floating through space, lifeless.

It was terrifying, not being able to do anything. He knew the machines in charge of this part of the battle were faster and smarter than him, but he couldn't help feeling as though he should be doing something. Waiting for death to take him was not something he was very good at.

The seconds between the ships passed both in an instant and in an eternity, but before Tev could rationalize what was happening, the other members of his squad were turning their bodies, preparing for a hard landing. Tev did the same, pointing his feet toward the rapidly growing *Hellbringer*.

It was hard to measure speed in space, but Tev absorbed the impact with his exosuit-enhanced legs. Operating quickly, his squad double-checked their landing location to ensure they were on the right part of the *Hellbringer*. After confirming the correct touchdown, they placed the rocket up against the hull, transforming it into a small breaching charge. Tev stepped back with the rest of his team and watched as there was a short flash, and then there was a hole in the hull. One by one they stepped into the hole, their magnetic boots pulling them down into the ship.

Tev was the last, and before he dropped, he took one last look at space. There was some debris still remaining between the two ships, but it was hard to believe they had just passed through some of the most dangerous space around. Tev was reminded of accidentally passing through the lair of a predator once when he was younger. He hadn't even known the danger he was in until afterwards.

Bringing himself back to the present, Tev dropped into the ship, his weapons out, ready to fight.

BY THE TIME Tev came down, the rest of his team had already formed the perimeter, their arms extended. The weapons they were using were the same ones Tev had used in his fight with Kenan back on his home planet. The barrel was attached to his arm, and the targeting reticle was one of the few things he could see on his display.

They waited for a moment, and Tev figured that Aki was looking over schematics and using his sensors to see if anyone was coming. If their intelligence was correct, they should have some fierce fighting ahead of them.

Tev could almost hear the frown in his commander's voice. "Everything looks clear. All sensor readings show that the hallways are empty."

Tev understood Aki's fears. They had been expecting heavy resistance. If no one was here to fight them where were all the suits? Where were their opponents?

The lack of resistance seemed to confuse Aki. For a few moments they all stayed in position, scanning their fields of fire while their commander relayed his findings back to the *Destiny* for instructions. After a few moments, he spoke again. "Okay. They aren't on *Destiny* either, so we don't know what's going on. Our orders are to keep heading towards the bridge and try to take the ship over."

The members of Tev's squad all looked at each other, nervousness on their faces. To Tev, it was just like being in any other hunting party. When they encountered the unknown, fear soon set in.

The commander read their body language, even in the exosuits.

"I know, I don't like it either. We're going to keep this simple. Move slowly and make sure you're checking your corners. I refuse to walk us into an ambush. Is that clear?"

There was a chorus of assent, and the squad started

moving. Tev took the rear, walking backwards and making sure that no one came up behind them.

They walked the hallways, strangely silent. Even Tev, with his limited understanding of the functions of jumpers, knew something was wrong. Walking the hallways of the *Destiny*, you always passed somebody, no matter what time it was. Jumpers were busy places, and to walk through empty hallway after empty hallway was disturbing.

Eventually, that fact got to Tev's commander as well. He called for a stop.

While Aki got in touch with Captain Absalon, Tev tried to contact Kindra, who responded instantly.

"How far are we?"

"If your objective is the bridge, you're just over halfway there. You haven't seen anyone either?"

Tev shook his head, then remembered that she wouldn't be able to see the gesture. "No. It's eerie, like being in an empty ship."

"I don't like it, Tev. Be careful."

It was obvious advice, but he knew she didn't know what else she could say. He focused his attention as Aki's voice came through his helmet. "Our orders are to keep going. None of the other teams have encountered resistance yet, either. I'm not liking what's happening here. We're going to move even more slowly, clear?"

The chorus of assent came back, but this time it was softer. There was nothing more challenging than facing an opponent you didn't understand. Tev knew exactly how it felt. It made a predator feel like they had become the prey.

Two more empty corridors, and one of Tev's teammates called for a stop. "Hold on, all. I've got something faint on my sensors here. I'm reading trace amounts of explosive residue."

Aki didn't hesitate. "Everyone, back ten meters." Tev became the front of the line as the group retreated the way they had come.

Tev paused about ten meters away from where he had been, and the rest of the team came to a stop behind them. Each of them turned rapidly, trying to see if anything was coming their way. But the corridors were as empty as ever.

Tev's commander turned to the woman who had reported the explosive residue. "Use one of your snoopers."

The woman, Murphy, nodded and reached to her waist, where several balls were strapped. She detached one, pressed a button, and tossed it gently forward. The snooper, which Tev had never seen before, floated in the middle of the hallway, held up by some force Tev didn't see or understand. Slowly, it moved forward.

Tev didn't want to look foolish in front of his team, so he asked Kindra instead. "Kindra, what's a snooper?"

"It's a small device that has a lot of sensors on it. They're expensive, so we don't use them too often, but it can find things while keeping your team safe."

Tev nodded, forgetting again that Kindra couldn't see. She seemed to understand though, and remained silent as Tev watched the proceedings.

The commander spoke, "Murphy, what readings are you getting?"

Murphy replied. "I don't like it, commander. I'll feed you the info, but there's something..."

Murphy's words were cut short as the hallway in front of them exploded, filling with fire that rushed towards Tev. Tev, caught completely off guard, didn't know how to react, and the flame washed over him before he could make a move. He could feel the heat, but it dissipated quickly, and as soon as his sight came back to him, he was looking at a gaping hole in the hallway. Surprisingly, he was unharmed.

His first instinct was to check his team, but he was in the rear and could see easily. All four of them were standing. Aki, who had been in the front of the squad, turned around, and Tev saw there was shrapnel sticking out of his suit in at least a dozen places. Tev worried for a moment that perhaps his commander had been killed, but he seemed to move without problems. None of the shrapnel had pierced his armor. But Tev knew, if they had been closer to the explosion, at least some of them would have died.

Aki's voice came over all their helmets. "General message to all teams. *Hellbringer* contains traps. Explosive devices utilizing shrapnel. Proceed with caution."

Switching back to his team's frequency, he spoke again. "Why would they go to the trouble of setting traps in their own jumper? If they are as powerful as we think they are, there's no reason at all for them to resort to such measures. They should be able to set up checkpoints that would kill us all with no problem. They shouldn't need to do anything like this."

Tev saw where Aki was coming from. Something was wrong with this entire mission, but *Destiny* kept ordering them onward. Even Tev's commander wasn't sure about how to proceed. In the end, there was no way to go but forward, so forward they went.

They had turned through two more corridors when they came upon their first roadblock. Scrap metal had been piled high across the hallway, and as soon as they poked their heads around the corner, people opened fire from small holes in the scrap. Everyone took cover behind the corner, and thankfully no one was hurt. But they were stopped.

Aki spoke to the team. "There's no other way to the bridge that doesn't involve a whole lot of backtracking. We'll need to go through."

Another of Tev's teammates pulled a rocket from his back and loaded the tube. He was their heavy artillery, and the boyish part of Tev's heart was excited to see what would come of it. The teammate stepped into the hallway, launched his rocket, and continued his momentum so that he ended in the opposite corner. If nothing else, he would split the focus of the fire onto both sides of the hallway.

Tev heard the explosion, the noise dampened by the sound system in his suit. Immediately, the team received the order to advance, and they did so. The scrap metal hadn't been piled too thick, and the rocket had blown completely through it. Tev saw one exosuit down, with a steel beam through its chest. Tev's commander stepped over him and fired a few rounds into the helmet, to end the pilot's misery.

Tev was a hunter. He had never been a part of a war before, and while his prey had sometimes fought back, he had never hunted humans before. The nonchalance of the commander's actions disturbed him. It had been cold, emotionless. The least someone could ask for was some emotion at their death. But here, there was none.

Tev didn't have any time to process the event. His team was moving forward, and Aki spoke again.

"Let's get moving, people. We need to take that bridge, double-time."

The team moved quickly, but after turning down just one more corridor the commander signaled a halt. It lasted longer than any halt should have. They were in the middle of a corridor, exposed in all directions. Tev knelt down into a crouch while keeping his weapons trained on the hallway they had just come through.

Something was wrong, and Tev felt like he was being left in the dark. He opened his channel to Kindra. "Do you know what's going on?"

"There's a lot of chatter passing between the teams and *Destiny* right now. I'll patch in."

About thirty seconds later, Kindra was back, distress in her voice. "They think the entire ship is one large trap. Some teams have found crew in sleep in preparation for a jump."

Tev shook his head. What was going on here? Despite his ability as a pilot, he didn't have the slightest understanding about the strategies and tactics of space combat. All he knew was that nothing he had seen thus far made any sense.

His commander's voice overrode his connection with Kindra. "Okay, team. We've got a situation here. It seems like this might all be a trap. But we're close to the bridge, and Captain Absalon wants to know if we've got any chance at all of taking this ship. That means we need to move, now. Murphy, lead with a snooper. We don't have time to go slow, not anymore."

Their careful advance became a sprint through empty hallways. Tev was forced to turn around, unable to keep up while keeping his eyes focused behind them. The empty ship, which had once been eerie, was quickly becoming terrifying. Tev could sense the change in his teammates.

He had listened to the stories Kindra had told him of how scared her people were of jumping without drugs. Apparently, it caused madness and insanity, and was one of the greatest fears of any person who traveled through space. Tev didn't understand exactly what happened during a jump, so he didn't understand the deep-seated fear. But even though he didn't understand it, he could feel it among his team. They were professional pilots, used to danger and combat, but the mere prospect of jumping without drugs had them more on edge than Tev had ever seen them.

They made it to the bridge in the space of only a couple of minutes, but when they got there, they found that the door was tightly sealed. Not only was the regular door sealed, but an additional door had come down around the command center, preventing any easy access.

Murphy spoke quietly. "My sensors aren't picking up any signs of life behind the door, sir. There's no one in there."

Tev was now certain. They planned to jump, and jump soon. Otherwise, the bridge would be crowded.

Tev's commander came to the same conclusion. "Fine. What's the likelihood of us being able to cut or blow our way in there and take over *Hellbringer* before she jumps?"

Murphy shook her head. "With this ship's AI, and the blast shield between us, I'd guess the chances are close to zero. Maybe if we had the full jump sequence, but there's no way that's true. They had to have initiated it before we even began our attack. This had to be their plan all along."

Captain Absalon's voice came over all their helmets. "Attention, all pilots onboard the *Hellbringer*, we are detecting signs that the jump process is already well under way. You've all got about seven minutes before *Destiny* needs to pull away to avoid being in the jump field. Get back home, now!"

The urgency in his voice couldn't be mistaken, and it was backed up by Tev's own commander. "You heard the captain, people! Move!"

What had once been an orderly operation turned into a panic. Tev and his team sprinted to get out of the ship. They were limited less by their speed and more by the narrow corridors. The commander allowed his suit to crash around corners, and everyone else followed, looking like pilots who had drunk too much before the mission.

A countdown timer popped up in the corner of Tev's vision, concerning him further. He wasn't sure how long it had taken them to get to the bridge, but it felt like a long time. Trying to get back out in so little time would be almost impossible. He pushed the thought out of his mind. It wasn't something he could worry about. What he needed to do was focus on getting out. He put all his attention into piloting the suit, making sure he was moving as fast as he could.

As the team ran, they were separated by about two meters apiece. It was the standard that Tev had been taught in his training with the team, making sure that in conditions like these, each pilot had time to react to the events happening to the others in his group. Tev was still in position in the back of the line, covering the rear.

They were running down a straight section of corridor, Murphy just a few steps ahead of Tev, when a pressure seal shot down in between them. Tev tried to stop, but it happened so quickly he didn't have a chance. He ran into the door, alerting his team ahead what had happened.

Murphy turned around. "Commander, pressure seal just trapped Tev behind us."

Tev could hear the panic in Aki's voice. "We can't worry about that right now. Tev, connect with *Destiny* and try to find an alternate route home. We'll see you back there."

With that, the commander took off running down the hall. With one last glance at Tev, Murphy did the same. Suddenly, in the space of only a few seconds, Tev was alone.

"Kindra. I need another way out."

"I'm working on it."

It was ten long seconds by the clock that Tev had in the corner of his vision before Kindra responded.

"I'm sorry Tev, I can't see any way to get you out of that ship in time to meet up with *Destiny*."

TWELVE

KINDRA FOUGHT the urge to hold her head in her hands. Even though the *Destiny* had to move away, it would still take some time for *Hellbringer* to spin up its jump drive. There had to be options. She linked up with Eleta, who had been following the events down at her station in mechanical in the *Vigilance*.

"Any ideas?"

Eleta didn't respond right away, and Kindra was tempted to repeat her question, but before she could, her friend responded. "Maybe? I have an idea, but there's no guarantee it will work."

"What is it?"

"It'll be faster if I just chip in." Eleta connected herself to Kindra's secure channel to Tev. "Tev, can you hear me clearly?"

Kindra wanted to slap her palm against her forehead. Of course he could. But he responded in the affirmative.

"Good. I need you to follow the directions to this place. Go as quickly as you can."

Tev hesitated, and Kindra figured she knew why. The

directions Eleta was giving him led back toward the bridge. If he wanted to escape from the ship, it was exactly the wrong direction to go.

Kindra chimed in. "Trust her, Tev. If there's anyone who can get you out of there, it's going to be Eleta."

In the corner of her screen, Kindra saw that Eleta was attempting to upload several large data packets to Tev's suit. Kindra opened a private channel to her. "What are you doing?"

"Tev's going to encounter a number of locked doors where he's going. I've written a few programs that can help him out."

"Why didn't you load them earlier?"

"They were something I didn't want Fleet to know I had. A bit of a result of Derreck's requests to us. We're probably going to get in a lot of trouble for this."

Kindra understood. Regardless, it was worth it to get Tev off that ship. But then another question came to her mind.

"Wait. If you had this, why not just use it on the pressure seal that separated Tev from his squad?"

"Pressure seals are a different system than bulkheads. My programs won't touch them."

Kindra nodded. She supposed the difference in systems made sense. Together, they watched as Tev worked his way past the bridge and into the heart of *Hellbringer*, into engineering. As Eleta had predicted, the door was locked, but she guided Tev through the process of linking his suit to the door. After a few tense moments, Tev was in.

Kindra watched the entire process from her screens, unable to do anything but offer her silent support. She was far outside her area of expertise. She took a moment to thank their stars for Eleta. Whatever hacks she was running were high-level.

Eleta spoke to Kindra over their private channel. "Kindra, can you tell me what direction *Hellbringer*'s main laser is pointing?"

Kindra wasn't even sure how to look that information up, but with a little bit of digging into the battle net, she was able to query *Destiny*'s AI, who answered her.

"It's pointing into the middle of nowhere."

"Excellent."

Kindra watched, interested, to see what Eleta was up to. She was giving directions to Tev, and he was following them to the letter, but Eleta never bothered to explain why she was doing anything, or what her programs did.

Suddenly, every alarm in *Destiny* seemed to go off at the same time. Red lights were flashing, and Captain Absalon's image appeared in her neurodisplay, overriding everything else. "All hands, battle stations. I repeat, all hands, battle stations. Prepare for impact."

Once his image disappeared from her view, Kindra could hear Eleta chuckling softly in the background. "What the hell is going on?"

Eleta didn't explain. "Don't worry. We're not under attack, although I didn't consider the fact that *Destiny*'s sensors would pick up on that. Oops."

Kindra, confused, decided to trust Eleta. She didn't go to battle stations, but instead remained in her command chair, watching what Tev was doing.

From one perspective, it wasn't very exciting. He was at a console, a wire from his suit connected to a plug that had been exposed by tearing open some paneling. Physically, he wasn't doing much, just shifting his weight from foot to foot.

From a desire to do anything, she opened her channel to him. "How are you doing, Tev?"

"Fine?"

She could tell he was just as confused as her, but she didn't have any additional comfort to offer him.

Suddenly, all of her attention was focused on *Vigilance* and her screens. Even the dropship was shouting warnings now. Large laser emissions had been detected, jumper class. At first, Kindra thought perhaps everything had spiraled out of control. *Hellbringer* was attacking *Destiny*, breaking every iota of law and decency that existed in the galaxy.

Kindra had never been on a ship that was subjected to laser attack, but from everything she could tell, nothing had happened. The screens flashed again and again, and Kindra sealed up *Vigilance*. Even if *Destiny* was destroyed, maybe, just maybe, they could live through this.

As quickly as it started, the warnings stopped streaming across her display. She ran a quick diagnostic on her ship, but everything seemed to be in order. *Destiny* was in one piece, as was her own command. Whatever had happened, Eleta had been right, they weren't really in any danger.

"Eleta, what did you do?"

Eleta didn't respond to her, instead focusing on giving Tev further directions.

Eventually she got her answer. "I had Tev do an emergency discharge of their capacitors, several times over. The easiest way for the ships to do that is to discharge their main laser. We didn't have access to any weapons protocols, so we weren't able to aim the laser at all, but being as you told us we were safe, I just had him fire the laser over and over again. Now they don't have any energy to jump."

Kindra nodded her head in appreciation. Such an idea never would have occurred to her. Once Eleta explained it thought, it seemed obvious, but it still wasn't anything she ever would have come up with. "Nice work. Now what do you have him up to?"

"Well, I figured that when they wake up from their sleep, Tev is going to have a lot of furious rebellion people after him. I ordered him to the shuttle bay. We're going to have him steal a shuttle and come on over."

Kindra admired the simplicity of the plan. "Will that work?"

"So long as Tev gets back here before they figure out what's going on when they wake up. There's no way of telling for sure, but based on the timing of their jump sequence, Tev should just be able to make it back here before they wake."

"Won't their AI prevent him from leaving?"

"Maybe, but I was able to hack into their clearance codes from your little expedition over there, and I'm utilizing a ton of *Destiny's* AI to keep *Hellbringer* occupied."

Kindra actually laughed out loud as Tev boarded a shuttle and took off. She realized the programming that was going on behind the scenes was incredibly deep, but from a visual perspective, it was almost ridiculously easy.

It was only a matter of minutes before Tev was in space, safely between the two ships. Eleta reported that he had passed the point of no return, and Kindra collapsed back into her chair, not even realizing how tense she'd been during the entire ordeal. She shook her head and laughed.

JUST WHEN KINDRA thought it was all over, Derreck's voice came over the intercom. "What the hell is going on?"

Kindra tried to sit up straight, but it seemed like too much effort. "What do you mean?"

"For the past hour, I've been trying to access the command net, but I've been locked out the entire time, and now that it's back, I'm getting all sorts of very strange, very disturbing messages."

Kindra didn't even know where to start. "I'll tell you later."

Derreck seemed to be wrestling with something, but eventually gave in. "Very well, Derreck out."

Eleta spoke next. "Kindra, we might have a bit of a problem here."

"What do you mean? Is Tev okay?"

"Yeah, he's fine. He'll be aboard *Destiny* in a few minutes."

Suddenly, Eleta's feed cut out, which caused Kindra to sit straight up. What could have happened to cause that? Did they have saboteurs on the ship?

Kindra was surprised when she heard the airlock to the *Vigilance* cycle open. She hadn't triggered it, but someone had forced it open from the outside. Her instinct was to try to find some sort of weapon to defend herself, but that was silly. She was aboard her own jumper, and they knew no one had broken in. She pulled up the video feed and saw that it was Captain Absalon.

Kindra shook her head. She wasn't sure what Absalon was doing on the *Vigilance*, but right now, she didn't care. She laid back in her seat and covered her eyes, reflecting on how close they had come to losing Tev.

When she turned around, she was surprised to see Captain Absalon, not alone, but with two exosuits next to him. "What's going on, captain?" She couldn't help her rebellious streak, as much as she knew it was going to get her into trouble.

"Commander Kindra, under Fleet Regulation 86.3.4, I hereby order your immediate arrest."

KINDRA HAD ALWAYS KNOWN that the brig existed on jumpers, but she had never really spent any time thinking about it. Most of the time, it was used as a holding cell for people who had a little too much to drink on their off-hours. By and large, there wasn't much need for it.

She had to confess, she had been expecting something a little different. The brig on *Destiny* was a single large room, well lit, with some comfortable beds and a small privacy area for personal hygiene. Everything was monitored in more ways than Kindra cared to count, but it wasn't a half-bad space.

Her confinement was made even better by the fact that she wasn't alone. Eleta was next to her, dressed in a simple set of shirt and pants that matched Kindra's. Kindra was trying to remember the last time she had seen Eleta outside of some sort of Fleet uniform. It made her sad. Of all the people aboard *Vigilance*, Eleta was probably the person she had the most in common with, but they were friends only in regards to work. They never went on shore leave together.

They had plenty of time together now. At first, Kindra had wanted to talk about what had happened. She had tons of questions, not the least of which was what she had done to justify arrest. She had no idea what regulation Absalon had cited at her, and he had been tight-lipped as they dragged her down to the brig.

Kindra had tried to probe Eleta, but she hadn't said anything, and it was only after about a half hour of trying that Kindra figured out she didn't want to say anything that would further implicate them. Eventually Kindra took the hint, embarrassed it had taken her so long to figure it out. She wasn't used to being under arrest. Her rebellions had always been petty, but at heart, she was square.

It wasn't long after they were put in the brig that Derreck came to visit them. Kindra assumed it was his first order of business after getting everything finished up with his suit.

Derreck walked into the brig, and the first thing he did was come up and give Kindra a huge hug. Kindra frowned. It was entirely out of character for him. For everything they had been through in their years of service together, Derreck always kept his demeanor professional. Regardless, Kindra accepted the hug, comforted by the embrace.

After just a moment, Derreck stepped back and gave Eleta a hug as well. The surprise on her face was worth everything that had happened to them so far today. Kindra smiled.

They sat down, but Derreck made it clear he didn't have time for a long visit. He wanted to make sure they were doing well, and let them know he was doing all that he could to get to the bottom of what had happened.

Kindra couldn't resist any longer. He had to know more than she did. "Derreck, why are we even here?"

Derreck and Eleta shared a look that indicated that Kindra needed to catch up. There was something obvious that she was missing.

Derreck chose his words with care. "Well, we're still investigating what happened today, but it appears that somehow, some very illegal software was used in combat today, resulting in the discharge of anti-ship weaponry from a hostile capital ship. If the perpetrators are ever discovered, there might be a set of laws and treaties which would almost certainly require that said perpetrators are thrown out of an airlock."

Kindra was taken aback. She would never have guessed that their actions would carry such severe consequences. A glance at Eleta, though, made it clear that her friend had already considered it. She wasn't surprised by anything that Derreck said. A whole host of questions sprinted through Kindra's mind. Did they get some sort of trial? If they didn't, why were they still alive? It was obvious Captain Absalon knew exactly what had happened. They had spoken over secure channels, but it wouldn't take an investigative genius to put the pieces together and recognize who was responsible.

Some small part of her recognized that this was not the time or place to ask questions. Derreck's voice was calm and reassuring. "Don't worry. I'm working closely with Captain Absalon to figure out what happened, and we will clear your good names before long. Is that clear?"

Kindra nodded her head, not sure what else she could do.

"Good. Now, get some rest, you two. We're going to be very busy moving forward, and I want you two to take this opportunity to get prepared for what comes next."

With that, Derreck left, leaving Kindra with far more worries and concerns than she had when she had first been thrown in the brig.

THERE WAS no clock in the brig, and after pulling up the clock on her own personal display several times, Kindra gave up. There was simply nothing to do, and Eleta seemed drawn inside herself. Kindra was grateful when the lights dimmed, indicating it was time for bed.

After lying sleepless for a time, Kindra heard Eleta stir. "Kindra, are you awake?"

A part of Kindra, the part of her upset that Eleta hadn't spoken more than a few words to her all day, wanted to not respond; but she was desperate to have a conversation, to know how her friend was feeling.

"Yeah, I'm awake."

"We should be able to talk freely now. Derreck slipped me a small piece of my equipment when he came in. I don't want to use it too much, but we should have a little bit of time."

Kindra's first reaction was one of anger. The whole reason Derreck had hugged her was so that he would have the cover to slip something to Eleta? The man was horrible. Jealousy raged, and she wondered why Derreck hadn't brought anything into the brig for her.

It took a few seconds, but eventually rationality prevailed. What would Derreck have been able to bring her anyway? She was a biologist, far out of her comfort zone. A test tube wouldn't do anyone any good here.

The first part of their conversation was quick, and Kindra was happy to hear that Eleta was feeling fine. She had appeared sullen all day, but in reality she had just been bored and frustrated at not being able to speak openly. Once Kindra was reassured on that point, it opened up the way for her to ask the question that had really been on her mind since Derreck had come in.

"You knew the consequences of what you were doing, didn't you?"

"Yes."

"So why did you do it?"

"Tev is part of our crew, and that was the only way I could think of to get him off safely."

The answer seemed overly simplistic to Kindra, but she was willing to let it slide. She wasn't the type of person to push her friends for deeper answers than they gave. Fortunately, after a few seconds of silence, Eleta went deeper on her answer herself.

"Perhaps this will sound silly to you, Kindra, but your actions have changed my outlook in the past few months."

"What do you mean?"

"The actions you took when Kenan went rogue, back on Tev's planet? I struggled with those for a very long time. When it all happened, it happened so fast I don't think I really had time to think about it. I didn't like the decisions you made, not at first. My philosophy was much more that crew needs to stick together no matter what. I felt like you were betraying Kenan, even though what he was doing was horrible.

"Your decision to go after him, to use Tev the way that you did, it wasn't just a crazy idea. It was also honorable. You put the good of strangers, aliens you had never met before, over the life of your own crew when it was the right thing to do. I didn't see it at first. I'm not sure that I could have. But that was the right action to take. I think a part of me recognized that even at the time, which was why I didn't make more of a fuss.

"But when you asked why I did what I did today, yes, part of it was because Tev is our crew, and we should do everything we can to save him. More importantly, though, I did it because leaving him behind was wrong."

Kindra didn't know how to respond. She hadn't expected anything so emotional from Eleta. It was a side of her that Kindra rarely got to see. "Thank you for telling me.

For what it's worth, I'm grateful that you did what you could to save him."

There were a few minutes of silence, but Kindra felt as though the entire atmosphere had changed. Where once the brig had been confining and tense, it was now open, as though the air were easier to breathe.

Eleta spoke. "There's something else that bothered me when it happened, but I haven't really been able to put my finger on why until recently. The pressure seal that fell in front of Tev, almost trapping him? That doesn't happen. There weren't any other seals in our way, and the fact that it closed just before Tev ran through it is beyond suspicious. The AI on that ship had to do that intentionally. It's the only thing I can think of."

"What are you saying?"

"I've been thinking about what happened on the assault on that ship. Something still isn't adding up, but it seems to me that their plan was to try to jump out while most of our suits were aboard. Logically, the only reason they would do that would be so that they could try to take the suits after the jump, after all our pilots lost their minds jumping without sedation. But the AI seemed to be singling out Tev."

"Are you saying that the *Hellbringer* was trying to capture Tev and his suit?"

"I think so, yes."

Kindra let the idea sink in for a while. She couldn't fault any part of Eleta's logic. As always, it was sound. But she didn't like the conclusion that her friend had reached. It was an amazing amount of trouble to capture one person. She thought again about her brief conversation with Captain Nick and his mention of a weapon. Was Tev the weapon he was so worried about?

THE NEXT DAY they didn't have long to wait before Derreck entered the brig with Captain Absalon. Kindra had a sudden desire to wash her hair and make herself look more presentable.

Derreck was wearing a grin on his face which made Kindra feel almost immediately at ease. As always, her captain had come through, saving the day again.

Derreck spoke first. "Well, it's been quite a while since I've had to bail somebody out of jail, but I suppose it's worth it for you two, huh?"

Kindra shook her head, a smile on her face. "I don't know, sir. We might be more trouble than we're worth."

Derreck laughed. "Oh, there's no doubt of that. Come on, let's get you out of here and showered up. I don't want to spend too much time too close to that stink."

As soon as they stepped out of the brig, Captain Absalon turned around and gave the two girls a harsh stare. "What you two did makes me uncomfortable. I know you were trying to save Tev, and Derreck has assured me that you two checked to make sure the laser wasn't pointing at us before firing it, but I can't stress enough that type of behavior will no longer be permitted on the *Destiny*. You two won't be thrown out of an airlock, as much as that might allow me to sleep more soundly in my own bed, but you are going to be confined to the *Vigilance*, at least for the near future. All of her connections to *Destiny* are being monitored, and I can assure you that if you try anything like that again, it will not work. Are we clear?"

Both women stood up straighter and saluted. "Yes, sir!"

Kindra fought an urge to laugh. It had been a very long time since she had saluted, and the entire practice seemed silly to her. Fleet was getting too formal for her tastes, she decided.

With a scowl on his face, Absalon spun on his heels and walked away, almost knocking over a passerby in the process. Kindra stifled a giggle. Part of it was knowing she was safe again, but part of it was just the humor of the entire situation.

Derreck didn't waste any time. "Come on, you two. Let's get you both inside the *Vigilance* before he changes his mind."

As they walked, Derreck filled them in on all the new developments.

"Absalon will never admit this out loud, but thanks to you two, and Tev, I suppose, we are now in an entirely different situation than we were before the battle. We're almost fully charged, and they aren't. Now we have an advantage over them. It's changed the dynamics of the entire chase."

Kindra tried to absorb everything she was hearing. She was glad they would make it to Tev's planet first. That was one problem, at least, that they wouldn't have to worry about.

"For now, you two can get some rest and catch up on your daily work. But I want *Vigilance* ready for launch. There's a lot of different factors at play, but I want to make sure we're in the best possible condition."

Derreck looked as though he was about to leave them, but Kindra couldn't let him leave without at least a word. "Derreck, I realize it may not mean much, but thank you for having our backs."

He nodded. "You two did the right thing. Now we just need to do it again so that Tev and his people can live in harmony with the rest of us, instead of as our slaves."

THIRTEEN

TEV HAD ALWAYS BEEN good at waiting, even if he didn't like it. As a hunter, he often had to wait for a very long time for his prey to make its move. When animals got spooked they liked to sit silently in one place. At times like that, when you knew the animal was nearby, it was often best to wait, to let it make the next move.

Out here in space, away from the places Tev was familiar with, it all fell apart on him. His ability to wait, to remain calm, was compromised. Now, all he wanted was action. He wasn't sure if it was because the stakes were higher or because the process was so unfamiliar, but all he wanted to do was move, to attack, to fight something.

Derreck had noticed it during a small training run two days ago. Tev had been too aggressive, not thinking clearly, and Derreck had punished him for it, beating him in simulation after simulation. Derreck had offered words of encouragement, but that wasn't what Tev wanted. Tev wanted an enemy in front of him, a target to aim for. This endless waiting, punctuated by moments of excitement, was getting to him.

They knew something was coming. Tev had set the *Hellbringer* back in the attack a few weeks ago, but he hadn't stopped them, not by any stretch of the imagination. They just didn't know when or where the attack might occur.

When the moment came, it came quietly, Kindra whispering in his ear.

"Tev, Derreck wanted me to get in touch with you. The *Hellbringer* just jumped in-system, and it looks like she's making a hard burn for us. It looks like we'll be in combat within the next five hours."

Tev was always amazed at the differences in scale between the combat he was used to and the combat in space. In his world, if you had a few seconds of warning, that a lot. Now, although Kindra's voice was strained, there wasn't much urgency. If his past encounters were any indication, he had time to lie down and take a nap before there was any need for him to even get suited up. Kindra's next words confirmed his guess.

"The combat meeting is in three hours. I'm to let you know to get ready. They'll want you on this one."

Tev confirmed the message. There was more that he wanted to say, questions he wanted to ask, but he couldn't bring himself to do it. It was time for action.

Tev forced himself to think on different subjects. It was easy, when so much of your time was your own, to let your mind wander in circles that spiraled ever-downward. He needed to think about protecting his people. The time was running short for him to be able to do anything, and he still hadn't figured out how to approach the situation. The problem was that Fleet, or the *Hellbringer*, was more powerful than all the people on his planet. They didn't have the technology to fight at this level.

The problems he faced were myriad, but he only knew one way to face them. Head on, and one at a time.

IT FELT like he had just been here, and in truth, it had only been a couple of weeks. He and the other pilots were all assembled, and it was painfully obvious that there were fewer than there had been the last time.

The reality was tough for Tev. Everyone here was risking their lives for his people. His people, who had no idea the chaos that was about to be visited on them, even under the best circumstances. He didn't know these pilots, not personally. He'd met a few of them, and trained with his own squad for some time, but even though they had shared danger, they weren't friends, not comrades who would lay down their lives for him.

In the last battle, they had lost friends, people they cared about. And for what? For the chance to be first down to Tev's planet? It didn't make sense, not when he thought about it.

But the world he found himself in made little sense anymore. It was a world beyond what he was used to, a world with new rules, both spoken and unspoken.

His musings were interrupted by Captain Absalon coming into the room, bringing with him a deafening silence.

"Ladies and gentlemen, I believe we're going to be in it for real this time. Here's the breakdown: The question that has been on everyone's mind lately is why the rebellion ship is using such unique strategies for dealing with us. The command staff has been running different scenarios with *Destiny*'s AI, and we're pretty certain the most likely scenario is that the rebellion has been running a complicated bluff the entire time. The reason they invited us over wasn't to deal, but to present a show of strength. We believe they are in the same situation we are, where they are bringing far more suits than pilots. Like us, it seems that they expect that Tev's people all might prove to be exceptional pilots.

"The problem is that we have no way of knowing how many pilots they do have. From the information we've gathered and the battles we have seen so far, it could be as few as eight. If we're wrong, they could have well over a hundred. We don't have enough data to make an educated guess.

"Which brings us to our current problem: *Hellbringer*, as you all know, is burning hard for us, and it looks like she means business. If her course holds steady, we're going to be scraping hulls in about two hours. They've decided this is the battleground, and I'm fine with that. We're not going to go on offense again. The same trick rarely works twice. Today we're playing defense, and we're going to be setting up some strategic chokepoints to send them through."

Absalon pulled up a display of the *Destiny*. Tev saw that several areas of the ship were highlighted, but with his limited knowledge of the ship as a whole, the highlighted sections made little sense to him.

"Here's the plan: All crew will be evacuated to battle positions, leaving most of the hallways near the exterior of the ship wide open for you all to play in. There are several points they will have to go through to get to critical systems. We'll be defending those with everything we've got, in addition to having a couple of back-up points.

"We're also going to have some back-up procedures ready. What I'd really like is for us to be able to handle this the old-fashioned way. They board us and we take them all out with better pilots and better positioning. But we might get overwhelmed. The jump drive is running hot, though, and if it comes down to it, we will make an emergency jump of the ship. I'll give as much warning as I'm able, but there may be real unpleasantness ahead."

Tev felt the attitude in the room change with the captain's words. He still didn't understand the fear everyone felt. He was surrounded by soldiers, people who made a living training for and delivering war. How was it that they could face death with a stony face, but the idea of traveling made them lose their spirit?

There was time for questions, and there were many. The pilots on *Destiny* were strong warriors, and Tev had noticed that their preparation was always excellent. It reminded him of his own hunts. The best hunters he knew didn't boast about the actions they were about to perform. Instead, they sat quietly, off in a corner of the camp, checking their bow to make sure it hadn't cracked and that the string was still tight. They sharpened their knives. When it came time to hunt, they were the ones who had earned the glory, not those who had bragged about it.

Tev's mind drifted during the questioning. He was trying to learn more, but the strategies of space combat didn't make sense to him. For now, he would follow his squad and their directions. They might not be as close as his clan, but he trusted them, and they trusted him. He wouldn't be led astray by them, not in combat.

He noted that his squad and Derreck's were in different places again. Derreck would be defending the bridge, the last line of defense before the ship was taken over. Tev, on the other hand, was supposed to be near the hull of the jumper, in a position that was sure to see plenty of combat.

After the meeting adjourned, Derreck came up to Tev,

and for a few seconds, the two of them stood there, enjoying a companionable silence. Tev liked Derreck, a lot. He liked the man's cool demeanor and sense of honor. He would have made a tremendous hunter, someone Tev would have taken with him any time. It made him smile, this idea that he had to travel farther than any hunter before him to find the perfect hunting partner. Their eyes met, and exchanged the words they'd never feel comfortable saying out loud.

Derreck extended his hand. "Be careful out there. I have a bad feeling about this one. Protect yourself, okay?"

Tev nodded. "Do the same."

Derreck nodded, and with one last, vigorous clasp, they split apart, each to their own suits.

TEV STOOD BEHIND A BARRICADE, the entire docks spread out in front of him. His suit had been modified since the last time he piloted it. As usual, his right arm held the rifle he recognized. But on his left arm was an even longer rifle, extending beyond his hand. Aki had explained it to him as they were suiting up. It didn't fire the same metal that his rifle on the right fired. It fired shots that flew faster and straighter than the ones he was used to. Aki said that it was for fighting at long distances.

Tev asked why it had been given to him. None of the other members of his squad had one, although he did see that they were also carrying a wide variety of other weapons that he hadn't seen before. They were throwing everything into this defense.

"Well, we don't have too many of these, and as much as it pains me to admit it, you are the best shot in the squad. It's also the most similar to what you're used to, so it made sense. I suppose it also keeps you a little way from the rest of the fight, and that's important as well."

Tev understood that last part. The rest of his squad was down in the docks, behind barricades specifically designed for repelling boarders. The fight would be most intense down there. Tev was twenty meters above them, also behind cover. It was a much safer position than where the rest of his team would be.

Part of Tev's vision was filled with information from the battle grid. Kindra was talking him through most of what he was seeing on a separate channel. Tev found her voice comforting as he waited for the battle to begin. He didn't have any real desire to fight, but he wanted to get home, and he would do anything to make that happen.

"*Hellbringer* is pulling up right next to us. Wow, that's really close."

Tev smiled. Kindra couldn't help but say exactly what was on her mind, all the time. It was one of the things he liked about her. She couldn't lie if her life depended on it.

On his display, various lights disconnected from the image that Tev knew was the other jumpship. Kindra let out a short whistle. "They aren't trying to sneak people in like we did. That's an armored dropship. They're planning on knocking down the front door."

Tev didn't always understand exactly what Kindra was saying, but he knew enough. A big ship was heading their way. Suddenly, on Tev's display, there were many, many more lights surrounding the dropship.

"Oh, no!" The awe and fear in Kindra's voice was obvious.

"What?"

Kindra took a moment to respond. "That's a lot of suits.

You know how we thought maybe they didn't have many pilots onboard? We were wrong."

Tev didn't have any time to reply, because his own radio started squawking. It was Tev's commander. "Okay team, be ready to fall back to position Bravo, quickly. They're bringing in a lot of suits, and we're going to be the target right at the tip of their spear. Hit them hard, hit them quick, and then we bug out. We aren't in a position to deal with what they are sending our way."

Derreck's voice intruded at the same time, and Tev suddenly had more information than he could process. "Kindra, get the *Vigilance* ready to launch. Put all of its defenses on code red. Nobody, and I mean nobody, gets close. Hold for further orders."

Tev didn't know everything that was happening around him, but without warning, the port door opened in front of him. They'd already pumped all the air out of the hangar, so there wasn't any effect.

Tev's commander spoke. "They're bringing way more firepower than the hangar doors can handle. Might as well let them in and prevent some damage that wouldn't even slow them down anyway. Don't worry, people."

For the first time, Tev could see as the enemy dropship approached. A series of explosions blossomed across the hull of the ship, brief in the vacuum of space. It was beautiful, in a way that Tev couldn't quite explain. The ship was beautiful, and the destruction that licked across the hull was also beautiful.

Tev readied his weapon, the sound of the suit preparing for battle reassuring. He wouldn't fail. He would make it back home, no matter what.

The enemy dropship landed in the hanger, the landing

gentle considering they were in a combat situation. Tev's commander had placed his squad well, and they were able to cover most of the dropship's exits. There were a few moments of peace while they waited for the chaos to ensue, and Tev took a final, deep breath before the world erupted in noise and fire.

The dropship's doors opened and suits came pouring out. Behind the dropship, several suits floated in, coming to land in the hanger on their own. Below him, his squad opened fire, covering the doors of the dropship with metal death.

Just as though he was hunting, Tev's senses focused. He picked a target, a suit near the rear of the boarding party. He rested the reticle over the suit's head and mentally pulled the trigger. The head disappeared and the suit collapsed, but in the middle of the firefight nobody noticed. Tev drifted over to the next target and repeated the process.

Inside he was cold. A part of him recognized that he was killing people, something he had only done once before. But seeing them in their suits made it easy, made it possible to think of them as being something other than human. He found his next target and fired again, and then once again.

Finally, someone below must have figured out what was happening. Tev heard the rounds strike around him. Of all his team, the height and cover he was behind made him the hardest to hit. He focused on another target, and another round sent the suit crashing to the ground.

Tev pulled his focus back. It was easy to only see one thing at a time, but it was also the way that people got killed. He took a moment to take in the entire battle. His squad was doing everything they could to hold off the much larger boarding party. All of their weapons seemed to be firing continually; and rockets, grenades, and other explosives were launched with deafening regularity towards the dropship. For a moment, it almost seemed as though they might be able to hold back the advance.

The dream disappeared as quickly as Tev's hearing once the enemy dropship opened fire. Tev hadn't expected it, but within moments he was hiding behind his barricade as the dropship unleashed a tremendous amount of firepower in the hold. The barricade, which to Tev had once seemed sturdy and dependable, shook against his suit like a blanket in the wind. Tev, more scared than rational, leapt from cover and rolled behind a thicker steel box. His timing couldn't have been better, as an explosion enveloped the place he'd been just moments ago.

An eternity later, the firing stopped, and Tev's hearing returned to normal. His suit had deadened the sound for him, the only reason he could still hear anything at all. There was plenty of movement below, and when he poked his head around, what he saw sank the slim hope he had left.

The dropship was disgorging three, no, four, enormous machines. They moved like exosuits, but were so much larger.

"Heavies!" someone shouted over the intercom.

Aki didn't hesitate. "We can't stay here any longer. Retreat to checkpoint Bravo. Arm the traps, maybe it will slow them down. Tev, can you cover us for about ten seconds?"

Tev acknowledged and took some deep breaths. More than anything, he wanted to stay behind cover and wait for everything to be over, but before the battle he had made a promise to himself. If this was what it took, so be it.

"Mark."

Tev stood up and pivoted, giving himself a clear field of view of the battleground below. He raised both arms, and let his right arm with the main rifle spray the entire area without concern. That was the cover his teammates needed, but he knew the odds of getting a fatal blow were slim. He focused on his left arm, bringing his targeting reticle up over the cockpit of one of the heavy machines. He could see the man inside, and he pulled the trigger in his mind.

The result wasn't as dramatic as he'd expected, but his rifle had the power to punch through the cockpit. The heavy sank to its knees, some type of automatic shutdown.

His elation lasted only for a moment, and then his world became a living hell. His actions had worked too well. Every single suit down below seemed to fire on him, and Tev stepped backwards, out of line of sight, as bullets whistled in front of him. Below him, the deck shook, and as Tev stepped backwards again, trying to get to checkpoint Bravo. Then the entire deck collapsed around him as he was swallowed up by flame.

FOURTEEN

KINDRA WAS FROZEN IN INDECISION.

Day after day, she considered the decisions she'd made, but day after day, she was able to push her guilt aside. There was always a duty to do, a task that needed to be completed. She was never in a place where she had to make life-or-death decisions. Derreck was her commander, and she always had the shield of his orders to hide behind.

When the battle came to them, her shield disappeared.

Kindra sat on the *Vigilance*, in exile from her own jumpship. She had company, at least. Eleta was on the bridge with her. She watched the battle unfold, her attention divided between several viewscreens. On one, she had Tev's feeds pulled up, and on another, Derreck's. On the third she could see the battle readout of the entire situation. She was a part of this battle, and yet her actions had separated her from the rest of the jumper. The dissociation in real life mirrored her mental state.

Eleta sat right next to her. In the preparation for the battle, the two of them had been forgotten, or at least, that was what Kindra told herself. They had been sealed in their dropship by Absalon's orders, and that seal had not been broken. Perhaps he figured they were just as safe there as in the center of the ship with the rest of the non-combat crew.

For now, there was nothing they could do, and Kindra wasn't certain she even wanted to do anything. She wanted to get back to Tev's planet and explore it more. The last thing she wanted to do was see more bloodshed. Wasn't space big enough for all of them?

She had convinced herself that supporting Tev was the right action to take, but she hadn't been forced to consider the consequences of what that support might be. How far would she go to protect him and his people? She hadn't answered that question, not even for herself.

Kindra tore her eyes away from the viewscreens and watched as a dropship came into the hanger where the *Vigilance* was docked, settling in softly. She had watched the ship come in the entire way on the battle net, but seeing it there, in her hanger, wrenched her gut in a way she hadn't expected. Danger, from a distance, was very different than danger right outside your door. Flashes of light filled the bridge as the suits stationed in the hanger opened fire on the enemy dropship.

She could hear the firefight, both on her screens and outside her ship. The exchanges were intense, and she wondered if she would be able to hear any shots taken against the *Vigilance*. She pulled up another screen with diagnostic imagery. So far, everything read green across the board. She wasn't surprised, but she was grateful. Dropships weren't nearly as valuable to humanity as jumpships were, but they were still prizes. The rebels would want to take the *Vigilance* intact if they could.

Kindra's sight was drawn back to Tev's screen. The fight happening there was insane. She could see that Tev was firing, and the viewscreen displayed just how successful he was. He was so many things, but one aspect she sometimes forgot was that he was a warrior unlike any they had seen recently. He was good.

A glance at Derreck's screen and the tactical readout confirmed that so far, the fight was restricted to the hangers. But, if the screens were telling the truth, they were far outnumbered.

Outside the *Vigilance*, the fight increased in intensity. The gunfire was almost constant. Kindra had never lived through anything like it before. She looked over at Eleta, and they shared a look of uneasy comfort.

Her chair shook as explosions rocked the ground outside. A glance at her monitor showed that *Destiny*'s troops were retreating. Two of the four in the squad had been killed, more than they could afford to lose.

On Tev's screen she saw the heavies unload from the other dropship. She had heard about heavies and seen pictures, but had never seen one in reality. She watched in horror as Tev launched an all-out assault on the rebels. She shook her head, horrified by the knowledge that he was completely outclassed. Seconds later, his screen erupted in flame and went dark.

Kindra screamed, her mind working on autopilot. She checked all the other channels of information, but she wasn't getting anything from Tev's suit. No vitals, no video, no audio. Either he was gone or all of his communications had been knocked offline.

In that moment, Kindra made a decision. She wouldn't sit on the sidelines. No longer would she try to push her decisions off on others. She wasn't some helpless damsel. She might not know how to pilot a suit, but she could solve problems, and she would take a stand against those who thought Tev's people were nothing more than pilots for their weapons. She looked over at Eleta, who was appeared to be in a state of shock. "Do we have anything that will make their life hell?"

Eleta nodded. "We could unleash our new defensive measures into the hanger."

"Do it."

Eleta hesitated.

"What's wrong?" Kindra was surprised by the edge in her own voice.

"It's just that, that's a lot of people."

Kindra, driven more by frustration and rage than by reason, navigated the weapons control panels herself. If Eleta wouldn't do it, she would be more than happy to. She found the controls and commanded the AI to target enemy suits. She held fire until the AI had the best targeting solution. She hesitated just for a moment. A part of her recognized that if she did this, there was no turning back. She would be a killer.

Kindra opened fire.

Vigilance erupted, small turrets throwing out thousands of pellets at tremendous speeds. It tore up over a dozen suits in less than two seconds, destroying the hanger in the process. The enemy didn't even have time to react.

Kindra didn't feel anything.

FIFTEEN

TEV'S WORLD SPUN, a kaleidoscope of flame and gravity. He crashed onto his side, an impact only dulled a little by the suit he was wearing. He tried calling out to Kindra, but there was nothing. Something must have happened to his suit to prevent him from communicating. Grunting, he called out for a report of the suit, and the suit responded by flashing a display in the corner of his screen. There were yellow markers around the suit, indicating non-critical damage. All he knew was that he needed to avoid red. As long as he did that, he'd be fine.

His second thought was that he needed to move. He had crashed to the deck below the one he had been shooting from. He was still above the battlefield, but it would be much easier for the boarders to reach him. The rest of his team would be waiting at Bravo. He just had to make it there in one piece.

Tev stood up, and immediately a hail of gunfire converged on his location. He felt several impacts, one of which cut through the armor on his right bicep. Tev felt the pain flood through his mind, but he couldn't allow it to distract him. He half-ran, half-stumbled towards the nearest bulkhead. It opened to his suit as he got close and he threw himself through. The door closed behind him, and for the moment, he was safe.

Tev took the time to catch his breath and his bearings. There was a general ache throughout his body, but his arm felt as though it were on fire. What he wanted to do was sit and fall asleep. What he did was get back to his feet and ask his suit for directions to Bravo. Arrows came up on his display, and he started walking as fast as he could.

He made it to the barricade without problem, and his teammates let him through. Tev's commander looked him over. They stood a step apart from one another until Aki realized Tev couldn't hear him. He stepped forward and put his helmet against Tev's. "Are you okay? I can't get any information from your suit, and you looked pretty banged up."

Tev replied, "I'm shot through the arm, but otherwise, okay."

"Okay. It's good to see you. We were getting a little worried."

Tev took his position and double-checked his suit. It seemed like everything was going to work, but his right arm was sluggish. That could be a problem. In the close quarters of the hallway, the rifle underneath his right arm was far superior to the long-range rifle on his left, but there wasn't any time to do anything about it. Tev could hear the sound of the other suits approaching, and it wouldn't be long before battle was joined again.

The loss of communication had a strange effect on Tev. He had walked into this battle as part of a team, including Kindra in his head to keep him company. But now, even though he was surrounded by people who were friends, he felt alone, isolated, in a bubble of silence even though he was sure his team was chattering back and forth. Tev had felt alone before, especially since he'd left his planet, but he had never felt this.

It was a profound sense of isolation, as if he were in the plains that the elders of his clans talked about, nothing but grass for as far as the eye could see. Sorrow and a sense of resignation washed over him. The barricade they were behind was strong, but it would not last against the forces arrayed against it. Behind this, there was nothing but the hallways that led to the bridge and to engineering. No more cover.

Tev was pulled from his reverie by the shaking of the floor. He imagined that one of the traps his team had set had gone off. He could hope, at least. Who knew how effective they'd be?

Another explosion rumbled through his feet, and he knew they didn't have too much time left to wonder. It would all be over for them soon. Tev decided that with few other options, he would fight the best he could. He would show them the strength of a hunter from his clan.

He didn't have long to wait. A suit came around the corner, appearing unconcerned about its fate. Tev was faster than anyone else on his team. He raised his left arm, and a single shot streaked through the suit's chest. It collapsed to the ground. In the next few seconds, the entire hallway became a hail of metal. Their barricade was holding, but it wouldn't for long. One of Tev's team launched a handful of grenades, and for a moment, there was peace. Tev looked around and was surprised to see Aki on the ground, a clean hole through his helmet. He didn't even have time to feel remorse.

The attack commenced again, and Tev stood straight,

his left arm out, as suit after suit came around the corner. Tev's side was pointed towards the enemy, and he felt the impacts as he was hit by several rounds. He grimaced through the pain, but his aim wouldn't be thrown off. Calmly, he picked off the attacking suits, one at a time. The rifle wasn't meant to be used at such close quarters, but Tev's aim was impeccable, and his shots always went through the armor.

Off to his side, Tev saw another one of his teammates fall, but it only registered in the farthest corners of his mind. He didn't react until he was pulled back down behind the barricade, just as one of the heavies turned the corner. Tev got off one shot, but he wasn't able to hit the cockpit, and his shot did nothing but fling armor off the heavy.

He didn't understand why he had been pulled down. His eyes took in the scene and saw that Murphy, the last member of his team, also had a number of holes in her suit and was bleeding freely from them. It hit Tev, like a punch that he never saw coming, that suddenly he was the last member of his team, one of the last people standing between the rebels and his home planet.

Tev's first instinct was to stand back up and unload both of his weapons at the cautiously approaching enemy. The hail of steel had become a trickle, their enemy uncertain whether or not they had killed everyone. His teammate seemed to be trying to say something, forgetting that Tev didn't have any comms. She grabbed his helmet and slammed them together.

"RUN!"

With that, she shoved Tev forward. Some part of Tev seized on her intent. Their barricade was going to be overrun, probably in a matter of minutes, if not seconds. She was sacrificing herself for him, for his people. Tev focused on his movement, turning at the first corner as a burst of gunfire chased him. Another round struck his suit, but when he called up diagnostics, he saw that although he was almost entirely covered in yellow, he had still managed to avoid any red.

Tev paused around the corner, catching his breath and deciding what to do. His mind told him to run. He knew he couldn't change the direction of the battle on his own. But there was another part of him, the part that wanted to be the best, to be greater than anyone expected he could be. It wouldn't let him run, not when he could still make a difference.

A massive explosion rocked the hallway, and flames licked past Tev's suit before disappearing. Murphy had set off all the ordnance she had left. It was a noble sacrifice, and he thanked her for what she had done.

Not for the first time, he wished that he could talk to Kindra one last time. She was a woman torn between her desire for knowledge and the understanding of what that knowledge cost. He wanted to let her know that it was all going to be fine. She would be heartbroken over his death, but she had to know that he went willingly. It had always been his choice.

Tev took a deep breath. It was time to join the final hunt.

SIXTEEN

KINDRA'S MIND was focused on the viewscreens. Beside her, Eleta seemed to be in a state of shock over what they had done, but Kindra didn't have time. She had done what was necessary. Her only concern was what the other dropship in the hanger would do.

Kindra figured she would help it decide. She opened a missile tube on *Vigilance*. The enemy dropship had been kind enough to land directly in front of them, so Kindra could snap off a shot in a moment. There was no way she would miss. It would destroy quite a bit of *Destiny*, but Kindra was willing.

The enemy dropship seemed to sense her intent. It took off and glided back out of the hanger, heading back toward the rebel ship.

Kindra shifted her attention to Derreck's screen. It made little sense for the dropship to pull off the ship. She knew she had dealt the rebels a blow, but it couldn't be that easy. If anyone would have any answers, it would be him. When she looked, though, she saw that his helmet was off-center and the view was all askew. She worried for a moment before realizing he was just holding the helmet under his arm. Curious, Kindra turned on the audio pickups to match the visuals. She saw he was on the bridge of the *Destiny*.

Derreck wasn't speaking, and she had to turn the gain up to hear the background chatter. What she heard chilled her blood.

"Sir, *Hellbringer* is pulling away. Both dropships are in pursuit, and they are going to dock in the next few minutes."

For the first time, she heard Derreck's voice. "What are they up to?"

Absalon responded. "I'm not sure. Your XO decimated half of their attacking force with her damn antics, and although I am going to kill her for using her defense systems inside my ship, I can't deny it was effective. The other half is making their way through the ship, but they are taking heavy casualties, and *Hellbringer* looks like she's abandoning them."

"There's no way they would just retreat. Not after sending a force like that after us."

"I agree. That's why I'm concerned."

There was relative silence for a few moments before Absalon continued. "Spool up the jump drive. I want all non-essential personnel to go under, now. How long until the assault force breaches the bridge?"

Another voice called out. "At current rate of advance, maybe about ten minutes."

From the tilted helmet perspective, Kindra could see Absalon looking at Derreck. "You've jumped once without drugs, right?"

Kindra didn't hear Derreck respond, but she assumed he was nodding. Her ears perked up. She had always heard rumors that he had done it once, but it was something he refused to speak of. "If I jump this ship, will the assault force be able to reach us before we wake back up?"

Derreck's voice was soft. "It took me days to come back to myself. If they don't kill themselves first, we'll be able to clean up easily."

"Good. We'll pull the same trick on them they tried to pull on us. Who do we still have out there?"

In the corner of her viewscreens, Kindra saw the order come through her own terminal to prepare for jump. It was a strange experience, to be present, albeit virtually, as the orders were given, and then see them come through her screen.

Her attention was drawn back to the report Absalon was getting, "... only unit left is Derreck's guarding the bridge. All others have been eliminated. We are getting readings that indicate a battle is still in progress on deck four, where the first assault force came up against Aki. There's only one suit that's still mobile, but we can't communicate with it. It's registering as the alien's though."

Kindra almost fell into her viewscreen. Tev was still alive, fighting the assault all on his own. But they were going to jump, and he didn't have any way of knowing. She wanted to scream, but no one would hear her.

Another voice called out on the bridge. "Sir! Torpedo tubes are opening on *Hellbringer*. I'm reading four nuclear signatures, sir!"

Kindra didn't think her stomach could drop any further. No one fired on a jumper. If it happened, the offender would be pursued by everyone in the galaxy. There wouldn't be any safe harbor. Nick had seemed like a reasonable man, and she couldn't understand why he would go to such ends to make sure they didn't get to Tev's planet first.

Absalon's voice was cold, a side of him Kindra had never seen before. She knew he was a war hero, but she had never seen this. "How long until estimated impact?"

"Assuming typical launch sequence, four and a half minutes, sir."

"Set jump timer for three minutes, ensign. Make sure everyone knows that's all the time they have. Everyone's going under."

Kindra could see the timer start in the corner of her own viewscreen, but she was focused on the drama happening on the bridge. Derreck and Absalon were standing chest to chest, and from Kindra's perspective, all she could see from Derreck's helmet camera was the sleeve of Absalon's uniform.

"You're going to kill him."

"And I wish there was another way, but if we don't jump, this entire ship dies. Come on, Derreck, you know this is the only way."

Derreck swore, but he took a step back. Kindra was able to see more of Absalon, and she could see the emotion barely contained on his face. The two men didn't say anything else, and for a whole thirty seconds, they stared at each other. Kindra watched the countdown clock nervously. She'd need at least a minute to get from her seat to under sedation, but Derreck would need more. There wasn't any way he could warn Tev though. There wasn't any way any of them could.

"Torpedoes launched, sir. Four nuclear signatures."

Kindra couldn't believe it. They were under nuclear attack.

"Get under, Derreck."

"Yes, sir."

Derreck turned and started running. Underneath her the gravity shifted as the *Destiny* started a hard burn away from the torpedoes, trying to give themselves as much time as possible. The last words Kindra heard from the bridge were a question from captain Absalon. "Are they going to be in our jump field?"

She didn't hear the answer as Derreck tore out of the bridge to the nearest bunks.

Kindra looked at the clock. There was only a minute and a half until jump. She needed to get going, too. Eleta had already followed the orders.

Her mind raced. There had to be some way of warning Tev, but her mind was frozen in place, focused only on the numbers counting down in front of her. She swore, feeling a sudden cowardice. She stood up and sprinted towards her bunk. As she ran, some part of her mind was trying to think of how to save Tev, but nothing came. She could only save herself.

As she lay down in her bunk, Kindra hated herself. She felt the needle penetrate her skin, and she took one last look at the clock. Fifteen seconds until jump. The drugs took an average of five seconds to flood the system under emergency dosages. She had made it, but Tev wouldn't.

Kindra raged against life as her world went black.

SEVENTEEN

TEV WAS JUST ABOUT to sprint back out into the hallway when blue lights flashed in the halls. The event halted his motion. Blue lights meant that the ship was about to jump, but that couldn't be right. Why would the ship jump when it was under attack? If everyone was so scared of it, they'd want to wait until they were safe in their bunks, wouldn't they?

Tev didn't have time to worry. The lights only flashed a few minutes before the jump, so he knew there wasn't anything left to do. Whatever everyone was scared of, he would face it, and he'd face it with the courage of a hunter.

When the *Destiny* jumped, Tev didn't feel any physical sensations. But it felt as though his mind and spirit were torn out of his body, thrust onto their own journey. He wanted to vomit, but there was nothing to vomit, no food to regurgitate. He didn't understand what was happening. It was the worst feeling, but a part of his mind recognized that it was only a feeling, not rooted in any physical experience.

Time ceased to have any meaning for him, but a small voice, something in the back of his soul, screamed at him. It felt as though he was digging, digging to find a truth hiding beneath the surface. When he pulled the voice out of the dirt, its message was as confusing as everything else that was happening to him.

You've been here before.

Tev didn't understand. He was in a space that couldn't be understood. But then his perspective shifted, as though he had turned just a fraction of a centimeter to the right, and suddenly, something resembling order came to his disjointed thoughts.

He was standing on top of a high place. Perhaps it was the highest place. It certainly felt higher than any mountain he had ever climbed on his own. A cold breeze cut through his body, slicing through his skin as though it was nonexistent.

A memory of a dream shot through Tev's consciousness. A flash of recognition. He had been here before. He turned, and the woman was there, just as she had been the last time. Lys, goddess of the hunt.

Her lips didn't move, but Tev was assaulted by sounds, indistinguishable. He saw a ship moving through space and found that he had the language to describe what was happening. It was the *Destiny*, floating in space, and suddenly, it seemed like it was the most important thing that had ever happened, the most important ship in the history of humanity. Tev shook his head against the onslaught of emotion. It was just a ship, but it wasn't. It was the piece on which the future of all people rested.

Tev forced out words, an almost physical effort. "I don't understand."

Lys' lips didn't move, but her voice rang through Tev's mind, crystalline in its clarity.

"You do."

Tev looked down and saw a planet underneath him. It was familiar, something else he had once seen. Was it the planet he had come from? He had only seen it the once, when he had flown away from it with Kindra.

The planet fell away from him, and again Tev fought the battle between the physical and the imaginary. His mind screamed that he should be feeling vertigo, but there was no sense of movement, nothing at all.

It wasn't something he saw, so much as it was something he felt. As the distance increased and Tev could see more and more stars, he understood. The clans were spreading. They were hopping from star system to star system, no longer limited to their home planet.

When he thought of a home planet, his stomach twisted, as though it was wrong. Deeply wrong.

He was back on the mountaintop, and Lys stood by him, beautiful and deadly. With just a glance, Tev knew that her bow was stronger than his, that she never tired of the chase. She was the perfect hunter, the best that had ever lived.

"What do I do?"

She turned to him and smiled, a smile that pierced him and brought him to his knees. No woman would ever match Lys' beauty or attraction. All others were just pale reflections of true beauty, and Tev's heart broke at the sight.

Lys leaned over him, and Tev was intoxicated by every part of her. She exhaled softly, and her breath smelled like a spring morning in the woods. Her lips moved, and this time, it was more personal, more meaningful than anything he had ever encountered before. It was as though she actually there. He could feel her breath, hear her words in his ears, not in his mind.

"Hunt. Farther than you ever have. Better than you ever thought possible. Hunt."

Echoes of the past crashed against his mind. It was similar advice to that he had gotten last time.

Lys stood up, and her sudden absence nearly destroyed Tev. He couldn't stand to be more than a few centimeters away from her. It was cold, as cold as death.

Tev's world shifted again, and he felt as though he had been slammed back into his body. He looked around, the effort causing him to almost scream in agony. He was back in the hallway of the *Destiny*.

REALITY WAS difficult to return to. For the first few seconds, it hurt to move any part of his body. It was a difficult feeling to describe. After most jumps with drugs, it felt as though you were reconnecting with your body, where everything was just a moment or two behind your command for it to move. This was like that, but worse. He would command his arm to move, and it seemed like it took a minute or two to move. Inside the suit, it was even worse.

Tev didn't know how long he took to struggle back to his feet. In so many ways, everything was the same, but Tev felt that he was a very different person than the one who had been present before the jump. He didn't have the words to describe it.

He heard a rifle go off in the hallway adjacent to him, dragging him back into the present moment. Tev peeked around the corner. He counted eight suits moving. Six of them were normal, and two were heavy. One suit fired at another, and then there were only seven. Tev waited, but although they were moving, they didn't fire anymore. They might not have the mental ability to do so.

Tev was driven by something stronger than him, something larger. He moved quickly, his motions as smooth as they had ever been before. He turned the corner and locked on to one of the mostly immobile suits and pulled the trigger. The suit stopped moving. Tev kept moving, mentally pulling the trigger every time his reticle passed over one of the moving suits. He climbed up on one of the heavies and shot a round point-blank through the driver's compartment.

Behind him, Tev heard movement. The last remaining heavy was moving. It staggered as though it were drunk, but some part of the pilot had recognized a threat and moved to deal with it.

Tev was moving even before his brain recognized the danger. It was a good thing, as a row of large shells ripped up the heavy he was standing on. Tev got out of the way just before the shells cut his suit into ribbons.

Tev's mind raced, a liquid calm settling over him. He'd never experienced anything like it, a calm deeper than any he had known. He tried to bring his left arm up, but the pilot had seen what Tev had done. He rotated his torso, so that Tev didn't have a line-of-sight on the cockpit. Tev held his fire. If he couldn't break through, there was no point in firing. He wrenched his right arm up and over and pulled the trigger, just to keep the other pilot aware of his presence. The shells tore up armor but did no real damage to the heavy suit.

He wouldn't win this way. More shells tore through the space around him, another one striking his right arm. The shell tore through his armor and injured arm, rendering it entirely useless. The pain was incredible, and Tev almost lost control of his suit. It also meant he had lost his best weapon for close range.

Tev debated running for cover, but he knew he would never make it. The shells continued to chase him as he circled the heavy in the hallway, and if the heavy had even a second to catch up to him, Tev wouldn't make it. His only chance was in his greater mobility.

Tev launched himself at a wall, kicking off it with a force that caved it in. He redirected his speed quickly, allowing himself to fall to the ground and slide to the opposite wall. As soon as he wedged his foot into the corner, he launched himself up and over the heavy, which was still trying to turn fast enough to track him. The heavy tried turning back again quickly, but Tev could tell the pilot was disoriented.

Tev came up right in front of the cockpit, placing his hand against the shell. The pilot of the heavy paused, knowing in his last moment that there was nothing he could do in time to stop what was about to happen.

Tev pulled the trigger, and the hallway went silent.

THE SILENCE WAS EERIE. Like everyone else, he had never been on a ship so soon after a jump. To the best of his knowledge, he was the only one alive and awake on the ship. He wandered the hallways, lost in thought and shock.

The men he had just fought against didn't have a chance. The pilot of the heavy, maybe, but he had taken life that didn't pose an immediate threat to him. He had never done that before, and he found that it didn't bother him. That in itself bothered him most of all.

He didn't understand the vision he had seen. He didn't know what he was supposed to do. There was no telling if it was even real of not. He was lost.

His arm hurt, fires of agony shooting through his body every time he moved. Finally, he stopped. There wasn't any place for him to be. He sat down in a random hallway, one that looked to his sight the same as any other. He didn't plan to, but he fell asleep quickly, exhaustion and blood loss finally overcoming his will.

When he woke up, it was to the helmet being pulled off his head. He startled, but he saw Kindra's face in front of his, and he immediately settled down.

Their eyes met, and Tev knew that something had changed for Kindra. For the entire journey, she had been torn in two about her decisions. But now her eyes were clear. She had made a decision and had figured out how to live with it.

Tev didn't have words, his mind, body, and spirit spent beyond endurance. Kindra's hand lifted up his head and his gaze, and she spoke calmly.

"Don't worry, Tev. I'll take care of you."

Tev smiled and gave in to exhaustion.

EIGHTEEN

THEY WERE ALL, including Tev, bandaged and broken, gathered in the *Vigilance*, one jump away from Tev's home planet. If all went according to plan, *Destiny* would jump in about eight hours, and shortly thereafter *Vigilance* would pull out of its berth and take Tev back to the home he had left long ago.

This time they were gathered because Kindra had called them together. Ever since their final battle with the *Hellbringer*, Kindra had been thinking about one problem, and one problem only. How could they save Tev's people?

She thought she had a solution, but it would require the cooperation of everyone. At some point in the future, it might even require mutiny. Kindra was willing to pay the cost, and she thought the others would as well, but she had to know.

Alston, as she would have predicted, was the first to speak up. "So, why are we here today? What vague sedition do we have planned this week?"

Kindra heard the loving sarcasm in his voice and was

surprised. She still didn't know what drove their geologist, but it was clear he was just as invested as any of them.

Kindra's response was given in kind. "You'll be happy to know, Alston, that this time I called us together, and I have a very specific sedition in mind."

Alston raised an eyebrow in interest, and Kindra continued.

"I've been thinking a lot about what we can do for Tev and his people. Eleta has finished decrypting the colonization plans, and they are a good news-bad news situation. Fleet is certainly considering colonization, but any action is years away. But I think all of us understand that no matter what happens, Tev's people are in an unfortunate situation. They are sitting on one of the most habitable planets we've ever found in the galaxy, and they don't have the ability to defend it. No matter how benevolent Fleet is, the temptation is too strong.

"Believe it or not, I think the best solution is to let Fleet's plan go ahead."

There were several intakes of breath around the table, but Kindra charged ahead. She had suffered countless sleepless nights considering the problem, and she was certain her idea, while certainly not ideal, was the best way forward.

"Look, there is a historical precedent here. A very long time ago, back on old Earth, countries on the continent of Europe explored and conquered much of the globe. One of the reasons they were able to do so easily was because they had better technology than most of the rest of the world.

"But what if they had encountered a level of technology equal to their own? It's hard to answer such a question, but we have to imagine the era of colonization would have looked much different.

"I propose that we give Tev's people our level of technology. Fleet wants them to pilot the exosuits? Fine. Let's train them to be the best exosuit pilots the galaxy has seen. Then they have the strength to negotiate a better deal with Fleet."

There was silence around the table as everyone considered Kindra's argument, weighing it against their own beliefs and plans. Derreck made the logical leaps first. "At some point in time, your plan means that we might need to choose sides."

"Possibly. I still hold out hope that Fleet will be wise and we won't have to. But yes, if the conflict goes so far, I would ask us to choose a side, and to fight against Fleet."

Derreck looked to Tev. "What would your people think? Would they adopt our technology to protect themselves?"

Tev's answer was certain. "We don't always welcome new ways. But if this is a matter of survival, and given enough time, I will convince them. I have no doubt we will adopt your technology."

Derreck nodded and scanned the rest of the room. "This has to be unanimous. I don't think I need to underline the consequences of this decision."

Surprisingly, it was Alston who spoke first. "The way I see it, we're just following Fleet's orders." He smiled at his own joke.

Eleta looked carefully at Tev and at Kindra. "It's the right thing to do. I'm in, too."

Derreck grinned. "So be it. As planned, we'll load up the *Vigilance* with every remaining exosuit and start training Tev's people. Then we'll wait and see how Fleet responds. If the worst should happen, we can use *Vigilance* for orbital defense, but we can all hope it never goes that far. But we will protect Tev's people and his planet."

The meeting disbanded, and Kindra felt proud. Proud of her service, proud of her actions, and proud to be part of the crew of the *Vigilance*. Tev's people would be protected, and Fleet would do right by them. She chose to believe in that future.

EPILOGUE

TEV STOOD on the observation deck of the *Vigilance*. Off in the distance, a large dot grew slowly as they approached his home planet. He fought the urge to scratch the itch of the cast his arm was in. Kindra had tried to explain their technology to him, but all he needed to know was that if he left it on, his arm would be healed.

There hadn't been any combat since the jump that Tev lived through. They hadn't seen any more signs of *Hellbringer*, even though they hadn't destroyed it. Derreck told Tev they thought that perhaps they had killed too many of the rebel ship's pilots. They knew it was still out there, but it was in hiding for now. *Destiny* patrolled the jump points, waiting for a sign of the rebellion ship.

On board the *Vigilance* were all but four of the exosuits *Destiny* had brought along. The suits were a symbol of the transition coming to Tev's people, whether they desired it or not. Tev's clan, and all the others, were about to be thrown into the future.

Tev didn't care about any of that. There would be a time where it would become his focus, but not yet. He could only think about the jump. Kindra, of course, had been obsessed by what had happened. Few people ever kept their sanity through a jump, and to her knowledge, never before had it happened when a full biology lab had been so close at hand. Kindra had run him through more tests than he had thought possible. He had been poked and scanned more times than he ever wanted.

Kindra had been fascinated, and she had told him about some of her theories, but Tev didn't pay attention. His mind was in other places.

The soft hiss of the door announced someone's entrance, and Tev could tell from the steady footsteps that it was Derreck.

"Kindra told me you'd been up here for hours."

Tev looked over at Derreck. If there was anyone on this ship who would understand him, it would be the captain. But he wasn't sure what he had seen was something he should share.

Together they looked at the planet as it approached. It had been years of travel, and Tev wondered what was in store for him when they returned.

Derreck seemed to read his thoughts. "Are you nervous?"

"Yes."

"You've done a lot for us, Tev. I don't know what will happen when we land, but I want you to know that you always have a home here, no matter what."

Tev nodded his appreciation, but that wasn't what he was concerned about, and Derreck seemed to pick up on it.

After a long time, Derreck spoke. "It changes you."

Tev knew Derreck was speaking about living through a jump. Kindra had told him that Derreck had lived through one earlier. He nodded.

"When it happened to me, I thought my soul had been torn from my body. I'm not spiritual, but I didn't have any other language to describe it. I don't know how you came through as well as you did, but I know I came through different. It was as though I was stripped of everything. There was no place to hide. I could only be me, and nothing else."

Derreck paused and looked at Tev. "Does that make sense?"

Tev nodded. He understood how Derreck felt, and he saw Derreck's shoulders lift, as though a burden had been lifted from them.

"Do you want to talk about what you saw?"

A part of Tev wanted nothing more. He wanted to share his vision with someone, but he couldn't bring himself to do it.

"Not today."

Derreck nodded. He was about to turn around, but Tev softly put a hand on his arm to stop him. "Was it real? What I saw?"

Derreck shrugged. "I don't know. But I've explored a lot of space, and every day I learn about just how little I am sure of. What's real is what we say is real."

Tev took a deep breath. It was hard to find balance, out here in the black. But he had a clan who would help light the way.

AFTER EVERYTHING THAT HAD HAPPENED, landing back on his home planet seemed almost anticlimactic. There was no danger, no combat or risks necessary. The *Vigilance* landed in the same place it had landed two years ago, and after the required safety checks,

Tev almost ran out of the ship to touch feet on his home planet again.

It all came crashing back to him. The sights, the sounds, and the smells. It was the smells he missed the most. The fresh scent of the trees, a hint of moisture in the air hinting at a storm that had just passed. He stripped off the moccasins he wore around the ship, digging his toes into the soft dirt.

They had spoken at length of what to do upon arrival, and although it pained Tev, they had decided it was best to wait for the people to come to them. Derreck had burned long and hard on reentry, and so anybody should have been able to see them come in. It would take them some time to come to the ship, but Tev estimated it would be no more than four or five days before they received a visitor.

For the first time in years, Tev made fire on his own and sat around it, surrounded by a new clan. He was surprised to find that even here, back home, his thoughts had changed. Kindra, Derreck, Eleta, and Alston were now his clan. He wasn't sure if that meant his first clan wasn't his anymore, but he didn't dwell on negative thoughts. It was good to be back.

That night Tev cooked food from the ship over the fire for them. The evening was, as all things had been in his life recently, a strange mixture. The food of the aliens over the fire of home. They ate and spoke, *Vigilance*'s sensors watching over them.

As the sun set, the rest of the crew retreated to the ship to sleep for the night. Tev went back in with them, but he went to his bunk and pulled out his old kit. He always kept his knives sharp, but so much else had been unused since he left. He took it all back out and made camp, watching the stars that made up Lys spin lazily over his head.

After five days, Tev started to get anxious. The rest of the crew were running experiments, their time filled with activity, but Tev had none of that. He had covered the surrounding ground time and time again. Derreck had suggested he wear his suit, mostly patched up from the battle wounds, but Tev refused. Not here, not when his people could come out of the woods at any time.

That night, Tev sat around the fire alone, whittling sticks. Off in the woods upwind and in front of him, he heard a twig snap, and his senses instantly became alert. He didn't react, forcing himself to whittle as though nothing had happened. He sniffed the air, and there they were, careless.

It was too easy. It was a trap. Tev stood up and pulled a small pistol from his waistband, finding the target he knew would be there about fifteen paces behind him. It was Xan, as deadly and graceful as ever.

Out of the woods a voice called to him, a voice Tev had worried he would never hear again. "I told you that he wouldn't let himself get soft." It was Neera.

Tev didn't dare take his eyes off Xan. The hunter smiled and laughed. "I guess you're right, again."

Certain that he wasn't in any danger, Tev put the gun back in his waistband.

He turned around to see Neera step out of the trees. She was two years older, but she was still beautiful. Holding her hand was a small boy, who looked unmistakably like her. Tev squinted. Not just her. Her and Xan. His heart sank, his dreams of her waiting for him dashed for good. But he forced a smile on his face. He wouldn't let sorrow ruin this reunion.

Neera returned his smile. "Welcome home, Tev."

PART THREE
PRIMAL DESTINY

For Justin

ONE

TEV LANDED SOFTLY, considering the fact that he was wearing an exosuit that weighed twice as much as he did. The rocky outcropping he had jumped from was almost ten meters overhead, but his muscles, enhanced by the artificial strength of the suit, absorbed the impact with ease.

The jump itself held no significance to Tev. He had made dozens just like it in the past week alone. But the feeling of freedom he experienced while wearing the suit was addicting. He moved faster, jumped higher, and was more dangerous than he had dared to dream when he had been younger.

Tev was the complete master of his environment. He was the apex predator, afraid of none of the beasts that once kept him awake at night. To know that he was the most dangerous predator freed his mind from the background hum of fear that had once been a constant companion.

Tev snapped out of his reverie as he heard the approach of his opponent. Unlike Tev, who was quieter than a breeze, his opponent crashed through the environment, heedless of the noise he created. That was the danger of the suits. If nothing could harm you, you lost the skills you once relied on, skills that gave you an advantage, even armored.

To his credit, Xan, Tev's opponent, showed no fear in the face of a challenge. He had been pursuing Tev for several minutes now, and Tev could tell by the sound of Xan's footfalls that the big man had no plans to slow his chase. As Tev predicted, Xan took the drop a few moments after Tev had landed.

Tev leaped out of the way, less out of fear for his own safety and more concerned about Xan having a flat place to land.

Xan hit the ground Tev had just vacated with tremendous force. Xan was huge, and Tev had been surprised to discover the *Vigilance* carried a suit large enough for him to squeeze into. Together, man and machine outweighed Tev by a substantial amount, but for a moment, it looked like Xan would be able to control the impact from the fall.

The moment lasted less than a heartbeat. Xan hadn't fallen straight down, his drop maintaining some of his forward momentum. That energy transferred to his landing, and he crashed face first into the ground. Without armor it might have been a deadly blow. Fortunately, Xan was protected, the metal skin of the exosuit dimpled in several places, a testament to Xan's willingness to push the edges of his ability.

Tev aimed his rifle at Xan and pulled the trigger, just to drive home the point. There were no rounds in the weapon, but the computers would register the hit all the same. He didn't stick around for more than a few seconds. The lesson wasn't over yet. He jogged down the crevasse they had leaped into, looking for a place to climb or jump back up.

Behind him, Tev heard Xan struggle to his feet. He

knew from firsthand experience that such falls hurt, even armored, and he didn't envy Xan the pain he must be feeling. But Xan was a hunter worthy of the stories told about him around the campfires, and Tev could hear the chase begin again.

Distracted by the sounds behind him, Tev missed on his first attempt to jump out of the crevasse. Cursing his own lack of focus, he leaped and grabbed the ledge just as Xan turned the corner, careening off the rock wall towards him. Tev pulled himself up and over the lip just as Xan lunged to tackle him.

Tev got to his feet as Xan sprang from the bottom of the crevasse to come down right beside him. The move startled Tev, who hadn't believed a jump of such height was possible. Xan landed awkwardly, stumbling forward as he fought to find his balance.

Tev seized the opportunity, pushing gently on Xan's back, laughing to himself as the larger hunter fell to the ground once again.

This time, Xan was back on his feet in an instant. He lashed out with a fist aimed squarely at Tev's head. Tev saw the blow coming and leaned back, allowing the roundhouse to pass in front of his face. He watched in amusement as Xan's momentum twisted the big man.

Xan was, by most accounts, an excellent pilot, but Tev was pushing him harder, trying to get him to pilot the exosuit like a second skin. Xan still forgot to restrain himself in some of his movements, which led to a loss of balance. In a real fight, such mistakes would be fatal.

Xan seized on Tev's moment of distraction and grabbed his right arm, twisting it into a powerful throw that sent Tev flying back towards the crevasse. Instinctively, Tev extended his hands and tucked his head, turning his short flight into a dive roll. He came to his feet less than a meter away from the edge of the crevasse, and Xan's thundering footsteps were a powerful clue to Tev's immediate future.

Tev used the forward momentum he still had to lean into a soaring leap across the chasm. The crevasse was about three meters wide, and unpowered, Tev never would have made the jump. With the suit Tev landed on the other side with ease, his footfalls as light as ever.

Tev turned to see Xan making the same jump. With the power from his short sprint, Tev could already see Xan was going to overshoot him by at least two meters. The other hunter hadn't realized that truth yet, and he raised his fist to pummel Tev as he arced through the air.

The more experienced hunter stifled a laugh as Xan went barreling through the space in front of him. The large man landed lightly, though, and quickly turned towards Tev. This time, instead of a roundhouse, he came in with a strong series of jabs, where a lack of control wouldn't twist him off-balance.

The idea was a good one, but Xan's execution was poor. Tev retreated a few steps and then stopped and bobbed down, allowing a right jab to pass over his left shoulder. With one quick move, Tev grabbed and controlled Xan's wrist, pulling it down as he lifted his hips up. Xan went crashing onto the forest floor, and Tev thought he heard the big man let out a small groan.

Xan tried to get back to his feet, but Tev opened the radio channel between them and spoke in their shared language, a language that still sometimes felt alien to him after the months he had spent among Kindra and her people.

"That's enough for today, Xan. If we go much longer it's going to be difficult for them to repair our suits."

Even with the armor on, Tev could see the tension evaporate from Xan's body as he allowed his frame to collapse back against the ground. "Thank Lys. I'm tired of getting beaten by you."

LESS THAN AN HOUR LATER TEV, Xan, and several other hunters gathered in a small circle. This small group represented the best pilots their planet possessed, each one responsible for training several others. In the terminology of Kindra's people, they were lance commanders.

When Tev first started training his fellow hunters several months ago, he and Derreck had quickly come to the realization that by themselves, they couldn't train everyone as quickly as they wanted. Most hunters could pick up the basics of piloting a suit in a few days, but to protect their planet, they needed far more than just the basics. They needed to be the best pilots the galaxy had ever seen.

Derreck was the one who proposed the solution. They chose the best pilots from their volunteers. These were the warriors that Derreck and Tev spent the most time with. After a training session, the lance commanders had the responsibility of going back to their lance and teaching the concepts to their team.

Becoming a lance commander was an honor, but keeping the position was a challenge. The title and responsibility was given to whichever student Derreck and Tev considered the best pilot in each lance, so there was constant friendly competition to be the top of the squad. The only one who had kept his position in the top of his lance was Xan, but that was to be expected from the greatest hunter in all the clans.

As the warriors relaxed into deep squats, Tev took a

moment to laugh at the incongruity of it all. They were deep in the forests claimed by Tev's birth-clan, and the hunters all wore traditional garb, clothing that Tev wouldn't have given a second thought to three years ago. They wore skins of the animals they had killed, many wearing a minimum of clothing due to the heat of the summer days. Tev was no different. He wore a pair of pants and nothing else. Even his feet were bare.

But they weren't gathering around a fire, as his people had for so many generations. Instead, they gathered around a holographic projector replaying scenes from Tev's and Xan's skirmish. The clash of the traditional and the alien would have been bizarre a few months ago, but it was quickly becoming a new normal. Outside of the circle, Derreck stood.

The captain of the *Vigilance* wasn't flexible enough to sit in a deep squat, and his uniform set him apart from the rest of the assembly. Despite his status as an outsider, many of the hunters looked up to the captain. Time and time again, Derreck had given the perfect advice to each new pilot. Many of the hunters were almost equal to Derreck's skill with the suits, but his real gift was as a teacher, a role revered among the clans. Even Tev, who could pilot circles around Derreck, frequently came to the captain seeking guidance.

Tev settled into a squat and picked apart the duel with the commanders. As was his custom, he started with a broad question. "What do you think was the primary reason I defeated Xan in this duel?"

Several answers were suggested, but all were timid. This reluctance came up whenever Xan was involved. The big hunter was a legend, and outside of a suit, Tev was certain the man had no equal on the planet. Xan's fame made many of the students hesitate to criticize him. One young woman, though, had no such problem. Tev called on her.

"Mara."

The woman reminded Tev in many ways of Neera, once the love of his life. Like many of the men, she wore only the minimum necessary to be appropriate, and even a quick glance at her confirmed her physical strength. Unlike Neera, her dark hair was cropped short, and her eyes were sharp and focused as she watched the replay.

"Xan still struggles to control his strength in the suits. Because of that, his attacks and movements often throw him off balance."

Tev agreed. Using a small remote, he brought up Xan's leap across the crevasse, which had sent him flying in front of Tev.

"Look here. There's no doubt of Xan's strength. He's proven it many times over."

That statement was very true. At night around the campfires there had been many impromptu wrestling matches, and even Tev had been ground beneath Xan's great arms more than once.

"The challenge with such strength is that the suit amplifies everything we do. It's a problem each of us need to solve, but it's even more challenging for the strongest among us. The good news is, once Xan masters his control, he'll be able to jump farther than any of us. So, how do we solve this problem?"

The ice broken, the hunters started speaking up, sharing practices that had worked for them and brainstorming new ways around the problem.

This was the part of the reflection Tev most enjoyed. He had started the conversation, but the hunters, in their pursuit of mastery, had no problem taking the lead from him. Ideas bounced around the group and were constantly refined and improved. Tev and Derreck made suggestions, but the weight of improvement was shouldered by the hunters themselves.

After almost an hour of discussion, Tev broke the commanders up. Each of them would spend the afternoon with their lance, practicing and improving upon what had been discussed this morning. It was their new routine, and a demanding one at that. Few of the hunters here had seen much of their clans or families since volunteering.

Unfortunately, the clans and families would have to continue waiting. Tev wouldn't stop training his hunters until they could defend their planet from the threats from space.

THE DEBRIEFING DONE, Tev offered to walk with Derreck back to the *Vigilance*. Their pace was slow, both of them lost in silent thought. At times, Tev winced as he stepped on an exposed rock or root. He had lost the callouses on his feet in his years in space, the surfaces of Derreck's world smooth and even. They were growing back, but if his attention wavered, he was liable to step where he would injure himself.

His weak feet were just another reminder of how stranded he felt. As a youth, he had always wanted to explore, his travels often taking him to the edges of the land of his clan. He had so desperately wanted to cross those boundaries, to explore as far as his feet could carry him. Two years ago that desire had come true in the most dramatic fashion, and he had volunteered to go into space. But in space, his attitude had changed. His driving desire became coming home, to walk the well-known paths and feel the familiar surge of excitement as he tracked his prey.

But Lys, the goddess of the hunt, was unkind to him. The world he returned to was different from the one he left. He had been foolish to think nothing would change. Time always pushed forward, and life didn't pause like one of Kindra's holodramas. You couldn't just leave for years and hope to find the story in the same place.

His feet had become soft and nearly useless. Neera married Xan, joining their two clans into one of the strongest the storytellers could remember. The two of them had a child, a young boy who showed all the promise of having two well-regarded parents. Tev wasn't shunned upon his return, but he wasn't welcomed either. There was no feast for his return. Shet, Tev's mentor, was no longer strong, but old and sick.

Tev thought about home and what that idea meant. When he was a boy, home had been the place he wanted to escape from. Home was small and confining, full of rules Tev hadn't fully understood. In space, on board the *Vigilance* and its parent jumpship, *Destiny*, home had always been here, on his home planet among his clan. Home was the place he longed to return to.

He didn't know what home was anymore. Perhaps it was just a feeling, a sense of security, love, and acceptance. All he knew was that whatever home was, he didn't have one. He was trapped between two worlds, part of both but welcomed by neither.

They were almost halfway between the hunter's camp and the dropship when Derreck stopped walking. Tev came to a halt beside him instinctively.

Derreck's voice broke through his reverie. "How are you doing, Tev?"

Tev turned to look at his captain, a term he didn't even know two years ago. For others, such a question might simply be a way to start conversation, but that wasn't how Derreck thought. The captain shunned empty words, so if he asked, it was out of genuine concern.

Tev looked back at the camp they had come from and looked forward to where the dropship stood. Derreck seemed to read the hunter's thoughts.

"You know you are always welcome on the *Vigilance*. All of us would love to see more of you."

Tev shook his head slowly. "I don't belong there any more than I belong there," he said as he gestured towards the camp.

He appreciated that Derreck didn't try to fill the silence with meaningless words. Another man would have protested, would have argued Tev did belong among his crew, but not Derreck. He understood that as welcome as Tev was on the *Vigilance*, he was still an alien.

Derreck's voice carried clearly on the afternoon breeze. "Acceptance will take time, Tev. We haven't been here long, and there's been a lot of change. Someday there will be a new normal. The process is hard, but life will get better."

"And if it doesn't?"

The expression on Derreck's face shifted, and Tev knew the captain had come up with a new thought.

"What if your problem is a matter of perspective? You're trying to fit into one of two existing groups, but what if you considered it differently? You aren't an outsider caught between your first home and your second, but instead, you're the first of a new generation."

Tev let the idea sink in. He liked how it sounded, but his heart didn't believe it. He gave Derreck a sad smile, to let him know the effort was appreciated, and together they continued toward the ship.

When they reached the *Vigilance*, Tev took a moment, as he almost always did, to admire its clean lines. Even after months on the planet, the dropship still seemed so out of place, an alien artifact on an otherwise natural world. But even though the ship's appearance was unnatural, Tev couldn't help but be impressed by the design. Derreck's people were capable of beautiful creations, once one developed an eye for them.

Derreck walked up the cargo ramp into *Vigilance*'s hold, but Tev didn't follow. Derreck turned around and looked down at Tev. "Aren't you coming in?"

"No." Tev looked back down the hill towards the encampment, where the first sounds of afternoon training could be heard whenever the breeze stilled. "I need to keep practicing, otherwise they'll be better than me soon."

Derreck gave a single laugh and turned around, calling behind him as he did. "Fair enough. Don't be a stranger, though."

Tev waved and turned back towards the encampment. His statement to Derreck had only been half-true. He did need to practice, but he knew a storm was coming, and his people needed to be ready. He wouldn't give them a break until they were, and he wouldn't take one either.

TWO

FROM HER PERCH in the command center of the *Vigilance,* Kindra watched as Tev and Derreck said their farewells. She could have turned on the external microphones to hear what the two men were talking about, but looking at their hunched shoulders and close proximity, she guessed the conversation was private.

Tev turned and walked back towards the makeshift village that had sprung up in the past few months, and Derreck continued up the ramp alone. Kindra watched Tev as he picked his way back down the rocky path, his gait slow but steady.

Kindra stood up and paced the small command center, her quick stride covering the length of the room in just three steps. She fought the urge to play with her hair, a habit she'd been trying to break for over a decade now.

One of Kindra's strongest desires was to help Tev. She was responsible, at least in part, for everything he had gone through in the past few years. She had been a part of the survey team that had explored Tev's planet and made first contact. It had been her decision to bring Tev onto the

Vigilance when he had been gravely injured in a battle with Derreck. Kindra didn't believe in fate, but since that initial series of decisions, it felt as though everything that happened was preordained.

Kindra pressed her palms to her forehead, trying to clear the thoughts from her mind. She was well aware that Tev felt that some greater power was in play, but she was more rational than he was. Everything that had happened, everything, was a matter of cause and effect, nothing more. But still...

The biologist shook her head, hoping the action would reframe her thoughts. It didn't, but it did throw her hair, longer now, into her face. She hadn't cut it since they left Haven a year ago. *Vigilance* had the facilities to do so, but she had wanted to try something new. She liked the way longer hair made her look, but she still wasn't used to it.

The problem, as she saw it, was that Tev wasn't willing to open up to her. He wasn't cold or aloof or even rude. On the surface, their friendship was as strong as ever. But Kindra wasn't interested in shallow pleasantries. She wanted to know what was running through Tev's mind, and he wasn't sharing with her.

Kindra blamed the jump. Prior to their arrival upon Tev's planet, their jumpship, the *Destiny*, had been in an ongoing firefight with a jumpship from the dying rebellion, the *Hellbringer*. The fight had culminated in an attack on the *Destiny*. Tev had been fighting enemy exosuits when Captain Absalon, the commander of *Destiny*, gave the order to jump to avoid a nuclear missile strike.

No one jumped while they were awake. The biological mechanism still wasn't understood, but jumping caused most to go mad. Those who didn't usually flirted with the edge of insanity before somehow finding their way back.

Derreck had survived a jump before, but he was the only one Kindra knew who had made it, and like Tev, he didn't talk about that moment.

Kindra forced herself to sit down and order her thoughts. She had been over all of this with herself countless times, a loop her mind seemed more than content to let run on repeat forever. She admitted to herself that she was worried about Tev, but stopped herself there. In her experience, people didn't change except on their own. All she could do was continue to let him know she was there, and mean it.

Besides, she still had work to do, work that any exobiologist would kill for. She was studying an alien planet, filled with life in a way that no other explored planet was. Over the past few months she had collected hundreds of samples. If not for Tev, she gladly would have lost herself for weeks in their study.

She heard Derreck before she saw him. She suspected he had made a quick tour of the ship, taking a few moments to check in with all the crew and get updates. Kindra knew the behavior was automatic now, a practice so ingrained in him he didn't even think about it. Such small actions were what separated Derreck from merely good captains.

He poked his head in, as though it wasn't his bridge. Even though he had quite a few years on her, his grin still held a hint of boyish charm.

"Hey."

"Hey yourself."

Derreck stepped onto the bridge and settled into the captain's chair with a heavy sigh. Kindra used the moment as an excuse to ask what was on her mind. "How is he?"

Derreck swiveled his chair around so he was facing her. He didn't answer right away, his gaze studying Kindra before responding. She didn't mind. She was a terrible poker player, and she knew Derreck would see to the heart of her question, but her desire to keep updated on Tev was strong.

"He's struggling. There's a lot on his mind right now, and he's trying to shoulder the burden of preparing his people alone. He's doing excellent work, but the task would be a lot to ask from any person, and Tev's already been through too much in the past few years."

Kindra almost laughed at the inadequacy of the understatement. Tev had gone from living in a primitive society to discovering they weren't alone in the stars. He had learned how to pilot an exosuit, flown into space, lived on a planet that was thousands of years ahead of his people technologically, and fought and killed to protect his home. Yes, Tev had been through too much.

Derreck was twiddling his thumbs, and Kindra waited for him to order his thoughts.

"I don't know if there's a way for him to find a home anymore. There's no doubt that he likes and respects this crew, but I'm not sure he'd ever feel at peace here. Our lives are simply so different from how he was raised. He can't go back to his old life, either. He is certainly respected, but he's no longer one of them. I worry that our actions have destroyed his life."

Kindra heard the weight of responsibility in Derreck's voice. She didn't think her captain should bear the burden he did. He had been in a coma when she made the decisions that transformed Tev's life. Perhaps it was one aspect of leadership she never understood, the drive to take responsibility for everything that happened under your command.

Derreck finished his thought. "Maybe all he needs is

more time, but I just don't know. Have you spoken to him about it? He's closest to you, after all."

Kindra wasn't sure what gave her away. Perhaps she glanced away from Derreck. Maybe she shifted her posture slightly. But somehow, as he watched her, he understood.

"Ahhh." Derreck was at a loss for words. "I see. Have you said anything?"

Kindra gave her captain a pointed glance.

"Right. Of course not."

The silence between them grew awkward, and to break it, Kindra said, "Aren't you going to quote a regulation at me?"

Derreck's grin returned to his face. "Like it would matter to you. Besides, I think we can all agree that we've gone far beyond any regulation Fleet ever dreamed up. I don't know what to tell you."

It threatened to become awkward again until a message flashed across both of their neurodisplays. Derreck laughed. "Saved by *Destiny*. Shall we hear what Absalon has to say?"

Kindra nodded, and the two of them stood up to take the meeting in the conference room.

THEIR "CONFERENCE ROOM" was also their mess hall. The *Vigilance* certainly wasn't small, but most of its space was given over to scientific equipment. Space was always at a premium, and many areas of the ship did double duty. The mess hall was the only place large enough to fit multiple people around a table, and so a holographic projector had been set into the table.

Unfortunately, sometimes that meant upkeep at annoying times. Both Kindra and Derreck had received a message from *Destiny* requesting a meeting in fifteen minutes, and the room looked like some of the crew had just finished lunch. From a glance, Kindra guessed the guilty culprit was Eleta. The table was filled with opened packets of rice and steak, one of Eleta's favorite meals.

Kindra cleared off the table while Derreck entered authorization codes for the meeting. The doors to the hall sealed and darkened, causing Derreck to shoot Kindra a suspicious glance. She shrugged. Her notice hadn't said anything about the meeting being classified either. Regardless, in a few moments the hall was completely sealed off from the rest of the ship. Kindra hoped Alston, the ship's geologist, didn't get hungry any time soon.

The hologram came to life at the appointed time. Absalon was a stickler for timetables, even out here hundreds of light-years from the nearest Fleet outpost.

Absalon looked as though the time out in space was starting to get to him. Though his voice was as sharp as ever, his eyes looked tired. Less than a week had passed since their last routine check-in, and they weren't due for another for three days. Taken together, Kindra guessed something serious was on the horizon.

After a few seconds of small talk, Absalon asked for updates. Kindra and Derreck glanced at each other, and Derreck went first.

"Nothing new, sir. Tev continues to train the local population. I know I've expressed this before, sir, but they're *good*. Although we'll need an actual analysis to say for certain, Kindra's theories about Tev's adaptability to the suits seems accurate. He's still the best, but there will be a few catching up to him before long."

"How good are they?"

"Sir, they're regularly rolling in combat now. It doesn't even slow them down."

Kindra thought Derreck's comment was an odd statement, but Absalon's jaw almost dropped to the floor. "To be clear, you're saying 'roll' as in 'somersault,' correct?"

Derreck nodded, a smile growing on his face.

"I've never heard of such a thing. You're going to have one of the strongest military units in the galaxy if what you say is true. How do you think they'll hold up to combat situations?"

Derreck thought for a moment. "It's hard to say before putting them in the field. However, per our previous encounter here, I don't think they'll have any problems under fire."

Kindra noticed Derreck suppress a small shudder. In that previous encounter, Tev had almost killed Derreck, and Tev hadn't even been wearing a suit. Her captain's assessment was accurate. The hunters weren't afraid to fight. If the time came that they had to, they wouldn't break under the strain.

Absalon's eyes shifted to Kindra. "What's your update?"

"More of the same, also, sir. The life on this planet is related to life on Earth. Every sample I've tested shares at least some DNA. But at the same time, life here is also different. Even though I can recognize some of the DNA strands, everything I study is a new species."

"Care to make any guess how that happened?"

Kindra rejected the offer. "I'm as lost as you are, sir. When we were on Haven our findings were confirmed. Humans have never been in this part of space before."

Absalon stared off into the distance for a moment, probably looking at something off-screen. "I keep hoping that we'll find the answer to this mystery, but it seems that won't be the case. I wanted to meet with you two to discuss a new strategy."

Kindra perked up, and she forced her body to relax. There was always the fear that *Destiny* would somehow turn on Tev's people. Such an action was less and less likely with every passing day, but still, Kindra couldn't shake the fear. Tev's people were more able to defend themselves now, but they were still heavily outclassed.

Absalon didn't notice any change in Kindra's posture, but he seemed distracted by other information. Holos were the best way to communicate over a distance, but they were still a distant second to meeting in person.

"I'm concerned by the fact *Hellbringer* never jumped in-system. We may have reduced their forces when they attempted to take over *Destiny*, but we certainly didn't finish them off; and as a ship, our last data indicates *Hellbringer* was as capable as ever. For all the effort they took to get here first, it's hard to believe they would have given up.

"We've been discussing it as a crew up here, and we'd like to jump to the planet Mala explored on our first trip. We believe there is a chance they bypassed Tev's planet entirely in favor of it."

Kindra was confused, and Derreck echoed her thoughts. "Why would they do that? I was under the impression our intelligence was certain they were heading here."

Absalon shrugged. "We have nothing certain to go off of. Personally, I think Tev's planet was their primary target, but after we defeated them the second time, they had a change of heart. Perhaps the reward was no longer worth the risk. They knew that Mala found traces of civilization. They might have thought it was worth exploring."

Kindra glanced at Derreck, then forced herself back to Absalon. She might not be the best poker player, but even she could tell that Absalon was lying. The answer was too easy, too casual. *Hellbringer* had lost dozens of lives trying to get to Tev's planet, lives they could afford to lose even less than Fleet could. They wouldn't have casually decided to go visiting another planet instead.

She suspected Derreck picked up on the lie too. He was better than her at such things, and if she knew Absalon was lying, he would too. But he was a better poker player, and his voice and demeanor betrayed nothing untoward.

"I think it's a good idea to have our bases covered, but what if they are there? You're not equipped to fight *Hellbringer*, and Tev's people certainly aren't prepared to fight in space yet."

Absalon agreed. All but four of *Destiny's* functioning exosuits were down on the planet being used by Tev's people. Alston and Eleta were working on making more onboard the *Vigilance*, but Absalon knew nothing about that. If it came to a fight, *Destiny* was outclassed by *Hellbringer* in every way. "This is nothing but a recon mission. Our capacitors are fully charged, and if there's any danger, we jump right back out."

Absalon paused, as though a new thought had just occurred to him. "I suppose if *Hellbringer* isn't there, I might allow Mala some time planet-side. She's been itching to fly her ship, and we could always use more information. At the longest, we'd be gone a month."

Derreck looked over at Kindra, and she knew what he was thinking. If something happened to *Destiny*, they were stranded out here. It would be years, at least, before Fleet knew something was wrong and sent out a rescue.

Absalon seemed to read their minds. "Derreck, in preparation for this little trip, I'd like you to come up and pick up the distress beacon. If something happens, you'll need it more than us."

Kindra saw the logic. They only had one jump-capable emergency beacon. *Destiny* could jump away from danger, but their little dropship couldn't. If they had the beacon, they could at least get word back to Fleet about what had happened. It would still be years before a rescue, but it would be fewer years than the alternative.

"Very well. I can probably leave in the next few hours. I can be up to you by tomorrow."

Absalon and Derreck discussed logistics for a few moments before the meeting ended, but Kindra had already tuned out. Absalon was hiding secrets from them, but that didn't surprise Kindra. But she really wasn't sure how she felt about being left hundreds of light-years from home without a way back.

THREE

TEV FINISHED up his afternoon of training. The day had been busy. After leaving Derreck, his first priority was training on his own. While most of his time was spent training others, he did his best to reserve at least an hour a day to work alone. The others were quickly catching up to him, and Tev was determined that they'd never succeed. If he wasn't the best pilot, what did he have left?

After his own session he visited as many of the lances as he could, giving suggestions and advice to the other hunters. He remained with each lance for as long as needed. He didn't speak much, but instead demonstrated new ideas. Words were cheap, but actions carried weight. It was the same way he had learned to hunt years ago.

What most excited Tev was the new system of combat that developed among the hunters. When Tev had first piloted a suit, he had only received a bare minimum of training and support. Later, Derreck had personally trained him, and some of that training had gone against Tev's instincts. Derreck, like most of his people, relied too much on range, armor, and their weapons.

Tev had grown up in a world where the only ranged weapon was a bow. He was used to getting in close to his prey. The ranged weapons on the exosuits were excellent, but they were easy to learn, and somewhat wasteful. Tev's trainees mastered them in short order, but they also mastered using cover and mobility to limit the effectiveness of the weapons.

What had developed over months of practice was a new system of combat that alternated between ranged attacks and close, personal infighting. The new style was far superior to what Derreck had tried to train into Tev, and it pushed the suits to their limits.

The entire process was remarkable. One lance would develop a new strategy, tactic, or trick. They would use it during mock battles, and if it worked, the idea spread like a fire in dry grass. Every lance was competitive and fought to be the best, but when the sun set, they all came together and shared what they had learned. In this way, their advancement was beyond what Tev had even thought possible.

Derreck only saw the tip of the spear. Tev and the other hunters trusted him, but he was still an outsider, and wisdom dictated that a smart hunter always kept some surprises a secret. Derreck knew they were excellent pilots, but he didn't realize just how far they had advanced.

Tev's day had been full, and he was already looking forward to resting around a campfire. The last thing he expected that evening was a call from Kindra. She told him that *Vigilance* was heading up into space for a few days. Tev could tell there was something else from the tenor of her voice, and he waited for her to bring it up.

"Would you mind if I spent the next few days in the camp? There's some more experiments I'd like to do."

Tev was torn. As much as he could, he tried to keep his worlds separate. He had his people, and he had Kindra's people. When the two met, he felt the challenge of his unique position more sharply. But his weakness was no excuse to deny a friend's request.

"We'd be happy to have you."

Tev could hear the smile in Kindra's voice. She told him she'd be down to the camp early that evening and signed off.

She arrived just when she said she would. The last of the lances was shuffling into camp, exhausted from another demanding day of training. The sounds of exosuits powering down blended with the soft roar of their nightly bonfire and the smells of pig roasting nearby. Xan's lance had been responsible for the evening meal, and as much as it pained Tev to admit it, the big hunter was almost as good at cooking as he was at hunting. It was no wonder Neera had fallen in love with him.

Kindra came into the camp carrying a small backpack full of gear. Tev didn't react outwardly, but he approved. The few times Derreck had come to spend the evening at camp he had brought a backpack that looked almost as heavy as an exosuit. Kindra, at least, traveled lighter. Tev told her to find any open space and set up her tent. She did so in short order and joined them at the fire, sitting on a fallen log beside Tev.

"What are we having? I'm starving."

"Pig tonight. Xan is cooking, and he's very good." Here, in the camp, Tev spoke his own language. He was fluent enough in Kindra's that he could have spoken without the aid of the translator, but he couldn't set himself apart like that. Not here.

Kindra didn't say anything about Tev's language choice, which he appreciated. They sat together in companionable silence as everyone gathered around the fire. The meal would soon be ready, and the excitement was building. All of them had been active all day, and their hunger was about to be sated. Kindra seemed content to simply enjoy the atmosphere.

The meal began, and Xan cut off the best parts of the pig for Kindra, including the cheek. Kindra didn't hesitate, but threw the meat down her throat, making appreciative noises. Tev had noticed while on Haven that Kindra's people only focused on a few cuts of meat, and he was pleased to see she accepted the cuts offered without complaint. Xan also grinned his approval.

She was, in many ways, a remarkable woman, Tev supposed. Lately he had been very self-focused, but she was always present when he needed her, and he sometimes forgot she had left most of her people far behind as well. Tev had been to the society she came from, and to say it was different than his own was a tremendous understatement. She had made sacrifices too.

The conversation was wide-ranging and casual. One of the lances had brewed a strong fermented beverage that immediately relaxed the hunters. Most evenings were spent discussing training, but with Kindra present, the subjects changed. She asked about their hunting methods, and they were happy to oblige with story after story, each one slightly more unbelievable than the last. Kindra's translator could decipher their language, and Tev translated her questions to the group.

Neera, who sat next to Xan, asked Kindra how her people acquired their food, and Kindra struggled to explain how their markets worked. Tev's people had no concept of money, and so it was a challenge she eventually gave up on. Tev tried to fill in the gaps as best he could.

As the evening progressed, Tev realized that for the first time in his memory he could look at Neera with Xan and not be jealous. He smiled quickly to himself, thinking that it was good to be happy for a woman who was and always would be a close friend.

Kindra asked another question about hunting, and finally one of the hunters replied, "If you are so curious about our ways, there is no better way to learn than hunting yourself. I'm sure Tev could show you how. He once was well-regarded as a hunter, if he hasn't lost his skills."

Tev studied the smiles around the campfire. Didn't they realize the danger they were in? He couldn't spare the time to go hunting. "If I leave, who will prevent you all from shooting yourselves in the feet?"

There was a gentle laughter, but the other hunter persisted. "We will be fine. Game in this area is still plentiful, so it shouldn't take you more than a few days, even with one who has never hunted before, eh?"

Tev sensed the challenge for what it was. He had proven time and again he was the best exosuit pilot, but that wasn't the path to respect among the hunters. He sighed as he understood what was really being said. The contest had been laid in front of him. Bring back a respectable kill while escorting one who had never hunted. The feat would be difficult, but among the assembled hunters, nothing less could be expected. If he wanted to continue to lead them, to earn their trust, he had no choice.

Tev's response was light. "Very well. I suppose I need to show you how that is done as well."

The challenging hunter grinned, and Tev could see his decision had been correct. Around the fire, there were several subtle nods of approval.

Tev looked over at Kindra, studying her in a new light.

She seemed to understand the subtext of what was happening, and had the wisdom to remain silent on the matter. Tev estimated his chances. To her benefit, Kindra walked lightly for one of her people, and didn't breathe as heavily as some of them. With training, perhaps she could even become a hunter. The thought had never occurred to him before, but it felt right. He could do this.

Tev spoke to Kindra, loudly enough for everyone to hear. "Would you like to go on a hunt? We can leave tomorrow morning. Xan can oversee training for the next few days."

Kindra smiled, and Tev saw it was filled with genuine excitement. "I'd love to."

As the fire burned low, the hunters continued to share their stories. Tev noticed that Kindra seemed more welcome here than Derreck, and he wondered why that was. He suspected it was because Kindra didn't project any superiority. She recognized that here she was the outsider, not the expert. Derreck couldn't quite pull off the same feat.

They retired to their tents late that night, the entire evening an excuse to relax more than they usually allowed themselves to. Kindra walked with Tev away from the fire and whispered to him when they were out of earshot. "You don't have to do this, you know."

Tev looked up at Lys, the familiar pattern twinkling in the sky. He wished he had more answers, but he didn't. Not yet. "Yes, I really do."

THE NEXT MORNING Tev woke up with the rising sun, yesterday's late evening notwithstanding. The hunter came awake immediately and rolled out of his tent, preparing their supplies for the journey. He basked in the silence of the early morning, the other hunters still asleep after their festivities. Nearby, songbirds chirped their morning greetings to one another and a soft breeze rustled the tops of the trees.

Tev paused his packing for a moment to take in a deep breath of the fresh pine smell. The refreshing scent was always strongest in the morning. He had been back on his planet for several months already, and most of the time, he didn't spare too many thoughts for his home environment. But occasionally, a moment like this one would strike him, and he would realize all over again how much he had missed these places.

Kindra's world and life were composed of right angles and smooth surfaces. Her people had lost touch with what their bodies were capable of. Although his time with them had been fascinating, he could never live among them. Not happily. He was grateful his path had brought him back home, back to the places that calmed his mind.

After another deep breath, he went back to work, a small smile on his face. By the time he was done the camp was stirring, and the noise of the hunters woke Kindra.

She didn't take long to prepare. Together they were packed and ready to go before the sun even crested the tops of the trees. Tev said a few words to Xan, but the other hunter knew how to maintain the training. Knowing him, Tev would be welcomed back with open arms by the hunters eager to escape being under Xan's thumb. Tev's most pressing concern regarding the training was that the others would catch up to him in the few days he'd be gone.

They left without fanfare. Were it a larger hunt there would have been a small ceremony, a blessing of the hunting party. This hunt, though, was only about confirming Tev's skills. The other hunters would consider the task no more than a chore to be completed.

Tev's thoughts diminished the further they got from the camp. The Tev who was consumed by fear for his planet, the one who acted as a liaison between the *Vigilance* and his people, slowly evaporated. In his place, the old Tev reasserted himself. With every step, he became more immersed in the present moment, in the sights, sounds, and smells of the forest.

Kindra picked up the basics of hunting more quickly than Tev expected. When they left camp, their pace had been rapid, but as they entered areas where game would be more plentiful, their fast walk became slow and methodical. Tev showed her how to walk properly: how to check her footing before she made each step, how to brush aside dried leaves and twigs, and how to keep a close eye on low-hanging branches that she might hit as she walked under. He spoke softly about breathing silently. While hunting, stealth was far more important than speed.

She learned fast, but Tev could see the physical exertion was taking a toll on her. Kindra was in fine shape by the standards of her people, but she had never moved like a hunter, and even though the pace was slow, it was physically taxing. The sun was nearing its peak in the sky when Tev called for a break.

Their meal was simple. Dried meat from a previous hunt, some fruit and nuts that had been foraged from the area, and water from a nearby stream. While they ate, Kindra asked questions about hunting, and Tev answered as well as he was able. At times the task was challenging. Hunting wasn't something he explained very frequently. He had demonstrated often, but to put his life's passion into words didn't come easily.

He had just finished explaining the importance of staying downwind of prey when Kindra went silent. Tev allowed her the space she desired for a few minutes, but from the way she stared blankly off into the distance, he knew something was on her mind. Finally, he asked her.

She startled, almost as though she had forgotten he was there. "Even though I've known you for years now, I keep underestimating you."

"What do you mean?"

"There's this mindset that is very easy to fall into. We've got technology that is so far ahead of everything your people have accomplished. Because of that, it's easy to think that we, as a people, are more advanced. But the truth isn't that simple.

"Take hunting, for example. When I first learned that you were a hunter, my thought was that it wasn't a very demanding task. When I read about hunting in books, it sounds so simple: find an animal and shoot it. But this morning has taken all of my focus and all my strength, and we're just beginning. When you say you are one of the best hunters, I'm only now starting to understand what that means."

Tev felt a flush of pride in his gut. Derreck may have spent the most time with the hunters, but Kindra was the closest to understanding them. Kindra's thoughts made Tev feel like it might be possible to build a true bridge between the two cultures. Perhaps there might be a real chance for coexistence.

The moment passed, but Tev couldn't help but watch Kindra as he let her lead the next section of their journey. His heart and mind were stirring, but he couldn't bring the thoughts to the surface. With a small amount of dismay, he forced himself back to the matter of the hunt.

Tev was torn about what, precisely, they should hunt for. He knew there were deer in these woods, and plenty of small game, but he feared such easy prey wouldn't prove himself to the warriors at camp. There were boar deeper in the woods, but the deeper one went, the more danger one was in. Kindra, although a quick study, was still inexperienced, increasing the risk further.

He didn't see any other option, though. The hunters didn't have the time to decide who was best qualified to lead them. There was no telling when they would need to defend themselves. If Tev could bring back a boar while Kindra was with him, his leadership would be unquestioned, and they could focus on training and protecting their people. Tev took over from Kindra and led them deeper into the forest, hesitation heavy on his heart.

By mid-afternoon they had discovered traces of a boar. Tev gave Kindra a quick lesson on tracking, and let her take the lead once again, testing her new skills. Tev's practiced eye saw that the tracks were over a day old, so the risk of Kindra actually running into the boar was slim.

Kindra proved to be a natural. Her scientific training made her an excellent observer, and she was willing to take her time to ensure she didn't make mistakes. At times, Tev wondered how good of a hunter she could become if she had more time, or how good she would be if she had grown up like he had. Tev suspected she would be excellent.

While Kindra tracked, Tev kept an eye on their surroundings. Like most new hunters, Kindra was so focused on tracking that the rest of the world fell away. Her face was close to the ground, and she moved from sign to sign with an intensity that made Tev smile. She reminded him so much of himself when he had been younger.

At one time, Kindra turned to him and grinned, her joy

at the experience obvious. Tev grinned at her in return. She was discovering the same passion that had driven him for most of his life. He had planned on taking over from her, but she was enjoying herself too much.

In the late afternoon Tev sensed that something was wrong. Kindra had been tracking the boar almost to perfection, but the environment made Tev nervous. Something was off, something he didn't recognize at first.

When he realized what he had noticed, he cursed himself. His skills had rusted with disuse. The forest was too quiet, the birds and creatures unnaturally still. He heard a bird cry to the west of them, and now that he was paying attention, he recognized the call as one the bird made when it spotted a predator.

Tev didn't panic. Such a reaction would only make the situation worse. The wind was coming from the east, so a predator to the west would most likely have their scent. What predators were in the area? The only ones Tev could think of were the big forest cats. They were uncommon, but were one of the few creatures that would attack hunters. They were almost fearless in that regard.

He considered their options, which were limited thanks to Kindra's presence. She was a good tracker, but would be less than useless if the cat attacked. Thinking of Kindra made him realize she was moving farther ahead of him, so focused on tracking she didn't even notice he had stopped following. He ran up to her quickly, the noise causing her to snap out of her focus.

Tev put a hand on her shoulder. "We are being hunted."

Kindra pulled out her sidearm, a look of fear on her face. She offered it to Tev. He reached for it and then stopped.

"No. I must face this my way, or I can't return to the camp."

Kindra glared at him. "Even if it costs you your life?"

Tev didn't have time to explain himself to her. "It's better if you use the weapon to protect yourself. I have these." He held up his spear and knife.

Kindra opened her mouth to argue, but Tev put his finger to her lips. He needed to figure out where the cat was, and soon. Fortunately, Kindra seemed to understand the urgency in his gesture and remained silent. Tev focused on the sounds of the forest.

The woods were still quiet, and if Tev had to guess, he would say that the silence was surrounding them. The predator was close. From experience, Tev knew he wouldn't hear the cat itself. The beast was too good of a hunter. He tightened his grip on his spear and turned slowly around, trying to spot any movement that would give the animal away.

Behind him, Kindra's breathing was ragged and loud. If they had been hunting he would have been upset, but as it was, he understood. Experience and willpower were the only two attributes keeping his fear in check. That, and the knowledge that his skills were all that separated them from an eternal hunt with Lys.

A realization dawned on Tev at that moment. He didn't want anything to happen to Kindra. His own life was important, but he was suddenly certain that if he could give his life to keep her safe, he would do so gladly.

The cat didn't give him time to fully process his thought. Tev only heard the animal as it made its leap. He spun quickly, the cat coming at him from his left side. He couldn't move fast enough to stab the animal with his spear, but he knocked it sideways and away from them.

The spear shivered in his hands. Tev took the beast in with a glance. He had never seen one so large before. The animal landed softly on its feet and Tev glanced at his spear. Only luck and quick reflexes had seen them through that initial attack.

The cat leaped again, this time at its closer prey, Kindra. Time slowed down for Tev. Kindra was between him and the cat, and there was only a small window to try and stab his spear through. He thrust without hesitation and everything happened at once. He felt contact in his arms as the spear sliced through the fur of the cat. Kindra dove to the side, her reflexes not quite quick enough to avoid the attack. The pistol went off in her hands, but Tev saw that from the angle she was holding the weapon that she wasn't even close to hitting the target. Kindra's dive moved her away from the deadly jaws, but couldn't get her out of the way of the claws, which raked the right side of her torso and arms.

Tev spun as Kindra fell, putting himself directly between her and the cat. He held his spear straight out, the cat eyeing him warily. The hunter had hoped that his cut was deeper, but it looked to be a shallow wound. The cat wasn't hindered by the injury at all.

Tev knew that when the attack came, it would be sudden and without warning. He was right. The cat went from a slow crawl to a full sprint in a moment, leaping from tree trunk to tree trunk. Tev turned around as quickly as he was able, but his movement was hindered by Kindra attempting to stand. The cat leaped at him again, and Tev's reflexes were just quick enough. This time he planted his spear in the side of the cat, which let out a ferocious roar of pain. The cat attacked as soon as it landed, ripping the spear out of Tev's hands.

Tev ducked to the side as the cat clawed at him, drawing his long hunting blade in one smooth motion. The cat landed and turned. The animal was slowing down, but every moment it was alive, it was a danger to Kindra, who had collapsed back to the ground in shock.

There was one way to end this quickly. Tev stepped in towards the cat, an action that went against every gram of self-preservation he had. He angled towards the injured side of the cat, easily dodging the half-hearted swipe from the animal. Tev brought his blade up and across the neck of the animal, and a few moments later it was sprawled on the ground.

Tev knew the animal was dead, so he didn't waste any time getting to Kindra. He rushed to her as she attempted to sit up, and she fell back into his arms. His eyes ran over her quickly. She had lost a decent amount of blood, which explained her inability to stand again. Otherwise none of her injuries seemed fatal. If he could clean and dress her wounds, she should be fine.

His eyes met hers, and she saw the fear in her quick, darting eye movements. He laid her down gently, keeping her injured side elevated and out of the dirt. "It's going to be okay, Kindra. I'll be back in a moment to fix you up."

With that, he sprinted into the woods, looking for the materials he would need.

TEV RETURNED in only a few minutes. Fortunately, the area they were in was well-covered with vegetation, and those plants which were difficult to find were a constant companion in his bag. He cleaned her cuts with water, finding that only one on her arm was deep enough to be of concern. He considered trying to stitch the wound closed, but decided against it. Tomorrow they could return to camp and to the *Vigilance*, where they had much better ways of treating injuries. He would clean and bandage it.

Kindra was a much better patient than Tev was. She sat through his ministrations without complaint. He tried to be as gentle as possible, but his hands weren't often called on to heal. He was convinced she was still in shock. From the moment he had warned her to the moment of the attack had only been a few minutes. She'd just barely avoided severe injury.

"How are you?"

Kindra was shaking, her eyes unfocused. She didn't respond.

Tev unpacked her tent from her backpack. The setup was simple, and he had watched her put it together several times before. He unrolled her sleeping bag and escorted her into the tent. Inside, she continued to shiver, and Tev sat down beside her and wrapped his arms around her. Awkwardly, he pulled the sleeping bag around them in an attempt to warm Kindra up.

They sat together as the sun went down, Kindra's shock slowly wearing off. The moon was bright in the sky, penetrating even the thick foliage of the forest, allowing both of them to see within the tent.

Eventually she turned around and faced him. "Thank you."

Tev simply nodded. "You're welcome."

He wasn't expecting her to kiss him. He wasn't expecting to return her affection. But he did. Slowly, she pushed him down to the ground, and he didn't resist.

FOUR

THE JOURNEY back to the camp and the *Vigilance*'s landing pad took them two days. They were slowed down a little by Kindra's wounds, but more by the fact that Tev had to lug an enormous dead animal behind him. Their progress was slow, but Kindra didn't mind. She needed time to think through the events of that evening.

Tev's attitude was both convenient and frustrating, and Kindra was reminded again that she was dealing with someone whose upbringing couldn't have been more different from her own. He didn't make mountains out of molehills. They had spent the night together, and that was that. He didn't treat her any differently in the morning. He didn't avoid eye contact or act ashamed, nor did he pressure her into anything again. In all respects, it almost seemed as though the night hadn't happened.

At first, Kindra thought she should be offended, but that reaction seemed inappropriate. Eventually, the scientist in her surfaced, and she started asking questions.

"Tev, how does marriage work in your clan?"

The hunter laughed, a feat somewhat impressive

considering he had been dragging a large cat's corpse for several kilometers. "It's complicated, and many clans have different customs."

Kindra didn't press. The two of them played this game of question and answer often enough that she knew he was simply organizing his thoughts.

"Marriage generally happens between the clans, to keep new blood flowing in. Occasionally the elders will approve of a marriage within the clan, but most often marriages strengthen ties between neighboring clans. It is far more difficult to fight with another clan when you have such ties."

"But what about love and desire?"

"They play a role. No one is ever forced to marry against their will. Xan and Neera are an excellent example. There is no doubt there was desire present, but their bond is important to the two clans they come from. Their marriage is an ideal example."

Kindra couldn't stop herself before the question came out. "But what about you and Neera?"

Tev turned his head around and gave her a sad smile. "I have loved Neera almost my entire life, and I believe she loves me, too. When I was younger, I desired to marry her, but it was always unlikely. My love for her remains unchanged."

Tev must have seen the confusion on her face, and realized the heart of her question for the first time.

"Yes, we have been together, but it was not condemned. A child would be frowned on outside of a marriage agreement, but it would still be raised as one of the clan's own."

The more Tev tried to explain, the more confused Kindra became. Tev frowned as he thought of another way to describe his culture.

"There is a difference between your culture and mine. In yours, the individual is all-important. In mine, there is more of a balance. The needs and desires of the individual must be balanced by the needs of the community. Nowhere is that more visible than in marriage."

Kindra sighed, regretting she had asked the question in the first place. She needed to be much more direct. "What about us?"

Tev stopped and turned around completely to face her. "I care for you. If you are asking about marriage, I would have to think about it, and we would certainly need to consult with the elders of my clan."

Kindra raised her hands, forcing herself not to backpedal. "No, no, no. Nothing like that. We don't need to talk about marriage."

A look of relief passed over Tev's face. His focus was on other matters at the moment. He turned back to the path and continued walking, leaving Kindra lost in her own thoughts.

Tev's attitude was refreshing, if perhaps difficult to accept. She was unused to relationships being so simple. His declaration of care was straightforward, his open honesty a distinct change of pace from the dance of relationships she was familiar with.

That night they slept in separate tents, and Tev didn't seem upset or disturbed by the fact at all. The next morning it rained, but they made it back to camp by mid-afternoon. *Vigilance* had already returned from its brief stint in space.

Tev's return was greeted with some fanfare. The upside to being attacked by the cat was that Tev had brought back game greater than any of the other hunters had expected. Not only was Tev's position solidified, their respect grew for him in an instant. He tried to be modest, but Kindra saw the flush of pride the adulation gave him.

Despite his hero's welcome, Tev escorted her to the *Vigilance* right away. Both of them wanted to ensure her wounds weren't more serious than they appeared. They left the camp, Tev promising to return for evening festivities.

Fortunately, a few minutes in the medical bay was all the time Kindra needed. Tev had washed her wounds well and had prevented infection. Kindra's cuts were healed in minutes, Tev watching in fascination.

When the healing was finished, Kindra noticed Tev looking around. She forgot sometimes this was where Tev had first met her. He had been gravely wounded, but they had healed him, setting off a chain of events no one expected.

"We've come a long way since we first met, haven't we?"

Tev ran his hand over one of the medical pods. "Yes, we really have."

His voice was soft, as though he was lost in his memories. After a few moments, he shook his head, coming back to the present. "I should return to camp. Will you be fine?"

Kindra patted her arm, recently healed. "Good as new. Go back and enjoy your celebration. You've earned it. And Tev?"

"Yes?"

"Thanks for taking me hunting."

Tev grinned, an infectious smile. "It was a pleasure. You'd make a great hunter."

With that, he was out the door and out of the ship, leaving Kindra alone to reflect on the past few days.

KINDRA'S first order of business was to find Derreck and report. She gave a fairly full accounting of her adventure, leaving out the personal details. He enjoyed her story, but he had even more exciting news for her.

"We picked up the emergency beacon without any problem, and *Destiny* jumped away as soon as we were outside of its jump field. On a whim, I asked Eleta to look into what was stored on the beacon, and we made a discovery. The beacon is full of information for Fleet, including private logs from Absalon himself. I've had Eleta hack them." Derreck looked incredibly pleased with himself, like a child who had figured out what his birthday gift was before he received it.

"How is that even possible? Why didn't we just do that while we were docked on *Destiny*?"

"Eleta knows the details, but from what I gather, the encryption protocols are different. On *Destiny*, the files were secured by the AI, which Eleta didn't think she could get past. The encryption here is much more straightforward, and with the help of *Vigilance*'s AI, she thinks she can crack it in a day or two, and we can figure out what Absalon's been hiding from us."

If the plan worked, they would be able to clear up the remaining confusion they had about their journey. Throughout the trip and the conflict with the *Hellbringer*, it had always seemed like both jumpship captains, Absalon and Nicks, had information that they didn't. Kindra, for the first time in her life, was doubting Fleet; and the knowledge contained in the beacon would go a long way towards either easing or confirming her doubts.

Eleta discovered the information in short order, and the next day the four remaining crew of the *Vigilance* gathered around the mess hall table as their systems engineer shared what she discovered. They ate as they talked, and Kindra almost had to laugh at how much their discipline had slipped in the past few months. Derreck usually forbade eating during meetings.

Eleta said, "So, as all of us know, Mala lead a dropship mission to another planet as we were exploring this one. Originally, it was thought the other planet was an even better candidate for intelligent life based on signals coming from the planet's surface. They didn't find a civilization, but they did find the remains of one. We didn't know exactly what they found until now."

Eleta was enjoying herself, holding the knowledge over everyone until they were on the edges of their seats.

"Mala and her team had to leave before they were able to make any substantial discoveries. However, they found possibilities that, if true, could change our entire civilization."

Derreck was getting frustrated by Eleta's gentle teasing.

"Get to the point already."

Eleta laughed. "Fine. Although they didn't find anything specific, they found indications of two technologies that could reshape our lives. The first is a new type of AI, potentially superior to our own. The neurological modeling is completely different than what we use, but if it works, it would both be faster and lighter in terms of resources than our own AIs. That technology gives rise to the second possibility hinted at in some of the archives: new equations for jump technology."

Alston spoke, "What does it mean?"

Eleta shrugged. "There's really no knowing. Mala and her team had to leave before they could dig too deeply. All Fleet has are hints that these technologies exist. Perhaps we're looking at incremental improvements, or maybe we're looking at leaps beyond what we can fathom. What I wonder about is what the civilization that left this technology behind is like now. We're looking at discoveries that are at least a thousand years old."

Derreck focused them on the problem at hand. "More importantly, if Fleet has this information, the rebellion does as well. Maybe Tev's planet wasn't the goal. Maybe they were always aiming for the second planet."

Kindra stood up and stretched her muscles. Her arm still itched from where the cut had been healed. "The only way to know for sure is to ask Captain Nicks, and who knows if he'd even tell us the truth. Does this change anything we do?"

Everyone shook their heads. Whatever was happening light-years away, their goal was still the same: Prepare Tev's people to deal with outside influences. Knowing what Fleet was hiding was useful, but the secrets they uncovered didn't change anything. At least, that was what Kindra hoped.

KINDRA PRESSED her palms against her forehead, trying to push out the cobwebs that gathered in her mind. More than a week had passed since the *Destiny* left and she had gone on her adventure with Tev, and the memories were still as fresh as the moment they had happened. Whenever she closed her eyes she saw the cat jumping at her. Other times memories of Tev replayed themselves. Between the competing dreams she had difficulty sleeping at night, and when she did sleep, it was a shallow, restless slumber.

The problem was made worse because she felt as though she had little to do. In one respect, that idea was false. Every day she was running experiments that brought in a lifetime's worth of data. There were mysteries and enigmas to be solved, enough to keep the entire field of exobiology occupied for decades.

But she had a hard time focusing on that aspect of her mission. Their real mission, as she saw it, was to prepare Tev's people for the arrival of either Fleet settlement or the rebellion. In regard to that mission, she had less to do than anyone else. She dealt with injuries as she could, but Derreck and Tev focused on training while Alston and Eleta attempted to build new exosuits using the equipment on the *Vigilance* and the wealth of materials from the planet.

Kindra sat up in her bunk. Sleep wasn't going to happen tonight, so there was no point in staying here. She might as well get some work done. Kindra padded softly down to the biology station and sat at her terminal. There was something in the back of her mind that was bothering her, but she couldn't put her finger on it.

She leaned back in her chair, letting her mind go blank. Experience had taught her that trying to force her intuition to the surface would only end in failure. By letting go, she could see more clearly.

Something about the attack was bothering her, a detail out of place in this alien world. One moment her mind was empty, the next the picture was clear as day. Her heart raced as she pulled up some files on her terminal. She couldn't remember the name of what she was looking for, but she was quickly able to narrow down her search until she found it.

Kindra almost fell out of her chair. Her first instinct was to rush to Derreck and tell him what she thought, but she calmed herself. She needed more than images. DNA would confirm her hunch.

On the screen was an image of a large cat, a species of

leopard from Old Earth. The animal that had attacked them wasn't the same, but it was eerily similar. Not only did this planet have humans, but it also had other creatures similar to Old Earth! She dug a little deeper, and found that the leopard species pictured had gone extinct before humans had even left the solar system.

Kindra didn't have any explanations, but the itch in her mind finally subsided. She would get to the bottom of the mystery of this planet if she could.

On a whim, Kindra went up to the observation deck to look at the stars. It was the one activity that always calmed her mind enough to go to sleep. More than once she had fallen asleep on the observation deck.

The night was cloudless, and the image was crystal clear. Kindra hadn't grown up on a planet as populous as Haven, but she had grown up in habitations where the sky was rarely seen. The simple act of watching the stars grounded her, gave her a perspective she didn't otherwise have. She saw them all the time out in space, but seeing them through atmosphere was different. The stars twinkled and came alive.

Suddenly, in the corner of her vision, a bright sphere of light exploded, covering a small portion of the sky for a few seconds. Kindra blinked as her vision adjusted and information started flying across her neurodisplay.

The *Destiny* was back, and it was under attack.

FIVE

TEV HAD BEEN sound asleep when the explosion lit the sky, but he heard of it in short order. He was roused from his slumber by the commotion in the camp. Everyone was awake and looking up at the stars with an air of expectation.

No one would ever accuse the hunters of lacking courage, but the hunters were human, and they feared the almost-magical powers of Kindra and her people. The power to light up the night sky and turn it to day, even for a moment, was so far beyond the abilities of even the best hunter as to be unfathomable. Though they interacted with the technology daily, Tev was reminded that the exosuits were just a small slice of the new world bearing down on the clans.

Tev tapped the small earbud that was an almost-permanent fixture in his ear these days. It opened a channel directly to the *Vigilance*. Within a moment, he had Kindra's voice in his ear, a welcome reassurance.

"*Destiny* was attacked by *Hellbringer*, which was patrolling the other system we explored when we came to visit last. They launched nuclear weapons at *Destiny* again, and she jumped away just in time. Unfortunately, one of the nukes got caught in the jump field and exploded at the completion of the jump. We're still getting damage reports in. The *Destiny* is battered, but from what we're hearing, the ship will be okay."

"Has there been any sign of the *Hellbringer* following?"

"None yet, and we're keeping our sensors running all the time."

Derreck's voice jumped into the conversation. "Hi, Tev. I heard Kindra getting you up to speed. Do you want to bring the lance commanders up to the *Vigilance*? We need to plan our next actions."

Tev agreed and cut the connection. Kindra's people had plenty to do, and he needed to calm his own people. Explaining the situation took more time than he would have liked, but there were so many concepts the hunters were new to that Tev spoke for almost an hour. Finally, he felt as though he could leave them and their entire endeavor wouldn't fall apart. He gathered up the lance leaders and led them towards the ship.

Tev was reminded of his first efforts to introduce the new technology to the hunters. Some of them, like Xan, had already experienced the exosuits, and so the exposure came as less of a shock. But there were many hunters who had never seen the suits, and had only heard unbelievable stories. Gathering the hunters who would become the exosuit pilots had been an arduous task.

From the looks on the faces of the lance commanders, getting them into the *Vigilance* for a meeting might be just as much of one. Again, Tev felt like an outsider among his own people. He so often underestimated just how challenging these days were for most of the hunters.

Tev had watched how the other hunters had adjusted to

the arrival of Kindra and her clan. For most of them, the extent of their exposure to the aliens was Derreck and the exosuits. Derreck was easy enough to accept. Although he was profoundly different, he looked like them and shared many values with them. The exosuits, in the eyes of many of the hunters, had simply become the latest tools of the hunt, like a very advanced bow. Because of their limited exposure, they never considered the full ramifications of the technology they used every day.

The *Vigilance* was a sharp reminder of those ramifications. Its sleek, unnatural beauty contrasted starkly with the quiet grandeur of the forest and mountains the hunters called their home. The mere presence of the ship forced them to confront a greater truth: the universe was so much bigger than they thought.

Though their eyes darted back and forth with anxiety, none of the lance commanders would be the one who voiced their fears first. Tev laughed to himself as he walked easily up the ramp into the *Vigilance*. Behind him, there was a slight shuffling of feet. None wanted to be first, but at the same time, none would admit weakness by being last. After a second or two, Xan followed behind Tev, leading the charge.

Derreck greeted them at the top of the ramp and led them into the mess hall, where he started to offer food. Tev put his hand on the captain's shoulder and gently shook his head. Perhaps Derreck's action was polite, but no business would get done as the hunters studied the strange food and drink. Better to be rude and get to the heart of the matter.

The captain seemed to understand, and he began the discussion at once.

"I assume Tev has told you everything that has happened. For right now, nothing has changed. The enemy did not pursue our ship, so for now, everything is the same as it has been. However, because of the attack, I have been thinking. Each one of you is an excellent pilot. But that is true only on the ground. I want to take you up into space to practice fighting there."

The only reason the room didn't erupt in an uproar was that no one wanted to admit their fears. As Tev glanced from face to face, he saw discomfort and terror, and Derreck's proposal was greeted by silence. Tev looked at the captain.

"What changed your mind?"

"The attack reminded me that battles don't just happen on the ground. If they did, I would be content with the training you're doing. But if they simply leave their ships up in space, there's nothing you can do. All your training will be for nothing if you can't fight in space as well as on the ground."

Tev agreed. Convincing the hunters would be no small task, but Derreck was right.

The captain continued, "If we're going to train in space, we should do it now. *Destiny* can support all of us up there, but I don't know how much longer that will be true for. We should leave immediately to be safe."

Tev agreed, and he asked Derreck to leave the room as he sat with the hunters and explained what was being asked of them. As expected, the discussion did not go well. Tev knew how much he was asking of the hunters, but he didn't see any other way. Eventually the group bent to his will, and they left the *Vigilance* with their heads drooping, faced with the task of talking with each of their lances. Tev would follow soon after to take the brunt of the questions. He smiled briefly to himself as he imagined just how chaotic the training was about to get.

THE YOUNG PILOT was named Dez, and Tev was giving him a very quick and very dirty lesson in space combat. Their suits were still in training mode, armed only with powered-down targeting lasers that simulated real rounds. Despite that fact, Dez was trying everything he could to kill both Tev and himself.

In the space beyond, Derreck piloted the *Vigilance*, picking up stray exosuits that had wandered away from the battlefield. He had been far busier than any of them expected.

Although the nukes hadn't destroyed the *Destiny*, they had damaged it more severely than Tev first believed. The jumpship had never been beautiful, but the close call had crushed the outer levels of several decks. The good news was that the damaged part of the ship made for an excellent training ground.

The hunters picked up jumpship combat quickly. They moved well in the tight spaces, and with artificial gravity, the change in environment wasn't as dramatic as in space, which was an entirely different beast. There, they were almost as dangerous to themselves as they were to enemies.

The primary challenge was that the hunters refused to give in to fear, even if that fear kept them alive. Tev vividly remembered his first forays into space with the exosuits: the elevated heart rate, the vertigo, and the feeling of helplessness. If not for the support of several pilots, Tev wasn't sure he would have overcome the sensations. His first attempts had been timid and careful, almost the opposite of the other hunters. Derreck was the only person keeping many of the pilots from flying into the infinity of space.

At first, Tev had watched the other hunters and

believed himself to be too fearful. Although the hunters would have killed themselves without support, they learned new skills faster than Tev had. But after a few training trips into space, Tev realized he had been wrong. The other hunters weren't any more courageous than him. The difference was, they had someone they could model their development after. Tev had learned spaceflight the hard way, step by terrifying step. He hadn't been sure it was possible for him to pilot the exosuit in space. After all, he didn't have the same nanotechnology coursing through his brain that Kindra and her people did. For the others, though, Tev proved that it could be done. His painful experiences had laid the foundation for their accelerated learning. When viewed in that light, Tev was grateful for his suffering.

Even with their accelerated learning, Tev was much better than anyone else. It was a matter of experience. He didn't doubt for a moment that given enough time and opportunity he would be overtaken. But he wasn't going to make it easy for them. As Dez shot by, Tev turned his attention to the group floating beyond.

"What is the mistake that Dez is making?"

Neera's voice returned through the intercom. "He moves too fast, without control."

"Exactly. On the ground, we became used to how the exosuits moved in gravity. Out here, forces are much stronger." Tev's display let him know that Dez had finally gotten turned around and was jetting back at him. The young hunter's movements were improving, but Tev could still see the erratic course changes. Dez learned quickly, but not quickly enough to best Tev.

Tev took a moment to continue his lecture, both to get the point across while he still had time, and to intimidate

Dez into making a mistake. "There is nothing wrong with speed in space. In fact, the faster you can fly, the harder you are to hit, both for big ships and for other exosuits. However, speed must come after control. I would rather see you move like a scared elder than a young child while you are learning. Control, then speed."

Tev punctuated his comments with a short, powerful thrust. He shot in the direction of his feet just as Dez got his aim lined up. Dez flew through the space where Tev had been, his simulated rounds missing completely. Had his rifle really been firing, thrusters built into the arm of the suit would have fired in an attempt to negate the spin imparted by the rifle. Tev lined up a single shot, which punched through Dez's armor without problem. In response, Dez's suit froze, a technological simulation of death.

Tev set up groups for mock battles. He matched better pilots with worse ones for one-to-one skirmishes. Then he took a group of four pilots who were of middling ability and took them off himself. When he was certain that everyone was set, he focused on his own training.

Tev had been experimenting with different strategies for fighting multiple suits. In their late-night conferences, he and Derreck shared a common concern, a concern that when the enemy came, whoever that was, Tev and his hunters would be vastly outnumbered. If they were going to have a chance of maintaining their independence, they couldn't just beat other pilots in single combat. They had to defeat large groups of exosuits.

So, while others trained, Tev took a group every day to practice new techniques himself. The other hunters eagerly waited for their chance to be a part of the group, for the chance to defeat Tev, even if they outnumbered their lead pilot.

Today's plan was to test out a new contraption, designed for them by Alston and Eleta. Tev struggled to find the language to describe it, but it looked like someone had stuck a group of metal balls together in a bundle. Each of the balls had a small set of thrusters, almost so small as to be laughable. Each held enough propellant to last for about three seconds of flight. Then they would become magnetized and explode upon contact. Today, of course, none of the balls held any explosive, but were weighted as if they did.

In theory, the balls would act as small self-guided grenades. But they had several limitations, which was why they needed to be tested. They would only fly for a few seconds, so to work, Tev had to get several suits into close proximity. They were only designed to fly in zero gravity, and would be less than useless once on board a jumpship or dropship. There would be so much metal in the walls the balls would just stick where they were launched, killing the pilot who released them.

However, if they worked, they could potentially be used to take out several exosuits in space at once. Tev needed to see if they could be effectively used in combat.

The four hunters circled around him, and Tev watched their movements. He needed to accomplish two tasks. He needed to bring them all close enough that the balls would have a chance of working, and he needed to stay alive while he did so. Derreck, safe from the *Vigilance*, signaled the beginning of combat, and dead space came alive. Tev fired his thrusters, almost at random, allowing his exosuit to bob and weave through the void.

One of the concepts the other hunters were only slowly starting to grasp was the fact that space was truly three dimensional. Hunting was a three-dimensional task as well, but it was generally restricted. Most movement happened only in two dimensions, and very occasionally in the third, moving up and down. In space, up and down were just as valid, and beyond that, up and down were entirely relative. Getting one's head around the new mental concept was challenging at best, if not almost impossible in some cases. Tev used the confusion to great advantage, being sure to utilize all the room he had available to him.

At first, the other hunters tried to keep their distance, relying on small movements to try to keep themselves safe. Against a weaker opponent, such a strategy might have kept them alive, but Tev's aim was impeccable, and their movements weren't terribly random. Tev managed to wing two suits in short order. He probably could have gotten simulated kills, but that wasn't the point of today's exercise. He already knew he could snipe his opponents at a distance.

The hunters realized quickly they weren't going to beat Tev by keeping their distance. They didn't know what Tev was trying to do, so they fell into his trap all the more easily. One exosuit led the charge, darting inside the protective perimeter they had been keeping. Tev fired a few shots in the pilot's direction. The hunter had been flying straight, so it would have been easy to hit him, but Tev wanted to bring them all in close. He needed them to believe they'd be safe coming in closer, where their own rifles were more dangerous.

His plan was flawless. One by one, the other suits came in, and soon they were dancing an intricate, fast-moving series of encounters. Tev narrowly avoided being slammed into by one pilot who got too close. He fired wildly, allowing his shots to pass by the other pilots. Every time he missed, their confidence grew, and they moved in tighter and tighter. Tev kept one eye on his display, which was a simulated image of the surrounding space. There was a light red rim around the projected range of the grenades. More than once, Tev almost had all four opponents in the red, but never quite.

He singled out the problem. Three of the pilots were now comfortable close in, and Tev's evasions had to become more and more dramatic. Regardless of the difference in their skill levels, fighting so many pilots was a challenge, and there was a lot of simulated ammo flying around. At one point, one of Tev's opponents even took out the arm of one of his friends. But the fourth pilot was less comfortable, and he flew in and out of the danger zone in long passes. He wasn't close often, and when he was, another pilot was always out of range. Tev needed to put a stop to the pattern.

Tev kept dodging, at one point kicking gently off another suit. He was reaching the limits of his ability, and if the fight continued much longer, the other hunters might get suspicious. Tev was surprised they weren't already. The fight had been in progress for almost three minutes, and Tev still hadn't killed a single one of them. He tracked the fourth pilot as he came in, burning at a moderate speed. At least the pilot's flight was steady. Tev waited for another agonizing few seconds before hitting all his thrusters, shooting up and towards the approaching pilot.

The younger hunter didn't have a chance. Tev grabbed his arm and fired his thrusters, spinning them both around. He threw the pilot towards the other three suits, which were all following Tev. It took Tev a few moments to regain control. The forces he had put his suit under were severe even for him. But once he did, he launched himself towards all four suits, dodging erratically. He took two hits as all four opponents trained their rifles on him from the same direction, but none of them were fatal. Tev dialed up the speed, his thrusters all the way open. As he passed through the center of the group, he triggered his weapon, and the balls detached from their place on his back. Tev allowed his momentum to carry him away from the group, slowing himself down patiently. He watched his readout. Four confirmed kills, all within a second of one another. Tev couldn't restrain his smile. The weapon certainly wasn't perfect, but it worked.

With Tev's battle over, he took a moment to survey the rest of the training. Most of the matches were finished or in their final stages. Derreck was flying to and fro, catching all the strays. Tev was thinking about which scenarios to run next when he heard Derreck.

"Tev, round up the hunters. The *Hellbringer* just jumped in-system."

TEV MET with Derreck and Captain Absalon on the bridge of the *Destiny*. This was the first time he had ever been invited to a commanders' meeting, but because of the training he was running, he had become the head of the exosuits.

Absalon wasted no time in catching them up. "*Hellbringer* jumped in-system about an hour ago. The ship jumped in on the other side of the sun, and it's burning towards us. We haven't heard anything yet from them, but there's little doubt in my mind Captain Nicks plans to attack again."

"Do we have any clearer an idea about what forces we're going to be dealing with?" Derreck asked.

"Yes, and the answer isn't good. They still have a large

number of exosuits, both normal and heavy models. At least three times as many as we do."

Derreck frowned. "If they have that many suits, why didn't they attack us with them on the race here?"

Absalon shrugged. "That's really the question, isn't it? I don't know the answer, but I suspect that because *Hellbringer* is the last rebellion ship, Nicks is doing everything in his power to keep most of his forces in reserve. Every unit they lose is a greater cost to them than every unit we lose, even though they have far more suits and firepower."

Derreck didn't seem to like the answer, but he turned back to the displays showing a map of the system and the position of the two jumpships. Tev could see *Hellbringer* coming closer.

"So, what do we think Nicks is going to do?" Derreck asked.

Absalon pulled up information on the *Hellbringer*. "Again, I'm not sure. One of the big questions that I have is how many nukes he has left. He's fired six at us so far: four during our initial confrontations, and two during our previous match. Nicks has made it clear that he has no problem destroying *Destiny*, and that fact is perhaps one of the most concerning of this battle. In direct jumpship combat, *Destiny* can't hold a candle to *Hellbringer*. Their ship has better armor, weapons, and speed. If Nicks has more nukes and launches them at close range, there's very little we can do. However, if he gets in close and tries to take over *Destiny* with exosuits, I think we can surprise him. No one would expect Tev's people to have made as much progress as they have."

"So your plan is to wait and see what they decide to do?" Derreck's voice was incredulous.

Absalon fixed the dropship captain with an icy stare. "I understand that being reactive doesn't appeal to your sensibilities, commander, but we don't have enough information to make a better decision."

"We could attack."

Tev answered that one. "You know we can't do that, Derreck. They'll be on guard against attacks." Tev vividly remembered their last attempt to take over *Hellbringer*, the endless corridors filled with traps and ambushes. "Also, if the hunters are going to fight up here in space, I'd much rather it be in a place where they can take defensive positions. This will be their first real battle, and there's no preparing for that. Better to give them every advantage we can."

Derreck paced the bridge, his frustration evident. Tev watched him, always curious to see how the man reacted. Tev and Absalon were right, and Derreck knew it, even if the thought of waiting for the enemy to make the first move rankled him.

Absalon ignored Derreck and focused on Tev. "Get your pilots ready. At his rate of burn, Nicks will be in combat range in about two hours. By that time I want you all suited up and near *Vigilance*. If the situation gets out of control, I'll try to cover your escape."

Tev nodded and was just about to leave the bridge when a voice got his attention. It was one of the many bridge officers. "Sir, there's something here I think you should see."

Absalon turned to the man. "What is it?"

"We didn't notice this at first, but *Hellbringer* left one of its dropships on the far side of the sun. It must be running quiet to have evaded our detection, but the AI just caught a glimpse of it before it ducked back behind the sun."

Absalon stroked his chin. "That's odd. Do we know anything else?"

The bridge officer shook his head.

Absalon glanced back at Tev. "Don't worry about it. We'll figure everything out up here. You just need to focus on preparing your people."

Tev nodded and was out the door.

THE TWO HOURS seemed to pass in no time at all. In Tev's memory, the battles he had been a part of on the journey home had been slow and ponderous affairs. At one point, he had even napped as the two jumpships got in position to fight. But then he hadn't had anything to do, either. He had a lance commander who told him where to be, and his only responsibility had been to fight to the best of his ability. Now that he had command, those hours were spent very differently. He rushed all over the ship, trying to prepare his fighters for whatever was coming. He gave last-minute tips to everyone, and it wasn't until he encountered Xan that his nerves began to calm.

Xan placed an enormous hand on his shoulder. "Tev, this is no different than a hunt. Treat it as such."

He took a deep breath. Xan was right. He called all the hunters together, and they formed a small ring in the center of the hangar outside *Vigilance*. Tev looked at Xan. "Would you say the blessing for us?"

Xan bowed. Typically, the blessing was only given by the elders, but there were no elders in this group. By singling out Xan, Tev bestowed on him an honor he wouldn't see in his own clan for many years, if ever.

Xan said the words they all knew by heart, asking Lys for her blessings on this new hunt. Normally faithful, Tev opened his eyes and looked around, the juxtaposition of his two worlds giving him a small sense of vertigo. The prayer of Lys, uttered within this world of steel and fire. Tev was disoriented, but only for a moment. Then the two worlds, once separate, blended together into something else entirely. He didn't have the words to describe the sensation, or the time to decipher what it meant, but for just a moment, Tev felt an overwhelming sense of being home. He closed his eyes and chanted the final words of the prayer, feeling a small peace descend on his racing mind.

When Xan finished the prayer Tev gave the rest of the hunters a few moments of silence. Then he raised his head and spoke in a clear voice, the words flowing out of him like water. "Hunters. We are on a hunt greater than any that has come before. You have worked hard, and you are ready for what comes next. Stay calm and stay strong, and let your aim be true."

Without a word the hunters broke apart, each to their own exosuits. The battle would be upon them shortly.

Tev climbed into his own suit and powered up. His display came to life in front of his eyes, and soon he saw the situation as it developed. His greater authority gave him access to the command channels, so he could hear what was happening on the bridge. He closed his eyes and listened.

Tev could hear the nervousness in the silence of the bridge. All the advantages were in the hands of Captain Nicks and the *Hellbringer*. *Destiny* was prepared to respond, but they weren't sure what they would be responding to.

The silence stretched out, each second another nervous breath within the confines of his suit. On his display there was a thin line that indicated the maximum range of *Hellbringer*'s nuclear weapons. The dot that represented the enemy ship passed the line without incident, and Tev started to think they might get a chance at fighting. But it didn't mean anything, not yet. Captain Absalon was fairly certain the *Hellbringer* couldn't have too many nukes left, and if they did they would wait until the last possible moment to fire.

Derreck gave Tev the command to spread out his hunters, and Tev didn't question why. He gave the orders, and the six lances of four suits each spread out throughout the *Destiny*, prepared to repel boarders.

Tev's attention was drawn to his display, which had suddenly lit up with dozens of tiny lights. The battle between the two jumpships had begun.

The lights distracted Tev, so he switched back to his combat display, which was much more barren. He left the audio channel open so he could hear the news.

The bridge was still largely silent, which surprised Tev. He knew that Derreck and his people let the machines do most of the fighting for them, but it was surprising how much trust they put in their technology.

The floor rocked underneath him, and on his audio channel he heard the report. "Missile strike penetrated our point defense system, outer hull, decks six and seven. Bulkheads are sealed, sir."

There was no audible response.

Another officer spoke. "Sir, *Destiny* is reporting the attack is concluding. It requests guidance, sir. Counterattack or defensive?"

Tev heard Absalon reply. "We don't have the missiles to get past their defenses. What does *Destiny* think?"

"Three percent chance of penetrating defenses. *Destiny* is better electronically, but we're solidly outclassed when it comes to weapons. *Hellbringer*'s electronic interference isn't even slowing us down."

"Defensive positions. We're not going to waste what missiles we have."

Tev wondered what was going to happen next, but he didn't have long to wait. The report came in from the bridge. "Sir, *Hellbringer*'s launching a dropship, arrow class."

The sensitive microphones caught Absalon whispering to himself. "Where the hell did they get an arrow class from?" Out loud, his voice was commanding. "Unleash everything on that dropship. Try to kill it before it breaches our hull."

Tev couldn't contain his curiosity any longer. He pulled his original display back up, and he saw a single pinpoint of light speeding towards *Destiny*. Their own ship launched dozens of missiles towards the dropship, and it looked for a second as though the space in between the dropship and the jumpship was a solid block of light. Tev turned the display back off. The information didn't help him at all.

Absalon spoke to Derreck. "Get everyone to the breach point of that ship."

Derreck relayed the order to Tev, highlighting the points where he wanted exosuits stationed.

Tev passed along the order and started running towards the point his display indicated. The walls of the *Destiny* were a flat gray, and without directions it would have been difficult for him to find his way.

He was one of the last to arrive. Many of the others were already in position. Tev didn't get there a moment too soon. As soon as he was in position, the whole wall of the ship started to cave in. Tev had never heard of an arrow-class dropship. He didn't know what they were capable of, didn't know that they had made their name by boring directly into jumpships and depositing their soldiers. But he learned quickly as the event unfolded in front of him.

The sound was tremendous, a wailing screech of metal so loud even Tev's audio system wasn't able to dampen the sound to a more bearable level. Instinctively, Tev closed his eyes as the sounds of tearing metal assailed his ears. He forced them back open. He needed to see what was happening. Even with his eyes open, Tev wasn't sure he wasn't dreaming.

The walls gave way to the pointed hull of the arrow-class ship. Once the ship had broken through *Destiny*'s armor plating and into the hangar, it opened up, like a deadly flower unfolding. Inside were four enormous machines, exosuits Tev had learned in their last engagement were known as "heavies." Tev frowned. Four heavies were a considerable force, but was also much smaller than he was expecting. From his vantage point almost directly in front of the breach, he could see deeper into the ship that had broken into the *Destiny*, and there were no other exosuits.

The arrow class reversed its direction, pulling backwards as the hull folded back on itself. The breach, which had been mostly sealed by the presence of the other ship, rapidly depressurized the hanger. Tev watched as emergency bulkheads closed all around them, trapping their entire force within the hangar, at least for a few minutes. His perspective shifted, and it occurred to him that all his well-trained hunters were now locked in a small space with some of the most powerful exosuits in the galaxy. The next few minutes would be a trial by fire.

It almost felt as if Tev's thought triggered the firefight. Any sense of order evaporated immediately as the room erupted in fire and metal. These exosuits were equipped differently than the ones Tev had fought against before, and when the four heavies took a moment to face each other, showing boxy objects on their back Tev had never seen, he knew something was wrong.

Derreck's voice came over the general channel before Tev could say anything. "Take cover!"

Tev's instincts took over and he threw himself behind a steel plate purposely designed for the purpose. He was almost fast enough. In the corner of his vision he saw the boxes open and hundreds of small missiles shoot out, heading in all directions. One struck Tev directly in his left leg, and plenty of others struck all around him. His view was obscured by fire and smoke, and his helmet cracked as it was struck by shrapnel. His leap would have landed him on his side, but the explosion on his leg twisted his body in mid-air. Tev didn't know which way was up as his body careened across the floor and walls.

He hoped that the others had fared better. As the last one into the room, he had been distracted by everything happening and hadn't had a chance to get behind cover. With any luck, the others hadn't been so foolish. Agonizing seconds passed as Tev fought to get his bearings once again. His head was ringing, and his leg didn't seem to be obeying his commands. Finally, he remembered how to move his head, and he sat up and looked down at his leg, fearing the worst.

The damage was bad, but it could have been far worse. All of his armor had been stripped from a large part of his left leg. His bare shin was showing, and there were several deep cuts bleeding profusely. As Tev came to awareness, he could feel the armor on his lower thigh constricting, attempting to keep blood loss to a minimum. From what Tev could see, the suit's efforts weren't too successful.

There was an even more challenging problem, though. Most of the suit had been blown away, including the parts that helped move the lower leg. Tev's foot was still encased in his armor, weighing more kilos than Tev wanted to count. With an extreme effort, he could move his leg, but not much. In terms of combat mobility, he was useless.

Tev remembered he wasn't alone.

The sounds of gunfire returned to his ringing ears, and he forced himself to look away from his leg and find out what was happening.

He was in some sort of hell.

He was sitting up, not even behind cover, as the four heavies laid down a blistering field of fire. If any of them saw him, his life would be over in a moment.

Tev froze, worried that any movement would attract attention. To try to hide or not? Indecision made him a statue.

No one else was moving. Were they dead? Injured? Or just taking cover?

Tev's thoughts ran in circles, out of control and yet returning to the same place over and over.

His leg. His life. His hunters. Kindra. His leg. His life.

Derreck's voice pierced through the fog of his shock, abruptly ordering his thoughts. The captain's voice was cold and calm, ice in the middle of a hot summer's day.

"Tev, get behind cover! Most of your hunters are fine, but they're hiding. They need to remember that they have armor now. They can start taking shots, but they aren't listening to me."

The voice gave him purpose, a list of tasks to accomplish. Get behind cover. Give orders. One task at a time, Tev's mind returned to normal.

He looked around. There was a steel plate he could

hide behind just a few paces behind him. He risked a glance at the heavies and saw that he had a clear shot on one of them. Tev had a different weapon than most of the other hunters. Instead of an automatic rifle, he had a single-shot rifle, far more powerful. It was the weapon he had been given by his former lance commander, and he had developed an appreciation for its abilities.

The heavies had made another modification to their armor. Their cockpits were better armored than the last. They had learned. Tev wondered if the extra armor would be enough. With the speed of thought, he raised his arm and rifle and centered his targeting reticle on the cockpit. The round sped from his arm and the heavy collapsed. He had his answer.

His action attracted the attention of the other three heavies, as he knew it would. Tev planted his good leg, his right leg, down on the ground, and shoved himself backwards. He could hear the screech of metal on metal as his exosuit slid across the decking towards the steel plate. He reached cover just as hundreds of rounds of ammunition made the place he had been sitting a death trap. Even behind the steel plate, with all three heavies focusing their fire, he wouldn't have more than a few seconds. But hopefully it would be enough for everyone else to regain their courage.

Tev spoke for the first time since entering the battlefield, and even he was surprised by the sound of command in his voice. "Hunters, your prey is in front of you. They are dangerous, but they are prey. Time to hunt."

For a long, fear-filled second, nothing happened. More rounds punched through the steel that protected him. Tev believed Derreck that most of his people were still alive, but he hadn't seen any evidence of it yet with his own eyes.

Then the room came alive, exosuits running, jumping, and spinning behind cover. As they did, they took shots at the heavies, and as their confidence grew, so did their rate of fire.

At first, nothing seemed to affect the heavies. They had more armor than Tev and his hunters did, and they could shrug off rifle rounds like they were shrugging off bugs. The hunters might be becoming more confident, but they weren't becoming any more effective.

"Their weak point is their cockpits. You need to hit them there."

There wasn't any verbal response, but Tev risked a short glance to see the three remaining heavies struggle as round after round pinged off their new cockpit armor. The rifles the other hunters had weren't as powerful, but they made up for it in sheer volume.

The heavy pilots were very good. They kept moving, not letting themselves become a target for any one exosuit for more than a second or two. At the same time, they kept trying to hit the hunters, which was apparently a challenge for them. The hunters had remembered how well they could move in the suits, and they were leaping all over the hanger with almost reckless abandon.

For almost a full minute there was a stalemate between the heavies and the hunters. The hunters weren't piercing the armor of the heavies, but the heavies weren't hitting the hunters as they bounced around the room. The only casualty in the firefight, as near as Tev could tell, was the hangar itself. Spent shell casings littered the deck, and there were more holes in the walls than a team of repair techs could work on in a month. A random thought crossed Tev's mind that made him smile. Absalon was going to be furious about the damage.

Xan, of course, was the one who broke the stalemate. Tev watched the entire feat. He saw as Xan leapt from the upper decks, ten meters above the fight. He plummeted towards one of the heavies, his feet aimed squarely at the cockpit. The heavy must have had some warning, because it looked up and started shifting its position. But it was too little, too late. Xan adjusted his course with a small rocket thrust, and his aim was true. The huge hunter crashed through the armor of the heavy and straight through the cockpit, sending both exosuit and heavy crashing to the floor of the hangar.

Xan's idea had been effective, but he hadn't thought about how tangled up he would get in the remains of the heavy. The two remaining warriors turned to avenge their fallen comrade, and Tev shouted a command, all he could do. "Hunters! Protect Xan!"

Tev didn't need to worry. Xan had shown them the way to make the most out of their mobility. The hunters swarmed from the walls, giving up on trying to take the heavies out with their rifles. They darted in, slashing and grabbing at the heavies. One-on-one, an exosuit would never have the power to manipulate a heavy, but as they swarmed, they became more and more effective.

As soon as the hunters left the protective cover of the edges of the hangar, the battle was over. The hunters only needed a few minutes to make it official. Tev watched as they brought down the heavies and tore them into pieces.

Unfortunately, he didn't get to see the end of the battle, as he passed out from blood loss.

FOR A MOMENT, Tev felt like he was reliving a previous memory. He woke up and the world was black. He took a deep breath and shot his arms out, suddenly afraid he was locked in a healing pod again.

He didn't need to worry. His movement brought the lights up, gradually brightening so as not to hurt his eyes. He looked around, deciding he must be in the sick bay of *Destiny*. He had only been here once before, and now he was in a private room which he had never seen. But he recognized enough of the devices to be certain.

As his memory returned to him, Tev looked down at his leg, fearing again that the worst had come to pass. He wasn't sure he could take the loss of his leg. But his leg was still there, wrapped up in a healing cast similar to the one he once wore on his arm. He shook his head. This was, what, the third time Kindra and her technology had saved his life? Or at least saved a limb.

The door to his room opened, and for a second, Tev expected Kindra to walk through the door. If he had been on the *Vigilance*, it would have been her. But she was still down on his planet with Alston and Eleta, working with the clans to prepare for the arrival of more humans.

Tev's thoughts were interrupted by the nurse, who asked him several questions about his health. Fortunately, he felt fine. Outside of the initial barrage of missiles, he hadn't really been involved in the battle, so his leg was the only wound he had taken. She offered to give him medicine to put him back to sleep, but Tev wasn't interested. He asked instead what he was capable of.

The nurse shook her head and laughed.

"What's so funny?" Tev asked.

"All of you are the same," she replied. "The idea of resting and healing isn't very popular. If we don't give you the medicine, you all leave within a few minutes of waking up."

She ran a device up and down his leg and continued. "Fortunately for you, you are good to go. You will need to be in the cast for a few days to allow your leg to heal completely, but so long as you don't jump around or get in an exosuit, you can do whatever you want."

Tev thanked the nurse. Once she left he changed into his traditional garb. As he did, Derreck spoke through Tev's earpiece. "Hey Tev, glad to see you're up and moving around again. Absalon left orders to meet him on the bridge once you were up."

Tev acknowledged Derreck's order and went towards the bridge, pausing in sick bay for a few minutes to catch up with the injured. The ones still there were in worse shape than he had been, but it sounded as though the *Destiny*'s healing tools and staff would be able to heal all of them within the next day or two. Not for the first time, Tev was incredibly grateful for the new technology.

He thought about that idea while he walked towards the bridge. He still felt that Derreck and Kindra and their kind relied too heavily on technology. It had become more than a tool for them, it was an integral part of their lives. Such reliance wasn't healthy or safe, but it was still powerful. There needed to be a better way, a way for skills and technology to come together to improve life.

The exosuits were just such a technology, Tev realized. Take a hunter out of the suit, and the hunter was still dangerous. The hunter's skills were what guaranteed survival, not the suit. But give a hunter a suit, and their abilities increased several times over. With such power, a clan would never have to go hungry again. Tev held the thought in his mind and wondered if this thinking was what had led Kindra and her people to where they were today, utterly dependent on their tools.

Tev ended his wondering once he entered the bridge. Derreck was already there, as was Absalon. Together they gathered around the main table on the bridge, capable of projecting whatever the captain needed. Absalon pulled up a map of the solar system with dots indicating *Destiny*, *Hellbringer*, and an unknown ship all placed around the home of Tev's people.

Absalon, brisk as usual, got Tev up to speed. The attack they had repelled had been the whole thrust. The arrow-class had returned to the rebellion ship and not come out again, no more missiles had been exchanged, and *Hellbringer* had never fired her main weapon, a large laser capable of destroying *Destiny* with only a few shots.

"After this last attack, I'm fairly certain that I understand Nicks now. Mind you, I don't have any evidence of this, but I've tried story after story, and this is the only one that fits. When Nicks realized he wasn't going to outrace us, he tried to destroy us. I'm still amazed he'd go so far, but I believe he's a desperate man, and he doesn't have many options," Absalon said.

The jumpship captain continued, "Something changed when they visited the other planet. His priorities shifted, and he decided to make another attempt at capturing *Destiny*."

Derreck interrupted. "Why only four heavies, if that was his goal? If he has the forces you say, he could have taken us over easily."

"Good question, but I'm coming around to your own idea, Derreck. I think Nicks is aware that he has the only remaining rebellion troops. If he fails, the entire rebellion is over for good. Because of that, he's too cautious. He's trying to get huge rewards with small risk, and it just isn't working. I also think *Destiny* isn't his primary objective. I think it's a bonus for him. Now that his latest attempt failed spectacularly, I'm not sure what he's going to try next. I'm worried he might try simply destroying us. Tev and his people still have to be his ultimate goal."

Tev studied both men, but Derreck seemed to agree with Absalon, and Tev trusted their judgment. He was still a novice in regard to the galaxy and what drove most of its people.

"So the big question then is what to do," Derreck said.

Absalon nodded. "I believe we need to get *Vigilance* and *Explorer* off the jumpship."

Derreck saw Tev's question and answered it. "*Explorer* is Mala's dropship. It's similar to *Vigilance*." Turning to Absalon he asked, "You think it's that bad?"

Absalon looked displeased but stern. "I do. I have a hard time believing Nicks would try to take over *Destiny* again after failing twice. If he attacks again, it will be to destroy us. I have a few tricks left, but most likely, *Hellbringer* will win the fight. We'll keep *Destiny* manned with a skeleton crew, hopefully volunteers. We'll do everything we can to keep the planet safe, but should the worst come to pass, we can minimize casualties."

Tev grasped what Absalon was saying and was surprised. Were his people worth such a sacrifice? Tev understood how important jumpships were to the alien humans.

"You could leave." Derreck's voice was soft and hesitant. Tev had never considered the possibility that Fleet would simply abandon them. For the past several months all he had heard was how important his people were. It made sense, though, that at some point Fleet might cut their losses and run.

Tev studied Absalon. He hadn't spent much time with

the jumpship captain. Tev had always found the man to be aloof. He expected Absalon to jump at Derreck's suggestion, but he was wrong.

Absalon wouldn't hear it. "No. I appreciate the suggestion, but what is happening here is far too important. If we can figure out a way to bring Nicks down, the rebellion is over for good. He's the last head of the hydra. But if he succeeds here, the story is a very different one. Between the technology they probably acquired from the other planet and Tev's people as pilots, they could potentially wreak havoc back in central space. No, this is where we need to make our stand. We decide the future here."

Tev looked at Absalon with newfound respect. The man had always run a good ship, and he was well-liked by the people who served him, but Tev had never thought of him as a warrior. Today he was proven wrong. Tev respected the courage it would take to sacrifice one's life for a greater purpose. Hunters who shared the same qualities had songs written about them. Tev was no bard, but should the worst come to pass, he would make sure Absalon wouldn't be forgotten.

The captain of the jumpship continued laying out his plan. "All of Tev's hunters should be healed within the next day or two. Once they are cleared for transport, I'm sending everyone back down. We're going to load up the dropships with everything they can carry. My plan is to drop you when we have the planet between us and Nicks. Once you land I want you to go as dark as possible. I'll set up some tightbeam communications, but I want you all to be hard to find."

Derreck asked a few clarifying questions, but he and his captain were on the same page. They ended the discussion with a long list of tasks between them. As soon as the door closed behind them, Tev asked the question that had been bothering him since he had gotten out of sick bay.

"How many hunters died?"

Derreck met his gaze. "Three. Two were caught without cover when the first barrage hit, and a third was the victim of a lucky hit from one of the heavies. I'm sorry, Tev."

Tev stared at the floor as they walked. Three of his people had gone to the endless hunt with Lys. He would grieve for them later, properly, when he had the time. But he couldn't allow himself that luxury now. He had to prepare so that after he fought Nicks and his rebellion soldiers, they could never threaten his people again.

SIX

IT WAS dusk when the dropships made their final approach. From her perspective, Kindra thought they were coming in far too fast. When she had last spoken with Derreck, he told her they were going to try to come in as dark as possible. Apparently, that meant they saved their burn until the last possible moment. *Vigilance* was a fairly aerodynamic ship, and could glide a little, but *Explorer* simply dropped like a rock. Fortunately, both pilots knew what they were doing, and their side-by-side landings were gentle.

The past few days had caused Kindra to practically declare war on her emotions. Derreck had only given them the outlines of Absalon's thoughts, but the one fact that came through loud and clear was the knowledge that they might not have a way out of this system. That knowledge was hard to swallow, and each of the crew was dealing with it in a different way. Eleta went on an overnight camping trip, which was so out of character for her Kindra worried briefly about her sanity. Kindra had offered to join her, but her support had been firmly turned away.

Alston was, as always, completely unreadable. He went about his day-to-day tasks as though the news was of no more importance than the weather report. Kindra had just about given up on ever understanding him.

Kindra, for her part, threw herself into work, trying to think about anything and everything but the situation they were in. When they left for this mission, Kindra had told herself she would do whatever she could to protect Tev, his planet, and his people. She felt that she owed them that much. But the guilt that had once driven her had faded, replaced instead by very confused feelings for Tev.

She had been grateful when Derreck ordered the three of them to remain behind for what had started as a training run. She needed time and space to think. She dove deeply into her work, some of it necessary and some unnecessary. Anything to focus her mind elsewhere. Then *Hellbringer* entered the picture, and her heart sank considerably when she found out Tev had been injured.

The truth was, making a promise to do anything necessary was cute when one was safe at home. To realize that promise might mean her life, or force her to remain in one place for the rest of her life, was an entirely different dilemma. What did it say about her that she was willing to kill to protect Tev, but wasn't sure if she could stand living on his planet until she died? Such questions were troubling, and she did everything she could to avoid them.

The return of the dropships meant she wouldn't have much longer to do so. A decision would soon be required of her, and she didn't know what it would be. Until then, she figured she would simply take life one moment at a time.

IF THERE WAS one quality that recommended humans,

Kindra decided, it was their endless adaptability. Thanks to technology and willpower, there weren't many places that they hadn't called home. They had lived in the depths of the oceans, in extreme climates of all types, and in the void of space.

She expected more complaints from the influx of people, but there were few. As soon as Derreck and Mala landed, they had ordered the sites to go dark. Almost all their electronics were turned off, and those that were deemed essential were moved far from the landing sites and concealed, both visibly and electromagnetically, as well as they were able.

In effect, they had removed a fair amount of the technology from their lives, down almost to the level of Tev and his people. Kindra thought she would hear grumbling and discontent in the voices of *Destiny*'s crew, but she heard little. Instead, a new spirit seemed to seize the camp. People smiled as they walked past one another, and at night the huge bonfires became the center of everyone's attention.

Kindra was reminded, almost, of her days as a child before the rebellion reached her planet. Her dad had often taken her to a local park in the habitat. The park hadn't been much, especially compared to the world she found herself on now. Her memory wasn't perfect, but she didn't think the grass and trees covered more than a city block. In the confines of the habitat, even that was a wasteful use of space.

But Kindra had loved those trips, and more than once she and her father had spent the night there, sleeping on the grass as the lights dimmed in the evening. Now the memories were tangled up with the destruction of her family and her habitat by the rebellion, but she remembered how those nights felt, with what passed for open sky above her head. She imagined the feeling wasn't much different than what the rest of the crew was experiencing now.

She supposed part of the new spirit of the camp was a rejection of their situation. Anyone who spent time thinking about the dilemma they found themselves in would be dejected. If Absalon was correct, there wasn't much chance of any of them getting home, and there was no better way of ignoring that than focusing on day-to-day life on Tev's planet.

Sometimes Kindra forgot just how unusual Tev's planet was in the galaxy. After months of being on the surface, it became easy to take life on the planet for granted. A few crew members of *Destiny* had grown up on lightly terraformed agrarian planets, but not many. Even for them, the diversity of life and environments on Tev's planet was beyond what most had ever experienced. Planets like Tev's, with mountains, trees, animals, and open sky, were incredibly rare. A large part of the value of Tev's planet was that it would require no terraforming.

Kindra's thoughts vanished when she saw Tev sitting at the fire. He still wore the cast on his leg. Kindra had checked on him earlier that day, and for complete healing he had another two days in it. She was well aware the cast drove him to madness. That was almost all he talked about when she was examining his leg. Fortunately, he understood the importance of letting the leg heal all the way, so he didn't try anything terribly foolish. She knew he was looking forward to getting back into his suit and piloting again. It had been repaired faster than he had recovered.

The bonfire was enormous tonight. Kindra sat down on a log next to Tev, and he explained that some of Mala's crew had taken the task of building the bonfire a little too seriously. She smiled as the heat from the fire blasted her face. The logs used as chairs had been moved back, but not quite far enough, she thought.

There was something about a fire, Kindra thought, that bordered on magical. As she watched the flames lick the sky, she fell into a slight trance, her entire body relaxing. She startled a little when food was offered, but she accepted gladly. Although she couldn't put the feeling into words, she felt as though there was something so natural, so right, about sitting around a fire. Thousands of years had passed since humanity had needed campfires, but they still drew attention like a magnet.

Unfortunately, there was still a language barrier between Tev and his people and Kindra and hers. There had only been so many translators to go around, and so while there was some intermingling of the two groups, they mostly sat on opposite sides of the fire from one another. The separation didn't feel harsh to Kindra. The clans weren't acting malicious. But it served as a reminder that there was still a bridge that hadn't been crossed.

Tev, however, was in a fine mood. Kindra had only seen him briefly since they landed, mostly to look at his injuries. His duties called him away. Of the three hunters who had lost their lives in the attack on the *Destiny*, two suits had been determined to be salvageable, while the third was stripped for parts. When they started training they had selected a few alternates, but those hunters hadn't gotten much suit time. Tev had been supervising their crash course, while Xan led the training. Tev had also been spending an enormous amount of time with Derreck, often missing the fires while they made defensive preparations.

Tonight, Tev seemed relaxed, more so than she had seen him in quite some time. Tev shouted something in his own language, and another hunter stood up, while the rest of the circle quieted.

"What's happening?" Kindra asked.

Tev glanced at her as he stood up and moved closer to the fire. Kindra wasn't sure how he wasn't burning up. "We should exchange stories. This is a common tradition when two clans meet each other around a fire."

The hunter who had responded to Tev's call stood up and began reciting a story, one that, judging by the reactions of the other hunters, was a very popular one.

Tev began translating to those who didn't speak the language.

"Lys was the greatest hunter who ever lived. She never missed a shot, and could track anything from a bird to a boar. One day she was out in the forest, checking her snares, and she found a rabbit caught in one. Now, this rabbit, like most rabbits, thought himself very clever. As Lys approached, he said, 'Oh, greatest of hunters. I never thought one of your reputation would stoop so low as to use traps to catch your food.'

"Lys, knowing the mind of the rabbit, released him. The rabbit knew running wouldn't save him, so he relied on his wits. He spoke again, saying, 'Now, if only you had hunted me fairly, with a spear, I never would have been caught, and your honor would be intact. Give me one hour and then you may chase me. If you can catch me then with your spear, I will gladly give you the meat on my bones.'

"Now, Lys knew that the forest was filled with rabbit holes, and the ground was hard and dry, making it more challenging to track the rabbit. Letting him go would mean losing her prey, which was unacceptable. But when she spoke, her offer was more than generous. She said, 'You are right, of course. I have brought shame to myself by falling so low. But I can't agree to your offer, for you are injured from my trap, and I would have an unfair advantage. Let us make camp here for two days, and I will feed you and let you rest. Then, on the third day, I will give you an hour and then hunt you with my spear, as you wish.'

"The rabbit thought this might be another trap, but life is hard for a rabbit, and spending two days in comfort was too good to pass up. The rabbit agreed to the terms.

"On the third day it rained, a torrential downpour unlike any the rabbit had ever seen. The rabbit did not know that Lys understood the elements as well as she understood animals, and had known of the storm. Well-fed, the rabbit couldn't run as fast as usual, and the nearby burrows were flooded and unusable. Lys was able to easily track the rabbit's muddy prints, and when the perfectly-aimed spear pierced the rabbit, the rabbit finally understood that it had escaped one trap, only to fall into another."

There was a cheer from the other side of the fire. The story was very popular, and Kindra had to admit, Tev's storytelling skills were excellent. This was yet another side of him she had never seen before. But she didn't understand the point of the story. Don't use snares? Be smarter than your enemy? Rabbits are delicious? But she did enjoy listening, and a part of her wondered who among her group would share a story. Oral storytelling wasn't exactly an in-demand occupation within Fleet, and she assumed Derreck would be the one to speak. Most unpleasant tasks ultimately fell to him.

So she fought her jaw from hitting the floor when Alston stood up. Their geologist was as quiet and introverted a man as she had ever met.

Tev switched sides of the fire, so that now he was

translating the story into his native language. He waited for the geologist to begin.

"A long time ago, there was a planet. A beautiful planet, very much like this one. There were trees and mountains and water, more water than we can even imagine today. The moon shone brightly in the sky, reflecting the light of a distant sun.

"The people of this planet did not appreciate what they had been given. They ate more than they could grow or hunt, and there were too many people. One day, some very wise men said, 'This planet is no longer enough for us. We must go up there, into the sky, and start again.'

"These wise men were not always popular. You see, these people hadn't gone very far into the sky. They were afraid, and didn't have the courage to begin.

"The first people who left died, making people even more afraid. Finally, there was one man who had the courage to try again, and he succeeded. He showed the people that they could live in the sky, around other stars, if they wanted. Because of one man, the whole planet saw a new way forward. That one man saved all the people from dying."

Alston sat back down, and there was silence around the fire as Tev finished translating. Kindra saw many of the hunters were smiling. They liked the story. Kindra wasn't sure what point Alston was trying to make to the hunters. The story of Captain Zhou was well-known, and taught to all children. But why Alston selected it was a mystery beyond her.

Regardless, the exchange of stories was complete, and as the meal finished, both hunters and crew did the best they could to mingle and learn from one another. Kindra kept herself largely separate, content to watch the scene. It had all the awkwardness of a teenage romance, but it was powerful to see two different cultures coming together and trying to learn each other's ways.

THE EVENING WAS ALREADY LATE when Tev took Kindra by the hand and led her away from the fire. Such a simple gesture, but one made in front of both Kindra's people and his own. The Tev she had known the past few weeks never would have had such confidence, such a lack of concern for anyone else's criticism.

Kindra had no hesitations, either, and she took Tev's hand with pleasure and followed him out into the forest. What was happening was something she never could have predicted, but she didn't mind. There were times in life where the decision was easy to make, and this, at least, was one of them.

Later that night, they laid together on the grass of a small clearing Tev had brought them to. Kindra's head was on the hunter's arm, and she watched Lys chase the deer through the night. Her breath was deep and slow, a deep relaxation that seemed to seep into every corner of her body, loosening up knots of tension she hadn't been aware of.

She could stay here, if it came to that. She had been a part of Fleet long enough that she didn't have many friends left on the outside. Those she was closest to were all here, on this planet.

Kindra turned over and snuggled in closer to Tev. The evening was warm enough, but Tev's body radiated heat, making the evening even more comfortable. He was also watching the stars turn overhead, his face relaxed.

"What changed?" she asked.

He turned his head so he could look at her. "What do you mean?"

"Ever since you came back from *Destiny*, something has been different."

He turned his face back up towards the stars. "It's hard to explain. I worried so much about being torn between your people and my own clan. Up there, though, I realized it didn't matter. The problem was one I made myself. I was a part of two worlds. There was no changing that fact, so why worry about it?"

The hunter glanced at Kindra and continued. "I also realized what was important to me. Between my new understanding and my realization, my decisions seemed much clearer. I almost feel foolish that I didn't understand earlier."

Kindra grinned at that. "You can't hold yourself to too high of a standard, Tev. No one is perfect."

Before they fell asleep, Kindra had another question. She almost hated to ask it, but she wasn't some damsel who could just be led away from a campfire whenever Tev felt like it. "Tev, what are we?"

He stirred from his near-slumber, a confused frown on his lips. "Humans?"

She punched him lightly on the shoulder, not sure if he was joking or confused. "No, Tev. I mean, us. What are we?" She pointed to the two of them to make her point more clear.

Tev turned and looked her in the eyes. "I do not know the customs of your people, Kindra. Have I offended?"

She laughed and rubbed her eyes. The thought occurred to her that there had to be easier relationships out there. "No, Tev, you haven't." She tried to rephrase her question. "How serious is this for you?"

The intensity in his eyes almost made her laugh again. "I care for you, Kindra. Is there more that you need to know?"

Kindra shook her head. They could dance around such questions all night and never quite understand each other. She studied Tev, and knew that whatever may come, she didn't need to worry about how he would treat her. That was enough for now. "No, Tev. I know all that I need."

KINDRA AWOKE to Derreck's voice. She startled at first, but rapidly came to her senses.

"Sorry to disturb you, Kindra, but I need you and Tev to come to *Vigilance* right away."

Kindra rubbed her eyes. The stars still spun overhead, but the sky was just beginning to turn colors. They couldn't have been asleep for more than a few hours.

"What happened?"

"The *Destiny* was destroyed about a half-hour ago. We need to figure out our plan."

Derreck's simple statement shocked her into awareness. The *Destiny* destroyed? That changed everything about their situation. Her heart raced for a few moments before she got it under control. If Derreck could be calm, so could she. "Understood. We'll be there in about twenty minutes."

She looked over at Tev, who was sitting up, disturbed by the tension in her voice. Derreck cut the line, and Kindra quickly explained to Tev what had happened. His reaction was muted, but she knew him well enough by now to see that he was upset by the news. He understood what it meant for Kindra to have lost her jumpship.

Together they raced towards the *Vigilance*, darting quietly through the sleeping camp they had left the night before. The peace of the village stood in stark contrast to the icy terror racing through Kindra's thoughts.

They were the last to arrive, and while Kindra received a few knowing looks, nothing was said.

Derreck launched straight into his briefing.

"We have important decisions to make, and we have to make them fast. Our guess about Captain Nicks picking up some new toys was accurate, and he's just shown us part of his hand. Before the *Destiny* was destroyed, it managed to send one last transmission our way. Absalon had a fair amount of foresight, and he's given us more information than we had before. But I'll let you see what I mean."

Derreck turned on the holotable, and a miniature display of *Destiny*'s bridge came into view. The lights in the room were flashing red, a color Kindra had only seen a few times before.

"Sir, confirmed targeting."

The hesitation was visible on Absalon's face. "Hold fire."

Kindra brought her hand to her mouth to cover her surprise. What if Absalon's decision had cost him the lives of everyone aboard the *Destiny*? Granted, there were only a few officers left on board, but all lives mattered, and the ship itself was a treasure.

When the first blast hit, Kindra couldn't even tell. The ship didn't shudder, and everyone acted with a calm Kindra couldn't understand. She only knew the ship had been hit when Freya, Absalon's first officer, reported, "Direct hit from laser, sir. It carved a nice gash through the front of the hull, but nothing vital was hit."

Absalon's response was quiet. "Launch everything. Full AI offensive, missiles, and laser. Don't worry about draining the capacitors. We're not jumping out of here. Fire as fast as you can cycle the laser."

Kindra was reminded of her last experience of combat on the bridge of the *Destiny*. There was the same silence as the AI ran most of the battle programs. There was little for the crew on board to do. The bridge shook once, and Freya reported that one of their missile storage units had been hit by a laser.

Derreck let the whole holo play out, a sign of respect for those who had given their lives. There was little to note on the video. Combat between ships in space was a rather boring affair in many ways, and Kindra found herself focusing on the few crew that remained. They had to know they couldn't beat the stronger jumper. They were doing everything they could, and there was always a chance for success, but Fleet didn't promote gamblers, and those who remained in the fight knew they were facing their last moments.

Despite that knowledge, they went about their duties with the precision and attitude of a normal shift change. There were no tears, no crying. Every person had a job to do, and Kindra wondered if the routine and expectations provided them some sort of emotional shield against what was coming. She looked for signs of fear in their faces, and at times she thought she caught a hint of indecision and terror in their eyes, but it might as well have been her imagination.

Kindra had a hard time putting herself in their shoes. She didn't consider herself brave, although she had experienced what it was like trying to simply get the job done. But she had never been in true danger. She had never known that her own death was inevitable. If she could face that moment with half the composure of the *Destiny*'s crew, she'd be pleased with herself.

Freya spoke from the holo again. "We've got nothing left, sir. Capacitors are empty and missiles are gone. *Hellbringer* has stopped its assault and is pulling away."

"Did we hurt it?"

"Our laser was able to punch a hole through the armor, sir, but nothing vital."

"Come on, Nicks. What game are you playing?" Absalon asked.

The captain of the doomed jumpship didn't have too long to worry. It was another bridge officer who first noticed something unusual. "Sir, I'm reading one, no, two jump signatures in-system."

Absalon's face was the very picture of confusion. "Are you certain?"

"Yes, sir. One is very close to this system's sun, and the other, sir, is directly in front of us."

Kindra's mind raced as she tried to figure out what was happening. She could see Absalon doing the same on the holo. He knew something was wrong, but couldn't figure out what it portended. *Hellbringer* was the only combat jumper the rebellion had, so Nicks couldn't be getting reinforcements. Absalon knew he also wasn't getting any support, so who else could it be?

Absalon gave a command. "Get the ship out of here!"

It was too late. Everything happened in the space of a second or two. Freya's mouth hung open as she saw some piece of information Kindra couldn't make out. "Sir..."

"There's no way—," were the last words that Kindra heard before the holo cut out.

Derreck let a moment of silence pass to honor the fallen.

"That holo doesn't show us what happened, but that wasn't the only data that was transmitted. I'll make the files freely available to anyone who wants to look at them in detail, but from what I can tell, Captain Nicks used new technology. The report Absalon heard was valid. Two jump points were opened, or more accurately, the two ends of a single jump opened. The dropship Nicks dropped on the other side of the sun either pushed or attached rockets to a small asteroid. The rock picked up quite a bit of speed, especially as it dropped towards the sun. The first jump point was incredibly close to the sun, and the second, as you heard, was right in front of *Destiny*. That asteroid came hurtling at them with incredible speed and power, and they never had a chance. The rock tore through *Destiny* from bow to stern and barely slowed down. It's nothing but scrap metal now."

Mala was shaking her head. "There's no way that's possible. Such an action violates almost everything we know about jump physics. Jumping a moving object, aiming it, jumping so close to a gravity source. Everything you're saying is wrong, Derreck."

Derreck shrugged. "I agree, and yet, the data doesn't lie. You said yourself you had discovered hints of different jump equations on the other planet. It's not inconceivable that Nicks and his team deciphered them and figured out how to weaponize them."

Kindra was surprised by the look of fear in Mala's eyes. "Such technology would change space combat as we know it. If the ability became common, enemies could hurl asteroids at planets, and there'd be little to no warning. *Hellbringer* needs to be destroyed."

"Which brings me nicely to the question at hand. We can look over what has already happened all we want, but I want to focus on what we're going to do next. The way I see it, we have two primary options. We can leave the dropships grounded and hope to hide them, or we can lift off and take our chances in space."

Alston spoke up. "Either way you'll run into problems. Even basic geologic scans of the surface will eventually pick up the dropships. We can take steps to hide them, but you're still playing a game of hide-and-seek you're eventually going to lose. Unfortunately, you don't have any better hope in space. The dropships may have faster in-system speeds than the jumper, but don't have the weapons to do any damage."

Derreck studied Alston with an inscrutable look in his eye. "You've summarized the problem well."

Mala voiced her opinion. "Let's take the fight to them. I'd rather decide everything with a quick blow than hide for a time, not knowing when an orbital strike will take me out."

Derreck didn't agree. He laid out his idea, which was to wage guerrilla warfare against the occupying forces. They might be outnumbered, but on the ground, Tev and his hunters would have an advantage, and might be able to whittle the forces down enough to force a different outcome.

Tev also chipped in. "The hunters can warn the people. With the suits, we can cover the ground in little time. You all would be welcome among the clans."

The debate was short-lived. Even Mala acknowledged any attack from space was unlikely to succeed. Without *Destiny*'s AI providing electronic cover for them, the dropships wouldn't even be able to get close enough to drop the suits off.

The decision was made, and spacefarers and hunters alike bent to the task of defending the planet.

SEVEN

TEV FOUGHT AGAINST THE DECISION, but he was not allowed to act as one of the messengers. He was told in no uncertain terms that his leg still needed another day before it was healed, and nothing he said or did would budge Kindra's decision. As a compromise, they agreed that Tev could be the hunter who delivered the news to his clan after his cast came off. Using a suit, he would be able to make it to his clan's last known location in less than a day.

When the cast came off the next day, Tev almost raced to his exosuit. Kindra caught up to him just before he put on his helmet. "Tev, wait! Are you sure you want to do this?"

He was. The upcoming weeks and months were going to be difficult, and Tev needed to visit his clan one last time, if nothing else. He could use the guidance from Shet, his elder, as much as they needed the warning from him.

Tev leaped across the forest, his powered footsteps carrying him incredible distances. Without the suit, such a trip would have taken days, not hours. Finding the clan's campsite was an easy matter, and although they had moved on since they had been seen last, a clan was easy to track. If

Tev hadn't been able to do so, there wasn't any way he could have called himself a hunter. He found them about two hours later, as the sun was beginning to set.

As soon as Tev came to the first line of guards, he found a safe place and powered down the exosuit. His clan had a passing familiarity with the suits, but from the wary glances he received from the sentries, he knew he would have a better chance of acceptance if he approached without it.

Tev knew both guards, and although they took a few minutes to warm up, they eventually spoke about what had happened to the clan since his departure. Tev already knew most of the highlights, at least up until the point Neera had married Xan and gone off to live with his clan. Since then, it sounded as though little had changed. More hunters had started families, but such was the natural order, and the news didn't surprise Tev. In his absence, other hunters had assumed more responsibility among the clan.

When they reached the campfire, the reaction of Tev's clan was muted. Most hunters ignored him, and several children stared at him with undisguised interest. Tev imagined he was the source of many cautionary tales.

Although he had hoped for a warm welcome, he had not expected one. Change was difficult, and much had been asked of the clans in the past few months and years. He understood that it was the change the clans hated, not him, but change was hard to focus your anger on. The person who brought that change was a worthy substitute.

While he didn't fret about the reaction of his clan, he desired a warmer reception from Shet. He needn't have worried. The old man stood up and embraced Tev, tears glistening in his eyes. For a moment, they stood together near the fire, and Tev looked over his elder. The strength in Shet's arms was still apparent, and the spirit in his eyes hadn't dimmed, but even from a glance Tev could see the old man's health was failing.

The realization was saddening, but not unexpected. Shet was old, even for an elder, and none of them were getting any younger. His continued life was a blessing from Lys.

Shet led them away from the fire, and Tev was reminded of the last time he and Shet had spoken, before Kindra's people had arrived. The night had been much like this, a clear night as the campfire burned behind them. It was hard to believe that night had been years ago.

Tev spoke before Shet could say anything. "It's good to see you again, Shet."

"And you, Tev. You have been in my thoughts daily since you left."

The elder's response was everything Tev wanted to hear. He could feel a small amount of tension melt from his body, pleased that he hadn't been forgotten by his clan.

Tev told the story of his past few years, all the things he had seen and done. Shet listened with rapt attention, his eyes wandering far away, his imagination trying to picture the wonders Tev described.

Tev kept his summary as short as he could. Otherwise he would risk going on for days. Before long, Tev was caught up with the current situation, and he warned Shet about what was coming.

Shet took the news in stride, almost as though he had been expecting it. Tev supposed that wasn't really a surprise. The entire reason they had recruited exosuit pilots from the clans was because they expected a day like this to come. Just because it had happened sooner than expected didn't change much.

Shet, as was his way, dove straight to the heart of the matter. "You care for the girl, don't you?"

"Is it obvious?"

Tev could hear the mirth in Shet's voice. "I've known you since you were a babe, Tev. The only woman you've ever spoken of that way is Neera."

Silence grew between them, Tev unable to ask the question that was bothering him the most.

Shet prodded him. "So, what troubles you?"

Tev took a moment to search for the words that described best what he wanted to say. "Everything that's happened, I've come to believe, is right. I can't find a better word. True, perhaps?"

"But you don't trust yourself?"

Tev shook his head. He'd never framed the question that way, but the summary was accurate. "I still struggle to understand who I am and what I'm meant to do. There are still times I feel torn between two worlds. Am I a hunter or a pilot?"

Shet chuckled. "These outsiders have become a bad influence on you, Tev."

Tev fought the small surge of anger that welled up in him. He'd given Shet no reason to laugh. "What do you mean?"

"When you track an animal, do you doubt your senses or your instinct?"

"No."

"Then stop doubting yourself now. Trust yourself, and stop thinking so small."

Tev's confusion must have been evident even in the dark.

Shet continued. "This is something I've been thinking on ever since you left. Our way of life hasn't changed much in years, and I'm not sure it should. I will have to think on what you've learned, but it sounds as though I would still prefer our way of life over another. But we do need to change the way we think. We're not just clans anymore. There are others out there, and if we want to live in peace, we need to think of ourselves differently.

"What I'm trying to say, Tev, is that you aren't just a hunter or a pilot. You're both, and I suspect that will someday be true of more and more of us. Stop thinking with such small categories. If what you say is true, you're human, just like me, and just like the girl."

"She once told me almost exactly the same thing," Tev said.

"Then she's a very wise woman."

They both laughed at that, and a warm silence descended on the two men. Shet, surprisingly, was the one who broke it.

"There's something else?"

Tev nodded. "Are we doing the right thing? Is bringing these weapons to our planet and forcing the clans into a new way of life correct?"

Shet was silent as he thought. "That is a hard question, and one that I'm not sure has an answer. Who knows how our actions today will affect our children and our grandchildren? I only know two things. First, if you are doing the best you can, you should not worry about the consequences. If you are doing all you can, there is nothing more to be done."

Tev waited for the thought to finish. He was about to prod the old man when he spoke again.

"Second, you cannot take the weight of this entirely on your shoulders. We have decided to follow this path you have set us on, but you did not force us. The weight of the future is on all of us. When you went on your boar hunt, right before the aliens came, do you remember what I said?"

"You said I needed to trust the clan."

"This is still true. We have decided to follow your lead, so it is our decision as much as yours."

"Would you have done the same?"

Shet let out a short smile. "You are asking an old man if he has the courage of youth. No, I wouldn't have done the same."

Tev's heart sank, but then was buoyed moments later.

"But I would have been wrong, Tev. I wish there was another, better path into the future. But if it exists, I do not see it. You've done well, Tev."

Tev took a deep breath and released the last of his tension. Shet's words were exactly what he had needed to hear. Together, they slowly made their way back to the camp, both to give Tev time to catch up and to warn the clan of what was coming.

TEV GLANCED down at the abrupt drop below him. He was at least a hundred meters in the air, and he was only halfway to their destination. He wasn't wearing any armor, but even if he had been, he wasn't sure it would have protected him.

Perhaps volunteering for this mission hadn't been the smartest idea. He was a hunter of the forests, and although he considered himself a fair climber, he never scaled faces like the one in front of him. The climbing wasn't hard, exactly. The plateau wasn't a sheer cliff, and in many places he could crawl up without a problem. There were always good handholds and footholds.

But that didn't make the effort any less intense.

Overconfidence would easily get him killed here. The holds were large, but if he missed one and fell, odds were he wasn't coming back. The other three hunters that had come with were all native to this area, and glided across the rock face as though they didn't have a care in the world. Tev both hated and envied them.

Tev had wanted to be a part of the scouting party, because ... why? He was having trouble remembering how he had justified it to himself. Wanting to make sure they were careful? Whatever his reasons had been, he felt foolish about them now. There were other mountain clan hunters who had volunteered, but he had overruled them.

Unfortunately, the time had come and gone for him to change his mind, so here he was, stuck climbing a mountain as best as he was able.

Their decision to hide had influenced many of their other choices in the past week. *Hellbringer* didn't know there were any dropships planetside, and Derreck wanted to maintain that advantage for as long as he could. Fortunately, Nicks seemed content to let that happen. The *Hellbringer* had set itself up in a very high orbit. They couldn't be sure, but Derreck was relatively confident they hadn't been spotted, not yet. Nicks' caution was working against him again.

Hunters spotted at least one dropship that had landed, and when the news trickled back to the camp Derreck had urged them to scout out the advance party. The captain saw an opportunity to ambush a small group of pilots, and several days later, Tev found himself panting for breath in the thin air.

Abandoning the suits for this mission had been a controversial decision. Derreck had fought hard against some of the lance commanders to convince them. He had two thoughts: the first was that he had fought against hunters before, his first time on the planet. A hunter, by himself, could evade detection from a suit. If they took the suits, it would only be a matter of time before whatever sensors were on top of the plateau would pick up their approach. The advance party would notify *Hellbringer*, and the surprise would be spoiled. Derreck's other point was even less popular. The suits were valuable, and Derreck argued they shouldn't be used until needed. There were hundreds upon hundreds of hunters on the planet, but less than two dozen suits. The hunters wanted to use the suits because of the additional power and protection they provided, but eventually they capitulated.

No one was sure what they were going to find on the top of the plateau. They assumed there would be at least a few suits, but their rewards might be even much richer than that. If they were truly fortunate, they could take a vulnerable dropship. Their only report had been about the landing, and that had been several days ago.

The only way to find out was to keep climbing, so they did. Tev picked his way up the rocks behind everyone else, painfully aware he was holding up the rest of the party. He was the only one even breathing hard.

Not only did they need to climb the rock face, they needed to do so while remaining out of sight of the top. Silence was crucial. If they accidentally knocked a rock down the face, there was a chance the pilots on top of the plateau might notice it. Everything came together to produce a slow and torturous climb for Tev.

The sun was beating down mercilessly by the time they approached the top. Although he was certain the sensation was mostly in his head, Tev felt as though he had climbed much closer to the sun. He was positive that his skin was burning, but there was little to do about it now.

Moving a centimeter at a time, Tev and his companions slid their heads above the line of the plateau, seeing for the first time what Nicks and his crew were working on. From his vantage point, Tev saw one exosuit working on a machine. Although Tev couldn't identify the device, he suspected it was some sort of sensor to scan this area of the planet. Derreck had told him the practice was common when his people explored a new place.

Using hand signals, the other hunters told Tev to remain where he was. The rest of them were going to climb farther around the plateau, scouting for other suits or ships. Tev nodded his agreement. A part of him felt upset at being left behind, but he saw the route they were planning on taking, and he knew that even if he could follow, he would be a much greater risk. The hunter swallowed his pride and remained in place, occasionally rising slowly to see if the scene had changed. He fought the urge to check more often. The exosuits were wired to notice movement, and each time he brought his head up, he risked alerting the pilot if he moved too quickly.

The sun crawled against the sky, and Tev wished there was more vegetation up here. His skin was on fire, and there was no shade to be found. One time, when Tev poked his head over the edge of the plateau, he saw a second exosuit near the first. From their stance, it was obvious they were conversing, but both pilots wore their helmets, and Tev couldn't hear their radio transmissions.

The plateau wasn't too wide. Tev assumed it was maybe about a hundred meters across at most, and it stood as one of the highest points in the area. The plateau wasn't perfectly flat. One large fissure ran through the middle of it, and the ground on top was rolling enough to provide a fair amount of cover. If they decided to attack, stealth would be possible, if difficult.

Finally, the other hunters returned, so silent Tev almost didn't notice them approaching. Together they retreated a few dozen paces and conferred in soft whispers.

The others had circled most of the plateau, and had seen the entire top. There were three exosuits in a small camp. There was no dropship, which Tev was glad about. Such a prize would have been beneficial to their cause, but taking one with only four hunters was more of a task than he felt was possible.

Two pilots were focused on studying the machine they had brought with them. The third was the greatest danger, patrolling the top of the plateau at random. The hunters, bold as always, wanted to kill their enemies, even though Tev hesitated. He was the only one present who had ever fought against the exosuits by hand, and his memories of that bloody attempt were still fresh in his mind years later. Their only advantage now was that they knew how the exosuits worked. If Tev could see what models they were fighting against, he might be able to find a weak point. They agreed on a plan and moved immediately to implement it.

First, Tev needed to climb. He followed two of the hunters as they worked their way around the sides of the plateau. The fourth, Tev's partner, followed. Tev moved with care, making sure each hand and foot was secure before continuing. Better slow and safe than dead. His fingertips, unused to the demands placed on them, were tearing against the rock face, but Tev had to use them anyway. They climbed to where the fissure met the edge of the plateau, and Tev worked his way in. After a few minutes of contortions within the tight space, Tev finally found a position he could work with. He was able to put his full weight on his feet, a relief to his battered hands. His partner settled in next to him.

The two other hunters moved on, finding places on the edge of the plateau closest to the other two exosuits. Then the ambush became a matter of waiting. Tev focused on his breath, a slow intake, a pause, and an even slower exhale. The technique was one he learned as a child, and it calmed his heartbeat as he waited for his enemy to appear. Eventually he did, the pilot looking out over the vista in front of him, his back to Tev and the fissure.

Ever so slowly, Tev stood taller, until he could get a good view of the suit. Once he had a glance he slowly lowered himself, and not a second too soon. The suit turned around and continued its track, not stopping too long at any one place. The good news was, Tev knew what type of suit they were up against, and he knew the places the armor didn't cover. It would be a difficult angle, but he could hit it. He gave the signal to his partner, and they waited for the suit to show itself again.

This time, they didn't have long to wait. The pilot was moving around the top of the plateau randomly, and came back to the ambush point soon. Tev heard his partner scramble up the face of the plateau, and he heard the suit try to respond quickly to the new threat.

Their ambush was as simple as they came. The other hunter would approach from the edge of the plateau, drawing the attention of the pilot. While the pilot was distracted, Tev would leap up from the fissure and attack from behind.

Tev leaped and stumbled. His legs were sore from being stuck in one position for too long. Fighting against the pain, he focused on making a clean killing strike. The exosuit warned the pilot he was being attacked from behind, but the pilot couldn't react quickly enough. The suit was turning around, but Tev's vision narrowed, and his world became the point of his knife and a small slot on the back of the exosuit's neck where the helmet met the armor on the shoulders. The slot was moving, but Tev slid his blade within and thrust up. The exosuit collapsed instantly as the pilot inside died.

The top of the plateau became a hive of activity as soon as Tev drove the knife home. The pilot's companions instantly knew that one of their own was dead, and they seemed none too pleased by it. But their surprise was total. They had been on the plateau for days without incident, and suddenly one of their friends died without warning. Their confusion helped keep Tev and his hunters alive.

Tev sprinted for cover as the exosuits saw him and brought their weapons to bear. He dove as he heard the rifles power up, and he landed hard and rolled behind a small rise in the ground. He felt rocky shrapnel tear through the skin of his back as the rifles bore down on him. The spot he had chosen was poor cover, and the exosuits only had to take a few steps forward before they had a clear shot at him.

Fortunately, Tev's hunters came to his rescue. They pulled themselves up behind the exosuits, and the pilots started to spin to face the new threat.

As soon as he was clear, Tev pushed himself violently back to his feet and sprinted towards the exosuits, bloody knife in hand. The lesson they had been drilling into the hunters from the very first sessions was one of distance to an enemy. Most exosuit pilots were used to fighting at range. Close-quarters combat was often an issue of simply standing your ground and hoping your armor lasted longer than your opponent's. The hunters could take advantage of that.

The four of them swarmed the two suits, slashing at any joint they could reach while dodging out of the grip and clumsy swings of the pilots.

Tev attracted the attention of one of the rebels, who spun to face the hunter. He brought his rifle up, but Tev moved in close and ducked underneath, his momentum opposite that of the suit's arm. The pilot fired his rifle, but the shells passed harmlessly over Tev's head, even if the whine of the rifle did deafen him for a few moments.

Tev sliced at the elbow joint of the suit, his sharp blade cutting through the weak protection with little problem. The pilot overreacted, swinging his arm back, trying to knock Tev sideways. Tev simply ducked down low again, letting the arm pass overhead while he cut down at the exosuit's knee.

The pilot was getting wise to Tev's plan, and he kicked out, catching Tev by surprise. Tev fell backwards, the kick passing just in front of his face. Tev scrambled away, but the exosuit pilot was bringing his rifle up, and Tev couldn't move fast enough to get out of sight. Tev did the only thing he could think of. He rolled on his side as the rifle came to life, shells tracking closer and closer.

He was saved again by one of the other hunters, who seized upon the exosuit's focus on Tev to get directly behind it and drive a blade into the neck joint, an almost identical strike to the one Tev had performed on the first pilot. The exosuit crumbled as the pilot died.

There wasn't time to celebrate. One exosuit remained, and even one could kill them all if they weren't careful. Tev pushed himself to his feet again, certain he would be sore that evening. The four of them swarmed the final exosuit, but the pilot, who had figured out what had happened to his companions, was too smart to let himself get caught standing still, even for a moment.

One of the hunters risked too much and was struck by a flailing arm as the exosuit continued spinning. Tev heard the hunter's ribs crack, but Tev didn't think the blow would be fatal. The other three hunters redoubled their efforts, making sure the pilot didn't have enough time to aim at their injured friend. The hunters landed cut after cut, but they couldn't pierce the armor in any place fatal. Tev worried that a stalemate would only serve the exosuit pilot.

Apparently, the rebel didn't feel the same way. Maybe he was scared. Maybe he thought he needed to escape to warn the *Hellbringer*. Tev couldn't guess the reason, but the exosuit suddenly broke from the battle and sprinted towards the edge of the plateau. The hunters chased after, afraid at first that the pilot was just trying to create space to better use his weapons. They needn't have worried. With a soaring leap, the exosuit jumped off one of the steepest sides of the plateau.

Tev reached the edge just in time to see the pilot careen off a rock ledge. Perhaps the pilot had been aiming for it, perhaps not, but the result was the same. The pilot couldn't control his descent, and he plummeted through the sky, tumbling out of control. He hit the ground at tremendous speed, and even hundreds of meters up, the sound was loud. Tev watched to ensure the pilot wasn't alive. The odds of it were less than slim, but he needed to make sure. When the suit didn't move for several minutes, Tev was satisfied, and he went back to tend to his injured hunter. They had a long journey ahead of them to return to camp, but they had drawn first blood on the planet's surface.

AFTER THE RETURN JOURNEY, Tev was more than happy to fall into his tent and sleep through the night and halfway through the next day. They had taken turns supporting the injured hunter back down the plateau, and once they reached flatter ground they built a stretcher to carry him. Even so, the hunter wasn't small, and by the time they returned to camp, Tev was exhausted. But he didn't want to stop until he was back home, meaning a trek of several more kilometers.

Tev woke up to the sounds of daily camp life. Hunters were training in hand-to-hand combat, and Derreck was showing a group of hunters the different places they could strike an exosuit and potentially kill the pilot.

They would be bringing the new exosuits back today. The last action Tev had taken before he had fallen asleep was to have Eleta travel to the plateau with a group of pilots. She would be able to disable the trackers and initialize the suits for the new pilots. Having the two additional suits would be a welcome boost to their forces.

Tev didn't rush around after he woke up. He savored a slow afternoon before meeting up with Derreck after the training sessions. He thought he saw a hint of grey in the captain's hair, and wondered if the stresses of this new existence were starting to get to him. Together they returned to the *Vigilance*, where Alston was keeping watch on their surroundings.

The news wasn't as good as Tev had hoped. *Hellbringer* had detached two dropships, heading for two different points. It was still too early to determine where the landing zones would be.

Derreck's analysis was quick. "They'll be sending large forces this time. We needed several days to stop the survey crew, so they'll already have good information. Nicks will have a plan."

"What do you think he will do?" Tev asked.

"If I were him, I would be proceeding with my original plan. I don't think he knows we're here yet, but he must be suspicious that there's more happening on the surface than he guessed. If nothing else, he knows that your people pose a threat to pilots. Those two forces he's sending will be numerous, and if the plan is still to recruit your people, they'll be landing near the biggest clans and taking the young men hostage."

"We need to stop him before that happens."

Derreck shook his head, a sorrowful look on his face. "I don't think we can, Tev. If we try to fight them in the sky before they land, we'll be toast. *Vigilance* is as good a dropship as any, but with a jumper in orbit, the second Nicks knows we're here, we're dead. We won't even be able to get to the enemy dropships before Nicks blows us out of the sky. We have to wait until they land."

Tev hated the answer, but he trusted Derreck. "So, we just need to wait and see where they land?"

Derreck confirmed Tev's guess. "Yes, and then we'll let them know the exosuits are here." The captain stood up straight and looked at Tev. "Get the hunters ready. The time has come."

THE NEXT FEW days were an endless nightmare for Tev. After all the training and preparation, to be forced to sit and wait for Nicks to make the first move was agonizing, and Nicks' dropships didn't seem to be in a rush to reveal their plans. They had circled the planet several times, each time causing Derreck and his crew to hold their breath. They had camouflaged the dropships as well as they were able, but the result was far from perfect. Each pass risked revealing Derreck's surprise.

Fortunately, it seemed that the camouflage was good enough. The ships eventually found their landing sites, and Tev split his hunters into two teams. His group would take the landing site farther away. Xan would lead an expedition closer to their camp. Both of them would require several days of travel, with an additional three for Tev and his group. Travel time that Tev worried they didn't have.

The problem was made worse by the fact that even Xan couldn't attack until Tev and his team were in place. They only got one chance at surprise, and once they lost it, it was gone for good. Xan and his team would abandon their suits several kilometers from the landing site and scout on foot while Tev and his team raced towards their destination.

Tev was tempted to push just a little farther every day, but he didn't dare take the risk. When they got to the site, they had to be ready to fight. Traveling in the suits was still exhausting, and they slept well each night.

When they arrived, Tev had several of the hunters get out of their suits and scouted the second landing site. They brought back a young woman from the local village, who told her story in between bouts of tears. The enemy suits had come several days ago. The woman had been out picking food when they arrived, and had wisely hidden from their searches. But she had watched what happened inside the village. Homes had been burnt and several people killed. The clan was forced to serve the rebels in the suits.

"On the third day, several of the clan tried to attack them at night. They left the door to their ship open, with two empty suits next to it."

Tev, knowing the suits as well as he did, already knew where the story was going. The suits had a guardian function to protect pilots in just such a circumstance. The programming and firing pattern was very basic, but it would have been a complete surprise to the clan.

"They charged the door, but the suits fired on us, without any people in them. Many of my clan were killed, and the next morning, the leader of the ship came out and told us never to try that again. That was the morning he started forcing the young people of the clan to pilot the suits. He said that every time someone tells him "no" that he'd kill an elder. Since then, he's been showing some of the clan how to use the suits."

Tev stood up and walked away from the circle that had gathered around the woman. She was attractive, and Tev was certain no small number of his hunters were hoping to play the hero for her. Tev, though, had more pressing concerns. Everything they had worried about from the very first day was coming to pass. He climbed into his suit and used it to communicate with Derreck, hundreds of kilometers away.

Tev's only question was how best to stop what was happening. He assumed Xan was seeing the same behavior, and Derreck confirmed it. Tev mapped out the village for Derreck and gave him the best estimates for the number of pilots. The woman had said there were sixteen pilots, which made sense to Tev. It was a reinforced company, four lances. His pilots would be outnumbered, but Tev wasn't too worried about that. This was their home territory, and they were fighting to protect their people. They could make up the difference.

Derreck and Tev shared the same worry. The dropship was going to be a problem. It had enough weapons on it to turn the tide of the battle, or, in the worst-case scenario, decimate the village. Tev couldn't let that happen.

He and Derreck threw around a number of ideas, but everything came down to the same problem. They needed to get inside the dropship and disable it before they could affect a rescue.

Tev was the one who finally figured out a solution. "We could always just blow it up."

Derreck, with his natural inclinations, wouldn't think of it. Tev could almost hear the disapproval in the silence that greeted his proposal. Derreck viewed the dropships as a valuable resource. Tev didn't care about them in the least. Destroying them was the only way of guaranteeing they would have a chance. Derreck had to see that.

He did, but Tev could hear how much it hurt him.

Tev got out of his suit after signing off with Derreck and approached the woman from the hostage clan. He told her what he had planned, and although she wasn't eager, she agreed to take part. Tev gave her a bag of explosives after showing her how to use them, then ordered his hunters into their suits.

By the time the countdown timer in his suit was down to five minutes, Tev and his force were all in position. Now, all they had to do was hope that the woman had succeeded in her task. They would know soon enough. Unless Tev received some sort of clear warning, he wasn't planning on stopping the countdown. The explosives were going to go. The only question was whether the woman had gotten them where they needed to be. Tev hoped so. He wasn't sure he could take the blood of more innocents on his hands.

When the timer hit two minutes, Derreck checked in with him. Their attack would align perfectly with Xan's.

Xan and his team were in position, also with a plan to destroy a dropship. Tev confirmed they were also ready to attack, and their path was set for them.

Even though he knew the explosion was coming, the violence of it still caught him by surprise. The explosives had been shaped charges, and the woman had followed the instructions perfectly. Explosions tore through the hull of the dropship, fire and smoke pouring everywhere. Tev didn't need to order the attack. The hunters sprang forward of their own accord, rage in their hunting cries.

Tev hung back from the rest of the group. Every muscle in his body itched to be part of the fight, but Derreck had asked him to remain behind. Tev's rifle was accurate at long ranges, so in case of emergency Tev could still take part, but Derreck couldn't command both battles at once. If Tev ran into the battle he wouldn't be able to keep track of the larger fight. He'd only be able to focus on the part happening right in front of him.

Tev was immediately glad he remained to watch the village. The enemy exosuits responded in a way Tev had never expected. Almost as soon as their ship blew up, without any hesitation at all, they started firing their weapons into the village. Bullets tore through huts, and men, women, and children ran for cover that didn't exist.

Tev choked on his rage. He had never considered his enemy might start killing with such wanton abandon. His mistake had been in assuming they had some sort of decency. Tev watched as a young girl spun around, the force of a bullet punching her to the ground.

Tev's hunters exploded out of the woods surrounding the village a few moments later, but those few moments almost destroyed the entire village. Their rescue, such as it was, felt a failure even before it began.

The hunters had seen everything Tev had, and they tore into the crew of the *Hellbringer* with unquenchable fury. His hunters moved so differently than the enemy pilots. Tev sometimes forgot, after training with the hunters for as long as he had now, how different their fighting was from the pilots they fought against.

The enemy largely stood in place. They were, after all, wearing powerful suits of armor.

Those suits did almost nothing to stop the hunters. The hunters moved with grace and speed, getting in close to their enemy.

Tev saw one hunter slide into an enemy, crawling on top of the other pilot as soon as the suit hit the ground. A few seconds of fire from the hunter's rifle ensured that the enemy stayed down.

Another hunter leapt into the air, her elbow coming down on the unsuspecting helmet of another exosuit. The other suit collapsed immediately.

Four hunters, working together, all trained their rifles on one poor enemy suit, making it the focus of an incredible amount of damage. The enemy suit spun from hunter to hunter, trying to hit just one of them before it fell, riddled with bullet holes.

Almost as quickly as it began, it was over. Only one suit remained, and it held two hostages in its right arm. Tev zoomed in on the scene. From the markings on the suit, it looked to be the captain of the dropship they had just destroyed, now a burning wreckage to his back, protecting it. In his right arm two women struggled to get free. Tev recognized one of the women as the one who had given them the information, the one who had been responsible for destroying the dropship.

The other hunters were uncertain. The captain had

positioned himself well, and there was no real way to surprise him. But the captain had to know what he was up against. He had seen the way the hunters moved, and knew that even if he bought himself a few minutes of a head start, they would catch up with him. He had to know he was doomed.

The realization made Tev's heart race. As soon as the captain knew there was no way out, he'd kill the hostages. Tev had to end the stalemate before it lasted too long. Again, he was grateful for Derreck's advice, as it had put him in just the place he needed to be. The targeting reticle appeared in Tev's visor as he brought his rifle up, stabilized by the powerful strength of the suit.

The shot was a difficult one. Tev was several hundred meters away from the battlefield, and the captain was shuffling back and forth, either very anxious or nervous about snipers. Regardless, Tev was certain he would make the shot. He couldn't afford not to.

Soft sounds carried over the distance, and Tev realized the captain had turned on his speakers and was trying to command the other hunters to lay down their weapons. The man's mind, flooded with fear, still hadn't realized just how hopeless his situation was. Tev was grateful. He had a few more moments to line up his shot and wait for the captain to stand still.

Tev was a stone. His breathing was deep and steady as he pushed away everything that wasn't his aim and his target. Somewhere in the back of his mind, he heard some of his hunters opening a channel, trying to ask him for advice. He ignored them. None of them would act rashly, giving him the time he needed.

The captain's head danced across his reticle, moving from side to side. Sometimes the head of the woman who had been their ally was in it. Tev held steady through it all, waiting for just the right moment.

A voice came through his helmet. More alarmed. His hunters were starting to get on edge. Tev didn't have quite as much time as he hoped, but the fact barely registered.

The moment came as the captain stopped to point his rifle at something besides the heads of the women. One of the other hunters must have made a move.

Regardless, just for a moment, the captain stopped shuffling back and forth. He had hugged the women a little closer to him. Tev only had centimeters of margin to work with over a vast distance.

Tev pulled the trigger.

He held his breath for the moment it took his round to cross the distance between him and his enemy.

Then he saw the hole open up in the helmet of the captain, who dropped to the ground without a word.

Tev watched for a few more seconds as the women struggled free. They were both unharmed, as near as he could tell.

The clearing that held the village fell strangely silent, and Tev knew they had just started a war.

EIGHT

KINDRA LOOKED out on the scene before her with a strange mixture of pride and horror. Dozens upon dozens of wounded rested outside the *Vigilance* waiting to be healed. The violence of the past few days had gone well beyond the exosuits themselves.

Kindra remembered someone saying from her childhood, "When the warriors play, it's the innocent who pay." She hadn't liked the saying as a child, and she still didn't, but she acknowledged the truth of it, at least.

By all accounts, Tev and Xan had led two very successful raids. They had eliminated two dropships and over two dozen pilots. However many suits *Hellbringer* originally had, Nicks had to be running low by now. Their surprise had worked, but it didn't mean it didn't come with a cost.

In both villages, the enemy exosuits had fired upon the village as soon as they came under attack. Derreck had told her they must have had standing orders to that effect, because he couldn't understand why else they would resort to such horrific tactics immediately. Even worse, with Xan's group, one enemy lance had escaped out of the pincer of Xan's forces. They ran for an hour and found a second village before Xan and his hunters tracked them down.

The horror of everything that had happened was almost beyond comprehension, and Derreck had taken a huge risk to try to help. As soon as *Hellbringer* dipped below the horizon, he took *Vigilance* and launched, flying towards each of the sites to pick up the wounded and bring them back. His window had been small but he had just made it, every hold, nook, and cranny of the ship filled with wounded. Fortunately, it looked as though *Hellbringer*'s scanners hadn't picked him up.

Which led Kindra to the sense of pride she was feeling. In front of her, everyone was helping out, and there was no complaining, even among the gravely wounded. They had been working through the night and into the next day, and not a single person had asked for a respite.

Kindra was dead on her feet. Her sense of time had become distorted, and everything happened in slow motion. They were nearing the end of what they could do for the wounded, but until they reached that point, she refused to stop, or even sit down.

She was reminded, too much, of her childhood, and one of the worst days she had lived through. She and her family had been out, visiting the gardens of the habitat that her father so often took her to. Out of nowhere, a rebellion ship had jumped into the system and dropped an orbital bomb on their home hab, adjacent to the one they were in. The bomb hadn't been big. Habs were strong enough for the elements, but had never been designed to protect against weapons, at least not in those days. All they needed to do was poke a big enough hole and the hab was immediately destroyed.

Weeks passed before they could return to their home, and her dad, when he could summon the energy, joked that Kindra's love of plants had saved their lives. He was right, but Kindra's love hadn't done anything to save the hundreds of other residents. That day had been the first time Kindra had experienced death on any scale. It colored her entire childhood.

Sometimes, she was surprised she hadn't become a medic. Looking back on everything in her life, she could see exactly how she had made the decisions that defined her. After that day, she had wanted to avoid death as much as possible. Some part of her must have thought she had seen enough for a lifetime. She became even more fascinated with life and how it developed, and had guided her plans to that purpose, eventually bringing her to where she was today.

More than once, she had thought it would be useful to have more medical training. Today was certainly one of those days. Their healing pods were powerful medicine, but they only had four between the two dropships, and they were reserved for the most serious cases. Others needed to be healed using more old-fashioned methods, and several methods which Kindra had no familiarity with. Everyone who had any experience with healing was doing all they could, and that included any of Tev's people who could help. But Kindra was limited in what she could do and what she knew. Her role on a small ship meant she had a greater degree of first aid training than any of her colleagues, but to her mind, that still amounted to far too little at this moment. With more medical training, she might have been able to save more.

But that was why she had never pursued it, even though medical professions were in high demand at the time. She might save people, but she would also have to watch many die, and when she was younger, she hadn't been sure she could handle that.

Her experience with Tev had changed her, though. Saying she was comfortable with death was perhaps too much, but she had come to recognize it as a part of life, and she had come to terms with the fact she had ended life herself.

Alston shook her out of her reverie. Their geologist looked at her with a concerned look on his face. "Are you doing okay, Kindra?"

The shock of Alston asking her anything forced her back to the present. In the years she had known him, she wasn't sure she had ever had him ask her anything about her life, even as mundane as asking how her day was.

Kindra looked out over the wounded, seeing not only the pain, but the healing and concern that was present. "Yes, I'm doing okay. Thanks, Alston."

He nodded, an awkward question taking a few moments to escape his lips. "I was wondering if you could use some more help?"

Would wonders never cease? The rational part of Kindra's mind reasserted itself for a moment, and she studied their geologist. She had always thought there was more to him than meets the eye, but that thought was twisted ever so slightly, and she began to think there was far more to him than what she had believed. He was a quiet man who didn't seem to have a care in the world besides his rocks, but he had continued to follow the rest of the crew of the *Vigilance* without any hesitation whatsoever, even when they had contemplated treason. Then her rationality slipped just a little, realizing there was only one question that really mattered at the moment. "Do you even know first aid?"

Alston looked torn, as if she had asked him a difficult question. "Probably not as much as you, but I think I know enough to help, if you'll let me."

Kindra nodded. "Please. If you can help, we'd be grateful to have you."

Alston gave her a short bow, a gesture Kindra considered terribly odd, and scurried away. Kindra pushed the geologist out of mind. There was still work to be done. She went to the next patient, a young girl from the village Tev had gone to rescue. She had been shot, but during triage they had seen the bullet had gone straight through the shoulder, so she had been put down near the end of the list. Kindra cleaned the wound as best as she could and bandaged it with cloth strips that had been torn from spare uniforms. They had run out of bandages long ago, and if there were many more wounded, they would have to strip their own clothes off and dress as Tev and his people did.

When she was finished, the girl ran off, seemingly oblivious to the fact she had been shot. She ran straight up the ramp to the *Vigilance*, curious to explore the shiny object. For just a moment, Kindra wondered what kind of world they were going to build for the children of this planet. Would they be like Tev and be able to switch between two worlds, or would something different happen?

Kindra pressed her palms to her eyes, trying to force some energy into her system. Just a few more patients, and then she could allow herself to rest. When she went to look at the lists, she was surprised to see how close they were getting to the bottom. Had she passed out for a few minutes?

She heard Alston call another name, and her world got

even weirder. Alston was working on a young man who had a bullet lodged in his upper arm. With deft movements, Alston pulled the bullet out and sealed the wound. His hands were sure and steady, and as he called a new patient, their eyes met. Kindra didn't know what to say or do, and at the moment, she didn't really care. Alston was helping, and that was all that mattered. She mouthed a silent thanks to him, and then called for the next patient.

They finished less than an hour later. There would be far more work to do in the coming days, but everyone was stable, at least for now. They could all rest and regain their energy. Kindra spent a moment looking for Alston, but quickly gave up when she couldn't find him. She was certain he was hiding somewhere, but all she wanted to do was find her bunk and crash into blissful oblivion.

KINDRA WAS TIRED of living in fear. The journey returning to Tev's planet had been a miserable one. They had been relentlessly pursued by the *Hellbringer*, and one of the worst aspects of that chase had been the silence between battles. The silence wasn't peace. They were still in constant danger, only hours away from attack at all times. Every time they jumped, there had been a degree of fear that they would be attacked as soon as they arrived, before their jump meds even wore off. There was a very real chance that when they went to sleep for the jump they'd never wake up again.

The only way to deal with that creeping fear was to do your best to ignore it, to treat every jump like it was routine, to go about your day as if there wasn't a warship with the same destination as your own. Sometimes, you could even succeed for a few minutes at a time.

The fear wasn't the kind that froze you in place. This fear crept upon you slowly, invading your dreams, making you jump at everyday noises. It wore at you, nibbling gently at the edges of your sanity. Kindra had almost gotten to the point where she welcomed the attacks, because then at least she knew what she was facing.

Their current situation was the same. The *Hellbringer*'s orbit had changed, dropping into a low orbit suitable for bombardment and quick dropship release, and Derreck was certain that Nicks was getting closer to the truth, if he hadn't guessed it already. They would run more frequent scans of the surface, and it would only be a matter of time before an alert tech saw through the camouflage and ended this game of cat and mouse.

They weren't safe on the planet once they were discovered, and they certainly wouldn't be safe in space. The clock on their journey was winding down, they just didn't know how much time they had left. Like their race to Tev's planet, they knew the final fight was coming, and the silence before the storm was more frightening than the event itself.

Kindra did everything she could to keep herself busy. There were patients to check on, and she rotated the more serious cases through the medical pods as quickly as she was able. The activity kept her mind off the impending doom they all faced.

There was also the mystery of Alston. He had been an enigma for as long as Kindra had known him, but recently, that feeling had become even more pronounced. Something about him was off, but she couldn't figure out what. It was as though she was working on a puzzle and discovered extra pieces after she was sure she had finished it. She didn't know how they fit. Part of her worried that Alston posed a danger, but as she went through all her memories of him, she couldn't come up with any where he wasn't polite and helpful. More than once she turned towards the *Vigilance*, where Derreck was keeping watch on all the events surrounding the planet, but she couldn't bring herself to do it. She questioned her own judgment, painfully aware of the lack of rest affecting her thoughts.

Eleta would have been good to talk to, someone to share a woman's intuition with, but she was gone. She had left with Derreck on his rescue run to be dropped off at the site of Tev's battle. They were going to salvage every suit they could, giving the surviving and uninjured villagers the very basic training needed to pilot the suits. All of them—Tev, Eleta, the hunters, and the brand new recruits—were on their way back, but the progress was much slower returning than going. The pilots were too new and moved too slowly. They were still at least two days out. Xan's group wouldn't arrive until tomorrow, their own captured suits in tow.

Kindra was left on her own to stew in her thoughts. So she continued to check on patients, far beyond what was necessary.

The sun was beating down on them in the middle of the afternoon when Kindra saw Alston come out of the ship. He had been lying low for the past few days, acting exactly like the Alston she had always known. Kindra hoped he was just out to collect some rock sample, but his eyes focused on her, and she knew that wasn't true.

The medical camp was bustling with activity. There were the injured, starting to move around more, as well as dozens of caregivers, both crew from *Destiny* and villagers. Alston moved without hurry, allowing a group of children laughing with joy to run around him.

Kindra held her ground, trying to act as natural as possible.

When Alston finally reached her, Kindra was just finishing up with another patient.

Alston began to speak. "Kindra, I just wanted you to know..."

Kindra held up a hand to interrupt him. In the back of her mind, she noticed that his speech pattern had changed slightly. It was more confident, more neutral than she was used to.

"Alston, you're a mystery to me, but only one thing matters to me."

He fixed her with an inquisitive look.

"Are you with us or against us?"

The geologist held her gaze as he answered. "With you. Always."

Kindra was about to tell him something about that being everything she needed to know, but Alston's eyes narrowed in suspicion at something behind her. Kindra turned around and followed his gaze. A hunter was walking up the main path through the camp towards the ship. She wasn't sure what was making Alston so suspicious, but she looked at the hunter more closely.

A small alarm went off in her mind, but her rationality overrode it. There was nothing wrong with a hunter being in the camp. The man wasn't injured, but that didn't indicate anything. She was about to turn around and ask Alston what was wrong when she noticed something herself. The way the man walked was different.

The difference was subtle, but Kindra had spent a long time around the hunters, and one trait they all shared in common was the way they moved. They were always careful, always in balance, never stepping on a stone or twig without cause. This hunter was also in balance, but his motion was straight. His foot placement never altered, no matter what was in his way. The man was no more a hunter than Kindra was an exosuit pilot.

Kindra's mind raced with questions. If the man wasn't a hunter, who was he? How did Alston pick him out so easily? Why was the man here? Her mind repeated the questions, but she couldn't find an answer to any of them.

She wasn't going to get the time, either. The man who wasn't a hunter saw her looking at him, and his expression changed. He knew he had been discovered, and he broke out into a sprint.

Alston grabbed Kindra's shoulder and pulled her back towards the *Vigilance*.

Kindra, too confused to argue, followed.

The two of them ran, chased by the mysterious man. Kindra wasn't called on to sprint very often, and within a few seconds, her chest was heaving, her breath coming out in ragged gasps as she dashed for the ramp. She had never seen Alston run, but he was fast, reaching the ramp seconds before her.

Kindra didn't dare look back until she reached the ramp. Alston slapped the controls to bring the ramp up, Kindra tumbling forward as she lost her balance. She worked her way back to sitting, looking behind, expecting to see the man give up the chase. But he didn't. The man was incredibly fast, and he leaped and grabbed the ramp as it closed. He threw himself up and over the lip with ease, as though explosive pull-ups were something he did on a daily basis. Their attacker landed lightly on his feet.

She knew they were dead. Derreck was several seconds away on the other end of the ship, and the way this man moved made it clear he would waste no time killing them.

The man stepped towards Kindra, and suddenly Alston was there, moving silently between the man and her.

She thought the idea was brave, but she also knew it would cost Alston his life. The two opponents faced each other for a second before the tableau exploded into an action scene. The man struck out at Alston, but Alston wasn't there anymore. The geologist drove his fist into the man's kidneys, but the blow didn't seem to faze their attacker at all. Kindra saw Alston's eyes narrow.

The next exchange was too fast for her to see. Both men tried to strike each other, elbows and fists flying in close quarters. Eventually, the other man got hold of Alston's wrist and drove him to the ground. Alston rolled out of the throw, coming to his feet with a knife in hand. The man who wasn't a hunter grinned and closed the distance, heedless of the weapon.

Kindra's wits returned to her, and she started scrambling away from the fight, looking around the hold for some kind of weapon. If they could just last a few more seconds, they could survive. But her eyes darted around hopelessly, the hold almost entirely empty.

The fight resumed, and Kindra couldn't believe what her eyes were telling her. Alston was attacking with a renewed focus, and if the fight was determined by who was landing the most strikes, he was winning, by quite a bit. Alston's knife sliced and stabbed, red cuts and wounds opening up all over the other hunter, who paid them no more attention than if he was being bitten by a mosquito. Alston was tiring, and it seemed he hadn't done anything to the man. The hunter, their enemy, landed a solid kick to Alston's leg, sending him crashing to the ground, barely holding on to his knife.

Alston tried to struggle to his feet, but the last kick must have caused him more pain than Kindra realized, because he wasn't doing a very good job of standing.

The hunter moved in for the kill, but then part of his head disappeared. Kindra's eyes widened in shock as their assailant dropped to the ground, his remaining eye lifeless. She followed Alston's gaze, who was looking directly at Derreck, who had just come in, a weapon in his hand. A weapon that was currently pointing directly at Alston.

DERRECK LOWERED HIS WEAPON SLOWLY, his steely gaze never breaking contact with Alston's. His voice was cold. "Intelligence?"

Alston nodded.

"Figured. Are you with us?" The question was an echo of Kindra's.

"Yes."

Derreck studied Alston's face for a moment and then came to a decision. He holstered his weapon and came to help Alston up. "You okay?"

"Yeah, just got tossed around a bit."

Derreck looked over at the body lying in the hold. "Looked like he was enhanced with some pretty illegal technology."

"Effective, though. He would have killed us both if you hadn't shown up."

The two of them came over to Kindra and helped her up. Kindra, for her part, was still trying to process everything that had happened. The fake hunter she understood. He had to have been crew of the *Hellbringer*. But she stared at their geologist.

"Alston?"

The man she had known was gone, replaced by another man entirely. "Yeah?"

Derreck interrupted them. "Explain as we walk. We need to get to the bridge right away."

They walked together, Kindra helping Alston along the narrow passageways. He gave his explanation. "As Derreck has already guessed, I'm with Fleet Intelligence. I was posted with Derreck almost immediately after the rebellion."

"Why?" Kindra didn't understand. She had thought Fleet Intelligence was a myth. And Derreck was a hero of the rebellion conflict. There wouldn't be any reason to spy on him.

Derreck himself filled in the blanks. "They were worried about me. I went on a lot of secret missions, a lot of dark missions that would bring Fleet down if I spoke of what I'd done. They tried to get me a desk, promote me so high I couldn't cause any damage, but I refused. I only wanted to fly. Their only option was to send someone to watch me."

Alston confirmed Derreck's explanation.

Kindra was beside herself. Alston had already been on board the *Vigilance* when she had joined. He had been there almost as long as Derreck. She couldn't believe Fleet would trust one of their own heroes so little. "Are you even a geologist?"

Alston laughed. "Yes, although not a very good one. My job was to be part of the crew. If Derreck ever looked as though he was going to cause trouble for Fleet, I was to use my discretion in handling the situation."

Derreck translated. "In other words, you had permission to kill me."

Alston looked uncomfortable, but he didn't deny it was true.

Kindra stared at Derreck. Her captain had just found out that one of his crew, one of the men closest to him in the world, was a traitor who had permission from Fleet to kill him if necessary, and he was acting as though he had just found out it was going to rain. She put a hand on his shoulder and stopped him. "Wait a second. I know we've got decisions to make, but I think this is something we should take a minute and talk about. How can you be so calm about this?"

Derreck smiled. "I had my suspicions for a while, but I wasn't acting against Fleet ... until recently. Anyway, I knew I could trust him."

The captain tried to turn around and resume his journey to the bridge, but Kindra prevented it. "How?"

Derreck looked at Alston, the two of them sharing a look that indicated Kindra should have figured everything out by now. "He broke his own orders. Back on Haven, I talked openly about disobeying Fleet on this mission. And yet we're still here."

Pieces slid into place in Kindra's mind. Derreck had explicitly told them he was considering disobeying the will of Fleet, and yet they had still been allowed on the mission. The only way that would be true was if Alston hadn't said anything to his superiors. She considered the spy in a new light yet again. But she wasn't satisfied as easily as Derreck. She needed to know more. "Why?"

Alston's voice was steady. "We are a very small part of Fleet, but we wield incredible power. All of us are allowed to use our discretion as we see fit. Simply put, I believed in Derreck."

The explanation was enough for Derreck, but Kindra

still held reservations. Unlike Derreck, she had never suspected Alston, and the change was difficult to process. But then they were on the bridge and Derreck was looking at a projection of the planet. *Hellbringer* was currently in range of *Vigilance*'s sensors, and just a glance was enough to let Kindra know that the ship had changed course.

Derreck confirmed Kindra's analysis. "We need to get out of here. That operative had to contact Nicks before he tried to singlehandedly capture our ship. Nicks will be in a position for orbital bombardment in about twenty-six minutes."

So little time to make the decision. So little time to act. Derreck was as calm as she had ever seen him, but she imagined his mind was racing.

Derreck looked up at Alston. "If you're Intelligence, I assume you're a better dropship pilot than I am."

"Yes." Alston seemed to know what Derreck had in mind.

"I want you to take Kindra and get out of here. Stay out of Nicks' crosshairs, and use your best judgment."

Another look passed between them, and Kindra felt as though Alston and Derreck were long-lost brothers. They thought the same and knew how the other would react.

Derreck turned to Kindra. "You have fifteen minutes starting now before Alston takes off. Do whatever needs to be done to be ready."

Kindra had too many questions. "I thought you said we would be dead if we took off?"

"Probably. The jumpship will eventually catch you, and you don't have the weapons to stand up to it, but if you have mobility, you have a chance, slim as that might be."

"What about the others?"

"I'd love to do more, but there isn't time. Your fifteen minutes are wasting away, Kindra."

She hated being rushed, and her mind was still catching up.

"Aren't you coming with us?"

"No. No one down here has the skills to lead these people. I need to stay here. They recognize me and will listen."

Kindra wanted to pick apart the argument. She didn't want to take off without the rest of the crew. They were leaving Derreck and Eleta behind. And Tev. She wanted to be able to say her goodbyes, to get some semblance of closure. But she only had thirteen minutes, and there was too much to do. She bent to her work, afraid that she would never see most of her friends again.

NINE

TEV AND DERRECK sat around a campfire, surrounded by a small group of hunters and villagers. The past few days had been chaotic, but life was slowly starting to settle down into a new normal. Around them, clusters of two to four enjoyed the fire and quiet conversation. If not for the deadly danger in the sky, tonight would seem almost the same as any other. A soft breeze occasionally stirred the trees, and when Tev took a deep breath, he could feel the tension melting from his body.

Tev had gotten the message from Derreck as soon as the captain found out they had been discovered. Tev left one trained hunter to escort the new pilots while the rest of them made for the camp as fast as they could. They ran through the night and arrived the next morning, exhausted but ready to help.

Derreck's greatest fear had been that *Hellbringer* would begin dropping bombs from space. To save Tev's people, Derreck had them separate. That way, even if destruction did fall from the sky, they would only take out a handful at a time. The process had gone surprisingly smoothly, but had still taken a tremendous effort from the hunters in the exosuits, carrying large amounts of gear for kilometers.

Tev's hunters were spread out now, pairs of them accompanying many of the groups. At the present moment, there was little for them to do. *Hellbringer* was in space, and they were locked on the ground.

Tev feared for Kindra. She had been ordered to leave the planet with no warning, and she was in as much danger as the hunters on the ground. Nicks had all the advantages, and now they were stuck waiting to see what he would do next.

Lys chased her prey overhead, and Tev leaned back against a log, resting his head against the dead wood as he lazily stared into the sky. In his mind's eye, he saw Lys as he had in his visions. Everything that was happening here was necessary. He was convinced of that. What he wanted was some guidance, some reassurance that their fight was the right thing to do. Dozens of his people had already been slaughtered. Thousands more were at risk. All Nicks needed to do was give a command and their civilization would be over.

Tev knew they were balanced precariously close to the cliff's edge. He had spoken about the problem with Derreck in hushed whispers. Nicks had to decide whether Tev's people were worth the trouble. So long as he saw the benefit, he would leave them largely alone. But if he ever decided they wouldn't take his side, there was nothing stopping him from wiping them out so that they would never be used against him. Such an action was terrible to consider, but Derreck had assured him that Nicks was the type of person capable of making that decision. He was a true believer and would go to any lengths to keep the rebellion alive.

Tev glanced over at Derreck, whose gaze was focused far away. "What's on your mind?"

Derreck's eyes focused, and in a moment, he was back in the present, sitting around a fire with Tev. "I'm trying to think of any way to board *Hellbringer*."

"Why?"

"It would solve all our problems. We would acquire whatever jump technology he found, and eliminate the threat to the clans and to Fleet. All our challenges, solved with one smooth stroke. I just don't know how. If both our dropships attacked at the same time, one of them might make it to *Hellbringer*. We upgraded our point-defense cannons before we left Haven, so we'd have a chance. But that's an awful lot to risk, and the point-defense system won't do anything if *Hellbringer* brings its laser into play, which I expect it would."

Derreck stretched his elbows back, taking a deep breath. "I've been thinking about it for days now, and I just can't figure it out."

Tev wished he had an answer for Derreck, but there was none to give. Derreck was the only one on the planet who had any chance of figuring out how to attack the jumpship, and they both knew it.

Derreck looked over at Tev. "But I'm not the only one lost in thought. What's on your mind?"

"Nothing so important."

Derreck gave Tev a mischievous grin. "Thinking about Kindra?"

Tev nodded. "Among other things."

A comfortable silence grew between them, but Derreck was one of the few people Tev felt like he could talk openly to, so he opened up, more than he ever had.

"Being with her, it makes me feel like I'm home. Like I

have a place in the galaxy. When I'm with her, I don't feel like an outsider stuck between two worlds."

Derreck gave Tev a soft smile. "Have you thought much about the future?"

Tev shook his head. "Someday, perhaps." He couldn't bring himself to say anything about his greatest fear, but Derreck was no fool, and he saw something on Tev's face.

"What's really on your mind, Tev?"

Tev only debated for a moment. Derreck was the only other person he knew who'd been through anything similar, and so he spoke of the visions he'd had. Derreck listened intently, not doubting Tev's claims at all.

Tev spoke of his visions of space, and of *Vigilance* and *Destiny*, and how he believed that his people would eventually spread through the stars. The visions weren't rational, of course, but he believed them with his whole heart, even if he couldn't explain them.

"The part that haunts me though, is the claim that I'll need to hunt farther than any hunter who has come before."

Derreck frowned. "But haven't you already fulfilled that requirement?"

"I thought so, but why have I heard it twice? The second time, I'd already traveled to Haven and was on my way back."

"You think she meant death, don't you?"

Tev nodded, and Derreck leaned in closer, his eyes boring into Tev. "I can't speak to the accuracy of what you saw, or what any of it means. But you need to get that thought out of your mind. I've seen people like you, Tev. Soldiers who thought they were doomed. The belief becomes self-fulfilling. If you believe you are meant to die, you'll make poor decisions."

The advice was good, but Tev couldn't shake his fear.

Derreck laughed softly to himself. "Besides, if you are being literal about the vision, you can't mean death. There are a lot of hunters who have died before you."

The statement, simple as it was, shook Tev to his core, because it was true. If he had to hunt farther, death couldn't be the answer. Even though the night was as dark as it had been five minutes ago, Tev suddenly felt like sunshine was beating down on him. He had resigned himself to the worst, but with one quiet statement, Derreck had changed everything.

And then he did again. All mirth faded from his voice as he received a message. "*Hellbringer* just launched her third dropship down to the surface of the planet. I have an idea."

TEV CHASED AFTER DERRECK, who had left the blaze almost as though he himself had caught on fire. There was no place for him to go, though, and he suddenly stopped and turned around, almost bumping into Tev.

"I know how we end this."

"Slow down. Tell me."

"We take over their dropship and use it to sneak back aboard the *Hellbringer*. Then we take it over."

The plan sounded simple enough in theory, but Tev knew that every part of that plan would pose a tremendous challenge. And there was one question that was bothering him most of all.

"Why would Nicks even send a dropship down? He has all the advantages by staying up where he is."

The question stopped Derreck in his tracks. "I don't know for sure, Tev. All I have are my best guesses, and I don't know how accurate they are."

"What's your best guess?"

Derreck took a deep breath, as though he thought his answer would somehow upset Tev. "I've been thinking a lot about Nicks' tactics. Often, they don't make sense at first, until we look at them in a new light. His behavior on the chase over here was downright bizarre from our standpoint, but we don't think like him. He's in charge of the last of the rebellion. Of course he would over-value caution.

"I believe the same thing is happening here. His efforts to coerce your people into service have been half-hearted at best. I'm convinced that while Fleet thinks this planet is the prize, Nicks looks at everything differently. For him, your people and this planet are secondary. I think Nicks is after technology."

Tev was confused. "That doesn't make any sense. Your technology is hundreds of years ahead of ours."

"Yes, but there's always been something more going on, something we haven't even come close to answering, right?"

The hunter wasn't sure if the question was rhetorical or not, but Derreck answered it quickly.

"Let's start with facts. The signals that brought us out here in the first place. Your system is over nine hundred light years away from even our remote outposts. You don't know the history of my people, but we only developed jump technology about eight hundred years ago. Hold on to that for a second."

Tev tried to keep up. Derreck was speaking so fast it was challenging.

"Second fact. Both your people and another advanced civilization are found within forty light years of one another. We've been exploring the galaxy for hundreds of years, and I'll let you know just how rare that is. It's impossible. The odds of such an event happening are beyond crazy. And yet here you are. Even though your civilizations couldn't be more different, you have to be linked somehow. Hell, you even share the same DNA. With us too, which I can't even begin to explain."

"Are you saying that you believe our planet has some sort of technology Nicks is looking for?"

"It's the only explanation I can come up with that makes any sense. We received signals from both systems, which means at one point in time, your clans were capable of creating a strong electromagnetic signal. There's no telling what Nicks found on that other planet, but if he found a clue that would lead him to search for a technology on your planet, it would explain why he's made so little effort to recruit your people."

"But even if that's true, how does it affect us?"

"It gives us a window. Whatever Nicks is searching for must be difficult to find. Otherwise he'd have already grabbed it and left. Also, when we first came, we made detailed scans of the entire planet. Nicks has to have those, so again, if it was easy, he'd have already found it. I'm guessing whatever technology he thinks he's uncovered will take a few hours to get to at least. And that means we have a small window to try and take over the dropship while it's on the planet."

"The ship will be well-protected."

"Yes, but I think we both know that it will be our last chance. Once that ship finds what it's looking for, we'll be stuck in this system for a long time."

"So, it's everything or nothing." The decision was easy to make. The stakes were too high for anything but an attempt to finish this all.

THE PAST FEW hours had been beyond busy, and Tev

was exhausted. As soon as Alston had mapped the trajectory of the incoming dropship, word went out to all the hunters. They made all possible speed to the landing site, a mountain hours away. Tev and Derreck were actually some of the closest to the site, which was a great benefit to them, because they needed to carry Eleta. If Derreck's plan was going to have any chance, they were going to need her skills, and the fastest mode of transportation they had was the suits. She couldn't pilot, and she couldn't keep up on foot. The only other option was to carry her in their arms. She found the transportation demeaning, but acquiesced when it was clear there wasn't another option.

While they approached, Derreck was constantly communicating with others. Tev didn't know everything the captain was coordinating, but he knew Derreck was going to throw everything into this last-ditch effort to change the course of history. The hunters were only the tip of the spear.

Tev had battled with some of the hunters about attacking. They saw their duty as one of defense, and as escorts to the injured they fulfilled that duty. They didn't have Tev's perspective, one that thought far into the future. Nicks leaving with the technology did them no harm anytime soon. But sooner or later, more people were going to come to Tev's planet, and when they did, Tev had decided he would rather they be part of Fleet. Their actions here would reverberate throughout time, even if few of the hunters saw it that way.

However, all hunters spoke the language of revenge, and when Tev reminded them of how Nicks' pilots had fired on innocent villagers, the hunters were convinced. They didn't attack to save their planet, but to avenge their friends and family.

Hours later, they were gathered to the south of the *Hellbringer*'s dropship, which had landed in the foothills of a small mountain range. Pair by pair, the hunters trickled in, and Tev urged them to get what rest they could. Derreck was sneaking his way closer without his exosuit to get a better idea of what their enemies were attempting.

They were dancing delicately with time. Every hour they waited meant they had more of their hunters in position, but there was no telling how long it would take the dropship to find what they were looking for. They knew that the window was only open for a certain amount of time, but they didn't know how long that would be.

So, the hunters got what rest they could while Derreck took the lead. Tev was able to close his eyes, but he couldn't sleep. Derreck's call could come at any moment, and he needed to be ready.

As he often did when hunting, Tev slipped inside himself. He gently focused on his breaths, which became deep and long. All else was a disturbance, and he pushed those thoughts out of his mind. In time, his body relaxed deeply while still aware of what was happening around him. The practice, perfected over years of hunting, had proven its worth several times over. Tev knew that when he returned to full consciousness he would be relaxed and energized.

There wasn't long to wait. Tev had hoped they might have more time, but the dropship didn't want to be on the planet any longer than was necessary. Derreck told Tev he was returning, and Tev assembled all the hunters who had arrived. They weren't at full strength, but Derreck wouldn't summon them if he didn't need to.

Derreck was back in the makeshift camp within the hour. He donned his suit with practiced ease and displayed the site they were going to be attacking. Unfortunately, the position seemed easily defensible. The dropship was in a U-shaped valley, the walls rising a good thirty meters in the air. If they didn't want to destroy the dropship, there was only one reasonable approach, and Derreck reported that direction held traps and enemy soldiers. Even if their enemies weren't expecting an attack, they were prepared for one.

Tev looked at the pictures Derreck had taken. A plan was forming in his mind. He opened a private channel to Derreck.

"We could attack from the top of the valley."

"Tev, there's no way. First you have to get up there, and then you have to jump off. Exosuits don't make jumps like that."

"Our best pilots can. The suits can take the impact, Derreck. I'm sure of it."

Tev knew the only reason Derreck was even considering the option was because a frontal assault had so little chance of succeeding. "What do you propose?"

"Split the forces. I'll take the best pilots, you take the rest. You attack first, make them think you're the thrust, then we attack from behind. Not too complicated."

"I hate that plan."

"Do you have a better one?"

"No."

Tev opened the channel up to the public and called for volunteers. He explained how difficult the maneuvering was going to be, and he was excited to see that only the best pilots volunteered. The hunters were brave, but they knew their limits.

There was little else that needed to be said. Derreck led the diversion force, while Tev led their best around the opening of the valley. They started their climb, and the route quickly became difficult.

Behind him, pilots slipped as the steep terrain gave way under their armored feet. Tev tested the way, leaping up the side of the mountain, always ready to leap away should the landing start to give way. Each step was nerve-wracking, each one an opportunity for the entire attempt to fail. Twice Tev jumped to a position he didn't trust, each time managing to jump back before the entire spot collapsed. Their advance was slow, and every jump, from every person, had to be perfect. Tev began to worry they wouldn't get in position in time.

Fortunately, he didn't need to fear. The dropship was still in place as they reached the top of the valley. Tev risked a short glance over the lip. From up here, the drop seemed so much farther than it had seemed from Derreck's pictures. A moment of doubt crossed his mind. Perhaps they wouldn't be able to take that fall. But again, they had no choice. They had come too far to do anything different.

Tev let Derreck know they were in position. Moments later, the valley below him exploded in fire. He resisted the urge to look again. He ran the risk of being detected. Instead, he waited, trusting Derreck to tell him when to jump. The command came a few moments later. Tev relayed it to his hunters, and without giving himself time to think, he sprinted towards the edge and leaped.

For the first few moments, the jump was thrilling. He basked in the power of the suit, the feeling of flying through the air. But that feeling soon became one of falling, and fear gripped his heart. The ground was so far away.

And getting closer so fast.

Tev barely had time to remind himself the technique was the same as any other jump. He landed and pushed forward, his suit screaming at the stresses it was being put under. Tev felt the impact in every bone of his body, as though he had been punched by a giant. Then the pressure was gone and he was flying forward, diving into a roll he could barely control.

He didn't have time to see if the others made it. They had to. He was too disoriented to roll to his feet, so he finished the roll sitting up. In front of him, he saw the back of an enemy exosuit. Acting on instinct, he raised his rifle and pulled the trigger, sending a single round punching through the armor.

His world was one of gut reactions and brief visions. Every time he saw an enemy suit, he brought his weapon up, firing.

When the first rounds knocked him onto his back, he remembered he needed to move.

He rolled to the side as an enemy pilot tried to stomp his helmet in, pushing himself back to his feet.

His awareness widened, just a little, and he saw he wasn't the only one who had made the landing. There were others fighting by his side.

He also saw several exosuits motionless on the ground. Some hadn't made the jump.

Tev spun underneath the arm of an enemy, raising his arm and firing a round that traveled from the enemy's torso through his head, exiting out the top. He continued his spin, finding another enemy in front of him. He was behind the enemy suit, and a single shot killed that pilot as well.

His awareness widened again, and he realized there weren't many enemies left.

Derreck's shout cut through the fog of his mind.

"Tev! They dropped a bomb!"

Tev didn't have the time to process the thought. The

enemies that remained were clustering into a hole in the side of the valley. It wasn't a cave, the edges were too perfect for that. Pieces clicked in place, and he understood that hole was why they came. Why they had risked everything.

One of his hunters followed the exosuits in, and was immediately torn apart by concentrated fire. Attacking the few suits that were left would be a nightmare.

An unnatural calm fell over the battlefield as active combat died away. Tev and his hunters didn't dare to attack the hole, but the enemy pilots couldn't come out without losing their lives, either. Too late, Tev thought about the dropship. With all the enemy suits safely in the hole, the dropship could open up and tear them apart.

Just as Tev had the thought, Derreck came crashing past him. Tev followed, seeing the destination was the dropship. The doors were closing, but Tev and Derreck leapt inside. Derreck crashed through the narrow halls, too narrow for exosuits, before coming to the bridge. He leveled his rifle at the pilots. "Do anything and you're dead."

Derreck's argument was convincing. With his free arm, he inserted a connection between his exosuit and the dropship.

Eleta's voice came through Tev's helmet. "All communication from and relayed by the dropship has been paused. Give me two more minutes and I'll have control over everything."

Derreck glanced at Tev. "We've got five minutes until that bomb lands. It's going to be close."

"What should we do about the remaining enemy?"

Derreck's response was cold. "As soon as we have weapons control over the dropship, we'll seal the tunnel. We'll leave a few of your hunters behind to watch for them, but really, we just need them out of the picture until our assault on the jumpship is complete."

One of the pilots moved suddenly, drawing a weapon from a shoulder holster. Before the weapon could even finish clearing the holster, Derreck's rifle unleashed several shells into the man, the noise deafeningly loud in such a confined space.

Derreck focused on the other pilot and turned his speaker back on. "I don't need you. I can fly this ship myself, so don't push me."

The other pilot nodded, then hesitated, worried that even that much might get him killed. Tev was certain the man wouldn't try anything.

"I've got control of the ship," Eleta said on the radio.

Derreck turned to Tev. "Get everyone on board, right away. We don't have much time."

Tev went back the way they came as Derreck opened up the ship from the bridge. Tev stepped down and called the hunters to him. The first part of the mission was done. Now only the hard part remained. The remaining hunters answered his call, and Eleta emerged from her hiding place as well, her slim figure out of place among all the armored hunters.

There were so few of them left. Together, they took a moment to look over the battlefield at their fallen friends. All told, eight of them survived, and none of them were unscathed. They were too few to attack a jumper, but they were all that was left.

Suddenly, a second sun appeared on the horizon. Tev was frozen in place as the afterimages echoed in his vision. He had thought he was familiar with the power the weapons. Of Derrick's, but he was reminded yet again of just how little he actually knew. The destructive ability of this weapon was beyond anything he could comprehend, anything he could have imagined. The shock wave was nothing but a gentle breeze at the distance he maintained, but kilometers of land had just been leveled in a moment.

Derreck spoke. "At least it wasn't nuclear."

Tev didn't even understand how much power had been unleashed. He was still staring at the land that had been destroyed when he heard a new voice in his helmet, coming on over emergency channels.

"Tev. I imagine you are part of the assault happening on my dropship. You have now seen the power I possess, and that bomb was just one of dozens I have. End your assault on the dropship immediately, or I will continue." The voice had to be that of Nicks.

Tev didn't know what to do. If continuing the assault meant that level of destruction, maybe their attack wasn't worth the price.

"Tev, Eleta thinks she can simulate an all-clear from the ship. We're going to give it a try and see if they buy it. If they don't, we're not going to be able to sneak on *Hellbringer* anyway," Derreck said.

There were a few seconds of almost unbearable tension. Nicks himself came back on the channel to thank them. "I am grateful for your wisdom. I never wanted war with your people, Tev."

There was nothing else, and Tev waited to hear what they should do next. Derreck asked the question. "I think we should continue. Tev?"

He never thought the decision would come down to him. The risk was tremendous, and he couldn't shake the feeling his foretold death was closer than ever. Letting Nicks escape was easy, safe, and tempting. He could live on in peace on his home planet, the only future he wanted for himself. The future seemed so abstract. Why risk everything?

Then he thought to his visions, the commands to hunt farther than he thought possible. He saw his people spreading into space, and deep inside of him, he knew this moment was the crux on which the future hinged. They needed the *Hellbringer*, and as he looked at the fires off in the distance, he knew he needed to continue the hunt, even though he didn't want to. Nicks was his prey, and Tev wouldn't stop until the hunt was successful.

Tev turned back into the dropship, the last of the hunters to board. A stunned silence had fallen over most of them as they were confronted with the full power of their enemy for the first time. They watched the aftermath of the explosion with awe and terror.

"Let's go."

TEN

TO SAY that Mala was unhappy would be an understatement. In fact, understatement didn't go far enough. Mala was furious and depressed, barely holding herself together. Kindra supposed she could understand. Dropship captains tended to develop an attachment to their ships, anthropomorphizing them and making them more than what they were.

Mala had been captain of *Explorer* for longer than Derreck had been captain of the *Vigilance*. But they had to be rational, and they knew there was no way they'd get both dropships to *Hellbringer*. With *Vigilance*'s upgrades, it was the stronger fighting ship, and so Mala's ship became their shield.

There had been a tremendous argument when Derreck had made the suggestion. Technically, he and Mala held the same rank, so he couldn't give her any commands, even though Derreck had clearly been in charge of the expedition. Derreck had laid out his points calmly. *Hellbringer* was the only way out of this system, and it currently possessed technology which would change the structure of power in the galaxy. On both counts, they needed to board the enemy jumpship. The odds of both Fleet dropships being able to get past *Hellbringer*'s defenses was almost zero. Even getting one close enough to matter would be difficult. The best use for Mala's ship was as a shield.

Mala had raged at Derreck, but it was the rage of one who knew they were wrong. Derreck let her have her tirade, but eventually, she gave up her ship. The two dropships docked together for a few hours as the crew transferred everything useful over to *Vigilance*. As Kindra walked the halls, every corner was stuffed with clearly labeled crates. If this attack didn't work, at least they could still say that *Vigilance* was the best-equipped dropship in the history of Fleet exploration.

While they were transferring the materials, Kindra worked to prepare the medical bay once again. The room had been worked over well by the number of people using medical supplies while they were on the planet. Kindra organized what she could and cleaned as best as she was able. They were heading into the jaws of danger once again, and she supposed she had best be ready to perform what medical services she could.

The constant stress and danger were threatening to make her numb. Back on Haven, she had made a promise to herself that she would see this mission to Tev's planet through, but at times she worried that promise would destroy her. The cadet she had been in the Academy would barely recognize her today, and she always wondered if that was a good thing or bad.

Fortunately, she didn't have long to dwell on her life. Word came from Derreck that they'd be launching the attack soon. Mala's crew rushed to get the last material off her ship, leaving it a husk of what it had once been. Then they all transferred to *Vigilance* and broke dock. The deed was done.

Derreck's plan was simple. If they could take control of the enemy dropship, they would try to sneak back aboard the *Hellbringer*, a modern-day equivalent of the Old Earth legend of the Trojan Horse. At the same time, the remaining Fleet personnel would launch at the enemy jumpship, with *Explorer* providing cover from the worst of *Hellbringer*'s weaponry. Derreck hoped that they could create the illusion that Fleet was making one last-ditch effort to stop *Hellbringer* from gaining important technology. *Vigilance* would attack the enemy jumpship, fighting with whatever they had available. That was very little, unfortunately, but Nicks didn't know how their forces were distributed. He'd be forced to divide his own troops.

Kindra didn't like their role. They were essentially a decoy, but a decoy that had no way to defend themselves. Still, they were something, and they needed every advantage they could get their hands on.

When Derreck let them know they had captured the dropship and were beginning their ascent, Alston ordered everyone to red alert stations, then laughed. Their normal stations were all chaotic. Kindra and the exobiologist from Mala's crew bumped into one another as they attempted to sit in the same chair. After a few seconds of discussion, they got all sorted and ready for their burn. Kindra thought it was an inauspicious way to begin their final trip.

Mala had given her ship's AI its final commands, and Alston slaved the *Vigilance* to it. On their approach, the two ships would move as one. Their biggest concern was *Hellbringer*'s main laser. Their point defense system would do a decent job against missiles, but Mala's ship was their only shield against the laser. They weren't sure what level of protection it would provide, but it was better than nothing.

When the burn kicked in, Kindra was surprised. She had never experienced such strong g-forces in space. Granted, she had never tried a combat approach on a jumper either, so she supposed it made sense. She was pressed back, the chair doing everything it could to ease the pressure on her body. The chairs weren't as good as the beds they used when landing on planets, but they needed to be at their stations. The dropship's acceleration was limited more by their own bodies than by physics.

The force wasn't straight, either. At times, the AI would jerk them down, then to the side, or back up again. Behind her, Kindra heard someone struggle to hold down their food. She was suddenly grateful she hadn't had the time to eat before they began. On the screen in front of her, she could see the relative positions of all the players in this small war. The enemy dropship, currently commanded by Derreck and Tev, was slightly closer to the jumpship than they were. Just as they wanted it to be.

Combat began without a word. On her display, Kindra watched as *Hellbringer* launched waves of missiles at them, her vision filled with small dots. Some dots were racing towards them, and some were racing towards the jumpship. The bridge was strangely silent, everyone's eyes glued to the screens in front of them.

Mala's ship launched missiles of its own. Kindra watched their progress on the screen, confused as to why they weren't heading for the *Hellbringer*.

She turned to Alston. Suddenly, the ship kicked her further into her chair, and she grunted out her question against the tremendous hand trying to crush her body. "What are you doing?"

"Selling the deception," was his reply.

The missiles raced towards Derreck and Tev. She could imagine the other ship trying to defend itself, and one by one the green dots representing their missiles disappeared, as though her imagination was affecting reality. One of the green dots collided, and Kindra's first thought was that their deception had been too successful.

But Tev's ride wasn't over yet, and Mala's ship launched wave after wave of missiles, emptying its magazines as quickly as it could. It was as though the ship knew it didn't have long.

Mala's voice penetrated Kindra's thoughts. "*Hellbringer* is turning!"

Alston replied, his voice cold. "I see. Time to test this idea."

Kindra realized, a few moments later, they were talking about the jumpship bringing its main laser to bear.

Every second that passed brought them closer. *Vigilance* was burning at the limits of human endurance, and the gap was closing quickly. Kindra wondered if Tev was having as difficult of a ride.

"Brace for impact!" Alston yelled.

Kindra didn't know what else she could do. She was pressed deep into her seat already, and she wasn't sure she could even move if she wanted. But she appreciated the warning all the same.

Nothing happened.

At least, nothing new happened. They were still pressed into their seats and missiles were exploding all around them.

The acceleration suddenly stopped, and Kindra was

disoriented by the sudden change in her weight. Her breath came easily for the first time in what felt like forever. She realized she had been sweating from the effort.

"Max velocity reached," Alston reported.

Kindra frowned, her understanding of space physics not keeping up with the reality of the situation.

"What do you mean?"

Alston barely had time to reply as he scanned his screens. "Need to decelerate if we're going to dock."

Mala's voice was soft. "*Explorer* can only take one more hit, and then it's done."

Alston shook his head. "I'm sorry, Mala."

There wasn't anything else to be said.

Alston warned them all what was coming. "Prepare for deceleration. It's gonna hurt."

Their not-geologist wasn't wrong. The engines kicked in, and again, Kindra was pushed into her chair. She was confused for a minute, only realizing later the *Vigilance* had turned around 180 degrees to brake.

The ship shuddered, and Mala burst out with a short scream. Kindra was focused on breathing, but she knew Mala's ship must have just been destroyed. How long did it take for the *Hellbringer*'s main laser to cycle? Would they have enough time to reach the jumpship?

There wasn't any way to know. Everything was out of her hands. She was only along for the ride. And then she finally blacked out.

HER VISION RETURNED. How long had she been out? It was still so hard to breathe, as though a tight rope was pulled across her chest. She gulped hungrily for air, sweat pouring down her face.

Alston was screaming, but the sound was strangely soft. She had never heard Alston scream.

But he wasn't Alston, was he? He was someone else.

To her left, the emergency bulkhead slammed shut.

Her next breath came more easily, air filling cavities of her lungs that had been empty for what felt like days. Her vision cleared.

They had been hit. Probably by the laser.

She rolled her head to the side and looked at Alston. He looked wrong, there was something protruding from his shoulder. He spoke, grunting with effort as he did.

"Launch missiles. AI override, code three-four-two."

Kindra wanted to frown, but the burn from the engines slammed her even deeper into her chair, and she blacked out again.

When she opened her eyes again, the world wasn't in order. She should have been looking at her screen, but she wasn't. She was hanging from her chair, blood dripping down her hair. Her blood?

Kindra's world went black again.

EVERYTHING HURT. She knew she should open her eyes, but she was afraid that if she did, they would simply hurt more. The darkness called to her, warm in its embrace.

Alston's voice, strained, brought her back to the present. He was calling her name.

She tried to open her eyes.

Failed.

Panicked, she put more effort into what should have been an easy task. One eye obeyed, dried blood cracking and falling down. She tried to find words, to let Alston know she was okay.

"Alston," her voice croaked. It didn't sound like her at all. More like a robot was trying to imitate how she sounded.

"Are you injured?"

"I don't know."

Kindra used her open eye to start scanning her surroundings. It took her almost a full minute to process what she saw. She was hanging upside down, only the harness of her chair holding on to her. Everything around her was chaos, nothing in its place.

One by one, she moved her limbs and found them responsive. She was in incredible pain, but there were any number of explanations for that. She brought a hand up to her head and winced gingerly as she touched a cut. With extreme care, she felt around the cut. It didn't feel deep, but it had been the source of the blood. With the same hand, she traced the blood down to her eyes and peeled the layer of caked blood off her other eyelid, which then opened.

Another minute of orientation and she started to undo her harness. She bit back a yelp as she hit the floor, hard.

"You okay?" Alston's voice was concerned.

"Yeah. Just a hard fall."

She looked around. She was still on the bridge of the *Vigilance*, but it looked like a child had taken the bridge and tossed it around, then left it behind when her mother called her for lunch. Kindra was standing on what had been one of the walls of the bridge, one of her feet on the ceiling.

She looked for Alston, found the pilot's chair. All the angles were wrong, her rational mind wrestling with her previous experiences. Gingerly, she picked her way over towards the chair, gasping at what she saw.

Alston had seen better days. There was a shard of metal driven into his left shoulder, and his left arm hung limply at his side. He looked at her with a lopsided grin. "I'm afraid I'm stuck."

The shard had gone through his shoulder, pinning him to his chair. Even if he undid his harness, it would rip the shard through his body. To move him, they needed to remove the shard, although it would open the wound. Kindra didn't need to point any of that out to Alston. His look told her that he understood.

She looked around for bandages but found nothing suitable. Lacking options, she ripped the sleeves off her uniform. While she prepared, she tried to distract him.

"What did you do?"

"Their laser cycled too fast. After they blew up Mala's ship, they had enough time to fire once directly on us. They missed the engine, at least, but destroyed a lot of the rest of the ship. We weren't going to be able to withstand what I'd originally planned, so I ordered the AI to ram us into the *Hellbringer*. It worked."

Kindra looked around the bridge. She saw two bodies, not enough for everyone on board.

"The others?"

"Trying to establish a perimeter. Told them I'd wait." Alston laughed at his own joke.

Kindra was ready to begin, but she hesitated. "Are you sure you want me to do this? You might lose too much blood."

Alston nodded. "I think you're going to need me. It's worth the risk."

Kindra didn't argue. After seeing his moves in the hold back on the planet, she was pretty certain that even injured and one handed he was the most dangerous one among them. "Ready?"

Alston gave one sharp nod of his head. Wrapping her

hand so as not to injure herself, Kindra braced her body and pulled on the shard. Fortunately, it came out smoothly, although, as she had guessed, the wound opened and blood poured out. She hurried to pack the wound and wrap it as tightly as she could.

After she helped Alston out of his chair. The entire affair was ponderous and felt as though it was taking all day, even though she assumed only a few minutes had passed.

Together, they worked their way off the bridge.

There wasn't much of the *Vigilance* left. They had crashed somewhere near the middle of the *Hellbringer*, and Kindra was surprised to realize she recognized the hallway they came out in. They took cover behind debris with Mala and her two remaining crew. Kindra thought the five of them made a pretty lousy boarding party.

They didn't immediately encounter too much resistance. Kindra assumed Tev and Derreck had been successful and were drawing most of the attention towards themselves. Nicks would realize they were only a decoy, only send enough people after them to keep them pinned down while he dealt with the real threat.

Their situation wasn't good, but it could have been worse. Both the Fleet crew and Nicks' crew seemed content to trade the occasional random shot, but neither side was trying too hard. The rebellion troops only had to wait for a couple of exosuits to come and clean up, and Kindra and her team were directionless. Their whole goal had been to be the decoy, and they had completed that as well as they were like to.

Survival was the easier option, but Kindra wanted to do more. They needed to do more. She risked a glance up and down the hallway, amazed they had ended up someplace she recognized.

One thought cascaded over another, and suddenly she had a plan. She put her hand on Alston's good shoulder to get his attention.

"I know the way to Captain Nicks' office from here. There may be copies, or even the originals, of the technology he found."

Kindra's mind raced. If they could get access to that information, or even find a way to control it, the balance of power in the conflict would shift. They could hold it hostage, bargain for some sort of peace. She hadn't decided on the best way to use the technology if they found it, but there was no doubt it was the best chance of doing something that would make a difference here.

Alston seemed to have the same thought. "Which way?"

Kindra pointed down the hallway, where the rebellion soldiers were firing at them from behind corners.

Alston groaned. "Of course."

He looked around at the surviving crew. "I don't suppose any of you happen to have a grenade lying around, do you?"

His request was answered with blank stares.

"I thought not."

Alston looked down the hallway thoughtfully. The corner the enemy was using as cover was about ten meters away. He looked back at his own team. "Can you all cover me?"

They nodded, and Alston got ready to leap over the debris and sprint for the corner. "On three."

"One."

"Two." Alston took a deep breath and paused.

"Wait. None of you are going to shoot me on accident, right?" The concern in his voice was evident.

Mala looked like she might shoot him on purpose.

"Right. Three." Alston leaped up as everyone fired in tandem.

Their desperate gamble worked. Alston slid into the corner, his weapon out and firing. Kindra didn't know how he managed with the pain he must be feeling. But he had been right. Without him, Kindra wasn't sure how they would have gotten out of their predicament.

He struggled to his feet, trying and failing to hide his pain. The rest of them came after him, taking the weapons from the bodies of the soldiers. Better armed, it was Kindra's turn to lead the way.

She had only been here once before, but every turn was ingrained in her memory. Her heart had been racing that time, too, even though no one had been shooting at her. The fear heightened her recollection, and she moved with a surety that surprised even her.

They didn't encounter any resistance between their crash site and Nicks' office. Kindra figured it was most likely that almost all the forces were focused on Tev. She hoped he'd survive, but it was difficult to hold out hope for any of them.

The door to Nicks' office was locked, but that didn't seem to discourage Alston. He reached into one of his pockets and pulled out his datapad. He held it up against the door and it opened without hesitation. Kindra stared at him, amazed and slightly jealous. He shrugged. "Fleet has some nice toys."

Kindra stepped into the office first and made a beeline for Nicks' desk. She wasn't entirely sure what she was expecting to find, but his desk was as clear as it had been the last time she was here.

Alston was looking around the room, admiring the decor. Having been in the space before, Kindra didn't think much of it, but it was richly appointed. There were relics scattered throughout the room. Alston's eye was drawn towards a sword mounted against the wall.

"This has to be thousands of years old." He reached out to touch it but hesitated.

Kindra fought the urge to throw something at him. They had far more important things to do than admire swords right now. "Will you come here and use your pad to hack into the system?"

Alston shook his head. "No. The information won't be accessible from his desk. It's too valuable, and he'd want to keep most of it off the general ship network. Too risky."

The spy pulled out his datapad and placed it on the wall next to the sword. To Kindra's amazement, a slot opened, revealing several data sticks. She decided, immediately, that Alston was a much better spy than a geologist. Far more interesting as well.

Her sense of relief and success was quickly taken away. Outside, she could hear the approaching footfalls of a sprinting exosuit. Without being told, she knew their foray into the office had been discovered, and the rebellion soldiers were on their way to kill them.

With the others, she approached the door, weapon ready, just in time to see a type of exosuit she'd never seen before crash around the corner. She could see the markings on the suit clearly, and her heart sank even further. Captain Nicks had come to reclaim that which he'd found.

ELEVEN

TEV LOOKED out the window as their new dropship lifted off. He wasn't sure if he would see his planet again. He certainly hoped so. Everything he had done had been for this planet and the people who called it home. It seemed a shame not to return for another campfire.

He let the thought slip from his mind. The debris was still settling from the massive explosion, and the higher they got, the more gutted Tev became by the damage a single weapon had caused.

Nicks would not be allowed to live. Such an abuse of power had no fitting punishment in Tev's mind. Death was quickest, but if there was a worse punishment, Tev would have had no problem in administering it.

Such destruction affected more than just the people who lived in the area, although many had died. The true tragedy was in all the other life that perished. Trees, fish, bugs. Nothing could have survived a blast like that.

Nicks shared the same problem so many in Kindra's society seemed to have: They took far more than they returned. Their behavior was disgraceful, and Tev felt sick when he thought about the actions Nicks had taken just to prove a point.

His resolve hardened. They would take the *Hellbringer*, Nicks' pride and joy, right from under him. Then they'd kill Nicks. The thought brought a smile to Tev's face.

They passed out of atmosphere quickly, and Derreck pushed them hard towards *Hellbringer*. He told them to take their seats in some of the gravity cushions. The suits protected them from some the forces they were going to feel, but not all.

For several minutes, the ride was as smooth as any Tev had taken, but it didn't last. He heard Derreck swear under his breath, and the ship started jerking violently, acceleration pushing them in many different directions.

Tev was worried. Their plan hinged on sneaking onto the *Hellbringer*. If they were already being fired on, they had no chance. He asked Derreck what was happening.

"It's our own people. I guess Alston's really trying to sell the deception."

Moments later, Tev was slammed to the side of his seat.

"One missile got through. No permanent damage, though."

Tev hated not being able to do anything. He pictured himself on the hull of the ship, trying to snipe incoming missiles with his rifle. He knew he was being childish, but anything seemed preferable to being locked in a can with nothing to do.

The ride smoothed out, and Derreck took a moment to open a public channel and call to the remaining hunters. "Everyone okay?"

There were a chorus of affirmative grunts.

Derreck was silent for several minutes before he spoke again. "Okay, everyone. *Hellbringer* is taking over our systems for final approach. If we get through this, we'll be on board the jumper in a few minutes."

A minute later. "Our codes were accepted. Prepare for combat."

Tev released himself from his seat. As the others stood up with him, he took a moment and looked around. He was proud of all the hunters he had trained. They were learning more than just how to pilot the suits. They were learning about an entirely different way of life, and they had adapted. The hunters, he realized, were the trial. Could his people quickly adapt to new truths? If the men and women in front of him were any indication, they could. They would survive, and thrive, long after he was gone. The thought gave him comfort as the ship gently shuddered to a stop, inside the belly of their most dangerous enemy.

WHEN THE RAMP of the ship opened there wasn't any time for him to take in the sights. Derreck had warned them that at most they would get a few minutes before Nicks realized he'd been duped. They might not even have that long.

Their approach was unconventional. They only had eight suits, all damaged, to take over an entire jumpship. The odds weren't in their favor, and if they stuck with conventional tactics, it would only be a matter of time before they were overwhelmed.

Generally, an assault would take place using groups of four suits, overpowering the enemy one step at a time. Derreck didn't want to concentrate their forces that much. Instead, they were going to make the most out of the hunters' mobility. The plan was to split into four groups of two, with two pairs taking different paths to the engine room and two pairs taking different paths towards the bridge.

Both objectives were down in the bowels of the ship, as was customary. Derreck's instructions were simple. "Keep moving. Kill what you can, but movement is more important. Never let yourselves get pinned."

Derreck was with Tev. Each pair was comprised of the two who had trained the most together, and for Tev, that meant the captain.

Before they sprinted out of the dropship, Tev turned and looked at Derreck. "You think you can keep up?"

Derreck laughed, a short bark. "Probably not."

Tev led the way, barreling past shocked technicians as they approached to perform the standard post-landing routines. As the last pair of hunters left the dropship, the ramp closed behind them. Eleta would stay on board and use the dropship to work whatever technical magic she could.

He could hear the exclamations of the techs as they were nearly run over by the sprinting suits. The four pairs of suits went to different exits of the hanger, gone by the time the hallways started flashing red.

Tev and Derreck were in a wide hallway, big enough for both suits to run side-by-side. They encountered their first opposition a few corners in, a lance of suits that was preparing itself for an assault on the hanger.

Tev came around the corner at speed and brought his arm up instinctively. His first shot was rushed, the adrenaline coursing through his system. He hit the arm of one of the suits, spinning it around. His second shot was better, punching through the back of the suit and exploding out the front.

The lance was turning around, caught by surprise. A

third shot was clean, killing the second pilot. The remaining two suits were coming to their senses, bringing their own weapons up. Tev's fourth shot went clean through the center-of-mass of a third suit, and Derreck, finally turning the corner, peppered the fourth suit with rounds.

They paused for just a moment to check to ensure the pilots were dead. They didn't want anyone coming up behind them. Derreck couldn't resist a moment of good-natured ribbing. "Four shots for three targets, Tev? You're getting sloppy."

Tev didn't respond, his mind focused.

They kept going, sprinting as fast as Derreck could run.

The hunter heard their next opponent before he saw it. The unmistakable footfalls of a heavy exosuit reverberated down the hallway. Tev sped up and passed Derreck, rounding a bend and coming face to face with the heavy. The hulking machine was closer than he expected.

Tev snapped off a shot, but he missed the cockpit, and even his high-powered rounds wouldn't do much damage anywhere else on a heavy suit. He dove to the side as the heavy swiped at him with an enormous metal hand. The blow passed harmlessly overhead, almost hitting Derreck as he approached.

Derreck sprayed the heavy with armor-piercing rounds, but even those did little against the monstrosity. The heavy unleashed a barrage of fire, driving Derreck back and out of sight.

Tev came to his feet and leaped on top of the heavy, noticing for the first time that it had an extra layer of armor over the cockpit. Tev grasped the layer of armor and pulled. His focus, narrowed for just a moment, didn't catch the arm rotating up and around, slamming into Tev's torso and tossing him from the heavy as though he were a child's doll.

The action did have one unintended consequence, though. Tev's grip had been firm, and the additional force had ripped the armor off the cockpit, remaining in Tev's hands even as he crashed to the ground.

Tev gritted his teeth against the bone-jarring impact. As he started back to his feet, he saw the heavy level its cannon at him. Instinctively, he yanked the armor up in his hands, and less than a second later, shells pounded against it. Tev guessed the armor wouldn't hold out long against the onslaught, and he was right. Shells started punching through, fortunately passing overhead.

The barrage paused for a moment, and Tev could hear the softer sound of Derreck's rifle. Tev didn't have long. He kicked the armor at the heavy and watched as it bounced off without effect.

He scrambled to his feet just as the heavy resumed its fire. The pilot had labeled Tev as the threat and was after him first. A heavy could ignore Derreck's rifle for the few moments it would take to finish the job.

Tev couldn't give him that chance. He sprinted straight at the heavy, leaping as its cannon fired, deadly shells passing underneath him. Tev fired his own rifle, drilling a hole through the now-exposed cockpit. Unfortunately, he missed the pilot.

Adjusting in mid-air, he drew his right fist back, driving it forward into the cockpit of the heavy. The enemy pilot, acting on instinct, threw himself backward, taking the heavy with him. The action wasn't enough to save him. Tev's fist found its mark, and he landed on top of the heavy as the machine crashed to the ground. Tev drew out his fist, staring at the blood on his armored hand.

Derreck's commanding voice broke him out of his reverie. "Tev, it's got a self-destruct!"

Tev's eyes widened, and he leaped from the heavy, following Derreck around the bend in the hallway. The explosion came seconds later, fire chasing them down the hallway.

The flames quickly subsided, finding nothing on the ship to burn.

Tev and Derreck stopped to catch their breath. Tev was surprised to find he was exhausted. They had been pushing so hard for so long, he hadn't had time to consider the toll the constant combat was taking on his body. Eventually he was able to stand up straight. He didn't have much farther to go. He just needed to stay alive for a while longer.

They were just about to continue on their way to the bridge when Eleta opened a channel to them. "Hey, you two, someone just broke into Captain Nicks' personal office. He's on his way there now with two of his best soldiers."

"Kindra and Alston?"

"I would assume so."

The two warriors glanced at each other.

"Show us the way," said Tev.

TEV RAN, fear and anger mixed in his heart. He didn't want Nicks to get to Kindra before he could come and help. He also wanted to be the one to kill Nicks. As he ran, he glanced at his hand, seeing the blood there.

He rapidly outpaced Derreck. In the straight hallways, their speed was nearly equal, but Tev could take the corners much faster than Derreck could, and there were a lot of corners in a jumper. Eleta kindly put direction markers on his display, and Tev ran with reckless abandon.

He came across Nicks' bodyguards first, but he barely paused for them. They heard him coming and turned around, but by the time they completed the turn, he was already there. He lowered his shoulder and ran into them, knocking one into the other and sending both of them tumbling to the ground in a pile of arms and legs. Somehow, he managed to keep his feet under him, and he kept running, following the arrows.

"Derreck, I left you his two bodyguards."

He could hear Derreck's labored breathing. "Thanks."

With Derreck's confirmation, he put the two soldiers out of his mind. He trusted his friend and commander to handle them. His focus was only on Nicks.

He turned yet another corner, and there his enemy was. Tev knew immediately that it was Nicks. There was something different about his suit of armor, but Tev didn't have enough time at full speed to figure out what it was. He crashed into Nicks, sending them both to the floor and into a line of fire coming from the end of the hall. A few rounds pinged off Tev's armor, and he knew it was small arms fire he could ignore. If they were firing at Nicks it had to be Kindra and the remaining crew, anyway.

The two fighters got to their feet, and Tev got a real look at his opponent's suit for the first time. It wasn't a heavy, but it definitely wasn't a normal suit. There was far more armor than Tev had, but not so much that it wasn't agile.

A quick snap of Nicks' left arm brought up a cannon Tev hadn't seen before. There was a small *whomp*, and Tev sidestepped as something large shot past his face. He turned to watch as the projectile traveled down the hallway, far past the open door where Kindra was sticking her head out.

The projectile impacted and exploded, filling the hallway with fire and shrapnel. Fortunately, the fire didn't reach them, and at this distance, the shrapnel bounced harmlessly off Tev's armor. He worried about Kindra, but he didn't have time. That cannon would tear Tev apart unless he got close.

Tev raised his own arm and fired, but Nicks must have seen the motion, because he rotated his left arm, displaying a small shield. Nicks' prediction was accurate, and Tev's round buried itself in the shield, not even penetrating.

Keeping the shield up, Nicks raised his right arm, where a typical rifle was mounted. Tev sidestepped again, and Nicks tried to track him, bullets passing off to Tev's side. Unfortunately, Nicks' arm moved faster than Tev, and eventually the bullets struck. Tev felt a flare of pain as one tore through his side.

He needed to move faster. Tev leaped towards a wall, bouncing off his planted leg to drive himself towards Nicks. Nicks had his shield up in time and tossed Tev further down the hallway. Tev didn't even allow himself to come to a stop. He rolled over his back to his feet and snapped off another shot, but Nicks' shield was there to absorb the impact.

Tev had to try something different. Nicks wasn't doing anything fancy, but his suit was strong, and he was calm, predicting Tev's movements. Still, as Tev saw the left arm rotate and display the cannon again, he knew he had to stay close. He could take a few shots from the rifle, probably, but the cannon would certainly tear him apart.

He closed, dodging to the left and right to keep Nicks' aim off him. In a moment he was close enough to feel confident that Nicks wouldn't use the cannon. He jumped at the wall, and he heard Nicks' voice for the first time since the bomb was dropped.

"Old trick."

Except it wasn't. Tev planted one leg on the wall, as he had before, but he grabbed Nicks' shoulder as he did. Using his arm as a plant, he kicked, twisting and landing behind Nicks, still holding his shoulder. Tev pressed his other hand against Nicks' back, firing his rifle point blank.

Nicks twisted, trying to drive his armored elbow into Tev's helmet. Tev ducked and sidestepped, firing again into Nicks' armor at point blank range. He wasn't sure if his shots were penetrating armor, but he was scoring hits.

Nicks continued his rotation, and Tev caught the incoming left fist with his right arm, driving his own left fist into Nicks' torso, collapsing the armor at that point.

With a growl, Nicks redoubled the power in his caught left arm, and Tev experienced the full force of Nicks' suit. He was forced to use both arms to protect himself, and he was still driven into the ground.

For a long, terrifying moment, Tev was pinned against the ground, Nicks pressing down with incredible power. Nicks' right arm came over and the rifle hovered over Tev's helmet, Tev staring into the endless blackness of that weapon. He panicked, struggling desperately against the strength of Nicks' suit.

Nicks enjoyed the moment of victory a second too long, and Tev had an idea. He stopped resisting Nicks, moving his arms out of the way. As Nicks' left fist came crashing towards Tev, he managed to push himself slightly to the side. It wasn't enough to get out of the way of the falling fist, but he took the punch in the shoulder, screaming as he heard the bones in his left shoulder shatter.

Nicks opened fire with his rifle, but he had lost his balance, and his rounds dug deep into the floor next to Tev's head. Ignoring the flare of pain, Tev forced his suit to rotate, using his injured arm and shoulder as the pivot point. He drove his right knee up with all his ability, and the two of them started rotating. Nicks fell onto his back, Tev on top of him.

For the first time, Tev got a prolonged look at the cockpit as they rotated. As soon as Nicks landed on his back, Tev made a fist and powered it towards the cockpit, aimed directly at Nicks' head.

His punch crashed through the cockpit, and he got his armored right hand around Nicks' head.

At the same time, Nicks brought up his left arm, the cannon still attached.

Nicks stared directly into Tev's opaque helmet, and Tev closed his hand, trying to leap away from Nicks and his cannon as soon as the job was done. He heard the soft *whomp* again, and his world spun out of control before blackness swallowed him in an instant.

EPILOGUE

TODAY FELT like the end of a very long journey, thought Tev. Months had passed since they had taken control of the *Hellbringer* and killed Nicks. Most of the time had been used to make repairs, both to the jumpship and to the last remaining dropship. When this journey had started, two jumpers and five dropships had left central space. The loss of so much valuable material still shocked the remaining members of Fleet who were with them.

Tev felt the loss as well, but not the loss of ships. He felt the loss of hunters. Of the almost thirty that had started training with him, only six remained. Those six were battle-hardened veterans now, survivors of both land and space warfare. They would become the leaders of a new group of recruits, new hunters who would stand on the divide between worlds.

Tev felt like he straddled the divide every day. Some days, he could almost convince himself everything was normal. He sat around campfires at night and enjoyed the company of other hunters. But at night, hazy memories of his final battle with Nicks became never-ending nightmares.

He had been knocked unconscious by the final explosion. His final strike had killed Nicks, but it had almost cost him his life. Some injuries, like his shoulder, could be healed. Others could not.

Up in space, *Hellbringer* hung lazily. After Nicks died, the rest of the ship had surrendered in short order. Fleet possessed the jumper now, and the rebellion was effectively dead. The capture of the ship had changed everything, again.

For one thing, they had no lack of suits. Alston and Eleta hadn't slept for months, constantly working on repairing the damage they could. The pilots inside might have died, but the suits could often be salvaged. They had suits from the rebellion, including three heavies and Nicks' own hybrid suit, in addition to all the suits from Fleet that were still intact. Derreck was taking back two in case of emergency. Otherwise, everything was being left with Tev and his people. They would continue to build and prepare, readying themselves for the day Fleet came again. When Fleet arrived, as it inevitably would, they would be ready to bargain on a treaty.

Tev was making a last inspection of the suits, lined up in rows. Alston and Eleta had set up some equipment on the planet to make repairs to the suits, but Tev suspected the motley assortment would never look better than they did today. Both Alston and Eleta were leaving, and with them, most of the experience needed to repair the suits. They had tried to teach what they could, and left behind all the information needed, but there would still be a sharp learning curve for those of Tev's people assigned to maintain the suits in the absence of Fleet.

He heard a noise off to the side and turned his head. Derreck was approaching, a sad smile on his face. Tev came to a stop, momentarily losing his balance before finding it again. He cursed his artificial leg, which he wasn't sure he'd ever get fully used to.

Nicks' final act had almost doomed them both. The cannon had torn off Tev's leg, but it could have been much more. Tev had seen the images of Nicks' suit after the battle. Even if Tev's final blow hadn't killed Nicks, his last shot was suicidal. If not for Tev's quick reflexes and suit's healing tools, he certainly would have lost his life. On his darkest days, he wondered if that might have been better.

There had been days when he considered giving up and taking his life. The practice wasn't uncommon among hunters who felt themselves a burden on the clan.

Kindra and Derreck had stopped him. The entire team of the *Vigilance* had worked together to create the best artificial leg possible. It wasn't the quality of limbs available in central space, they told him, but it was the best they could do.

His greatest blessing was that he could still pilot suits. They operated on two levels: muscular and neural control. Tev couldn't use muscular control of his right leg anymore, obviously, but his neural control was strong enough that he could still pilot. He wasn't the best these days, but he was still good enough to beat most others.

He wasn't sure he'd ever be able to hunt again, though. His artificial leg was silent, but unwieldy. Walking wasn't usually a problem, but the dexterous movement required of a successful hunt was beyond him.

A year ago, such an injury would have destroyed him. Now, he wasn't so sure. He felt the loss, keenly. But he was more than a hunter now. Because of that, he was able to return Derreck's sad smile.

There was a slight awkwardness between them,

possibly a last meeting between two people who had become more than friends. They had fought side by side, and fate had driven them closer together than either of them had ever expected.

"Everything look good?" Derreck asked.

"Yes." That was the truth. The power arrayed in front of him would change their world forever, and he was hopeful they would guide that power well. "Derreck?"

"Yeah?"

"Have you had any luck decrypting the pod?"

Derreck shook his head. "No. *Hellbringer*'s AI isn't the most powerful, but it should have been strong enough to decrypt something within a few months. The fact that we've completely failed worries me, but we'll get to the bottom of it, you have my word."

The pod was the last mystery. Tev and some of the other hunters had finished the excavation Nicks had begun, finding a small, perfectly spherical pod embedded deep in the walls of the valley. It wasn't from their planet, but beyond that, there was little they could determine. It had successfully resisted all attempts at unlocking its secrets. *Hellbringer*'s AI reported that it could communicate, at some level, with the sphere, but that was all. Eleta was certain the pod opened, but even with months of attempts no one had gotten any closer to breaking through. Derreck was taking the pod back with him, so some of the planet-wide AIs could have a chance at it. Tev was simply grateful for the pod to be off his planet. His gut told him it was better off far away.

They stood there in the clearing, looking at the mixed assembly of suits before them. Tev didn't know what to say any more than Derreck did.

"Tev, I just want you to know, I will do everything in my power to keep your planet safe."

Tev didn't have any doubt about that. He was certain he knew Derreck's heart, and he knew the captain was the best defender his planet could have asked for.

"The jump technology we found gives us a powerful bargaining chip. I'll make sure that everything here goes public, and I won't stop until there's a guarantee your planet will be protected."

Tev turned slightly and put his hand on Derreck's shoulder, meeting his nervous gaze. "I know, Derreck. I trust you. If I didn't, I would have chosen to go back with you."

Derreck took a deep breath, accepting Tev's statement.

"I'll watch the elders, too."

Tev laughed at that. "Now, that task I'm not sure you're up to. I think peace between our peoples would be easier to accomplish."

The decision had been controversial, but necessary. Many of the clan leaders were uncomfortable entrusting everything to Derreck. They recognized the lengths the captain had gone to, but he was still an outsider. Several elders had decided to make the journey back with Derreck. They knew they might never return to their home planet, but they viewed the sacrifice as necessary. Derreck had acknowledged their desire and had no problem bringing them with.

Tev turned the rest of the way so he was facing Derreck. He extended his hand. "Thank you."

Derreck grasped Tev's hand and pulled him in, embracing him. Tev returned the embrace, and a moment later they separated.

Together, they walked towards the dropship, making its

final preparations for departure. You'd be able to find the location from kilometers away, the celebration was so loud.

Derreck had one final comment before they reached the edge of the gathering. "Take care of her, okay?"

Tev nodded. He would.

They resumed their journey, weaving their way through the crowds to the dropship. Clans had come from great distances, both to celebrate and to learn how their world had changed. Despite everything that had happened, only a small number of Tev's people had been affected directly by the conflict. The word had spread, bringing as many clans together as possible to educate them on what had happened and what might still come to pass.

Their progress was slow. Tev had become something of a legend as the celebration grew. The stories of his adventures had grown considerably in the retelling, until Tev was certain there were people in the clans who believed he had snapped his fingers and killed three men at once.

Because of his leg, he was easily recognizable, and no small number of people swarmed to him, both to see him and his leg.

Derreck was grinning as they made their way through the crowd. "Admit it, Tev, you love this."

Tev replied, in Derreck's language. "Once I might have. Now, I only wish to resume my life as peacefully as I may."

Derreck laughed. "I understand."

Finally, they made it to the dropship, where the elders were wishing their clans their final goodbyes.

Shet, promoted in importance due to his status as Tev's elder, climbed onto a podium as the crowd fell silent. Eleta had set up a projector and speakers so everyone around the gathering could see and hear the old man.

Tev watched with interest. He had known Shet since

the day he was born, but his new importance seemed to suit him well. Tev respected the old man. Shet practically commanded it from his bearing.

Shet began with the usual formalities. He thanked everyone for coming and acknowledged the distance they had traveled. He spoke of the changes that lie before them.

"Today, friends, marks a new beginning for our people. We have learned that we are not alone, but we have also learned that we have friends from the sky as well. Our paths have come together, and today we celebrate the fact that we no longer walk alone!"

Tev tuned out the rest of the speech as he felt a familiar hand in his. He turned his head and looked at Kindra, a grin on his face.

She had decided to remain, a decision he didn't fully understand, but one that he accepted. She said she had very little waiting for her back on Haven. Here, she could study the development of life on Tev's planet, a dream come true for her. She also said she wanted to stay with him.

For that, Tev was glad. He still feared that he was pulling her away from the rest of her life, no matter how often she reassured him. But, another side of him was grateful that they wouldn't have to say goodbye.

Tev heard the change in Shet's voice and returned his attention to his elder.

"As we watch our friends depart, we know that we still have much work to do. We have learned so much so quickly, but we must not be hasty in our decisions. We must decide how to use our new tools. Our clans will be closer than ever, and we must learn how to manage our differences.

"But although our challenges are great, I have hope for our people. We are strong, and we will face these new challenges with the same courage we face every day with.

Join me in honoring our departing friends and family one last time!"

The speech ended with a roar of applause, and the last of the voyagers stepped onto the dropship.

Tev wondered at the future. Working with Derreck, they had created a draft treaty to propose to Fleet. It granted them limited permission for settlement, but left a tremendous amount of power in the hands of Tev's people. If Fleet accepted, Tev's people would become one of the most powerful factions within Fleet overnight. There was no guarantee it would be accepted, but Derreck promised he would fight for it, and even Alston said he would use what connections he had to see a favorable result. Hopefully it would be enough to protect them.

That was the other reason for the elders. They would act as negotiators for Tev's people. They didn't have the authority to sign, which protected them from harm and coercion, but they would make sure their wishes were respected. They would have to be enough.

Tev's thoughts were derailed as the crowd slowly retreated to a safe distance and the dropship took off, leaving them all behind.

KINDRA LEANED BACK and rubbed her eyes, sore from focusing on the results of her tests. By now, she shouldn't be surprised by her findings, but she was. The DNA in most of the plants had chains she could trace back to Old Earth. There was other DNA as well, DNA she assumed was alien, but there really was no telling. There were days when she worried she would study this planet for the rest of her life and still not understand it.

The sound of laughter outside made her realize that the

sun was high in the sky. Tev and Dinah would have returned from their morning walk. They had probably been waiting outside more than an hour for mom to finish her work. Tev didn't like bringing their girl into Kindra's lab. He wanted her to be older before encountering her mom's technology. For her part, Kindra agreed.

Dinah was almost three years old now, and precocious at that. Tev sometimes joked that no tree was safe from her desire to climb, and Kindra had to acknowledge that her daughter's ability in the trees was amazing to watch. Every morning, Tev took her out and taught her about the forest. If her trajectory continued, she would become a hunter to rival her father. Kindra knew that if that came to pass, Tev would be overjoyed.

The sunlight was bright as she stepped out and she covered her eyes with her hand. Tev was tossing Dinah into the air and catching her, and Dinah was laughing uncontrollably. The laughter stopped when Dinah saw Kindra, though. Her laughter turned into a squeal of delight as she focused on her mom.

Kindra scooped up Dinah as she sprinted at her, wheezing a little as she bent over. She still wasn't used to her larger belly.

Tev came close and laid a hand on her stomach. Kindra hadn't felt the little one kicking yet, but it was only a matter of time.

Together, the three of them walked towards the hut that served as their home. As the head trainer of exosuit pilots, there wasn't any need for Tev to be nomadic. A small group of them had started what amounted to their own clan, with permanent lodging for each resident. Nearby, the hunters who trained in the suits had a semi-permanent set of huts they lived in while they trained.

Whenever she thought about it, Kindra had to stop and consider how much had happened. Derreck and the *Hellbringer* had left over five years ago, and there hadn't been any word since. Kindra wasn't terribly surprised. The only way to send messages through space was via jumpship, and they were far, far off the beaten path.

They sat down for a simple lunch of dried meat and berries. Kindra found the food delicious, another example of the change that had happened in her. She had never been large, but the work of surviving on Tev's planet had leaned her out, given her a physical strength she had never expected to have. Her tastes had changed, too. She preferred her food simpler, although there were certainly days where she dreamed of a nice glass of wine.

After lunch, Kindra took Dinah while Tev went to visit the training grounds. The afternoons were always the part of the day Tev treasured, for they gave him an excuse to pilot once again.

He came back that evening, and he dictated into his book as they sat around the fire.

It was Dinah, as observant as always, who noticed the star moving the wrong way in the sky. Tev smiled, and Kindra's heart skipped a beat. They were back, but what did it portend?

Kindra's neurodisplay activated, the first time in a long time. There was little need of it on the planet. She jumped a little at the surprise, then grinned as she relayed the news.

"Derreck's returned, and he's got a treaty for the planet to sign."

She laughed. "He also says he wants the elders off his ship. He's never traveling with them again."

Tev laughed at that as well. He had often told Kindra

stories of his youth, and she felt sympathy for what Derreck must have endured.

He stood, his balance on his artificial leg almost as good as it ever was before the battle.

Dinah spoke up. "Where are we going, father?"

Tev pointed up. "There, Dinah. Farther than we've ever gone before."

PART FOUR

REBELLION

REBELLION

KENAN LOOKED out over the fields surrounding the farmhouse. Derreck could see the younger man's face reflected in the plastiglass window. He looked unperturbed, as though the scene in front of them didn't spell disaster for their mission.

"Two scout ships. The new ones. They'll be fast, and they have better sensors than we have camo."

Derreck grunted. Kenan wasn't saying anything they hadn't already figured out. The statement was meant to fill the silence and ease the tension, if such a feat was possible.

The commander stifled a yawn. Every year it was getting harder to keep going, and he was tired from the moment he woke up to the moment he fell asleep. They had fought against the rebellion for seven years now. Millions dead, and the movement now had no chance of winning. But they still fought on, even if—in Derreck's opinion—all they were doing at this point was causing more harm to innocents.

The commander glanced up as the farmer, Zelig, came in. He was just over forty years old, and he looked every day of it. His face was weathered and worn. Gray had already seeped into the edges of his hair. The man was lean, no more than a few ounces of fat on him, and strong. He had been a manual laborer all his life, Derreck was sure, but that didn't mean he lacked for brains.

"Supper's ready for you two, if you want to come get some."

Kenan looked at Derreck, disbelief in his eyes. Zelig had to know just as well as they did what was occurring just a few kilometers away.

Zelig caught the look and smiled knowingly.

"Can't run, right?"

Kenan nodded. Their exosuits were nearby and well concealed, but even if they got to them, they wouldn't be able to escape. The scout ships would notice their energy signatures the moment they powered up. They could try to escape on foot, but once the scout ships discovered they weren't in the outpost, they'd start sweeping the surrounding area, and they'd still be caught. If they didn't want to fight, their only option was to lay low and hope the sweeps missed them.

Derreck resisted the urge to chuckle. Despite the fact that Kenan was a highly trained combat specialist, the farmer seemed to be the one with a better grasp on the situation.

Zelig proved him right a second later. "Then you might as well eat. Can't fight on an empty stomach."

Derreck sighed. He wished that were true, but the past few years of experience had taught him you actually could fight on an empty stomach. You could fight with a broken limb. You could fight with shrapnel rattling around your ribcage. There wasn't very much, in fact, you couldn't fight through. And they'd be fighting again soon, unless he missed his guess.

He ran through his options, displeased by all of them. Running, as already established, was out of the question. They could power up their suits and start to fight, but Derreck would rather avoid that outcome. Their mission was almost complete, and they didn't know if the rebels were even aware that the two Fleet commandos were nearby. It would take a good hour or two to clear the outpost, so they had some time.

Derreck stood up, thanking Zelig for the hospitality. Offering them a meal was more than just feeding them. It was a real risk, concrete proof to any rebel sympathizer that this man had sheltered Fleet troops. If that became public knowledge, Derreck didn't want to imagine what would happen to the lean farmer.

They came to the table, where Celia greeted them. She was Zelig's daughter, an excitable eight-year old who was fascinated by the strangers who had called at their farm that morning.

Derreck and Kenan were well behind enemy lines on Artemis IV, a nearly featureless planetoid whose value was as a planet that could sustain agriculture, providing the food the rest of the galaxy so desperately needed. It had a population of less than ten thousand, and every single one was involved in the growing, packaging, and shipment of food.

Zelig was no exception, and Derreck was reminded again that humanity had better find more habitable planets soon, because the farmers who grew the galaxy's food weren't getting much of it. Artemis IV had been held by the rebels for six months now, and almost every kilogram of food grown here was being sent to the war front. Fleet had decided it was time to reclaim the planet, but they couldn't use overwhelming force. The jump points to the planet were well-defended, and the cost would be enormous.

Instead they had jumped in on a single Fleet ship, disguised as smugglers. Fleet intelligence had worked with a local smuggling group before, and they had found a way to the planet's surface.

Their goal was to destabilize the planet, and that was what Derreck and Kenan did best. Zelig had been identified as a man still loyal to Fleet and respected in the community. Derreck had come to discuss how Zelig could cause trouble without bringing any back on himself. Kenan was mostly around to provide muscle and firepower.

Zelig was a widow whose wife had passed away giving birth to the child before them. He bore the burden of single fatherhood with a quiet strength and good humor. Derreck had never been a father and didn't have any plans to become one, but he couldn't help but respect the man. His life was tough, yet in the time they'd spent together, Derreck hadn't heard a single complaint escape his lips.

The four of them sat down to the table, an awkward arrangement of people if there ever was one. Kenan, taller than Derreck and wider than a truck, sat down next to Celia, who was a small blur of arms and legs most of the time. Derreck sat next to her, with the farmer sitting next to him. They made for a drab group, except for Celia, who wore a vivid blue dress that highlighted her eyes.

The main course was passed around the table, a simple meal of meat substitute. It was poor food, but all Zelig had to offer. The real treat, though, was potatoes with real butter. Derreck couldn't remember the last time he'd had either, and just the smell of the authentic food made his mouth water uncontrollably.

The meal was evidence enough they'd come to the right place. Zelig grew potatoes, but he certainly couldn't afford to buy them. The fact that they were on the table meant he didn't see any harm in taking some of the fruits of his labors for himself, above what the rebels gave him as compensation.

Conversation was strained at first. Derreck had completed his business with Zelig, and experience had taught him not to get too close to those on rebel-held worlds. Maybe it was the richness of the butter, but Derreck found himself asking Celia what she wanted to be when she grew up.

"I want to be a biologist," she said with a calm certainty.

Derreck raised his eyebrow at Zelig, who chuckled. "She's been obsessed with plants since before she could talk. I don't want her to have to be a farmer like me, so she'll study biology."

"You've got a special girl, here, Zelig."

The farmer nodded, the pride evident on his otherwise-stoic face. "I know it."

For a few moments Derreck was relaxed, enjoying the pleasant company and the simple but delicious food. Kenan wrecked the mood when he stood up and walked towards a window. "Cap, I think you're going to want to see this."

Derreck frowned and stood up, immediately surprised by what he saw. Off in the distance, flames were washing over the outpost, sending a pillar of light high into the night sky.

The two warriors stood in silence near the window, trying to comprehend a sight that shouldn't exist. Had the rebels firebombed an outpost they controlled? Had Fleet sympathizers started a fight that got out of control? Derreck had no idea what had happened, but the situation was dangerous and escalating quickly.

He turned to his subordinate. "We need our suits."

Kenan agreed, but as he pulled out his datapad, he stopped his commander.

"We're not going to have time." He thrust the pad in Derreck's face, and Derreck saw what he was speaking of. They had placed sensors around the farm that morning to warn them of any unwanted visitors. Now six signatures advanced slowly on the farm. They were trapped.

DERRECK THOUGHT QUICKLY, his face not giving away any of his fear. Somehow, someone had figured out where they were. He didn't know how. Maybe a satellite had caught an energy signature, or maybe somebody had talked. He knew another pair of operatives had been in the outpost, but it was an inferno. Whoever had been there, he wasn't optimistic about their chances now.

He had to focus on his own mission. He needed to keep Zelig alive if possible, but his primary objective was to get himself and Kenan to safety. They were a long way from any safe transport, though.

Given the speed with which the assault team had found this particular farm, Derreck had to assume that the team was coming in hot. They weren't going door-to-door searching for the Fleet operatives.

They couldn't get to their exosuits in time. They'd be taken out before they got there. So they had to fight the old fashioned way and hope they weren't too badly outgunned. Most of the rebels didn't have the training Derreck and Kenan had, but you didn't need it if you were armored and fighting against a flesh-and-blood opponent.

Derreck glanced at Kenan. "Did you bring your heavy rifle?"

Kenan shook his head. "Just my sidearm."

Derreck frowned. He was armed the same.

Just then, Kenan grabbed him and threw him bodily to the side. Derreck's world filled with fire and shrapnel as dozens of rounds punched through the wall he had just been standing against. The farm was sturdy, designed for hundreds of years of habitation, but it hadn't been built to withstand the force of even one high-velocity round.

Kenan yelled at the family to take cover, and to Zelig's credit, he grabbed Celia and pulled her immediately down under the table.

More rounds tore through the air above them, filling the room with particulates that made it difficult to breathe. Derreck rolled toward Zelig and his daughter and shoved them across the floor farther back into the farmstead.

The air around them cleared, but they were hardly safe. Kenan joined them, his sidearm in his hand. Against the firepower that seemed to be arrayed against them, his handgun seemed woefully inadequate.

Kenan glanced at Derreck. "I guess they aren't planning on taking prisoners?"

Derreck glared back. Kenan was one of those men that war didn't seem to affect. Derreck had met a few of them in his career, and he had never understood them. Kenan was always cool under fire, a witticism ready for even the direst crisis.

Derreck, on the other hand, could feel the rage boiling in his blood. This was why the rebels had to be defeated. They always went too far, willing to sacrifice even the lives of innocents to achieve their aims. Fleet wasn't perfect, but Derreck had never opened fire without warning or provocation on a family's house.

Using hand signals, Derreck told Zelig to stay where he was. The situation was hard enough to keep track of without the farmer moving around. Derreck and Kenan crawled to the back of the farmstead and exited, the occasional round still passing overhead.

Derreck motioned for the two of them to split up and work their way around the farmhouse from opposite sides. They knew roughly where all their opponents were, so there wasn't any reason to stay together for cover. Better to spread out the counterattack as much as they could.

Kenan understood and started working his way clockwise around the farmhouse. Derreck went the other direction. He made it to the front corner of the farm before he saw anyone, and he thanked the fates when he saw his opponents only had one exosuit, and an old one at that. The rebels might be vicious, and their spacecraft might be second to none, but they didn't have top-of-the-line exosuits, not yet.

Using his nanos, Derreck tagged the order of fire on his enemies. Kenan, on the other side of the house, did the same.

Derreck started a three-second timer, and when the clock hit zero, both men took aim. Derreck knocked down two rebels with two shots, and Kenan took out the other three unarmored soldiers, leaving only the exosuit to take care of.

Both of them broke from cover. The exosuit could, in theory, hit both of them at the same time, but the pilot had to focus on both to do so. They spread out wide, making it impossible for the pilot to pay attention to both of them.

As Derreck had hoped the pilot would, the exosuit turned entirely toward Kenan, deciding to kill one of them at a time. As it turned its back toward him, Derreck sprinted toward it, getting up close and sticking his weapon in the lightly armored joint plates underneath the armpit of the suit. He pulled the trigger several times, hearing the screams of the pilot inside as his bullets penetrated the weak point.

The suit swung around, but Derreck dodged the blow. Kenan, who had been angling toward the suit, came up behind, pressing his own handgun against the joint where the neck met the torso.

As soon as it began, the fighting was over. They had bought themselves a few minutes, at least, to figure out a way to get off planet.

DERRECK ORDERED Kenan into his exosuit. The big man would provide cover while Derreck checked on the family. Zelig was a well-respected man in these corners. The attack on his farm wouldn't go unnoticed, bringing the rebels more negative publicity. Their mission was complete. Now they just needed to get everyone to safety.

Derreck worked his way back through the weakened farmhouse, finding Zelig and Celia right where he had left them, as low to the ground as they could be. Both of them were wide eyed and short of breath, but they were otherwise unharmed. They had been fortunate.

For a moment, Derreck had gotten careless. He had been lost in thought when the fight started, and only Kenan's presence had saved him. He hadn't expected the rebels to open fire without even giving some form of notice, some chance to surrender. He wouldn't make the same mistake again.

The captain led the family out of the farmhouse, grateful to see Kenan on a nearby rise covering the area.

Once the family was relatively safe, Derreck went to where they had stashed his exosuit. He threw off the camouflage covering that prevented detection, folding it up and putting it back in its compartment. The suit was crouched down, its arms wrapped tightly around its knees in a tight ball. When Derreck's nanos came within range it activated, standing up and opening so Derreck could step in. As he did so, the suit closed around him.

There was a moment of shock as the suit synced itself to his nanos, but soon it pressed comfortably against his entire body. The suit wasn't the strongest available, but for infiltration missions, Derreck wouldn't have anything else. Kenan's was a little heavier, better armored with stronger weapons. It suited the big man well.

Derreck immediately turned on his suit's comms, establishing a secure link with the Fleet smuggling ship they'd come in on.

"What's happening, sir?"

Captain Lora's gravelly voice came back to him almost instantly. "The mission's been compromised, commander. Your orders are to evacuate immediately."

Derreck decided to stretch the truth a little. Despite himself, he had gotten attached to the farmer and his daughter. "Sir, I've got two high-priority informants in tow, permission to evac with them?"

The comms were silent for almost a full minute before her voice came back. "Granted."

Derreck breathed a sigh of relief. If they were left

behind, Zelig and his daughter faced torture and death at the hands of the rebellion.

He cut off comms and met with the other three, catching them up in just a moment.

Kenan only had one question. "They coming to pick us up, sir?"

Derreck didn't even have to respond. Kenan simply laughed. "Of course they aren't."

A plan started coming together in Derreck's mind. "Kenan, you ride support for Zelig. I'm sure he's got transportation that can carry the three of you to the outpost. I'll go ahead and pick us up a ride."

Kenan didn't have to ask any questions, his years of experience filling in the blanks. With his heavier suit, he could protect the family better than Derreck could, and his commander's lighter suit could move faster than his own. Derreck also had all sorts of special software in his suit that aided in the more illegal activities they engaged in. The shuttles had landed by the outpost, and they were the closest way off the planet.

Kenan's armored head nodded, and Derreck didn't need any special abilities to know the man was smiling underneath his visor. "Aye aye, Cap."

THEIR PLAN BEGAN WELL, which was as much as Derreck could have asked for. There was little point in discussion. The more time they gave the rebels to gather their forces, the less likely his small team was to succeed. Derreck took off immediately as Kenan talked with Zelig about taking a vehicle into the outpost.

As Derreck ran, he performed a diagnostics check on his

suit. The habit died hard. Even though he had run one just that morning when they arrived at the farm, it never hurt to know your equipment was in the best possible shape. As expected, everything was green across the board. Derreck armed his weapons, light rifles slung beneath both arms. They weren't much, but they were certainly better than nothing, and they'd have to do.

His sensors told him that the shuttles had landed on opposite sides of the outpost to disgorge their troops. That was good, because it meant the enemy would be more spread out. Unfortunately it meant they might have a second shuttle to contend with if even if they could steal the first. One problem at a time, though.

Against common sense, Derreck ran into the hellscape that was the outpost. Up close, Derreck could see that the shuttles had indeed firebombed the place. The fires burned at unbearable temperatures, and even inside his cooled suit Derreck could feel the oppressive heat. There couldn't be anyone left alive here, but there were still scout teams searching the burning avenues.

He had chosen to run into the outpost to confuse sensors, giving him a small element of surprise when he attacked the shuttle. Unfortunately, it meant his own sensors weren't working well. He turned around a corner and ran face to face into two rebel exosuits.

They stopped in surprise, but Derreck kept his speed. He slammed his armored right fist into the helmet of the exosuit on his right, crushing visor and skull alike. He didn't slow down, reaching behind him and firing with his left arm at the remaining exosuit. His aim was true, high velocity shells working their way up his opponent's back and helmet. When the suit collapsed Derreck knew he'd killed the man.

He didn't have much time. The loss of the exosuits would bring others swarming to the area, and Derreck had no idea how many troops were nearby. He kept running toward the shuttle at the edge of town.

Derreck stopped at the outskirts of the outpost, delighted that the shuttle was only guarded by two exosuits and two unarmored rebels. He scanned his surroundings quickly and opened a secure channel to Kenan.

"How's the progress?"

"Two kilometers out. We can be there in less than five minutes."

They could do this. Kenan and the family were close, giving Derreck just enough time to hijack the ship. He let Kenan know where he was and then closed the channel. He believed that being a leader meant knowing when to give orders and when to let others make their own decisions. From here on out, Kenan could make the calls. He would know what to do.

Derreck took a moment to plan his assault. At first he thought about attacking the unarmored rebels first to even the playing field a bit, but then discarded the idea. They would be easy to eliminate. The real threats were the exosuits, and they had to go first.

The commander stepped out of cover and raised both his rifles, centering his reticles on the enemy's head. His rifles opened fire just as the enemy realized he was there. Many of his rounds missed, but a few connected, and that was all it took. The exosuit collapsed and Derreck moved his focus to the other one.

He gave the rebels credit. They had been surprised, but in less than three seconds, they were all firing at him. The unarmored rebels were firing at him with anti-infantry rounds, which pinged harmlessly off his armor.

The enemy exosuit was another matter. His rounds were heavier, and Derreck felt the bullets rake across his chest, like being punched a dozen times in less than a few seconds. Warnings flashed across Derreck's vision, but he ignored them. His suit was still moving and the shots had hit where his armor was heaviest.

Derreck started walking sideways, strafing as the enemy exosuit tried to lock on to him. Another round tore into his left arm, severing one of the actuators and causing the arm to lock in its current position.

In return, Derreck unloaded both rifles at the enemy exosuit, rocking it backward as it stood in place. The two combatants kept firing, Derreck moving and his enemy stationary, waiting to see who would break first.

Fortunately for Derreck, his sustained barrage quickly overwhelmed his opponent, dropping the other exosuit to the dirt.

Without wasting a moment in gloating, Derreck focused his attention on the remaining two rebels. One had stood his ground, and Derreck sent one burst into his chest, almost tearing him in half. The other rebel had realized the futility of attacking Derreck with infantry weapons and was running towards a crate that no doubt held heavier fare. Derreck shot her in the back as he walked toward the ramp of the shuttle.

The ramp was starting to close, the pilot recognizing the danger he was in. Derreck easily leaped up to it and walked up it as it finished closing. Instead of stopping Derreck, the pilot had sealed himself in with his enemy. Derreck made his way to the cockpit, grateful this particular shuttle was mostly storage space, allowing him ease of movement.

When he came into the cockpit the pilot fired once at him, the bullet harmlessly ricocheting off his helmet.

Derreck punched the pilot lightly, but even though he tried to be gentle, he worried that he had killed the man.

Derreck cocked his right wrist down, revealing a slender connector. He inserted it into the shuttle's mainframe and waited patiently as his suit's specialized software went to work hijacking the shuttle's security. His suit let him know it estimated the hack to take about two minutes.

Less than a minute later his comms came alive, Kenan's ice-cold voice breaking the silence of the shuttle. "Cap, that other shuttle is lifting off, and I'm getting readings of movement on the edges of the outpost."

Derreck swore as he pulled up Kenan's sensor data. The rebels had organized a coherent counterattack, and if Kenan's sensors were accurate, they still had quite a few suits to contend with. He glanced at his readout. His suit was counting down the seconds, estimating another minute and ten seconds to control of the shuttle. Derreck wasn't sure they had that much time.

EVERYTHING WENT to hell really fast. Derreck was more or less locked into place. If they wanted to have any hope of getting off this planet, he needed to stay where he was. But no matter how good they were, they didn't have the firepower to take out the force that had been sent against them. Derreck guessed most of the on-planet rebel forces were here.

He needed to take off, and do it fast. He stepped out of the suit while it continued to work. He squeezed around the tight cockpit until he was in the pilot's chair. Then he strapped himself in, ready to start a rapid launch sequence the moment he had control. Once he had done all he could to prepare, he pulled up Kenan's sensors to see what was happening outside.

His grip tightened on the joysticks of the ship as he saw what the big man was facing. He had managed to get the transport into the outpost, but it had been tipped over. Derreck pulled up visual and saw that everyone had survived. They were huddled behind the transport and taking heavy fire. Zelig's eyes were wide with fear, and Celia was in the fetal position, her hands covering her ears. Derreck didn't have to imagine the horror she was going through. He had been there once, too.

Kenan was trying to fight them off, but it was a losing battle. He was being pinned and flanked, a strategy as old as it was effective.

Worse, the second shuttle was coming around towards Derreck and the hijacked one. If he didn't get control of it soon, it would be a pile of molten slag. The commander guessed the only reason the others hadn't opened fire yet was because they weren't sure who was in control. Shuttles were fairly precious to the rebels, and they wouldn't fire on one without good cause.

Derreck opened comms. "Kenan, you need to retreat. There's an alley ten meters behind you. It should allow you to break their flanking maneuver."

"Roger that, Cap." Even facing the most desperate situation, his voice was calm and steady.

Derreck watched on visual as Kenan coaxed and encouraged the family to get up and start moving. He stood up and unleashed a devastating barrage of firepower that sent the rebel exosuits for cover, at least for a moment. He led the way across the field of fire, making his way to the alley. Derreck watched, not even realizing he was holding his breath.

Kenan was several meters ahead of the family. His exosuit helped him move faster than any unassisted human. He had just rounded the corner of the alley when a rocket streaked out from behind, exploding against the building Kenan was standing next to. Derreck lost sight of the family as Kenan was blown backward, deeper into the alley.

Just then Lora's voice broke his reverie. "Commander, we've got new orders. Fleet sees an opportunity to take out most of the rebel garrison on this planet, and we're taking it. You have one minute to evacuate." Her voice cut off as soon as it came on.

Derreck was furious. Lora's warning was nothing but a courtesy. He knew what she meant. A bomb had already been dropped from orbit. They didn't expect any of them to escape. She was giving him a minute to accept his end.

THERE WAS TOO much to do and far too little time to do it in. His suit notified him it had control of the ship, and Derreck's hands flew over the controls, beginning the start sequence in less than five seconds. As the computer came up, Derreck's first action was to pull up the weapons systems and unleash a flight of missiles at the approaching shuttle.

The sky lit up with fire as Derreck yanked on the control stick, shooting his shuttle high into the air.

As his sensors came online, warnings started flashing across the displays. Lora hadn't been exaggerating. The sensors were picking up the incoming weapon, already in atmosphere.

Derreck fought the urge to scream in frustration. He

needed to make decisions, and he didn't have the time. He opened comms to Kenan. "Kenan! Sitrep!"

"I'm alive, Cap. Lost track of the family, though. I think they were far enough behind me. They should be safe."

"They're dropping a bomb on the outpost, Kenan. We've got to get out of here." He glanced over at his display. The computer estimated thirty-eight seconds until impact.

Derreck turned down to the sensor screen, trying to see if he could pick up life forms. The sensors were picking up the energy signatures of the suits, but they weren't picking up any life.

The ship rocked as bullets tore through the hull. Derreck cursed, all his frustration and anger coming out in one word. He pulled up higher, out of the range of most weapons. He tried scanning again for life, but the flames and debris made it too hard to be sure of any readings.

"Kenan, I'm coming to get you. It's going to be a grab and go."

The big man's response was surprising. "Leave me, Cap. See if you can find Celia."

The idea was tempting. But there were only twenty-four seconds left, and Derreck couldn't be sure anyone else was alive. He knew he could save Kenan. He swore as he opened the ramp and dove the shuttle down.

"I'm coming, Kenan."

The shuttle slammed into the ground on the other end of the alley, away from the collapsed corner of the building. Kenan leaped on board just as the timer on Derreck's display hit zero.

The impact was a way off, well outside the boundaries of the outpost. Derreck wondered if the old smuggling ship just couldn't calculate impacts very well or if they had deliberately aimed for something just beyond the outpost. In the end, it wouldn't matter.

The sky flashed white, the screens of the ship automatically darkening to protect Derreck's eyes. A small ball of destruction grew into a wall of fire rushing towards them.

"Hold on to something!"

Derreck lifted off as gently as he dared. There wasn't enough time to close the ramp, and he wanted to give Kenan the second or two he would need to lock his suit onto a hold. He turned the ship so that he was pointing away from the blast. As he did, he looked down and swore he saw a flash of blue in the street below.

"Locked in, Cap!"

There was no time. The wall of fire was closer now, an apocalyptic vision. Derreck hesitated for just a fraction of a second before slamming the throttle all the way to full. The shuttle's engines whined as they kicked into power, and Derreck was pushed back in his seat, blackness creeping into the edges of his vision. Just when he thought he couldn't take any more, he eased back on the throttle and they slowed.

Derreck took a breath as he quickly unbuckled and ran back to the hold. Kenan was there, unlocking his suit's arm. The forces of the acceleration would have torn a man's grip easily, but the suit provided the strength necessary to survive the G-force.

Behind them on the horizon the wall of flame slowly dissipated, leaving afterimages on Derreck's retinas. The outpost was nothing but cinders now.

Kenan pulled off his helmet, the two men looked at each other, and both knew they had seen the same thing. Neither spoke, but Derreck sat down on one of the crates in the hold, staring off into the distance.

They had been serving together now for over two years, and they had been in some tough spots together. But Derreck knew their small two-person team would never be the same.

Kenan was quiet, his eyes locked in the same blank stare as his commander's.

The silence between them was heavy. Finally, Kenan stood up and slapped the button that closed the ramp. His voice was tinged with anger and despair. "Whatever."

He went to the other end of the hold and started taking off his suit.

Derreck watched the man, angry but understanding. He too slowly stood up and went to the pilot's chair. He opened comms, and Lora was on immediately.

"Good to see you made it, commander. There's one last packet of resistance on the other side of the planet. Please drop in and support our assault troops there. We're beaming you details now."

Derreck didn't want to fight. His weariness was more than bone deep. It rested on his soul, and there were days he longed for nothing more than to sleep forever. He wanted to leave these worlds behind.

With a sigh, Derreck opened comms and gave Kenan the briefing information. He programmed in their course, their shuttle shooting alone into the blue sky.

THANK YOU!

Thanks so much for reading! If you enjoyed the book, reviews are the lifeblood of independent publishing, and I would be grateful for your feedback.

If you are interested in FREE stories, access to giveaways, sales, and more, please visit www.waterstonemedia.net.

ABOUT THE AUTHOR

Ryan Kirk is the bestselling author of the Nightblade series of books. When he isn't writing, you can probably find him playing disc golf or hiking through the woods.

www.waterstonemedia.net
contact@waterstonemedia.net

Printed in Great Britain
by Amazon